THE MOON ALWAYS RISING

THE MOON ALWAYS RISING

a novel

ALICE C. EARLY

SHE WRITES PRESS

Published 2020
Printed in the United States of America
ISBN: 978-1-63152-683-1 pbk
ISBN: 978-1-63152-684-8 ebk
Library of Congress Control Number: 2019914837

For information, address:
She Writes Press
1569 Solano Ave #546
Berkeley, CA 94707

Interior design by Tabitha Lahr
Map of Nevis by Laurie Miller

She Writes Press is a division of SparkPoint Studio, LLC.

Alice C. Early is represented by April Eberhardt, Libra Nova LLC, dba April Eberhardt Literary, april@apnileberhardt.com; 415-309-0279

For Larry

and

in loving memory of Tom and Virginia

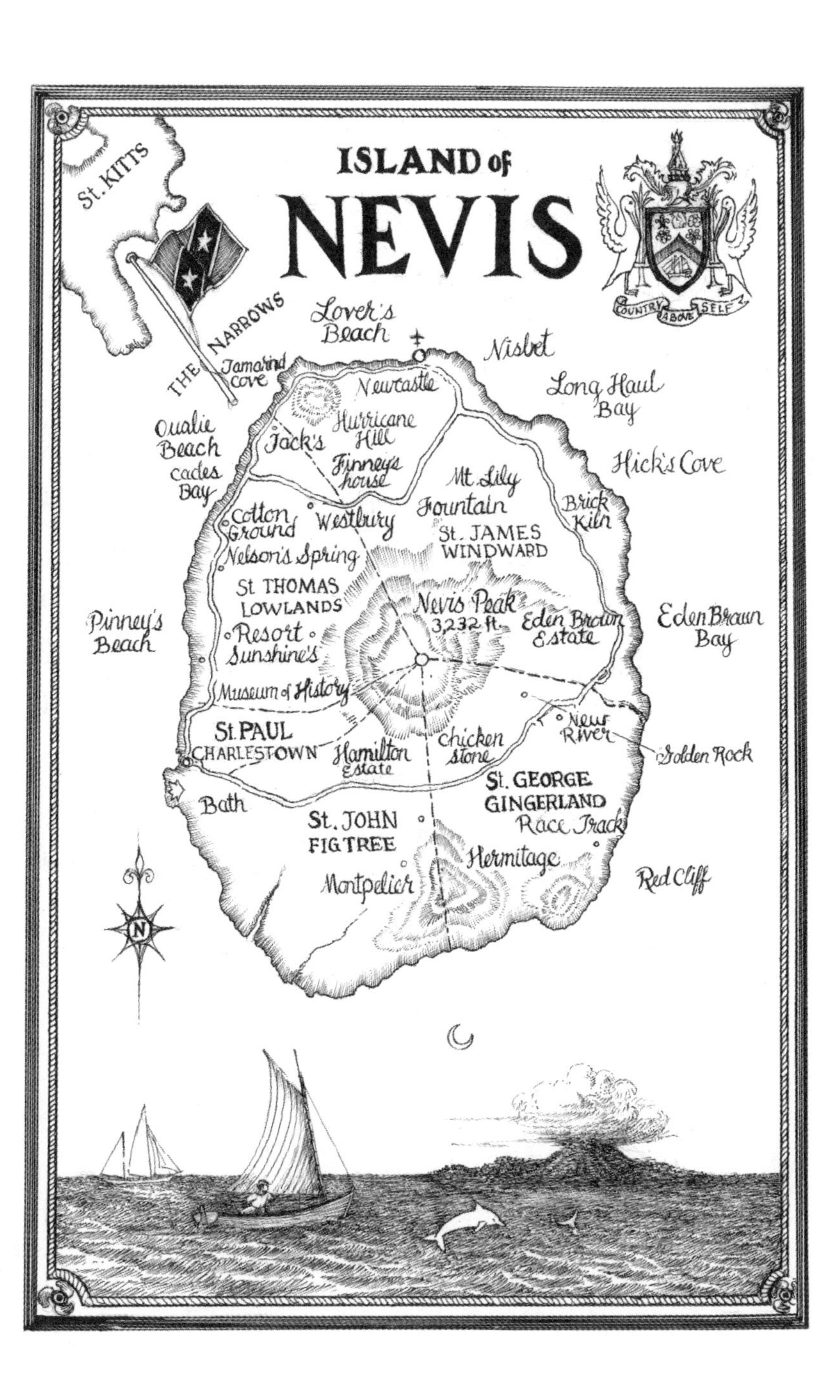
ISLAND of
NEVIS
St. KITTS
THE NARROWS
Lover's Beach
Nisbet
Long Haul Bay
Tamarind Cove
Newcastle
Oualie Beach
Cades Bay
Jack's
Hurricane Hill
Finney's house
Hick's Cove
Mt. Lily
Fountain
Brick Kiln
Cotton Ground
Westbury
St. JAMES WINDWARD
Nelson's Spring
St THOMAS LOWLANDS
Nevis Peak 3,232 ft.
Eden Brown Estate
Eden Brown Bay
Pinney's Beach
Resort
Sunshine's
Museum of History
St. PAUL
CHARLESTOWN
Hamilton Estate
Chicken stone
New River
Golden Rock
Bath
St. GEORGE GINGERLAND
St. JOHN FIGTREE
Race Track
Hermitage
Montpelier
Red Cliff
N
COUNTRY ABOVE SELF

EPIGRAPH

Nothing I cared, in the lamb white days, that time would take me
Up to the swallow thronged loft by the shadow of my hand.
In the moon that is always rising,
Nor that riding to sleep
I should hear him fly with the high fields
And wake to the farm forever fled from the childless land.
Oh as I was young and easy in the mercy of his means,
Time held me green and dying
Though I sang in my chains like the sea.

—Dylan Thomas, "Fern Hill"

AUTHOR'S NOTE

I have had the good fortune to visit Nevis annually since 1996. In addition to providing inspiration for *The Moon Always Rising*, Nevis granted me space and tranquility to write and edit much of this book. I grew to know and love the island, always recognizing how limited my visitor's grasp of its true heart might be.

My plot and character development were in baby stages when the events of 9/11 emptied the skies and changed our psyches forever. As I found it emotionally and intellectually impossible to set the book after 2000, I chose the Nevis of 1999–2000, when the "new" airport, island road project, and other major changes were in progress. Hurricane Lenny, which figures importantly in my story, devastated the Four Seasons Resort in November 1999. Damaged, rebuilt, and redecorated more than once since then, the Resort barely resembles that cluster of gingerbread cottages and simple wharf of the late '90s. While Jack's house is a complete fabrication, I've otherwise stayed true to Nevis geography and place names. In the twenty-first century, erosion, storms, and development have changed or eliminated some of the landmarks I mention. You can still get a Killer Bee at Sunshine's beach bar, but it's more of an establishment now, versus the brightly painted shack of yore. Through all these changes, Nevis retains its allure and rootedness. The setting in

The Moon Always Rising is so enveloping as to be almost a character, and many human characters are inspired by people I have known there. To be respectful of the island's history, people, and culture, I intentionally created in Els Gordon a protagonist who is by definition an outsider. This story is told exclusively from her point of view, with all the shortcomings of perception and understanding that creates. The Nevis I've depicted is, I hope, the Nevis that struggles and prevails, joyously if not always harmoniously.

CONTENTS

part one

CHAPTER 1

Nevis, West Indies

November 1999

The seven-seater plane roared over the Caribbean toward the green cone of the island where Els Gordon would serve out the sentence handed down by her boss: a week's holiday that chagrined her like a toddler's time-out. "If you don't get a grip before you come back . . .," the wanker had said. He hadn't specified the consequences.

The plane fishtailed low over a deserted beach rimmed with jungle before rattling to its landing.

Steam-room heat assaulted Els when she crossed the yielding tarmac, a jolt after the icy drizzle she'd left at Heathrow.

The immigration officer perused her form. "You neglected to state the purpose of your visit."

As neither business nor pleasure covered it, she stared at him too long before saying, "Penance?"

He regarded her, unamused, then checked the "pleasure" box. He peeled back the Scottish national flag cover she'd put on her passport, revealing its Westminster-issued European Union burgundy. After examining pages with entry stamps from the US, Asia, and South America, he found an empty spot and clacked down his stamp.

A cabbie hurried her to his taxi van in time to beat a dust devil that swirled across the construction zone, engulfing the terminal. Turning the van toward the ball of afternoon sun, he swept his arm to take in the scalped land and heavy machinery. "New airport gon' accommodate jets. Change fortunes for all a' we."

"Mind what you wish for," Els said.

"Even when we reach the twenty-first century, Nevis goin' always be Queen of the Caribees." He patted his chest. "And I am this little island's best ambassador. You want my special tour?"

"All I want is a cold drink and a hot bath," she said, already wondering how she'd survive a week in this tiny place.

When they crested Hurricane Hill, the sea spreading out before her was a wash of undulating sparkles. The brightness was invasive; she felt nature was strutting, taunting her.

"You here for the doctor meeting by the Resort?"

"Na, on my own," she said, recoiling from the thought that she might be walking into a convention of men as arrogant as the investment banking colleagues she'd left behind.

Just beyond the boundary sign for the Parish of St. Thomas Lowland, dung-splattered sheep milling in the road halted the van's progress in front of a cinder block wall. Higher up the hill, Els glimpsed a house nestled into the slope. Unlike the pastel concrete dwellings they'd passed, it looked ancient, a survivor with proportions that charmed her. Its weathered shingles and native stone walls stood in counterpoint to the riot of color poking through the garden's devastation. Plywood blindfolded its windows. An estate agent's sign dangled from the padlocked gate.

The cabbie snuck a peek at the house, waved his arm out the window, and yelled at the sheep.

"I'm in no hurry," Els said. "For once."

"Got to move on, miss." He leaned on the horn and whispered, "Lord, ley we pass *now.*"

With the ewes bleating encouragement, the babies huddled enough to clear a path. The cabbie drove away so swiftly he nearly clipped a straggling lamb. Els twisted in her seat for another look, but they'd rounded a turn and the house had disappeared.

"So, Mr. Ambassador," she said, "what's the story behind that place?"

He gripped the wheel and said nothing. A bit farther on, he slowed for a hairpin curve, tipped his head toward a seawall, and said, "Jack, he gone. But he ain't left yet."

"Jack's the owner?"

"Foh twenty years, mebbe." He tuned the radio to a preacher's oration and didn't speak again, leaving Els to ponder why this Jack would surrender such a treasure to rot and strangling vegetation, and why no buyer had jumped to save it.

She'd always told herself that love and attention could coax anything abandoned back to life.

The cabbie drove down the Resort's allée of palm trees and up to the Great House entrance. After handing Els's luggage to the porter, he whipped out a card reading, "Sparrow's Custom Tours. See the Nevis beyond the Beach and the Peak."

"The real Nevis," she said.

"Sparrow show you the sights, tell you the legends," he said. "Real, you gotta find on you own."

Needing no assistance pulling her small wheelie or finding her room, Els felt ridiculous tagging along behind Anthony, the porter dispatched with great ceremony by the front desk, who took the long way in order to point out the beach, pool, and dining pavilion. The paths meandered between plants that seemed to reach for her, their foliage in shades of green, burgundy, and purple, as if Gauguin had created the scene. When Anthony greeted two uniformed women and they replied in incomprehensible patois, Els felt an old stab of otherness.

"Welcome to Hibiscus Villa," Anthony said, and waved her inside. She eyed the romantic mahogany plantation bed and thought what a narrow, solitary dent she would make.

"What's this, the honeymoon suite?" she said. She felt as spiky as the arrangement of protea on the coffee table.

"Sometimes," he said.

She pressed a tip into Anthony's hand hoping to curtail his narration of the suite's amenities. He instructed her to enjoy her stay and backed out the door.

Alone with only the whir of the ceiling fan and pulse of the surf, she was rooted in the middle of the floor, unaware of how long she'd stood there when a discreet knock brought her back to the present. The young woman at the door with the name tag "Alaneesha" wheeled in a cart bearing a bottle of champagne in a sweating ice bucket and a frangipani blossom floating in a small bowl.

"Compliments of the management?" Els asked.

Alaneesha handed her a card that read, "Find someone to share this with. Loosen up and come back a new woman." It was signed "Coxe." Els wondered if "this" meant the champagne, the bed, or both. It was just like Coxe to assume anything could be righted by a good fuck, preferably while drunk. Fury sent a flush to her face, and she fanned herself with the card.

Alaneesha peered at her. "Ma'am, you okay?"

"Jet lag," Els said.

After Alaneesha slipped out the door, Els flung the card at the champagne and watched it sink into the ice bath. The frangipani's aggressive scent filled the room.

Mind what you wish for, Els chided herself. Festive champagne was hardly the cold drink she'd had in mind, and a hot bath, at the moment, might make her explode. She peeled off her sweat-dampened clothing, stepped into the shower, and stood under a cool stream until she felt rinsed if not cleansed. Wrapped in a huge towel, she went out to her terrace and shielded her eyes against the low sun, which made a couple strolling the beach hand in hand look dipped in toffee.

Over the past year, icy anger had frozen her grief into her bones, but recently the marrow seemed overwhelmed by the effort of this compression and had begun emitting a kind of fog, like dry ice vapors, that displaced the air in her lungs and slowed her brain. It was as if those noxious vapors were wreathing her words, further sharpening her already lacerating tongue. She'd begun messing up at work enough to give the ever-circling hyenas in her department a whiff of vulnerability.

Coxe had flashed his fake-compassion smile when he'd said, "I strongly recommend you take this opportunity to just get over, well, whatever it is." She'd imagined driving the Montblanc fountain pen he so fancied straight into his jugular. As if a few days of Caribbean frolic could erase all that had brought her to this point.

CHAPTER 2

Though she packed instinctively for business travel, she'd puzzled over what to bring on this junket, feeling naked without the armor of her suits. She pulled on a body-hugging coral dress with a low décolletage; the color amped up her copper hair and milky skin. After touching up the circles under her eyes, applying mascara and power lipstick, and dabbing on rose-scented toilet water, she squared her shoulders and lifted her chin. Her gray eyes stared back, defiant.

In the bar, name-tagged surgeons attempted the limbo to recorded music while their colleagues cheered them on. Els took a deep draft of her double Laphroaig, neat, splash of water. The scotch delivered welcome heat to her throat, her belly. When she caught a man farther up the bar ogling her, she locked eyes with him until she saw his flare of recognition. He said something to the bobbed woman next to him and walked over.

"Eleanor Gordon," he said. "Paul Salustrio. Goldman, New York."

Els held out her hand.

"Has it been two years already?" he said. "Where've you been hiding yourself since that ZarCom deal?"

While they shook hands, his eyes, a brown so dark that all expression drowned in them, were fixed on her cleavage.

"Mostly on a plane," she said.

"I was in London last month. Still trying to close that petro transaction we sparred about back then. Your boss brought a sharp young VP to the meeting. What's his name, Burgess?" He shook his head. "Watch your back with that one. He implied you were having some personal trouble." He gave her the investment banker size-up, part admiration, part domination. "You've lost weight."

For almost a year now, she'd been unable to sleep and uninterested in food; she'd compensated by burying herself in work. Though she'd dropped half a stone from her already lean frame, she often felt three times that was draped across her shoulders.

The woman joined them and slipped her arm through Salustrio's.

"Marlena," he said, "meet Ms. Gordon from Simon Coxe's team at Standard Heb. Or should I introduce you as Lady Eleanor?"

"Els will do," she said.

Marlena did not extend her hand.

"What brings you to paradise?" Salustrio asked.

"Coxe bought a week here at some charity auction with no intention of using it," she said. "Made a big show of sending me here as a birthday getaway."

"Alone?"

"My man couldn't make it."

That she was turning thirty-three was but a convenient cover. This birthday would arrive just before the dreaded first anniversary of a loss that had forced a question she couldn't answer: Who would she be now, since nothing she'd planned was going to happen?

She finished her drink and ordered a refill. "What pried *you* away?"

"The yacht had a week available," Salustrio said. "So, when's this birthday?"

"Tomorrow." When the bartender delivered her scotch, she dragged over a bowl of nuts.

"The mahi-mahi is fabulous," Marlena said.

"I was planning on eating a few of these nuts," Els said, "getting a little squiffed, and calling it a night."

Laughter erupted from the limbo crowd, one of whom had collapsed on the dance floor and had to be pulled to his feet.

"Look," Salustrio said, "how about a little celebration sail tomorrow?"

"You know I promised Louisa her first mani-pedi," Marlena said. She fluffed her hair and said to Els, "We agreed we'd spend our last day in the Resort, but he can never get enough yo-ho-ho."

"I'm no fan of boats," Els said.

"This isn't just any boat," Salustrio said.

"Humor him," Marlena said. "If he's ashore, he'll drive me and the girls crazy. I'll have the hotel send out some lunch."

Salustrio patted Marlena's hand. "Be on the dock at nine thirty," he said to Els. "Look for the zodiac from *Iguana*, probably a big Jamaican guy at the helm. She's the huge white ketch, likely flying a tanbark mizzen." He signaled for his check.

Els swallowed more scotch, thinking how self-important guys were suckers for jargon. Coxe would squirm when he found out that she'd gone yachting with his archrival. She raised her glass. "Cheers, then, to yo-ho-ho."

The man steering the rubber dinghy had blue-black skin and wore a crocheted hat stuffed with hair that resembled an enormous muffin. He was tall and sinewy, and his reflective sunglasses and silence gave him a sinister air. The sailboat was anchored beyond the rest of the craft. With its hull looming over them, the helmsman shouted a few unintelligible words and a blond sailor descended the ladder and stepped into the dinghy.

When Els stood up, the dinghy lurched on a wave and the sailor caught her hand and guided it to the ladder. "Welcome aboard *Iguana*, Ms. Gordon," he said. His accent was American. "I'm Captain Ingraham. Known to all as Liz. You've already met Jason, our first mate."

"Liz?" she said. "Does that get you into fights?"

He flashed a chipped-toothed grin. "Something does," he said. "Did." Nickname aside, he radiated full-on guy vibes—cocksure, ironic.

"I'm known to all as Els," she said.

The captain followed her up the ladder. He took her elbow as they stepped onto the deck, but she shrugged free, saying, "I'm fine," before stumbling into the cockpit and landing on a banquette. All around, ropes and wires slackened and tightened with the swells, much larger here than at the wharf.

Salustrio appeared in the hatchway, a cigar in his teeth. "Don't you just love these classic beauties?" he said. "This boat's a legend, a phoenix. Built in the '40s and nearly destroyed in St. Maarten during Hurricane Luis in '95." He stepped into the cockpit. "I tried to buy her and restore her myself, but nobody returned my calls. The owner's probably some money-laundering Colombian drug lord."

The engine rumbled.

"Mr. S, hook's up," the captain said.

Salustrio flicked his eyes over the white linen shirt and floppy pants covering Els from fingertip to toe. "Let's show Lady Eleanor what this baby can do."

After Liz had piloted the yacht farther from shore, he pointed the bow into the wind and turned the wheel over to Salustrio. Els was fascinated by the captain and first mate's energetic ballet, loosening this line and fastening that one; when Jason began pulling the main halyard hand over hand, he went nearly airborne between hauls. A huge, rust-colored sail glided up the mast, flapping and cracking in the freshening breeze. The boom swished over the cockpit. Everything on the boat was in clanging motion, and then the sails filled with a loud pop. The boat shuddered and swung toward St. Kitts. Liz took the wheel and switched off the engine, and there was no sound but the waves slapping the hull and the wind thrumming in the rigging. The yacht heeled slightly, leapt forward, and began slicing toward Basseterre.

They sailed to the southeast peninsula of St. Kitts, arid and uninhabited, and into a deserted cove, where Liz and Jason set the anchor and dropped the mainsail.

Salustrio pulled Els onto the stern deck. "Last one in is a puss," he said, and tossed his cigar butt overboard. "Hold the pickle." He grinned. "Maybe you're too much of a Brit to get my meaning."

"Nobody—Brit, Scot, or Yank—could miss it," Els said.

He struggled out of his polo shirt. Tanned flesh pooled above the waistband of his swim trunks.

While he unsnapped a section of lifeline and lowered the swimming ladder, she peered into the water. Near the beach, it was as aquamarine as any swimming pool, but at their anchorage it was a dark teal, its floor littered with brown humps that were hairy with seaweed. Driven by some unseen predator, a school of silversides broke the surface, their splashing like coins rattling. A strange pressure began to build around her heart.

"I'll pass," she said, and took a step backwards.

"I bet you've got a teensy little bikini under there just begging to get wet," Salustrio said. "If you can't swim, Cap stocks water wings for the kids."

"I was my S6 champion in crawl," she said.

"No excuse, then." He grabbed her elbow and heaved himself over the side. She reached for a shroud but caught only air, cried out, and tumbled after him.

The surface approached in slow motion. Terror squeezed the air from her lungs. When she tried to breathe, the air couldn't get in. There was a rushing in her ears. The sea closed over her. The water that had looked so clear from above became darker, thicker, as she descended. She tasted salt. Her trousers tangled around her legs and kicking only bound them tighter. It took all her strength to right herself and aim for the sunlight dancing on the surface, impossibly far away. Her lungs burning, she forced her leaden arms to pull for the dapples, and when she finally broke into the air, she inhaled water and began to cough and thrash.

She felt the concussion of someone entering the sea. A wave smacked her face. The captain surfaced next to her, pinned her to his chest, and stroked to the ladder. He placed her hand on the ladder rail and covered it with his own. "You're okay," he said. She felt his voice was coming from a great distance, though he was gripping the back of her shirt and speaking into her ear. "Listen to me. You're safe. Breathe. That's it. Breathe." He murmured reassurances until her panting subsided. When it did, he lifted her foot onto the bottom rung.

She managed to pull herself up, though she was shaking so hard she had to hug the sun-warmed metal after each step.

When she finally hauled herself onto the deck, she knelt and clung to a lifeline.

Salustrio, floating near the foot of the ladder, looked up. "The champ's a little out of practice." He rolled over and pawed toward the stern.

Liz climbed onto the deck and raked back his hair. His sunglasses dangled from their Croakies; there was a flicker of annoyance in his expression. He settled her on a banquette and draped a towel around her, and she drew it close, breathing through its folds and fighting to control her shaking.

"Breathe in while I count to ten," he said. "And out on ten."

She managed two breaths; the third caught in a sob.

Liz sat across from her and let her cry herself out, continually reminding her to breathe, while Salustrio splashed about below the stern. She was relieved he wasn't seeing her so undone.

"What's happening to me?" she choked out.

Liz crossed the cockpit and sat next to her. "Have you ever had a panic attack before?"

She shook her head, unwilling to trust her voice.

"You said you're a good swimmer. Is it something about the ocean? The creatures?"

Fearing she might dissolve again if she allowed him to be kind to her, she said, "Would it matter if I knew?" It came out snippier than she'd intended.

The color of his eyes darkened, like a blueberry with the bloom rubbed off of it. He looked away. She'd taken him for a younger man but now guessed he was in his late thirties. A scar interrupted his right eyebrow.

"Have you ever been snorkeling or diving?" he said.

"Never considered it."

"There's a dazzling world down there."

"Is that another of your services, guided tours of the briny deep?"

"Dare you to try it just once," he said. "You might be too entranced to panic." He rose and went below.

Hugging the towel, she rocked until the sun melted her terror and her breathing, if shallow, was dependable again.

While Els steadied herself against the galley doorframe, Liz dished up platters of lobster salad and grilled vegetables with an economical grace different from Jason's sinewy one. He'd changed into another *Iguana* polo shirt, dry except where its tails wicked up the dampness from his shorts. Billie Holiday, her notes bent and aching, sang softly in the background about wanting to try something she'd never had.

"Mr. S likes lunch on deck," Liz said, "but you've already had too much sun. Get out of those wet clothes. There's a robe in the master bath." He pointed toward a passageway to the right of the saloon ladder.

"I'm fine."

"You're goose bumps all over. You've had a shock. Do as I say."

She glared at him and considered resisting, but she'd already failed so dramatically to live up to her code—never show weakness—that courting further misery seemed pointless. She saluted, strode to the master suite, and rolled the door shut so hard it bounced open a crack.

Feeling better as soon as she'd shed her clammy bikini, she swaddled herself in the oversized robe and knotted the belt fast. When she returned to the saloon with her clothes rolled in a towel, Liz reached for them.

"I'll hang these on the forward lines," he said. "They'll be dry by the time we get back."

She handed them over, and he disappeared above.

She gripped the table edge. The clench in her chest gradually loosened, but she was still wobbly and disoriented. When Liz came down the ladder, she forced a smile. "You won't tell him? The tears, I mean."

"None of his business."

"Give me a task."

He handed her a cutting board with a baguette and knife. "You and Jason do everything?" she asked.

"When we're cruising we have at least one more mate, plus a sea chef," he said. "I sent the others ashore last night, thinking the Salustrios weren't going out today." He set an ice bucket with a bottle of champagne on the table next to a tray with cans of Diet Coke and bottles of sparkling water. That morning, she'd rescued Coxe's bottle from its tepid bath and stuffed it into her mini fridge, planning to toast her birthday alone later.

"Where do you all sleep?"

"Forward," he said, tipping his head toward a door marked CREW ONLY. He grinned and put on a Long John Silver accent. "With the sail bags and kegs of grog."

"You enjoy this rental captain game."

"We call it chartering." He handed her flatware and cloth napkins. "How bad could it be, getting paid to sail around?"

"Depends on who's paying," she said. She laid two place

settings precisely, folding the napkins and squaring the flatware. Salty air puffed through a porthole.

"Mr. S is better than many," he said. "I've put ashore more than one captain of industry who tried to be captain at sea too."

"Lucky you, being able to tell the likes of them where to go."

"Captain's command is law," he said. "Ancient rule of the sea. Thwart it at your peril."

"Aye, aye," she said with another mocking salute.

His hair dripping onto his collar, Salustrio lowered himself down the saloon ladder. He strode to the table, brandished the champagne bottle—Billecart-Salmon—and said, "Pink bubbles for the birthday girl."

"Never into pink," she said, "but I make an exception for champagne." Salustrio's taste in bubbly outshone Coxe's, but she steeled herself, guessing his agenda might be equally offensive.

When he popped the cork out the hatchway, it pinged off a shroud and plopped into the sea. After handing her a brimming flute and splashing an inch of champagne into a second, he glanced at Liz, who nodded and climbed up to the cockpit.

"*Cin cin.*" Salustrio clinked his glass against hers. "*Buon compleanno!*"

She took a big swallow, hoping the wine would calm her further. "*Grazie. Il dolce far niente,*" she said.

He took a tiny sip. "So you speak Italian besides Scotch."

"A wee bit," she said, intentionally upping her brogue. "At one time I hoped to be able to speak it with my mother. I'm told she lives on Ischia. Maybe you've heard of her. The painter, Giulietta Borelli?"

"I leave the artsy-fartsy stuff to Marlena," he said. "Funny, I always thought you were pure Scot, and that the legendary Sir Harald had been a widower for years."

"She left when I was two."

"So your hot-blooded mama was incompatible with one of the dourest men alive?"

"You'd have to ask her," she said. "How do you know Father?"

"By reputation." He plunked into the creamy leather swivel chair at the head of the table and gestured for her to sit at his right. He levered a Diet Coke tab, stuck a straw into the hole, and sipped, his gaze fixed on that same spot on her chest. "Maybe you were especially *terrible* at two? I'd believe it, given the temper you conceal under all that curvy cashmere."

She'd never confess, especially to the likes of Salustrio, that she'd always felt to blame for her mother's departure. Pulling the lapels of her robe closer, she gazed through the porthole at Nevis Peak and imagined the volcano's dormancy abruptly broken, its molten core blurping up and searing a path through the rain forest until it slid, hissing, into a boiling sea.

"Maybe I got that temper from her," she said.

Salustrio refilled her glass while he bragged of all the Caribbean islands he'd visited on *Iguana,* having chartered her every year since her restoration.

"Do you ever think of owning something here?" she said.

He tore off a piece of bread and tossed the rest into the basket. "You're too smart to get bitten by *that* ridiculous bug," he said. "Scratch the surface anywhere in the Caribbean, and all you find is poverty, corruption, incompetence. Governments a joke, economies unstable."

"You like it well enough to spend a bundle chartering this boat."

"The yacht's the thing," he said. "The setting just makes it go down easier with Marlena and the girls." He speared and waved a piece of lobster. "Living here would never match your fantasy. Stuck in the expat community of misfits and exiles. Impossible to become friends with the natives. Just because they smile at you, don't get to thinking they *like* you."

"I'm used to people not liking me." She finished her second glass of champagne and shook her head when he offered a refill.

He poured one anyway, then laced his fingers behind his head, leaned back, and thrust his splayed thighs forward in the chair. "You should have made managing director by now."

"I've been up two years in a row."

"They're keeping you slaving away on a promise while they promote guys like Singh and Carmody. Now that your father's retired from the board, you can probably kiss any hope of MD goodbye." He looked at her over the rim of his soda can. "If Coxe doesn't shitcan you altogether."

While she washed down a bite of lobster, she imagined the backbiting at work spreading throughout the City and Wall Street grapevines, the whispers reaching Salustrio and beyond. The champagne was turning her stomach acid and her head fuzzy. She pushed the glass aside.

"Why do you work so hard when everyone knows you don't need the money?" he said.

"That money is Father's."

"Hoping to prove you're more than just a sacred cow, then?" he said. "Maybe you should try working someplace besides your family's bank—a place that doesn't owe Sir Harald anything."

A gust of wind rocked the boat. The view captured in the porthole panned up Nevis Peak and back down.

"Like Goldman?"

"If you're hungry enough," he said. She caught a flash of glee in his eyes. Surely he knew Goldman was one of the few shops that could lure her from Standard Heb. He stood up, hiked his bathing trunks, and shouted, "Cap, time to head back."

"I need the loo," she said.

Steadying herself against the passageway paneling, she went astern, where she took refuge in the head. She sat for a while, listening to footsteps on the deck above, a chain rattling, and the engine purring. In the mirror—skin splotched from sun and wine, hair a wind-tossed copper mane—she looked bleary, vulnerable. She tightened the belt on her robe.

When she rolled open the door, Salustrio was on the other side, his hands on his hips and a bulge in his swim trunks. He stepped forward, blocking her way, grasped the tail of her belt, and tugged her toward him. He reeked of cigar and a musky cologne he hadn't been wearing before. "We could both satisfy our hunger," he said, leaning in to kiss her.

"Get off me," she shouted, slapping away his hand. Taking advantage of his stunned look, she planted her palms on his chest and thrust him backwards. He stumbled and landed on the foot of the bed. She yanked her robe into place, a flush racing from her breast to the roots of her hair. "I'll never be that desperate."

"Can't blame a guy for trying," he said. "Coxe said you put out for him big-time."

"You lying scumbags are all the same," she said. "I suppose you'll brag to him now, say you banged me silly all over that pristine duvet."

"First chance I get," he said. He stood up, hitched his trunks, brushed past her, and waddled toward the saloon.

"Everything okay?" Liz called from above.

"Ducky," Salustrio said. "Let's get the hell out of here."

Salustrio was in the cockpit, smoking another cigar and laughing with Jason at the helm. Her fury rising, Els imagined him hosting Coxe in the Goldman partners' dining room to trade lies of conquest.

Fighting the yacht's heel, she made her way back to the table, where she sat and rested her forehead on her arms. The boat's motion churned the champagne and lobster in her stomach. Nausea pulled at her tongue. Though she took deep breaths and lowered her head to her knees, she was light-headed, and both chilled and sweaty at the same time. She prided herself on holding her liquor and never getting airsick, even in the most turbulent conditions, but here her gyroscope had lost its bearings.

When Liz came down the ladder, she asked for a glass of water.

His glance was appraising. "You need to go topside."

She straightened and pulled her lapels tighter. "Don't tell me what to do."

"While you're on this boat, *Ms. Gordon*, I'll tell you what's in your best interest, and you'll do it." He took a ginger ale from the refrigerator and held it out to her.

"First you bully," she said, keeping her hands in her lap. "Then play nice."

"I'm responsible for everyone on this boat. Whether I'm nice or a bully is up to them."

"I'm going to lie down over there."

"You'll keep feeling shitty if you stay below."

"How the fuck do you know?"

"Twenty f-ing years at sea," he said. "Now get up that ladder."

Salustrio's laughter floated down from above and Els looked out the hatchway, wondering if the joke he was sharing with Jason was on her.

Liz took her elbow and pulled her out of her chair. "Do I have to carry you?"

"I'll thank you not to touch me again," she said. She climbed into the sunlight. As soon as she left the odor of lobster behind, she began to revive. When Salustrio glanced at her, she hesitated.

"Go forward," Liz said. "Away from that smoke." Carrying the ginger ale, a banquette cushion, and a towel, he led her to the bow and kicked aside a coiled line. He propped the cushion against a hatch cover. "Lie down there."

She sat down, pulled the robe over her knees, and hugged them. Liz dropped the towel onto the deck and nestled the ginger ale against the cushion. "You've had more sun than you think. Cover every inch. If you have to toss, aim that way." Under the jib, deep green water laced with foam sluiced by. "You'll be less queasy if you focus on something far away that's not going up and down." He squinted toward Nevis. "Try Jack's, that house sitting all by itself in the big patch of green."

She gazed at the house, intrigued to see it from this vantage point, and imagined its view of the expanse of sea and *Iguana*, a tiny copper arrow of sail crossing The Narrows.

Footsteps near her head and the anchor chain's rattle woke her. When she opened her eyes, she was looking into the crown of a baseball cap, its grommets like tiny portholes, which she assumed Liz had placed over her face. She sat up. Her folded clothing was next to her. Jason stood on the foredeck coiling a line, his elbow a jerking wing. He wedged the coil between the halyard and the mast. *Iguana* rode at anchor in deep water off the Resort.

The nausea lingered, a tension in the back of her throat. She stood up unsteadily, swished tepid ginger ale in her mouth, and spat it over the side.

"Sea sick is the worst kinda sickness," Jason said. He pronounced it "wust." His voice was deep; his Jamaican accent strong. "You feelin' bettah?"

"I can't wait to get off this tub," she said.

His sunglasses hid all expression. "May you wish be granted soon," he said, and went sure-footedly to the cockpit.

When she passed through the saloon to change into her clothes, Salustrio was bellowing into the ship-to-shore about a deal. He muffled the radio against his shoulder. "Cap'll take you ashore," he said. "I've got a situation here."

Liz stood with his legs apart, working the tiller behind his back. He steered the dinghy slowly, producing only a ripple of wake, and still Els gripped the gunwales and had to manage her breathing. She stared at a scar that zigzagged through the golden hair of Liz's left calf.

"Something went sour between you and Mr. S," he said.

"Your captain radar working overtime again?" she said.

"Servants are wallpaper with ears," he said. "I want *Iguana*'s guests to enjoy themselves."

"Meaning him or me?"

"Shouldn't be mutually exclusive," he said. "Most people use what they have to get what they want."

"What, you think like he does, that I would try to fuck my way into a job?" She turned around on the thwart so she was faced forward and stared at the slowly approaching wharf.

In her first summer at Standard Hebrides Bank, Coxe had insisted she go for burgers with him and some of the other new recruits—younger men, eager ass-kissers all. After paying the tab, he'd asked her to stay behind to discuss something important, to the unvarnished envy of her colleagues. Saying the topic was sensitive enough to require confidentiality, he led her into an empty function room. When he grabbed her breasts, pinned her against the closed door, and stuck his tongue into her mouth, she'd stomped on his instep with her spike heel and fled the restaurant. She'd agonized all weekend about facing the repulsive wanker on Monday, but he'd been unfazed, even jaunty, apart from a slight limp he faked occasionally ever since, always drawing chuckles from the guys. Every time, she seethed about the story he'd surely concocted and the impossibility of a rebuttal.

Salustrio's arrogance clung to her like a petrol stench. Her chosen career was a testosterone obstacle course, and the prize had begun to seem a meager reward for the relentless rigors of the race.

Liz snugged the dinghy against the wharf and tossed her tote onto the planks. She ignored his hand and sprang up as if out of a pool.

"There's a dare on the table," he said. "Have the guts to venture underwater."

"Pigs will fly first."

He revved the engine; blue smoke curled around his waist. "Then how about this one," he said. "Try going a whole hour without saying something bitchy." He sat on the dinghy's gunwale and sped back toward *Iguana*.

CHAPTER 3

Els rounded the planter of ferns and philodendron at the entrance to the dining room and saw, too late, the Salustrio family clustered at the maître d's podium. Challenge with a hint of apprehension flickered in Salustrio's eyes before he looked away.

Marlena waved her freshly manicured nails. "Paul said you had a lovely sail."

"He would," Els said, and strode out the side door and onto the spongy grass. From the safety of the dark garden, she looked through the French doors to see Marlena finger-wagging at Salustrio, whose shoulders, hands, and eyebrows were all busy shrugging.

Els strode to the beach and, sandals dangling from her fingers, dawdled along the line of chaises. She sat on the last one, out of reach of the lights from Sunshine's, the beach bar just beyond the Resort's boundary. Patrons stacked the bar three-deep and filled the picnic tables on the sand. Conversation and laughter mingled with Jimmy Cliff singing "You Can Get It If You Really Want." In her strappy dress, she felt all dolled up compared to Sunshine's T-shirted patrons. Though accustomed to eating alone all over the world, she couldn't brave this boisterous crowd tonight.

Someone near the water picked up the song's chorus—Liz, playing air guitar and singing in a tuneful falsetto. Behind him, Jason glided along in an erect, loose-hipped stride, sunglasses in place.

Liz saw her and angled toward her chaise. "What an unexpected pleasure, Ms. Gordon," he said. "Or is it Lady Eleanor?"

"Either beats bitch," she said.

"It's a fine line we *rental captains* walk," he said. "On the one hand, I take your shit, bite my tongue. On the other, I save you from drowning—you're welcome, by the way—and worry I might have to save you from Mr. S, who happens to be bankrolling my whole week."

"I can take care of myself," she said.

"Then why are you sitting here all alone? Is a crowded bar as scary as the deep, dark sea?"

"Both are full of predators," she said.

He looked into the throng. "I've never thought of it that way."

"We live in different food chains."

Jason, who'd been hanging back near the water, walked up. "Got to eat, mon."

Liz nodded. "Let us buy you dinner, Lady Eleanor."

"Els," she said. "Why should I want any more of your company?"

"Do you always make it so hard for a guy to apologize?" he said. "My parting shot was over the line."

"Did I miss the 'I'm sorry'?"

"You did," he said, and grinned. "I was provoked." He held out his hand. "We'll protect you from the denizens of Sunshine's." When she didn't move, he took her hand and pulled her to her feet. In the floodlights, his eyes were clear blue, unguarded. "Recovered your land legs yet?"

"I've been in a state all afternoon," she said. "Antsy and disoriented."

"Gotta let that attack wear off," he said. "Time for a Killer Bee. Captain's orders."

"No bossing," she said.

He released her hand. "On shore, we're equal."

She gave him a quick once-over. "Prove you believe that."

Led by Jason, they snaked through the restaurant to a picnic table occupied by three men in windjammer logo shirts. Liz shouted a drink order to a waiter who was maneuvering among the tables holding aloft paper plates that buckled under their cargo of food. Els sat at one end of the bench, Jason sat opposite her, and Liz perched on a palm stump at the end of the table. "Els," he said, leaning forward on his elbows, "this is Jimmy, Craig, and Spot, seamen of the *Wind Spirit* and reprobates all." Jimmy and Craig were ruddy preppies, but Spot's dark skin was splotched with pink, giving him a piebald appearance and making his nickname as apt as it was cruel.

The waiter set down bottles of Carib and a plastic cup. "Killa Bee fuh the lady," he said. "Watch out fuh de sting."

She lifted the cup and looked at Liz.

"Secret recipe," he said. "Heavily guarded."

"Zombie material—every kind of rum in the bar, with a splash of fruit juice?" she asked.

"Close enough." Liz banged his bottle on the table. "A toast," he called. The hum dropped a notch and patrons turned to stare. "To Lady Eleanor, who needs a little festivity on her birthday." He touched his bottle to her cup. "Riffraff such as we will do our humble best." The sailors and patrons toasted her.

She raised her cup. "*Sláinte.*"

"Slan what?" Liz asked.

"Any rental captain worth his salt should know every toast in the world," she said.

"It's Gaelic," Craig said.

"*Lou wai,*" Liz said.

"I got that one often enough in Hong Kong," she said, "until they learned I could keep up."

"Mebbe you hold you rum better dan champagne," Jason said.

"Maybe I'm better on land than on a careening boat," she said.

Jason looked toward the bar.

Els tasted the rum punch, its fresh nutmeg a pungent sawdust on her tongue. The restaurant's buzz resumed.

"What tales this time, lads?" Liz said.

"A Belgian scores some mega weed in Montego Bay," said Craig. "Thinks he's Spider Man and scrambles up the main rats, then gets the heebie-jeebies and grabs on like glue. Spot goes after him and the bastard freaks out."

"Imagine *that* face in the masthead nav," Liz said. "I'd be scared too."

"I had to go up there and talk the sumbitch down," Jimmy said.

"Been up to me, I'd have heaved him from the yard," Liz said.

Els tuned out and looked around. The bar was constructed of scrap wood and lattice painted in the colors of the Nevis flag fluttering from a nearby palm. Flags and pennants of countries, states, schools, football teams, and rums hung from the rafters. The speakers pumped Bob Marley. The Killer Bee went down as easily as pineapple juice.

The sailors excused themselves and regrouped at the bar. Jason exchanged a glance with Liz and followed them. He stopped their waiter, pulled out a roll of cash, and peeled off bills. As he moved through the crowd, people detached themselves from their companions to have a whispered word with him and shake his hand.

"Doesn't Jason worry about carrying around so much money?" Els asked.

"He lives in sort of a cash economy," Liz said. "And he *can* take care of himself." He moved to Jason's spot opposite her and held up his empty beer bottle to summon the waiter. When he came over, Liz asked for the menu.

"Mahi-mahi come in today, chicken, ribs, lobster," the waiter said, and looked at Els, who lifted her cup. He raised his eyebrows.

"The lobster here's the best on the island," Liz said.

"Go ahead, rub it in," she said, and ordered chicken.

By the time their food arrived, Liz had explained how *Iguana* split her year between the Caribbean and the Mediterranean and Els had admitted that her work took her all over the world, but never to the Caribbean. She'd also downed her second Killer Bee, switched to beer, and was famished.

Liz dug into his grilled lobster tail, prying the meat out with his fingers, while Els struggled to separate her chicken leg and thigh with her plastic knife.

"Forget your fancy manners, Lady Eleanor," Liz said. He tilted his head. "What kind of royalty are you, anyway?"

"Salustrio calls me Lady only to bait me," she said. "My father's a legitimate Sir. He was knighted for being a power in UK finance." She picked up her chicken leg, and soon her hands were bronzed with barbecue sauce. "I'm just a lass from the Highlands—at least, I was until I was exiled to a nun's school in Edinburgh."

"They teach you to swear?"

She smiled. "Nah, that was the evil influence of schools in London and Cambridge—Massachusetts, that is—and investment banking, first in New York and now back in London."

"You've lived around," he said. "No wonder you don't sound like our usual Brits."

"I'm a Scot, not a Brit."

"What's the difference, once you peel away the skirts and bagpipes?"

"Centuries of history," she said. "What stripe of Yank are you?"

"I come from *Iguana*." He drained his beer. His rumpled shirt, a cornflower-blue linen, was missing its top button. When he leaned forward on his elbows, a blue bead on a leather thong dangled from the opening.

"Dropped on board by the stork?"

"Other boats before that," he said. "Do you have family?"

"A father I adore."

"That's all?"

"I was raised by a nanny, a widow who moved in when I was two. She and Father have been shacked up for decades. She tried to mother me, but I wouldn't let her. She has . . . had . . . a son of her own."

"Your mom's dead."

"Might as well be." She tidied the mound of rice and pigeon peas on her plate. "Let's not get into that."

He cocked that scarred eyebrow, took her beer, and drank from it. The gesture felt challenging, intimate, playful.

She reached for the bottle even though she didn't want it back. "Get your own beer."

"You've had enough."

"Says who?"

When she pushed her unfinished dinner aside, a dog padded over, her tail waving figure eights, and Els cupped her chin. "Yir master wouldn't approve of me feeding ye from the table."

"She might starve without table scraps," Liz said. He pulled Els's remaining chicken off the bones and held a piece out to the dog, who took it delicately and slunk under a nearby table to eat it. "We're overrun with feral dogs," he said, "but Trixie's smart enough to hang out here and hit up the softie tourists."

"And the softie sailors," she said. "You're only encouraging bad behavior."

"Begging's a tough way to make a living," he said. He piled the bones onto his lobster shell and set Els's plate on the sand. Trixie finished the food and licked the paper plate until she had chased it out of the bar. Liz turned back to Els. "Do you like what you do?"

"Why do you care?"

His eyes darkened as they had on the yacht when she was snappish. She'd discovered his tell; she wondered what it signified. Hurt, reined-in anger? Maybe both.

"I only ask a question if I want to know the answer," he said.

The tables were emptying. A couple walked tipsily into the darkness, their arms draped around each other's waists, their hips bumping.

"I'm a scrapper," she said. "M&A is one scrap after another. Competition on the outside, colleagues itching to savage you on the inside. Addictive, in its own weird way." She ran her plastic knife blade in and out between the tines of her fork. "I crave some of what it gets me."

"The money," he said.

She shook her head. Work had become a place to hide, a reason to drag herself out of bed in the morning, a way to fill the days, the nights. "Belonging," she said. "The A-team. Work I'm good at. Respect, if grudging, from both sides of the table." A man at the bar started to sing loudly and off-key to a gaggle of laughing women. "The money is just a way to keep score," she said. "Everything is about keeping score."

When the last notes of Aretha Franklin's "Chain of Fools" faded out, she heard the surf fizzing onto the sand.

"Why the surprising nickname?" she asked.

"Why do *you* care?"

Touché, she thought. "Who wouldn't be intrigued by a macho guy choosing a flimsy name?"

"Nicknames choose you," he said. He gazed out at the boats. "I once had a pet green iguana named Curly." The music shifted to Linda Ronstadt's "Desperado." He mouthed a line of the lyrics.

"One of my favorite songs," she said.

"That voice'll stab your heart," he said. He listened for another line. "Curly and I spent a lot of time in bars. I'd challenge tourist guys to a game of darts, and, since I always won, they'd have to either kiss Curly or buy everyone a round of drinks."

"Did you challenge women?"

"Sure, but they had to kiss *me*. After Curly bit a guy, I left her on board. By then, people were calling me Lizard Man. When Jason and I took over *Iguana*—that was already her name—well, Liz just stuck."

"I thought iguanas were afraid of people."

"I got her as a hatchling and spent a lot of time with her."

"A lizard charmer," she said. *Patient, gentle, constant,* she thought. "Was she lurking with the grog while we were sailing?"

"Someone stole her."

"Desperado" ended; James Taylor's "Mexico" followed. Liz tapped the rhythm on his thigh. When the waiter signaled toward their empty bottles, he shook his head. "Got big plans for the rest of your time here?"

Getting that elusive grip, she thought, but she said, "Exploring."

"We're off at dawn for English Harbour, or I'd dare you to try sailing again."

"You couldn't get me back on that boat of yours, even on a dare."

"Your loss," he said. He rose and extended his hand.

She tried to stand, but her legs wouldn't cooperate.

"Not the first or last Killer Bee casualty." He helped her up and slipped his arm through hers. He smelled of beer, soap, and salt. He navigated her to the water's edge, where a bright lap of foam gleaming in the Resort's lights guided them back to the wharf.

"Did you make your birthday wish?" he said.

"If wishes were horses . . . ."

"Never miss a chance to wish."

She squeezed her eyes shut, pretending. Over her few childhood birthday cakes, she'd wished her mother would come home, and when it hadn't worked, she'd stopped making birthday wishes. Now, with all her plans upended, even if her current fog dissipated, she didn't know what future to wish for.

She wobbled and her eyes sprang open; he touched her shoulders to steady her. She reached for the railing and he let go.

"What terrified you about the water today?" he asked.

Underwater lights attached to the pilings cast arcs of turquoise in the otherwise black sea.

"I've always had this thing about dark water, but I don't think that was it—or all of it. Is there something spooky about this island?" Ever since her arrival, she'd felt porous and fragmented, as if she were cracking open. Drunk even when sober, and overly candid when tipsy.

"Could be just superstition, but I've heard people say there are magnets in the mountain that can cause clairvoyance or hypersensitivity to the supernatural," Liz said. "Or maybe what you feel is just that old Caribbean magic coaxing you to let down your guard."

They strolled to the end of the wharf.

"Jason beat me to the zodiac," he said. "I'll have to swim home."

"You're joking," she said, eyeing the inky water, the distance to *Iguana*.

"Got a better idea?" In one swift motion, he removed his necklace, looped it over her head, and said, "Many happy returns."

The warm bead fell heavily against her breastbone. She inspected it under the wharf light: a pentagonal shape, worn smooth. "You mustn't," she said. "This is some sort of talisman."

"It's a blue bead of Statia," he said. "Rare diving treasure. Too bad you'll never get down there to see any of it." He touched the bead, then dove into the water. He surfaced in a swirl of phosphorescence, looked up at her, and feathered his arms, which made him appear to sparkle. "See you around."

His words hung between them, more a question than a farewell. Els clasped the bead, the only impetuous birthday gift she'd ever received.

He stroked away, crossed the beams from several yachts, and disappeared into the darkness.

CHAPTER 4

Els insisted on sitting in the front passenger seat for Sparrow's tour, the first stop of which was the Culturama Bar, where he bought rotis to eat along the way. The aroma of curried vegetables partially masked the odor of diesel and open drains that pervaded the congested center of Charlestown. On the sidewalks, uniformed schoolchildren and bank employees crowded among women in dresses. She'd expected the island people to have a distinctive look, a tribal resemblance, and was surprised by the diversity.

When she mentioned this, Sparrow stared into the knot of traffic ahead and said, "Nevis people come down from slaves, miss." He pointed out a fenced empty lot near the sea and a plaque across the street. "Das where dey say dey used to sell dem. We come from different parts a' Africa. White masters like black women, so we mixed up with dem now." The traffic cleared and Sparrow maneuvered the van toward the courthouse. "De white people tek way we identity," he said. "So we hadda fin' a new one. We is Nevisians now."

Pricked by her own display of insensitivity and naïveté, she looked out the window at an elderly man soaking his legs in the hot spring below the remains of the Bath Hotel.

They drove around the island counterclockwise. Sparrow showed her the plantations, some mere ruins of sugar works, some transformed into posh hotels, each with a history both rich and cruel. She was charmed by the place names—Gingerland, Morning Star, Saint John's Fig Tree, Coconut Walk, Chicken Stone, Hermitage, Golden Rock—and the views of neighboring Redonda and Montserrat.

"That house we saw, the one that's for sale, must be as old as some of these others," she said. "Does it have a name too?"

"Trouble," Sparrow said. He pulled up in front of Nevis Pottery, where, he explained, the craftspeople worked with locally dug clay. He ushered her inside and told her she couldn't leave without a souvenir.

She selected a rustic horse, captivated by its energy.

Once they'd passed the airport and the cottages at Oualie Beach, Els began looking for the abandoned house, and as they climbed the hill toward its gate, she said, "Pull over there."

"Crazy to stop here," Sparrow said.

"Pull over."

With a whispered expletive, he stopped in the dirt strip between the road and the wall and looked at her. "Doan get out here, miss."

"Just a peek."

When she opened her door, he grabbed her arm.

"What's the matter with you?" she said.

"Jumbie doan want nobody 'round here."

She shook free and said, "Jumbie, whoever he is, will never be the wiser." She hopped out and went to the gate. The frosted flames of giant blue agaves stood sentry on either side of the drive. A Jeep was parked farther up the hill, the trunk of an uprooted palm dimpling its bonnet. The tree's dried fronds obscured the view of the house, but she could see wide stone steps rising to a covered gallery with a frill of gingerbread trim. Another fallen palm had sheared off a corner of the hip roof.

A bearded man stood at the end of the gallery beside a crimson hibiscus. Wedging her sandal between the boards of the gate, Els pulled herself up, waved, and called to him.

"Miss, who you talking to?" Sparrow said.

When she looked back at the house, the man was gone. She returned to the van and pulled out her tote.

"Get in, miss," Sparrow said. "Now."

"In a sec." Coralita vine had claimed most of the wall, nearly covering a sign warning "Beware of Gardenia." She opened the letterbox built into the wall with "Jack" painted on its door. Empty but for a spider's web and the bodies of its prey.

Sparrow hit the horn.

"Just hold your horses," she called. She took out her beach read, *Island of the Moon*, and scribbled the estate agent's number inside.

Sparrow shot her a look of pure terror, gunned the engine, and raced away toward town, swerving around a man on a donkey.

"You crazy son of a bitch," she yelled after him. She kicked a pebble across the road, followed it, and threw it as hard as she could toward the sea. It bounced off a boulder and plopped into an incoming wave. She gazed back at the house and garden, which evoked her favorite childhood stories—tales in which nothing was as it appeared—and wondered what secrets they held.

After waiting for a lorry to pass, she crossed the road again, clambered over the gate, and threaded her way up the drive around nests of desiccated palm fronds. The Jeep was hitched to a trailer cradling a small boat under a tarp. Beyond it, in the center of a gravel court, blue starbursts of lily of the Nile erupted from an enormous rusty cauldron. The property's silence was a presence, but when she listened, she heard doves cooing, birds whistling, a skittering in the brush. She smelled hot stone, damp earth, and the fragrance of gardenia, though she saw none blooming.

She climbed to the gallery where a cannon—too small for a weapon, too large for a toy—was mounted on a stone pedestal. Sitting on the top step, she gazed toward the sea until sunspots polka-dotted her eyelids. The view sent her into a fuzzy memory of azure sky between palm branches, the scents of gardenia and oil paint, and a woman singing in Italian, but she didn't know if she was remembering something real or wished for or dreamed.

A man was standing at the foot of the steps. She started, not having heard his barefoot approach, and stood up. "What the hell are you doing here?" She glanced down the drive, mapping the fastest route back to the road.

He chuckled. "Getting a front-row seat for the sunset," he said. "Just like you." *American*, she thought. *Midwestern*. There was a mocking confidence in his cocked hip and ironic smile. A gardenia poked from his shirt pocket; his trousers were cut off at the knees, the edges frayed. The sun at his back turned the locks escaping his stubby ponytail into a chestnut aura. He was younger than the bearded man she'd seen before, barely thirty.

"I'm not staying that long," she said, and hurried down to the court, skirting where he stood.

"The sunset's magical from here," he said. "It's why this house even exists. The fiery Sophia wanted this view. It was her joy . . . and her undoing."

"Sophia who?"

He poked his toe at a bed of ground cover the color of papal velvet, which was spreading headlong onto the gravel. "Unless someone inherits the obsession for this place, this garden will revert to cactus and weeds," he said. He climbed the steps, sat down, and gazed toward the sea with an expression of wondrous anticipation, as if the daily sunset was, in fact, a magic show about to begin.

"What is it about this place that would make my driver clam up and run off?" she asked.

"During the big hurricane last year," he said, "the owner was supposedly spotted on the seawall over by Tamarind Cove. No trace of him since. The locals believe he jumped into the sea, or let it sweep him away, and that his jumbie haunts this place. Won't set foot here, even to loot."

"Mr. Jumbie," she said, "is this Jack person's ghost, then."

"Do you believe in ghosts?"

"Fervently," she said. "I grew up in a stone pile in the Highlands. Been in the family for centuries."

He smiled. "Scotland: home of some of the best ghosts. Ever see one?"

"Once when we were children, my . . . friend . . . and I thought we'd seen something, but we couldn't be sure."

"Spirits are, like a lot of things, in the mind of the beholder," he said. "Only receptive people can see them. Smell that gardenia? The flower of secret love. That fragrance takes me back to junior prom, 1977. The last uncomplicated night of my life."

"I took you for younger than that," she said.

"I never said it was *my* junior prom." He settled back on his elbows.

Though she'd planned to wait for the sunset, the idea of being caught in the near dark with this stranger—at best enigmatic, at worst a complete nutter—clanged all her citified self-defense bells. She took a few steps toward the drive.

"Don't leave before the show," he said. "You've nothing to fear from Jack's jumbie, if that's what you're worried about." His gaze was tender. "Or from me." He hopped up, went to the cannon, and stared at the sun, which was oozing into the sea.

Els's glance bounced between him and the sun.

"Three, two, one. Bingo," he said. "See the green flash?"

"Where?"

"You weren't paying attention," he said. "Caribbean holy grail. If the horizon is clear, the sun makes a green flare just before she disappears. Doubters say it's just a trick our eyes play, a spin of the color wheel, but I believe it's Mama Sun's little good night wink. Some people think a green flash brings good luck."

"I ran through my luck a while back."

"Pay attention," he said, "or you might not recognize luck when it appears."

In the sky, high puffs of cloud were turning peach with purple edges, and a swirl of golden wisps hung in the west. "You should see yourself in this light," he said. "That red hair might burst into flame any second."

If he was going to flirt, she was going to run. "Enjoy the evening." Without waiting for a response, she headed down the hill at a purposeful and fearless pace, abandoning the obstructed drive for the more open grassy patches.

She hadn't heard him following, but while she was scrambling over the gate, he vaulted the wall; he was standing at the side of the road by the time she made it over. The gardenia was now behind his ear and he removed it, smiled rakishly, and set it on the ground between them. At close range she could see that he wore an earring, a tiny skull and crossbones with ruby eyes that seemed to glow from within.

He caught her staring at it. "A sailor's earring pays for his burial if he dies at sea."

She looked left and right along the empty road. He pointed down the hill. "The receptionist at Oualie will arrange a taxi to the Resort."

"How do you know where I'm staying?"

"Lucky guess." His hand over his heart, he made a little bow. "See you." He began walking toward Charlestown, whistling, "Begin the Beguine."

When she stooped to pick up the gardenia, she thought to question him about the warning on the gate, but by the time she'd straightened up again, the road was deserted.

CHAPTER 5

Cursing, Tony Hallowell struggled with the padlock and overgrown chain until his face had gone nearly as pink as the coralita vine. "Goddamn jungle swallows everything," he said. He propped the gate open with his knee.

"When was the last time you showed this place?" Els squeezed through the opening, avoiding Tony's belly. His breath smelled of this morning's mint and yesterday's rum.

"Never," he said. "Since Jack Griggs is only believed to have drowned, maybe on purpose, and no corpse ever turned up, the court has only just ruled his estate can be settled. What you see here is as he left it."

"No family?"

"No contact in decades, as I understand it. The heir's solicitor is handling everything. Mind where you step." He started up the drive. He was slack-shouldered, balding. Everything about him sagged.

"What's that enormous stalk with the orange flowers?" she said.

"We call it a century plant," he said. "There's a serious garden under all this mess."

"And the price includes everything?"

"'As is, where is,' as we say in the trade." He walked onto the court, planted his knuckles on his hips, and surveyed the roof. A solar water heater dangled from one of its fasteners. A green vervet monkey like those she'd seen at Golden Rock was sitting on it and glaring down at them.

"Is he part of the package?" she asked.

"Vermin," Tony said. "Bloody nuisance, all of them. Had enough?"

"I have to see the inside."

"I told you, I haven't the key yet."

"Who the hell does, then?"

"Jack, presumably."

She smiled tightly. "Surely you carry a tire iron in your car."

"Break the lock and leave the house open until I get a replacement?"

"You said yourself that nobody dares bother the place."

"Christ a'mighty," Tony said, and headed back to the car.

Els circled the house, snapping photos. She examined the stonework built into the hillside, which included a cistern, cracked and dry, with pipes feeding it from the roof. In the overgrown grounds were an outbuilding with its roof torn off, giant mango trees, and a row of gardenias as high as a hedge.

A hummingbird brushing her arm startled and delighted her. Its hovering produced a surprisingly loud whir. From the tiny bird she sensed acknowledgment, mutual curiosity, and welcome. They stared at each other until Tony's crashing through the palm fronds broke the spell, and the bird flashed green and zoomed off to gather nectar from the hibiscus.

Tony jammed the tire iron under the door's hasp and the screws popped away, along with a piece of the doorframe.

Els touched the raw wood. "Just look what you did."

"Relax, will you? It's not yours. Yet." He switched on his torch, wrenched open the door, and waved her through.

The kitchen was as cool as a cellar. Shelves with storage jars, an oilcloth thumbtacked to the table, three mismatched chairs in different paint box colors. Making its ghostly way up the wall was a sun-starved vine that had invaded between window and sill. A green gecko poked its head out of the cooker burner and puffed its golden throat; when Els stamped her foot, it retreated beneath the ring, reappeared on the stone floor, and sprinted under the fridge.

Tony pointed his torch toward some stone steps. "Be my guest."

With each step the temperature rose, the light dwindled, and a putrid odor became more pronounced. The next level was a single room. Light pricking through cracks in the shutters barely illuminated stout beams supporting the floor above.

Tony ran his torch over the ceiling like a lecturer's laser. "There's a quirky bathroom at that end, a bedroom in the middle, and a sort of study above here, if I remember correctly. Trust me, it's odd but totally unremarkable."

"Are you sure you're an estate agent?" Els said. She took the torch and examined the room: a big leather chair and ottoman, threadbare sofas, a refectory table, elegant proportions, crowded bookshelves, and something else. "Mother of God."

Tony hurried up behind her. "The crazy bugger must have been on one of his legendary tears."

The sisal carpet had been rolled back, and on the stone floor were the remains of a fire made from a smashed wooden chair. Mixed with the ashes and charred spindles were partially burned black-and-white photographs, all of young women, many of them nude.

"His profession, or just destroying the evidence before their husbands caught him?" she asked.

Tony picked up a photo. The flames had spared the head and torso of a bare-breasted teenager looking seductively into the lens, her lips in a pout. "He was a teacher, story spinner, tinkerer, ladies' man, brawler, intermittent drunk," Tony said. "But photographer? Not to my knowledge." He dropped the photo onto the pile.

"How do we get upstairs?" she said.

"I remember a stair starting somewhere over here," Tony said.

The paneled wall looked solid.

"A secret stairway," she said. "We have one of those at home. My favorite place as a wee lassie."

Tony pounded his fist against the paneling. Els snapped a photo of the room, and he jumped at the flash before pounding again. One of the panels gave back a hollow sound. They examined the seams.

"Door must be swollen tight," he said. "Surely you don't want me prying away at it. You'll just have to use your imagination."

"So did Jack, it seems," she said. "When I walked around the house, I saw a platform thing off the bathroom end that looks like a shower, but you'd have to climb out a window to reach it."

"I've always heard the place is one big Rube Goldberg," Tony said. Perspiration beaded his bald spot and mooned his underarms. "Let's get out of here."

Tony tapped the screws into place and hurried down the drive. Els lingered in the court to take a long look at the house; a lick of breeze carrying the scent of gardenia played at her shoulders.

Tony drove toward the Resort in such a hurry that Els braced her feet under the dash.

"How is it for you, living here?" she asked.

"Christ, Lauretta and I could go to a party every night during the season," he said. "The same little knot of expats, same old pigs-in-a-blanket hors d'oeuvres. Only thing that changes is who's sleeping with whom. No wonder we all drink." He turned in at the Resort gate.

"Is there any restriction on foreigners owning real estate?"

"It's encouraged," he said. He described the licenses, background checks, taxes, and fees associated with each.

"You call levies of sixteen percent *encouragement*?"

"The government sometimes throws in economic citizenship for buyers spending at least three hundred fifty thousand U.S. dollars." He slowed to let a golf cart pass. "Jack's wouldn't qualify.

Economic citizenship in the Federation goes only with new developments, most of them on St. Kitts. You'd have to petition."

"And the chances?"

"Any dealing with the government's a minefield." He stopped in front of the Great House and turned off the engine. The heat closed in immediately.

She opened her door. The air smelled of cut grass. "Remind me of the asking price."

"Seven hundred ninety-five thousand US dollars, all-inclusive."

"Offer them three fifty."

"They'll never take less than seven hundred."

"You forgot the ghost, not to mention the porn." Els flashed her deal smile. "The place doesn't have one intact roof. Lord knows what I'd find on proper inspection."

Tony started the engine. The vents spewed hot air that gradually cooled.

"Three fifty," she said. "Cash. No contingencies, except the license. Closing ASAP."

Tony leaned back and tapped his fingers on the steering wheel. "The license could take months."

"Assuming we cut a deal, I'll want to sign everything possible before I leave on Friday. You can handle any remaining details later. I'll wire the money."

Tony shook his head, but Els caught that broker's glint in his eye. She fished out a business card and scribbled the phone number at her flat. "And do inquire about that citizenship."

He studied the card before sticking it into a clip on the visor. "You'll hear from me."

"My breath is bated," she said.

The same fisherman had been on the Resort beach the previous afternoon, following the pelicans and scanning the shallows where they dove. His cast net dangled like a crinoline from his hand, the hem weighted all around with leaden teardrops. His dark skin was grayed with dried salt, his back broad, his legs bowed.

He stood thigh deep and peered into the water. A minute, two. When he swung his arm in a wide arc, the net sailed and landed in a perfect circle. He tugged the mesh closed, lifted it from the water, and carried it back to shore as tenderly as a small child. The low sun glinted on flashes of silver caught in its folds when he shook the catch into his bucket.

Els took out her camera and stood up. "Toss that again."

He looked at her. "Five dollars. US."

"You're joking."

"Local color ain't free." He slung the net over his shoulder. "It take years scraping for a livin' to make me this pictureful."

She lowered her camera and squinted at him. "Cheeky bugger."

He stared back, then smiled, a broad, generous grin. "Damn right." He moved a few feet away, cast another perfect circle, and let the net sink. She could have sworn he was posing.

After bringing in his last catch, the fisherman gathered up his gear and sat on a chaise at the end of the long rank. Tybee, the attendant whose job it was to adjust Els's umbrella, spritz her with spring water, and bring her drinks, dropped an armload of used towels and hurried to the foot of the fisherman's chaise.

"I should 'a guess this a you sorry ass again," he said, arms akimbo. He cut his eyes in Els's direction. She pretended to read. "Move along, man. The chairs for the guests dem."

"If you think there is *one local* that doan know the Resort policy on these fuckin' chairs," the fisherman said, "you even more chupit dan people say."

Tybee responded in rapid-fire dialect; all Els could understand was, "Don't interfere with me." Tybee's head was shaven; his stud earring sparkled.

"Where all you guests, anyway," the fisherman said. "Havin' a cocktail whilst you pick up they laundry?"

"I na kay wha' you say. I done with fishin'," Tybee said. "This job make more in a week dan you make in a month haulin' dem stinkin' pots."

"At least me ain' wukking fuh no white man."

"Zat true? Who you sellin' them fish to?"

"De white man my customer, fool, not my boss."

"You got to go. *Now.*" Tybee grabbed the fisherman's arm and pulled him off the chair.

"Tybee, something wrong?" a man called from the water sports pavilion.

Tybee glanced at Els. "I got it, Boss," he called back, then said in a low voice, "Doan mess me up, man."

Els stood up and walked over to them. "Tybee, would you be kind enough to bring sparkling water for me and my guest?"

Tybee hesitated.

"You heard me," Els said.

Tybee looked from her to the fisherman, then started toward the drinks kiosk. The fisherman sat down again and called after him, "Hey, Mr. Clean, ask the lady if she want you picture in you pressy uniform. Or maybe you make a better souvenir when you was haulin' them pots."

Els sat on the chaise next to the fisherman's.

"What you want with me, miss?" he asked.

"I want to know how living here is for you."

"You mean outside the gates a' this little paradise? You best ask a real local. I'm Anguillan. Been here only twenty-three years."

"That's local enough," she said. "How is the economy, from your perspective? Is the government competent?"

Tybee arrived with a tray. He poured a Perrier and handed it to Els, then set the tray down on the table between the chaises. "Watch that mouth a' yours, Uncle," he said, and walked away.

Els handed her glass to the fisherman and poured the other for herself. "A relative?"

"Uncle and Auntie are terms of respect for you elders, but never coming from him," he said. "He my wife's brother son."

"That sounded like a threat."

"No secret I disrespect dis gorment," he said. "Bunch a crooks and fools, including my wife's family. Especially my wife's family." His speech was peppered with a sort of nasal "anh?" but not as if to solicit her agreement or reply.

"I read about a secessionist movement," she said. Little Nevis trying to separate from the bigger St. Kitts, which dominated the Federation's decisions and sucked up most of its wealth, made her think of Scotland and England, perhaps equally disaffected and equally bound.

"We gon' win, too, maybe next time around," he said.

"What's your response to people who say this little rock is too small to be a country?"

"Way I see it, we more or less on our own anyway. Sinkits only do what good for Sinkits."

She raised her glass. "Here's to independence," she said, and felt a stab of passion for the Scottish cause that had cost her so dearly. She took a sip and tried to swallow that buzz of excitement along with the Perrier bubbles. "Call me Els," she said.

"Finney," her companion said, and sipped with his pinkie raised. He settled into the chaise.

"Did you know Jack Griggs?" she asked.

He watched a pelican glide by, its wing tips nearly grazing the water. "Sea claim the best a' them," he said. The pelican rose up, dove, surfaced facing the other way, twitched its tail feathers, and gulped down its catch.

"Indulge me with a little information," she said.

"Why you interested in ol' Horseshoe Jack?"

"He's intriguing," she said. "His house even more so. I'm a bit obsessed with it."

Finney looked at the yachts. "He a good friend. American. Here about twenty years. He about fifty when he take his leave."

"A serious drinker, I hear."

"When he wasn't sweetin' up the ladies?" He smiled at the memory. "He cherish every kind a' women. Old days, he sometimes keep several goin' at the same time, and somehow they doan claw each other up." His smile faded. "Near the end, though, things get messy."

"Catfights?"

"Last gyull he hook up wid, very young. Treat her bad."

"Violent?"

Finney looked away. "Gotta bounce," he said. He put his glass on the table and swung his feet off the chaise. "He was unbeatable at darts. Even blind drunk." When he stood up, his hand went to his lower back. He bent slowly to lift his bucket.

"Why 'Horseshoe Jack'?"

"He excel at horseshoes too," he said. "Enjoy you holiday, Miss Els." He settled his cap and walked toward the fishing shacks at Jessups. As he passed Tybee, who was lounging against the drinks kiosk, he walked taller and gave him the finger.

After sunset, Els ambled to the Resort's entrance circle. When Sparrow, who was waiting in the taxi queue, spotted her, he climbed hastily into his van.

She walked over to his window. "I could have your license pulled."

"I done tell you doan go up dere, interfere wid dat jumbie," he said, his eyes darting about as if to make sure the jumbie wasn't hiding behind her. "I gotta get outta dere. Sparrow doan mess wid spirits."

"Stranding me in a strange place when it was nearly dark?" she said. "I'll forgive you if you come talk with me for a minute."

After a few moments' hesitation, he followed her to a bowered bench and sat as far away as possible.

"I'm not infected," she said. "No jumbie came anywhere near me last evening."

He hugged his elbows. He was wearing a yellow bowling shirt with "Samson's Garage, Brooklyn's Finest" embroidered above the pocket. "They sneaky," he said. "You doan know if they right in the room wid you."

"They can't be scary if you don't know they're there."

"You not taking this serious."

"If I saw a ghosty thing, all white and floaty, I'd take it plenty seriously."

He hunched forward, his hands kneading each other. "Jumbies doan look like Casper," he said to the ground. "They got eyes like fire, no feet."

She leaned closer to hear him.

"They mostly go about in the dark, very quiet. They miserable spirits, can't rest no place, like to interfere wid people."

"Pranksters?"

"Demons," he said. "They come into you house, slide into you body, mess up you mind. My auntie husband jumbie take she over, and she went crazy and drink poison, kill sheself."

"So is her jumbie out there, too, united with her husband's in jumbie land?"

He looked at her. "Me not makin' joke."

"That was a serious question," she said. "Do jumbies harm people the way zombies do?"

"People say zombie and jumbie is spirit wha' can't join the good Lord in heaven 'cause they kill deyself," he said. "Me ain' really know bout zombie." He sat taller, spoke more loudly. "I hear dey got movies bout zombie eating people. Dat sound like stupidness."

Though zombies as suicides didn't jive with Els's dim concept of them, she just nodded.

Near the front door, a uniformed attendant stood motionless and observant, and Els wondered if a black cabbie and a white female guest engaged in intimate conversation had crossed some boundary.

"If I wanted to protect myself from a jumbie, Sparrow, what would I do?"

"Doan buy dat jumbie house," he said. He threw a pebble over the queue of vans and onto the grass beyond. This appeared to release some of his anxiety; after repeating the move twice more, he sat back in a more relaxed pose. "If you just can't live no place else, at least you got to pile sand in front all a' you door. Jumbie goin' stop to count every grain. Take dem all night. Dey forget all 'bout you."

A cab pulled forward and picked up a waiting couple.

"And put salt on the end a' you broom, but doan sweep at night," he said.

"I take you for a religious man, Sparrow. Surely your faith doesn't hold with all that superstitious voodoo."

"You could say what you want, miss, you doan know nothin' 'bout how it all work. But if people put obeah pon you or jumbie haunt you, you got to know how to deal wid dem." He put his hand over his heart. "I know I been saved by Jesus, but I still got to protect myself from evil spirits. You call dat superstition. I call it insurance."

Imagining the sultry air full of spirits, as thick and evanescent as the aromas of flowers, amused and comforted her.

Els started up the steps to the Great Room.

"Ms. Gordon!" a voice called from the car park.

She looked back over her shoulder and saw Tony Hallowell hurrying toward her. He motioned her to a secluded table near the pool and held her chair. Frangipani perfumed the air.

"Having fun?" he asked as she settled into her seat.

"I've read one tome of a romance novel. Nice escape, but that's all the sitting about I can handle," she said. "I've seen the sights and bought my obligatory piece of Nevis pottery. Any suggestions on how to keep sane for a few more days?" She caught herself in a lie; she'd become content just to stare at the sea for hours.

He dropped into the opposite chair. "A hard charger like you shouldn't leave here without climbing Nevis Peak," he said.

"I didn't pack my crampons."

"All you need is trainers and stamina," he said. "The trail starts over by Golden Rock in Gingerland. But don't attempt it without a proper guide."

She mused on the coincidence that this island's peak was the namesake of Ben Nevis back home, the mountain she'd climbed with her father when she was fourteen, its spectacular views being the reward for braving its icy hazards. Imagining her father's reaction to the news that she'd summited tropical Nevis Peak, she knew she had no choice but to attempt it.

Tony fixed her with his rheumy blue gaze. "The heir has countered at six fifty."

"She's keen, then," she said. She looked over Tony's shoulder at the peak, now dark against a pearly sky. "Go to four seventy-five," she said. "Still cash, same contingencies."

"That won't nearly do it."

"How the hell do you know?" she said. "I'm not going to negotiate against myself." She stood up. "I plan on exploring this little rock from stem to stern—maybe even to peak—for the next three days. You've got until Thursday evening, or the deal's off."

Els paid her guide and watched his beat-up Jeep pull away, glad to see the back of him as he'd talked incessantly for the five hours they'd spent climbing the mountain. But she'd been fascinated with his encyclopedic knowledge of Nevis and glad of his expertise and encouragement on the tough parts of the rocky and muddy ascent as she'd clambered from tree root to tree root and struggled for footing. They'd had only a few sunny minutes at the summit; during that window, she'd snapped a photo of the rainforest falling away to the distant sea and a small plane flying lower than where they stood. Then a thick mist had obscured the view, and she'd marveled that she was standing inside a cloud. Though she looked as if she'd spent the day mud wrestling, she was elated—pumped up with a kind of achievement she hadn't felt in years and eager to share her photos with her father.

The desk clerk handed her an urgent message to call Franklin Burgess at her office. Burgess, that younger VP whose cunning had been so apparent to Salustrio. The human loud hailer whose booming voice invaded all the cubbies and was known behind his back as "Foghorn."

She took a shower before ringing him. It was 22:15 London time, and he was still at his desk.

He announced he was taking over her transaction for Invicta's acquisition of Cornerstone and had a few questions. "Coxe's idea," he said. Even with the receiver as far from her ear as she could hold it, his voice assaulted her like a speakerphone on full volume. "He wants this kind of deal under my belt when I go up for MD."

"You scheming bastard," she hollered toward the distant receiver. "I've been gone all of four days, and you scoop a deal *I brought in*."

"He thinks you've lost your edge," Burgess said. "Fat chance; you're edgier than ever. It's your mind you seem to have misplaced. Besides, you can't be lounging in paradise and protecting your ass at the same time."

Nobody there's ever protected it for me, she thought. "If you're so smart, answer your own fucking questions." She slammed down the phone.

She sat on the balcony and drank a nip of Dewar's out of the bottle as the sun set behind the cloud-banked horizon. The sky took on bands of gray and lemon, and the day entered that half hour of luminous suspension she was coming to treasure.

She pulled out Resort stationery and began to write. Only after ripping up three drafts did she strike the tone she intended. Pithy, irreversible:

I RESIGN, EFFECTIVE IMMEDIATELY. APPLY VACATION AND SICK LEAVE TO REMAINDER OF 1999. IF YOU DON'T PAY REASONABLE BONUS, I HAVE THE GOODS ON YOUR F---ING WANKER ASS.

She drank another nip of scotch, took the memo to the front desk, and demanded that it be faxed immediately to Coxe. The clerk scanned the page and said, "You might want to sleep on this, miss."

"I won't sleep unless it's gone," she said, her giddiness too great to blame on two nips of scotch.

Tony Hallowell's voice was thick with sleep and maybe rum. "Who the hell is this?" he said.

"Your message said to call back tonight," Els said. "I've only just returned from an interminable dinner at Miss Ivy's. Do we have a deal?"

"Depends on you," he said. "Hold a minute."

She heard a muffled "It's the Jack's woman. I'll take it in the kitchen." She stretched the phone cord to reach the bathroom, slathered on cleanser with one hand, and wiped off her eye makeup with a tissue.

"They're firm at six hundred thousand," he said. "Net." She heard ice falling into a glass, water rushing, Tony slurping.

The deal had tipped. She smelled victory. But instead of the usual surge of triumph, she felt her bluff of a lifetime being called.

"Your promise of a clean deal was what did it," Tony said. "You just have to take care of all the nits and let her walk away with a tidy little check."

"Little, nothing," she said. "Fees, commission, lawyers . . . that jacks it up for me by what, fifty K?"

"Still a steal," he said.

Lacking her habitual mania for checking her numbers before agreeing to a deal, Els felt herself plunging toward commitment. To what, she wasn't sure—an alien place, a mysterious, needy house, an obligation as custodian of Jack Griggs's belongings and perhaps his legacy?

"Her solicitor won't promise to have papers before Tuesday," Tony said. "Don't plan on leaving before Wednesday, just in case."

"As it happens, I have the flexibility to stay a few extra days," she said. "Though I hear there's a storm brewing. I want to get out before it strikes."

"It's late for a hurricane," he said. "Probably just peter out to a little blow."

"You'd better be right, Tony," she said. "Tell them it's a go."

part two

CHAPTER 6

Scotland

December 1996

Once the priest had given the blessing to conclude Midnight Mass, Els slipped her arm into her father's and they let Burtie precede them down the aisle, past the waiting villagers and Cairnoch staff. In the last pew, Malcolm stood alone, watch cap in hand. Burtie picked up her pace at first, but she hesitated when she reached him, and he stepped forward and took his mother into his arms. He looked over her head at Els and smiled. Els felt her father stiffen.

Burtie stepped aside and straightened her coat, her face gone ruddy and her eyes full.

Malcolm extended his hand. "Sir Harald," he said. "I've only popped in to wish Mum a Happy Christmas." Their handshake was perfunctory.

After glancing at Burtie, Harald said, "You'll come in for a drink, then."

Burtie's smile was fleeting, grateful.

Harald and Burtie joined the priest on the steps to bestow both the Lord's and the Laird's Christmas blessings upon the departing congregation, leaving Els and Malcolm alone in the aisle. Malcolm's cheeks had the rosy spots that always bloomed when he exerted himself or was excited. The chapel was ablaze with candles, and in their gentle light, his eyes were their autumn sky blue and full of the amused curiosity that had been his habitual expression as a boy.

"*Fàilte*," he said.

"'Tis I should be welcoming you," Els said. "Where've you been hiding all these years, Mallo?"

"I could just as well ask you the same," he said, and pulled his watch cap over curls the color of rusted iron. "Since the Laird himself suggested it, let's have that wee dram together and share our tales." He offered his arm, and when she took it she caught a whiff of wood smoke, wool, and dogs mingling with the chapel's scent of pine boughs and melting wax.

As they strolled toward the house, he told her that his agricultural degree, courtesy of Harald, had landed him a position managing an estate to the north after Harald kicked him out. He visited Burtie at Cairnoch rarely, and usually when Harald was away.

"So you're still into the politics," she said.

"Deeper than ever. I've become quite the rabble-rouser," he said, grinning. "I believe Mum's tickled to think I might stand for office, but she'd never confess that to the Laird." He pulled her arm more tightly under his own. "When I come here, it still breaks me heart not to be runnin' yer lands as we'd always planned."

"Perhaps he'll relent."

"Not once he's declared his position publicly."

Up ahead, Harald was guiding Burtie through the front door, and for a moment they were caught in the portico light, a fond and aging couple, upright and proper. Though they'd been living in sin for years and fooling no one—Burtie a widow but Harald still technically married to Els's mother—they'd just taken communion.

"He makes his own rules, your father," Mallo said, and his undertone of bitterness sliced through her delight at seeing him again. Harald had shattered their childhood bond by sending Els to a convent school at eleven, where the girls had made fun of her boyish ways. Mallo had found companionship among the village lads and, at the holidays, was shy in her company. She believed she'd lost her only friend.

"How long have you known about them?" Els asked.

"I saw them in the bothy," he said. "I was about six." They veered from the chapel walkway onto the drive. "I was terrified he was killing her and that I'd be left an orphan. Then she commenced to giggling, which I'd never heard her do."

"And you never told me?"

"Never breathed a word of it to anyone. But some o' the laddies began cracking jokes behind my back, and I knew the whole village was in on it."

Els mulled over the news that her father and the young widow Burton, given shelter and work as her nanny, had become lovers when she was barely five. To the children and staff, she was Burtie, but Harald had always called her Mrs. Burton, or occasionally by her given name, Hannah.

"Who was the instigator, Burtie or Father?" She'd always imagined his mother the schemer who'd seen her chance at security, preying on disconsolate Harald after her mother's departure.

"He was," he said. "And got the better of the bargain."

"Did you also happen to know why Mum abandoned me?" she asked.

He shifted his grip on her arm. "Ye'd best ask Sir Harald about that."

"He made a point I was never to bring it up."

Instead, she'd plagued Burtie with questions, which had brought mumbled responses: "She is nae fit to be around children," or, "Let her stay with the Napoleons, where she belongs."

"Ma tells me ye've got a blazing career in New York," Mallo said. "Following in Sir Harald's footsteps, are ye?"

"He was probably a bit miffed when I chose investment banking instead," she said. "It was the hot thing when I finished business school. I had other offers, but Standard Heb was just starting its New York mergers team and gave me the best deal."

"Hard to believe he had no hand in that."

"He offered to put in a word, but I forbade it."

"Everything still on yir own terms, I see." He shouldered the heavy front door open and they stepped into the Great Hall, which smelled of cut greens and ancient stone, like the chapel. Harald and Burtie were in the study, tumblers in hand and feet to the grate. Firelight glinted in the glass eyes of mounted wildebeest and kudu heads and cast corkscrew shadows onto the coffered ceiling.

"Help yourselves," Harald said, no hint of welcome in his tone, and waved toward the drinks trolley.

They had no sooner selected their single malts—Laphroaig for Els, Glenmorangie for Mallo—when Harald stood up and said, "Past my bedtime. Mrs. Burton, may I escort you to your chambers?" He led Burtie out of the room, and Els smiled to think he was still pretending that Burtie slept in the third-floor suite given to her and three-year-old Malcolm when they first arrived. She imagined all the padding down the servants' stairs in the middle of the night and trysts in the hunter's bothy up in the hills. It was oddly erotic to think of their clandestine coupling happening right under everyone's noses.

Burtie pushed out of her chair, set her unfinished drink on the trolley, and looked at her son. "I'll see ye tomorrow, then?"

Mallo kissed her cheek. "If it fits in with yir obligations here, I'll fetch ye for tea in the village."

"That'd be grand," Burtie said. She looked at Els and Mallo appraisingly. "Ye've a lot a' catching up to do." She followed Harald into the Great Hall.

While they sat in the wing chairs with their feet to the fire, Mallo drew out Els's stories of the cutthroat world of New York mergers and acquisitions, which she embellished only enough to make him laugh. In the childhood tales they'd invented, the hero was always a boy, and she reveled now in being the one carrying the sword and slaying the dragons. He sat back and looked at her as if she was a font of enchantment; she was touched, and a little embarrassed, by the intensity of his listening.

"Ye've become the son Sir Harald never had," Mallo said, swirling his neat scotch.

"That should've been you," she said.

He stared into the fire. "At most, I'd have been a decently paid employee, smart on husbandry, lining his coffers," he said. "Surely ye've discovered for yourself that taking his money comes at a price." He stood and went to pour them both more scotch. When he returned her tumbler, their fingers on the crystal close but not touching, he held her gaze. She wouldn't let herself be the first to look away.

"The future—yours, mine . . . ours . . . Scotland's—lies in breaking from his way," he said. Excitement crept into his eyes, but he didn't smile. "I'm beginning to believe I've a chance in the election."

She took the glass from him. "Other than loving you as long as I can remember, tell me why I should vote for you."

"That's reason enough for Mum," he said, and flashed that grin again. "But ye've always been a far tougher nut than she."

For the next few hours, sitting on the edge of his chair, he countered her every argument against devolution for Scotland, challenging her to form her own opinions and step out of the Laird's shadow, and by the time they called a truce, she was more than a little swayed. When the case clock bonged three o'clock, its chime echoing through the silent house, Mallo rose to leave. He draped his arm around her shoulder and walked her through the scullery to the servants' door. As intimate as they'd been when children, she found the closeness of this tall, impassioned semi-stranger brand-new and unsettling.

"Come to Stonehaven for Hogmanay," he said. "I've got friends who can put us up."

"It's nothing but a sing-along and booze-up."

"Nah, not if we don't want it to be," he said. "Yi can't go back across the pond without bringing the New Year in with kin and seeing the fireballs."

In the dusting of snow that had fallen, the footprints of a fox crossed the drive.

"Promise you'll protect me from those hooligans?"

"On my honor as your sworn knight," he said, and made their secret sign.

She returned it solemnly, wondering if there was fealty, irony, rebellion, or mere teasing in his mention of their childhood games and difference in station.

He folded himself into a Lotus with a convertible top patched with tape. Standing in the cold, she watched his taillights cross the humped bridge over the lake and wind down the drive until he turned into the lane and was gone.

CHAPTER 7

To the strains of the pipe band echoing down High Street, the fire twirlers set aflame their wire balls stuffed with fuel-soaked rags and paper and began swinging them aloft and marching toward the harbor. Mallo's friend Will passed a flask. Mallo took Els's hand and pulled her through the revelers, keeping up with one hefty twirler who was crisscrossing his body with his chain, switching arms, and walking backwards. In the flickering light, Mallo's eyes were again full of wonder, and the splotches on his cheeks were as round and red as a cartoon clown's.

When they reached the Old Pier, the fire twirler's ball was still burning. He gave it one more heroic spin and launched it over the black water, where it flared and sank to the cheers of the crowd.

When the tower clock began to toll midnight, friends and strangers crossed wrists and clasped hands and raised their voices in "Auld Lang Syne." At the last verse, Els and Mallo locked eyes as well when they sang:

And there's a hand, my trusty fiere!
And gie's a hand o' thine!
And we'll tak a right guid willy waught,
For auld lang syne.

After the toast, Mallo was still holding Els's hand. He bent to place a New Year's kiss on her cheek, but she turned just enough for him to catch the corner of her lips. "Deirdre's famous for her black bun," he said. "We'll stop around there for first foot and another nip if ye've got the stamina for it."

"Lead on, my knight," Els said, and they strolled with the dispersing crowd back to Will and Deirdre's flat.

While they snacked on dark fruitcake and peaty scotch and Will, Deirdre, and Mallo debated the way toward devolution, Els studied Mallo for flashes of the tireless hiker, sharp-eyed eagle spotter, and tin soldier military strategist she'd once known. All of that boy was now wrapped into this man bent so passionately on their country's independence and carrying such bitterness about its social and class divisions. She represented all he wished to defeat, from relics of the feudal system to the financial strings that bound Scotland to the UK, and she mourned their unquestioning friendship of youth.

She drifted in and out of sleep to the rise and fall of their voices and laughter. When she woke at dawn, disoriented, she was caught in Mallo's embrace. He was spooned against her back on the sofa, both of them still dressed and a thick wool blanket wrapped about them. Before she'd been sent away, Harald allowed them to hunt with the men. She and Mallo would roll up in blankets near the fire and wake up buried in dogs. She snuggled deeper into him and slept again.

When they crested the rise with the view of the Munro to the east and Cairnoch House below, Mallo said, "Do yi fancy a *right guid willy waught* on this beautiful New Year's Day? I've no been to the Crag in years." When she hesitated, sluggish from too little sleep and too much whisky, he teased, "What, are yi too soggy from sitting at a desk to make it?"

She laughed, thinking of her daily runs around Central Park Reservoir to sharpen her wits for the battleground at work. "Ye'll be staring at my backside the way up and back."

"Just what I had in mind," he said.

She looked at the profile of the Crag in the feeble winter sun, already past its zenith. "Tomorrow," she said. "I'll meet you for breakfast in the village first."

She pushed herself to stay ahead of him, her long legs barely a match for his own, and they stopped for breath at a favorite outcropping with a view of the house and its western lands. At the Crag, they huddled against the wind. As when they were children, they searched for eagles, but none soared that day.

When the wind swung eastward, the clouds piled in the west began to race toward them.

"Coorie up," Mallo said, and started down the trail at so vigorous a clip that she realized he'd been holding back on the climb.

She hurried after him, making no comment when he detoured toward the old hunter's bothy, which was sheltered on two sides by huge pines and a rock face.

He waited for her at the door, then unhooked it and waved her in. Heavy mist followed them into the already dank hut. Empty beer and liquor bottles filled one corner, and a used condom topped the trash in the fireplace. The cot still sat against the wall, the blanket box at its foot.

"Burtie would never have left it in such a bourach," Els said.

"Nor any self-respecting hunter," Mallo said. He brought in wood and built a fire, and while she warmed herself before it, he took a tin cup to the nearby stream and came back with icy water.

"I don't smell snow in those clouds," he said. "But we should warm up a bit and go on down soon, just in case."

They stood close to the fire until she felt so warm she unzipped her parka. As she started to shrug it off, he slipped his arms underneath and around her back, pulled her toward him, and kissed her—as if he was asking permission at first, then again and again as she yielded and kissed him back.

He tossed away her parka and stripped off his own and they came back together, fiercely this time. An avalanche of desire—desire that had accumulated, flake by flake, over a decade—engulfed her. He unfastened the top button on her shirt, looked into her eyes again for assent, then quickly freed the rest.

They shed the remainder of their clothing. She felt shy in the gaze of this tall man with muscles taut from outdoor work. She'd last seen him naked—he nearly twelve and reedy, she barely ten—when they'd debated how a man could plant a baby in a woman, having watched the Cairnoch bulls, stallions, and dogs in action.

He pulled the cot closer to the fire and spread a blanket on it. "I've wanted this from ere I knew what to want," he said. He sat down, pulled her between his knees, propped his chin on her belly, and looked up at her. "Would ye indulge me and climb on top?" he said. "I want to be able to see all o' ye, so I can convince myself it's really you."

She pushed him backwards onto the cot and straddled his hips. He never took his eyes off her, which felt invasive, then teasing, then adoring as they burst through their old familiarity into an intimacy she found both thrilling and terrifying.

At the kitchen entrance, he backed her against the cold stone and they kissed until the sound of a car on the bridge made them spring apart. The car stopped out of sight near the main door, and he stepped back into her embrace. "Would ye ever consider comin' home?" he said. "The bank must have a spot for ye in Edinburgh or Glasgow. London, even."

"I've got to make managing director first."

"Ye always did want recognition," he said. He looked away toward the lake. "It's not only for myself that I ask. Ma starts the chemo next week."

"Cor," she said.

"It's in both her breasts," he said. "She's keeping all brave about it. She says it's the Laird that's terrified. At least he and I have that much in common."

"I can't remember her sick a single day."

"Good peasant stock."

She looked at him for the bitterness, but he'd said it with pride.

"Sir Harald's become that dependent on her," he said.

"He's as in charge as ever."

He looked into her eyes. "Ma says he's got to have his arteries cleared out. Blood constriction to the brain's made him a bit daft, but not so anyone but she and his banker could notice. Yet."

Her father ailing and dependent was an image she couldn't manage. "They were planning to keep all this from me."

"Wouldn't be the first time." He opened the door and they stopped in the scullery and kissed again. "I hope I've given ye at least three good reasons to come back soon," he said.

"One good, two scary," she said, and kissed him long and deeply. *Maybe all three scary*, she thought.

CHAPTER 8

March 21, 1998

It had been an exhausting day of ledgers, land maps, and financial statements, and when Ambrose Timmons finally rose from the cluttered dining table, the weight of responsibility for Cairnoch had shifted from Harald's shoulders to Els's. Timmons, ever the discreet family banker, barely acknowledged Harald's confusion and memory lapses, but Els's anxiety for the future and determination to shield the Laird's dignity grew with his every stumble.

"I believe I've earned a little lie-down," Harald said when they adjourned to the Great Hall. "Have a good trip, both o' ye." He embraced Els and shook Timmons's hand firmly, but his ensuing climb up the stairs was a labor.

Els saw Timmons to his car.

"'Tis a huge relief," he said, "knowing you have the picture now. Should anything happen."

"I can't very well run this place from New York *and* do my job," she said.

"You've a good man in Jamie McLaren," Timmons said as he slid into the car. "He'll step up."

"I'll spend more time with him when I'm back next month," she said.

Winter had loosed its grip, and on the Munro, the violet haze was creeping upward in the wake of retreating snowfields. Beyond the lake, a ring-necked pheasant strutted among daffodils that glowed in the late afternoon's slanted light.

She opened the door to what had once been her mother's bedroom and tiptoed over to the bed where Burtie lay. Through the closed door connecting to Harald's bedroom, she could hear him snoring.

Burtie opened one eye. She had shrunk but was as steely as ever. "Going, are ye?" she asked.

"I've a meeting in London in the morning."

"So you've said."

"I've asked Mary Partridge to come in every day for a few hours."

"No need for that."

"Just until you get your strength back."

"She'll be fussing all o'er me."

"Exactly," Els said. She started to kiss Burtie's forehead, but something in Burtie's downturned mouth deterred her and she patted her arm instead. "See you in a few weeks."

Just as the door was closing, Burtie said, "Have a good *meeting*, luv. And tell him he's to come see me as soon as he's through the lambing."

Els smiled, more comforted than annoyed that nothing got by Burtie, even though more and more was getting by her father.

As soon as Tommy, the youngest McLaren, dropped her at the Aberdeen airport and pulled away from the departures pavement, she sprinted to the car park and into Mallo's arms.

When he set a breakfast tray on the foot of the bed, she sat up and laughed at the mess they'd made of his tidy bedroom—clothing strewn about, an empty glass overturned in a patch of sun on the rug. The room smelled of wood smoke, coffee, and oranges. He'd put a single daffodil in a tiny vase on the loaded tray.

"Where did you find juice oranges?" she asked.

"I hear it's what the posh hotels serve in America," he said, and handed her a glass of pulpy fresh juice. Even on the coldest mornings, he walked around the house naked until he'd had his second cup of coffee.

"Trying to make me a regular customer?" she said. In the past year, she'd visited Cairnoch as often as trips to London and rare holidays allowed, but she could count on one hand the number of nights they'd spent in the manager's cottage that came with his job. She resisted the growing pressure to transfer, fearing she'd be out of sight, out of mind as soon as she left Coxe's immediate orbit.

Mallo joined her on the bed, savored a sip of the orange juice, and held up his glass. "When we're married, we'll have this all the time."

"Married, is it? Where was the bended knee, the sparkly ring?"

"Are ye such an old-fashioned girl under all those power suits? It's those novels ye read with bucklers swashing and wenches pretending to be coy."

He set their glasses on the tray, put it on the floor, and yanked away the bedcovers, releasing a funk of sex. He knelt and gathered her against him; she felt the confident beat of his heart. "Neither of us should be kneeling unless both of us are," he said. "The fact is, I can barely remember when ye weren't a part of my life. I no sooner lost me dad than I found ye. Then yir mum went away, and there we were with but two parents between us."

"I never thought of you as a brother."

"Ye were no sister to me, either," he said. "More like a voice inside me to keep me straight on what's worth gettin' into trouble for." He held her closer. "The fact is, now I've found ye again, all these big plans—my political career, making Cairnoch sound again—depend on us sticking side by side. So tell me now if I'm a hatstand. Are these fantasies I'm cookin' up all in me own head?"

"You're completely, totally, utterly a hatstand," she said. He relaxed his grip and sagged away from her, and she pulled him tighter. "But not about any of that."

He let out his breath. She leaned back enough to look him in the eye. His expression was guarded.

"I can't leave New York yet," she said. "This year they really owe me."

His border collie, Seamus, whined to go out. Mallo climbed off the bed, let him out the kitchen door, and returned, trailing fresh air. "A year today, Spring Equinox 1999, or as soon as ye have that title," he said. "Whichever comes first."

She stood up and embraced him. "Don't expect a raft of children," she said. "Proper mothering genes don't run in my family."

"Now who's a hatstand?" he said. "I've seen ye with the pups and lambs often enough to know better." He lifted her chin and looked at her. "Will we have each other, then? I feel the need to hear it."

"Aye, and forever," she said, and pulled him back to the bed.

CHAPTER 9

November 1998

Els burst through the door of the Aberdeen airport into the raw November evening and scanned the waiting cars. Instead of Mallo's Lotus, the family Rover sat at the curb.

Tommy McLaren got out of the Rover, went around to the passenger door, and helped Burtie to stand. Els was shocked to see how diminished she was, how the airport's greenish lights painted purple shadows beneath her eyes.

Dragging her luggage, Els hurried across the roadway and embraced Burtie, who seemed more coat than woman. "I hope I'm not too late to catch part of the celebration," she said. "The plane captain announced the voting results, but I can't wait to hear the details."

"Get in, luv," Burtie said. She sat down and pulled her feet into the car with some effort. Tommy took Els's luggage without his usual cheery greeting.

Els closed Burtie's door and climbed in the other side. "Just think," she said, "with what's happened today, by next summer we might have a Scottish MP in the family."

Tommy pulled the Rover into traffic. Burtie stifled a sob and took a balled hankie out of her sleeve.

Els grabbed her hand. "Something's happened to Father."

Burtie shook her head, unable to speak. Els met Tommy's eyes in the mirror and saw catastrophe in his gaze. She gripped Burtie's hand tighter.

"It's Mr. Malcolm," Tommy said. "All we know is what the inspector said when he rang. We came straightaway to fetch ye. There was a rumpus at the pub where he was drinking with his mates, cheering the results. A bloke who was backing unity in the referendum took today's vote personal. He had a knife."

Invincible Mallo. No tough could ever be his match, she thought. "He's in hospital, then?" she said. "Step on it, Tommy."

"Miss Els," Tommy said, "we're headed for the morgue."

Inspector Grainger ushered them into a small basement office that smelled of burnt coffee and formaldehyde. Burtie sank onto a chair. When Els declined to sit, the inspector leaned against the desk.

"The suspect followed Mr. Burton to the car park," Grainger said. "Witnesses report that he was inebriated and argumentative. Mr. Burton tried to reason with him, defuse the situation. The suspect stabbed him twice, once in the chest and once in the neck. 'Twas the neck wound that did him in, sliced an artery. Despite the medic's efforts, he bled to death in ambulance."

He went on to explain that the procurator fiscal would make his ruling, but given the number of witnesses and the obvious cause of death, there would be a criminal proceeding but no inquiry. The suspect had fled the scene but was a known quantity and would surely be apprehended soon. While he described arrangements for releasing the body, Els stared at the anatomical drawing on the wall and thought of the life that had coursed through Mallo's muscles, his strongly beating heart.

She kept her arm through Burtie's, though she wasn't sure who was supporting whom, and when they entered the identification chamber, all she saw was white—walls, lights, sheet. The cold invaded her bones.

"Show us," she said, and the attendant rolled back the sheet.

It wasn't Mallo lying there but a gray approximation with blue lips and a gash below his left ear. The only part of him that looked normal was his hair. She took his hand, as cold as the metal table, and made their secret sign, and when she let out her breath, the plume hovered over his face and dissipated. *This is how it is when a soul departs*, she thought. *He's waited for me.* She took a quick breath, hoping to trap a wisp of Mallo's essence.

Burtie nodded to the attendant and turned away, and the man carelessly replaced the sheet, leaving Mallo's hair exposed, an ember in the bleached space.

The sun filtering through the pines cast a feeble light over the coffin draped with the blue-and-white Saltire, the banner of Scotland. Cairnoch staff, past and present, their families, and many villagers gathered with Burtie and Els near the open grave, while Harald stood apart, his face stony. The few of Mallo's political cronies who'd shown up uninvited clustered as far from Harald as possible.

Els had taken charge of all the arrangements, including pressing Harald to let her bury Mallo in the family graveyard. Only when she'd said, "It'll go easier on Burtie to have him close by," had he reluctantly agreed.

She stared into the empty hole, its sides impossibly straight and tidy. The gravedigger had done his best for Mallo, a favorite among them all—even Harald, once.

Since leaving the morgue four days before, Els had been clenched—an attempt to hold on to the numbness she knew was keeping savage grief at bay. Now, she felt as if she were outside her own skin, observing herself with a bowed head, unable to recite the familiar prayers to a God who'd let one of His least worthy creatures take the life of one of His finest.

The priest intoned the final words of committal and sprinkled holy water over the coffin. His face awash in tears, Mallo's uncle Jerry Grimes and Richie Ahearn, a fellow stonemason, folded the Saltire into a tight triangle and presented it to Burtie. Cradling it like a newborn, she walked past Harald—he offered his arm, but she ignored him—and went up the path toward the house. The other mourners fell into line behind her, leaving only Els and the burial men who were waiting by the fence to close the grave.

She forced herself to go to the Great Hall, bracing for the condolences of those who thought Mallo was but her childhood friend. Only Burtie knew they were lovers; they'd kept their pledge to marry a secret from all.

Early the next morning, she hiked to the Crag. An eagle rode the thermals high above, and as she followed the bird's effortless soaring, she began to cry out the tears that had been frozen inside her. Much as she wanted to believe it was Mallo up there, flying so free, watching over her, she felt the certainty that he was really gone seeping into all the spaces the tears had occupied.

The numbness gave way to anger. Anger was supposed to be hot, she thought, but her rage was feral and icy. She raged at God, at Scotland, and most of all at Mallo for leaving her.

For two days Els slid between fury and a kind of blankness, avoiding everyone. She hiked every trail on Cairnoch's grounds and slept in the bothy, aching for the heat of Mallo's body spooned against her back. Her only company and confidant was Harald's favorite pointer, Ariel, and she poured out her grief and love to him and took comfort in his sympathetic eyes.

When she finally returned to the house, she found Burtie in the sitting room swabbing and polishing hard enough to have raised a sweat.

Burtie stopped and ran her wrist over her brow. "Got to get this done while I still can."

Perhaps Mallo's death had erased Burtie's best reason to keep fighting the cancer. Perhaps she knew her remaining days were few, even welcomed the end, and would keep that from Els too. Even though Els and Burtie hadn't spoken of Mallo in front of Harald since the falling out, they'd often discussed him when alone in the kitchen or garden. Since his death, however, Burtie had been unwilling or unable to say his name. Adrift and alone in her grief, Els longed to hear stories of Mallo, afraid they'd be lost forever when Burtie was gone.

Never one to ask useless questions, Burtie appeared untroubled by Els's two-day disappearance. "Ye've plenty right to yir sorrow, lassie," she said. "He would hae made ye a prize husband, no doubt about it."

Els looked at her, wondering if Mallo had told her their plans, but Burtie shook her head and pulled at the rag.

"Ye think I could hae missed all that fire and secret smiling right under me nose these last years? Ye think I don't know me own boy, and you like me own bairn as well?" She ran the cloth over a spotless tabletop. "Yir father and I've no spoken about you and him, but my own opinion is he would hae rejoiced for such a son-in-law, regardless of the politics." She walked over to Els, took her by the shoulders, and shook her gently. "Ye cannae heal yir heart by hanging about all peely-wally. Ye've got to get on wi' yir own life."

When her plane lifted off from Aberdeen, Els knew she would never again arrive home with the joyous anticipation that had filled her last two years. On the flight from London to JFK, she opened her briefcase and sifted through the papers and printouts, all urgent a week ago, that she'd ignored during her whole time in Scotland. She stared out the window and wished it were possible just to keep flying westward, reeling back time zone by zone, until the entire week had been erased, the assassin's hand never raised. When she looked down at her work again, two hours had passed. She'd chosen career and ambition over love, and now they were all that remained.

part three

CHAPTER 10

Nevis, West Indies

November 1999

While Hargrave Teal shuffled documents with stubby pink fingers, Els felt as much as saw the olive-green waves crash into the seawall and throw spray clear across the road to the car park that separated his restored colonial building from the Charlestown harbor. All the boats were gone. She wondered where *Iguana* might hide from a hurricane.

"Sign here, and again over here," Teal said. "There's the ticket." He straightened his stack of executed documents and glanced at the yellowed sky.

Tony Hallowell paced near the windows. "Don't drag this out, Gravy."

"We can't afford an error, now can we?" Teal said, winking at Els.

She scrawled her signature on the citizenship application and passed it back to him.

"As we agreed, everything on the property conveys with the sale," Teal said. "With one exception."

Els looked at Tony.

"My client believes," said Teal, "that certain highly personal items pertaining to her may have been in Mr. Griggs's possession, and she requests that you return them."

"I thought she'd never been here," Els said.

"Quite right."

"What sort of personal items?"

"She declined to supply a list, but said you'd know if you found them."

"When I'm not allowed to know her name."

"I grant, it's a bit unusual." Teal fingered his gold cufflink. "It's the only remaining issue."

"She sounds as crackers as Jack. Must run in the family."

"In point of fact, no beneficiary of Mr. Griggs's estate is of any relation to him."

"There's more than one?" she asked.

Teal pressed his lips together, as if he'd said too much. A gust of wind slammed the building.

"Very well, then," she said, "I'll keep a really sharp eye out, and you'll be the first to know, Mr. Teal, if I stumble across anything matching this precise description."

"Just so," Teal said, and placed the final document in front of her. "I'll inform my client that she can rely on your discretion in this matter."

Els gave him her deal smile. "You do that."

She tasted salt spray mixed with the rain as she and Tony hurried across the car park, dodging potholes brimming with water.

Safe inside the car, she wiped the condensation off the inside of her window and said, "I want to go to my house."

"It's not yours, officially, until all your clearances come through," Tony said.

"Who's to care if I just nip in for another look about?"

"We've got a major hurricane bearing down on us, in case you haven't noticed." He steered around a tangle of seaweed on the harbor road. Spume crashing over the seawall splattered the car. "Goddamn Gravy," he said, "just paying us back for pressuring him. You couldn't rush that man if you set fire to his tie."

Pinney's Hotel hugged the corner at the edge of town, and between its pink buildings Els caught a glimpse of the beach, now submerged, with waves reaching the thicket beyond. "Stringing it out, the bastard," she said. "Since it was on my nickel." In the crowded TDC home center car park, two men wrestled a sheet of plywood into a pickup truck.

"You could've had that relic for at least a hundred thousand less," Tony said. He switched on the defroster and ducked his head to peer through the widening clear spot on the windscreen.

"I underestimated you, Tony," she said. "Imagine, letting you wring that much out of me."

"You let your heart do the bidding," he said. "Cardinal mistake numero uno."

"My heart must be out of practice," she said. "Been out of commission for a year."

He slowed at the swale near the golf course, now running with muddy water. "You still paid less than it's worth." They were approaching the Resort now, and he put on his indicator light.

"We're going to Jack's," she said.

"Bugger," he said, and accelerated around the curve. "How are you imagining you'll get back here?"

"Taxi," she said. "Or I'll just stay there. Jack's has survived those recent storms pretty well."

"You'd better be joking," he said. "Mark my words, Miss City Banker, this Lenny is no Georges or Jose. It's going to knock the shit out of this side of the island."

"I can take care of myself."

At the hairpin turn at Tamarind Cove, where the waves battered the volcanic rock seawall, Tony stopped, then gunned the engine. The car dipped into the flooded swale, shuddered, and crawled slowly out the other side.

"You might want to go another way back," Els said.

"There is no other way."

Tony unlocked the new padlock and opened the kitchen door, releasing that fetid smell—a mix of ashes and something rank and animal.

"Ladies first," he said. The half-light of the stormy afternoon barely entered the house. "Jack was in arrears on his current. You'll have to settle that account too." He looked around the room, rubbing his arms. "Look, you really must go back to the hotel immediately."

"I've never had a property in my own name before."

"It's not even yours yet. I can't take this risk."

"I'm staying," she said.

He lit his torch and handed it to her. "With my compliments," he said. He went out but returned immediately. "Don't go anywhere near the ghaut—that ravine on that edge of the garden—or any of the others around the island," he said. "The mountain carved them out for a purpose over all these millennia. When this storm gets going, water, boulders, all manner of debris will come roaring down."

The door slammed behind him, plunging her into an eerie greenish darkness.

She opened the refrigerator and flashed the torch beam over jars and packets, all furry with green, pink, and black mold. Slamming the door immediately couldn't stop the smell from spreading into the kitchen.

She climbed the steps and cast the beam into the corners of the lounge. Some of the photographs had blown about the room, and she collected and arranged them on the refectory table. Jack's preferred subject was a girl in her late teens, blond and kittenish with erect breasts and a smile that was not at all innocent. Scrawled in pencil on the back of one photo was "S, Christmas 1977."

The flames had spared fragments: an Asian woman's boyish head and torso, a zaftig beauty, and a black woman's legs and feet. Els stacked the remains and weighted them with a tarnished brass candlestick.

The secret door in the paneling stood ajar, revealing a narrow stairway. She climbed up to a hallway that ran along the back of the house and gave access to three rooms, all facing the sea.

She swung the beam into the first room. A desk. A filing cabinet with an open drawer, its contents strewn on the floor. Bookcases on two walls, framed documents on another.

In the next room she found a brass bed, its mattress a desert camouflage of stains. A knot of mosquito netting swung over it, and a breeze turned the ceiling fan. The rain, coming harder now, clattered on the roof. Hanging by a chain from a rafter was a basket chair with a heart-shaped pillow in its seat.

When she forced open the bathroom door at the end of the hallway, wet wind rushed at her, carrying the smell of ammonia and filth. A monkey clung to the edge of a jagged hole in the roof and bared its teeth. The wind slammed the door behind her. A smaller monkey screeched and leapt from the back of a chair to the top of a wall shelf and up to the hole, where it huddled with the first one and hissed.

The stench was so strong she could taste it. "Get the fuck out of my house!" she yelled. The monkeys stared at her, blinking. Gnawed fruit, nut hulls, and monkey dung littered the floor. In the clawfoot bathtub, a mouse was decomposing atop a soggy pile of partially burned papers, and behind the tub a full-grown male monkey occupied a nest of grimy towels, his eyes glittering in the torchlight. When he jutted his chin and rocked forward onto his knuckles, she wrenched the door open and stepped into the hall, and the wind slammed the door behind her again. The screams of the monkeys pursued her to the bedroom, dissonant clarinet wails echoing above the growling tuba of the wind.

She latched the bedroom door and leaned against it. When her breathing slowed, she opened the cupboard doors and roamed the light over the clothing. She pulled a cotton blanket off the shelf, wrapped it around her shoulders, and returned to the kitchen.

In the storeroom, she found an orange oiler hanging from a nail; when she reached for it, her hand ripped through spider webs that clung to her damp fingers. She flapped the jacket hard, hoping to dislodge any creatures that might have taken refuge in it.

She set the torch on the kitchen table and pulled a pad out of her briefcase. "I could murder a cup of tea just now," she said. "Care to join me, Jack?" She tried the knob on the stove. A whisper of flowing gas. She found matches in a mason jar and lit the burner. A ring of blue brightened the room slightly; the odors of sulfur and gas reminded her of the kitchen at Cairnoch. She found tea bags in another jar and went to fill the kettle. A dribble of brown water slowed to a drip and stopped. Cursing, she killed the flame, pulled the musty blanket tighter, and began making lists.

The torch beam flickered and dimmed. She clicked it off and sat in the dusk, listening to the wind pummel the house. "Brilliant, fucking brilliant," she said.

Perhaps a failing torch was a harbinger of obstacles to come, but under her chagrin at having overspent so impetuously was a bloom of joy.

She slung her briefcase strap over her head, nestled the bag against her stomach, and pulled on the rain jacket, which reached almost to her knees. By the time she'd locked the padlocks on the door and gate, her hood had blown off three times, water had run up her sleeves, and her skirt was clinging to her legs, hobbling her stride. She stopped at the gate and tried to map in her mind the route back to the Resort—maybe two miles straight along the main road, hardly a daunting distance for someone brought up on mountain hikes, and surely she could hitch a ride for part of the way.

Before she'd gone a quarter mile, she'd twisted her ankle. Limping and leaning into the wind, she approached the turn by the seawall where Jack had supposedly disappeared. The flooded spot that had nearly swamped Tony's car was knee-deep now and growing with each wave that crashed over the wall. She rubbed her throbbing ankle.

A pickup truck with roof lights flashing crawled toward her. She stepped into the road and the driver stopped, rolled down his window, and looked her up and down. She realized the briefcase bulged enough to make her look pregnant.

"What in God's name you doin' out here?" he said. He was gray at the temples and wore a NevLec logo shirt.

"Give me a lift to the Resort?"

"You can't see the road's closed?"

"You could drive through that."

"I gettin' the hell back to Newcastle," he said. "Get in if you want a ride that way."

She climbed in and he turned the truck around.

"Boss says to check the poles out this way," he said. "When we gotta check them poles is after the storm finish wid dem, not before." He looked at her. "I drop you at Nisbet, just past the airport. They emptied out yesterday. They can find a bed for you."

"I just bought Horseshoe Jack's place," she said. "Let me off there."

"That no place for someone like you to ride this out."

"I'll take my chances on that sturdy old dame."

He made a low whistle. "Hurricane wash away one crazy owner," he said, "next hurricane blow in a new one."

CHAPTER 11

She slammed the kitchen door as if to seal out the breath of some enormous beast. In the failing light, she ransacked the cupboards and spread the food supplies on the table: three tins of evaporated milk, a package of spaghetti, a glass jar containing one sleeve each of Lorna Doone biscuits and saltines, jars of coffee, sugar, salt, and cornmeal. A plastic container with a few cups of cornflakes, cooking oil gone rancid, vinegar. A tin of sardines and another of Spam. Thin rations, but she'd survived in the bothy on cold tattie scones and Laphroaig.

Her search produced two lanterns and an Aladdin lamp, each with only a slick of fuel, the Aladdin holding a desiccated gecko that was curled around the base of the mantle. She collected all the candlesticks and rummaged through the kitchen drawers for stubs and matches. She set a bucket on the patio under the downspouts, and when she went back to collect it, the rain was falling harder and the wind was whipping the mango branches.

The wind squeezing through the hole in the roof created an eerie moan and sent a draft through the house. To silence the secret door's maddening rattling, she wedged it shut with a chair. The storm's noises were unnerving, made worse by intermittent crashes on the gallery roof that sounded like huge rocks hurled by a giant.

Though it was the darkest room, the kitchen felt the safest, so she gathered books, towels, pillows, and blankets and made a nest for herself in there. She set a pot in the storeroom for her privy. She'd found a rusty putter behind the big chair and kept it at hand in case the monkeys invaded.

Nibbling stale saltines, she wrote out a meal plan to stretch the supplies over three days, just in case. The best news was that the bar was well stocked, and she'd no aversion to drinking whisky neat.

After a tumbler of scotch, she fell into tormented dozing. Her house would be whirled away as by the tornado in *The Wizard of Oz,* carrying the screaming monkeys with it. Wind would rip off the roof and scatter Jack's nude photos up the mountain. Mallo was outside, pounding the door to get in, but she hadn't the strength to open it. She was in dark water, trapped in writhing fronds of seaweed.

A clap of thunder brought her fully awake and she felt she was on a raft, oddly stationary in a roiling sea. The closed shutters couldn't keep out the explosions of lightning, or the thunder that followed almost immediately. Half three in the morning, dark as pitch, and the world was an undulating roar broken by earsplitting crashes and the ripping and slapping of roof shakes. A scream of wood wrenching loose, nails losing their purchase, fibers separating, then a crash of timbers on the patio.

She'd dozed off reading a history of Nevis, leaving a precious candle to burn out. Chiding herself for wasting the light, she threw off her blanket, stood up, and pawed the table for the matches and a new candle stub. Her shadow jittered on the wall until she sheltered the flame with the hurricane shade. When she shouldered the door, it moved only a few centimeters. The storm hurled itself in through the crack, and she latched the door to silence the wailing.

Door blocked. Front door and gallery windows nailed shut from the outside. She was trapped. The ceaseless noise might drive her mad, but she was curiously unafraid, trusting of the ancient house's protection.

Without hope of further sleep, she made breakfast of rainwater tea and stale cornflakes in tinned milk and read how Nevis was dubbed Queen of the Caribees for outstripping the other islands in sugar production. A prize the British repeatedly fought the Dutch and French to retain, built on enslaved labor, its people freed to their own devices once emancipation robbed them of worth. Though trade, indenture, and fealty were woven into her family history, Els had never considered the plight of the millions of Africans wrested from their lands, families, and cultures and tossed into the furnace of greed to produce the riches of sugar, cotton, and rum. She wondered what guilt she shared and what she might owe to the people of this nation created by those who'd been dislocated and abandoned, but somehow remained unvanquished.

Mid-morning, the wind died and the sun broke through. Els pushed out the kitchen shutter and saw that the storm had thrown sections of the pergola against the building. Squinting in the rinsed daylight, she climbed out the window and over the wreckage.

The sky was cloudless, the agitated sea a deep sapphire. As Tony had warned, water cascaded through the ghaut, the mountain channeling the rain into lethal torrents and sending them barreling toward the sea. Birds fluttered and pecked in the smashed garden, and she wondered how such tiny, fragile creatures could have survived.

Under the searing sun, the garden was steaming. Smashed coconuts, the missiles that had crashed onto the gallery roof, littered the court. The monkeys emerged from the hole in the ridge, shimmied down the outdoor shower supports, and scampered into the jungle, and she wondered if they'd decamped for good or were only foraging for food and would soon reclaim her bathroom.

How quickly her opinion of monkeys had veered from adorable to verminous.

Each grass-edged stone on the patio held water reflecting the sky, a mosaic of tiny swimming pools. She stepped through the wreckage in the garden, gathering fallen coconuts and citrus fruit in her skirt.

The wind started to rise again, but from the opposite direction. A palm frond javelined past, and when she looked toward the sea, a wall of storm was fast approaching. The miraculous light was only the eye. The blue above quickly became a bruised gray. With its change in direction, the wind dislodged debris that had found a resting place and sent it flying again. She hurried back to the house and dumped her fruit through the window. She'd barely lowered in the brimming water pans, climbed in, and latched the shutter when the hurricane slammed into the house from the west.

She went to the lounge and flopped into the big chair, deep and enveloping, with a mannish scent. On the table at her elbow was a framed snapshot of three whiskery men cradling a mahi-mahi. All of them wore Blues Brothers sunglasses, fedoras, and goofy grins. She removed the photo from its frame, but the reverse revealed only the print shop's date: April 25, 1998. "Is one of these characters you, Jack?" she said.

She perused a stack of books and files on the table. One file, titled "Works in Progress," was stuffed with ideas, including a page ripped from a Nevis tour guide about Julia Huggins prowling the ruins of the Eden Brown Estate and mourning her love, who was slain in a duel on their wedding eve. A story more suited to an opera than anything she imagined Jack writing. In a book of Derek Walcott's poetry, a flattened cigar wrapper marked the poem "Ruins of a Great House," in which Jack had underlined the phrase "the leprosy of empire." On another page, beside the poem "Islands," he had marked the lines, "But islands can only exist / If we have loved in them."

On top was a well-thumbed paperback of *The Tempest.* She propped her feet on the ottoman, nestled deeper into the chair, and began to read, the cadence of the poetry a comfort against the wind's clamor.

By the afternoon of day two, still trapped and in half-light, she paced the house, opened drawers and books, and sat for a long time in the study. Jack's bulletin board, covered with snapshots of women and postcards from them, also sported a condom, a smile drawn on its tip, dangling from a pushpin. Rain on the roof no longer seemed romantic.

Evening approached, the blackness closing in again. Wherever she'd imagined she might be on the first anniversary of Mallo's death, it wasn't sitting in the dark hoping both she and her house would survive a biblical storm. She'd dreaded this day, mostly for fear it would be simply ordinary—a reminder that the world had gone on, leaving her dragging the weight of her invisible grief. The very drama of the lightning and rain comforted her, as if the heavens agreed that the world had been cracked asunder on this day one year ago.

She nibbled the last of the crisps and ate the sardines, and though she wiped her hands on a tea towel, the smell clung. She squeezed lime over her fingers and into her drink and licked off the sticky juice. Now well into her third rum and down to her last two candle stubs, she sat at the kitchen table and listened. The storm was abating. She pushed open the shutter. Rain still splashed onto the patio, but the wind had turned fitful. Clutching a sliver of soap, she climbed out the window and cupped the rain in her fishy hands.

Her face to the streaming sky, she let the drops pelt her eyelids and fill her mouth. She stripped off her clothing; the wind-driven water pricked her skin. She lathered all over and soaped her tangled hair, then threw her arms wide and felt the water dance off her shoulders and sluice over her breasts.

She tossed her clothing through the window and climbed in after it. When she lit a lantern, the kitchen filled with wavering shadows and she caught a glimpse of her naked silhouette, her curls wild and her body elongated and skinny. The last year may have reduced her to sinews, but they were tough and resilient.

After double-checking the shutter latches, she carried the lantern and putter upstairs and listened at the bathroom door. Wind, rain, but no monkey noises. In the bedroom, she pulled on one of Jack's shirts and rolled the sleeves. With the storm spending the remains of its fury and the monkeys vacated, she felt safe enough. She made up the bed with stained sheets worn soft and slid in, laying the putter against her hip.

She smelled cigar. When she opened her eyes, the darkness was velvety, absolute. Her tongue was furry with rum. She listened. The storm had moved on, but she sensed that its enveloping, terrifying presence had been replaced by another presence, equally formless.

A cigar tip flared, and in its faint light she thought she saw a man's face, disembodied, floating above the foot of the bed. She sat up, fumbled for the lantern, and struck a match, but she couldn't light the mantle and succeeded only in singeing her fingertips. She shook the match out and tossed it away from the bed. In its brief flare, the face was all beard and dark eyes.

"I just had to see if it was you," the man said, "who bought the house." His voice was raspy, barely above a whisper.

She took in a sharp breath. She struck another match and managed to light the lantern. He seemed to be jelling but cast no shadow. He was wearing a rumpled linen shirt. The expression in his eyes was apprehensive, needy.

She grabbed the putter.

"It all depends on you now," he said.

"How'd you get in?"

"You let me in."

Her mind raced through the house, thinking of ways in, ways out, something left unlocked. She checked the bedside table. No phone. She remembered phones in the study and next to the big leather chair. Hurricane. Lines down.

He swept the cigar to his waist and bowed. "I apologize for my appalling lack of manners," he said. "I thought it okay to help myself to one of these, but I should've asked the lady's permission to smoke." He examined the glowing ash. "I needed this," he said, "to steady my nerves." He took an ashtray off the dresser and rolled the cigar in it, sculpting the ash into a neat mound. His eyes glittered as if he was drunk or drugged. "I've got more at stake here than you do."

"Get. Out."

"Don't banish me, sweet," he said. He blew three smoke rings and watched them wobble and dissipate. He looked to be in his forties and was tanned and weathered, with dark curls falling over his forehead and pleading eyes. "I came to welcome you, but I've blown that completely. My charm isn't what it once was, obviously."

A gust of wind shook the palms. The surf raged.

"I should have let you settle in first," he said. He pulled on the cigar and exhaled toward the ceiling. "As Wordsworth says, I was given 'so much of earth, so much of heaven, and such impetuous blood.'"

She tightened her grip on the putter.

"I just can't get the hang of this." He stepped back until he was standing in the doorframe. Khaki shorts. Barefoot. "All the rules are changed."

He held the ashtray in his laced fingers like a precious vessel and looked at the ceiling. The smoke curled up his torso and wreathed his head. When he looked back at her, his eyes had lost their glitter.

They bored into her in a way that was familiar, seductive. "I should be good at befriending a woman as impetuous as I. A woman who glows in the sunset and dances in the rain. I was foolish to think we could take up where we left off."

The face and voice were vaguely familiar, his gaze like a remembered caress. "When have we met?" she asked.

"I was too tired tonight to get back to that younger me," he said. "This was the best I could do. At least I'm in my so-called prime." He shifted the ashtray to his left hand and pulled a small bouquet of blue flowers from the waistband of his shorts. He took a step closer.

"Stay where you are," she said, but she lowered the putter.

"Periwinkle," he said. "*Violette de Sorcier.* Protection against spirits, if you want it." He kissed the nosegay and tossed it onto the foot of the bed. "Some of them can be real pests, or so I hear." He bowed again. "See you," he said, his gaze on the flowers. "I hope."

He looked at her imploringly, saluted, and stepped into the hall, leaving behind a wisp of smoke.

The rum clotting her head, she hugged her knees and strained for any sound of his footsteps, but heard only the unrelenting surf and the rain, now a mere patter.

She threw off the sheets and, carrying the lantern and putter, checked every door and window. She lifted the receiver on the phone beside the leather chair. Silence.

Wide awake at three in the morning, again. The lamp burning up its last film of oil. She'd become used to terrifying dreams but had never suffered hallucinations, and she wondered what twist of alcohol-fueled imagination had produced this apparition. Deciding to blame the vision on the storm, or those magnets in the mountain, or all that silly jumbie talk, she curled up in the chair and dropped the putter onto the floor.

She listened to the surf hurling itself against the shore until the lamp faltered and spewed out an oily curl of smoke, and, in the absence of its light, she found she could see predawn grayness outlining the shutters. Reassured by the promise of an end to darkness, she settled deeper into the chair and dozed.

Daylight rimmed the windows. Els went to the kitchen and pushed open the shutter, letting in the clearest early light she'd ever seen. She was ravenous and desperate for the last of the coffee, even with tinned milk.

"Mother of God," she said, stopping mid-stride.

On the kitchen table was the bedroom ashtray, containing a fat roll of cigar ash. Next to it, *The Tempest* lay open with an earring, a tiny gold skull and crossbones, resting on the page. There was a pencil mark in the margin next to Ariel's lines:

Full fathom five thy father lies;
Of his bones are coral made;
Those are pearls that were his eyes:
Nothing of him that doth fade,
But doth suffer a sea-change
Into something rich and strange.

The house creaked, easing itself after clenching against the wind. She took the earring to the window and examined it, its ruby eyes glistening in the sunlight. She'd seen one before. Trespassing at sunset. That enigmatic young man. *A sailor's earring pays for his burial if he dies at sea.*

She ran upstairs and threw open the bedroom shutters. When she flapped the sheets, out flew a small bouquet, its stems bound with a knot of grass, the flowers gone limp. She carried it to the study, let in the light, and rummaged in the desk drawers. Curled photos, mostly of women. A checkbook showing a balance of $593.41, last check written September 12, 1998. A passport. She returned to the kitchen, grabbing the photo of the three men with the mahi-mahi on the way.

The passport, issued in Barbados in 1990, looked barely used. The man pictured there was older than the sunset fellow, younger than the apparition in the bedroom. In the photo of the three men with the mahi-mahi, the one in the middle was older still, but the resemblance was unmistakable.

Griggs, Elliott Jackson. Date of Birth: 30 July, 1949, Chicago, Illinois, USA.

Jack.

You let me in, the apparition had said. She wondered if that meant she was receptive, though she'd felt unreceptive to just about everything since Mallo's death. She held the earring and bouquet in her palm, weighing the superstition of banishment against the superstition of receptivity, knowing both were in the mind of the believer but wanting to surrender herself to this place, this house, and whatever secrets it might hold.

She climbed out the window onto the patio. Every wave wore a white cap, but the rising sun was changing the sea from mauve to blue. The peak's cloud halo was gone, and the sun sprang over the ridge and spilled down its western slope. The breeze brought an undertone of rotting vegetation. Mountain doves, cooing and answering to signal their survival, sat in the court like cinnamon sailboats, each with one wing raised to dry its cloud-gray flanks. The ghaut was a stream in spring flood.

The periwinkle leaves had lost their sheen. *Protection against spirits*, she thought. *If I want it.*

When she tossed the bundle, the breeze carried it into the palm wreckage. "Impetuous to a fault, Jack," she said. "That makes two of us."

CHAPTER 12

She picked her way to the gate, assessing the damage. Except for the pergola, the house looked much as before, but the garden was even more smashed and littered, and below the road, newly exposed boulders had trapped the remains of a fishing boat and a small sloop. There was no traffic. By the time a lorry full of workers rolled up to the gate, the sun had dried her damp clothing. The workers looked her over and elbowed each other.

"Give me a lift to the Resort?" she asked.

"You wanna job?" called a skinny man standing in the back. "They givin' good money ta help clean up."

One of the passengers got out and climbed into the back, and the other helped her into the high cab and climbed in after her. The men in the cab introduced themselves—Duveen, a line cook at the Resort, and Jaydon, the driver, a landscaper—and she sat wedged between their shoulders, the air heavy with their sweat.

The truck churned through the muddy streams gushing from the ghauts. People swarmed around roofless houses that seemed to have coughed up their contents onto lawns and into trees to dry.

"I trust the Resort wasn't too badly damaged," she said.

"Wrecked," Duveen said.

"Them waves was just bangin' and bangin', all day, all night," Jaydon said. "Smash it all away. Low Street flatten." He waited for an oncoming pickup to drive around a piece of corrugated metal. "Resort gon' lose all a' this season. But they sayin' all a' we got jobs in the rebuildin'."

"Rebuildin'?" Duveen chuckled. "Fust, we gotta spend the next six weeks shovelin' sand. Them guest rooms got sand all on top de beds. De swimmin' pool full up all to the divin' board."

"I coulda tell dem not to build so close to de beach," Jaydon said.

"Nobody axe you," Duveen said.

"No, but they shoulda," Jaydon said. "They shoulda axe Nevis people. I ain't no engineer, but I know which way water flow."

Patches of wet sawdust lined the Resort driveway, and sawn sections of palm lay in the ditches. Duveen helped Els down to join the guests milling among the taxi vans queued in the entrance circle. Jaydon tooted the horn and drove away, trailing a cloud of diesel exhaust.

From the Great Room she could see that the wharf, though mostly intact, was now detached from the beach, and the sand that had once united them was heaped onto the gardens.

The assistant manager pushed toward her through knots of guests and luggage. "Ms. Gordon, you gave us a lot of worry," he said. He glanced at her dirt-streaked clothing.

She found it oddly touching that anyone would care where or how she was. "I was perfectly safe," she said. "Sorry to be a trouble."

He told her the Resort had run on generators for four days to shelter and feed nearly a hundred stranded medical conventioneers. "I hope you were at least as comfortable wherever you were," he said.

"My discomfort was self-imposed," she said. "I need a bath and a meal."

"We are transporting everyone by launch to St. Kitts to meet charter flights."

"I won't be leaving right away," she said.

"We cannot ensure your safe passage unless you leave now with the others," he said. "The entire complex will be closed from this afternoon."

"I stand advised," she said. She watched him process her stubbornness and wrestle with his exhaustion and annoyance, attempting to hold on to his gracious demeanor. "I do appreciate your concern."

"Your belongings are in my office," he said. "I'll ask the cooks to prepare what they can and will give you access to a room, but it will be just as the previous guest left it."

"Nothing new there," she said.

She stood at the door to the Resort kitchen, a sanctuary of calm purpose and one of the few parts of the property that hadn't been ravaged by the hurricane. Three workers in hairnets were wiping down acres of stainless steel, all reflecting the lemony light. One of them dropped her rag and approached.

"Mr. Hendricks say you run off in the storm," she said, "and now you gotta eat." Her name tag read "Eulia."

"I've survived on stale biscuits and rainwater since the storm began," Els said. "I'd appreciate anything, Eulia." She pronounced it to rhyme with "Julia."

"Say it Yoo-leé-uh," the woman said. Her voice was deep, melodic. Her knuckles on her hips, she looked at Els. She had dark brown eyes fringed with long lashes, made all the more striking by her close-cropped hair. There was intelligence, pride, and challenge in the gaze. "Pleased to meet you, Miss Gordon from London."

"How do you know where I live?"

"All a' we know you not from there, though." She tied a splattered apron over her equally splattered uniform.

"What else do you all know?"

"You got a lot a' money, and you brave or crazy, buyin' Jack's place."

"I've got a lot less money now," Els said.

"Dey's all kinda rich," Eulia said, "and all kinda crazy."

The other two women tossed their aprons into a bin and strolled, laughing and waving, out of the room. The kitchen fell silent but for the hum of the refrigerators. Eulia said, "You sit over there. I go do what I can with what scraps we got left."

Eulia minced and mixed, every movement precise, economical, all the while humming snippets of hymns in a tenor range. Soon, Els sniffed sautéing onions and potatoes. In a few minutes, Eulia placed a frittata, breadsticks, orange slices, and iced tea on the table and sat down opposite, gesturing for Els to eat.

Els tried not to eat too greedily.

"You gon' live in that house?" Eulia asked.

"It's not fit for anyone to live in it just now."

"Jack leave a mess?"

"You knew him?"

"I used to . . . do . . . for him," Eulia said.

"Tell me about him."

Eulia dropped her eyes. "If you live in that house, you can learn everything he want you to know."

"What, did he leave clues?"

"Things he can't say, he write them down," Eulia said. "He say he write away all the pain from his mind right into those papers."

"He burned some things."

"He destroy in all kinda ways." Eulia refilled Els's tea, her gaze on the glass as she poured. "We wonder who he allow to buy that house."

"He could hardly handpick his buyer."

"Maybe he scare away more than looters," Eulia said. She stood up and occupied herself with cleaning the stove.

When Els was done eating, she thanked Eulia for the meal, but the young woman didn't look up until Els reached the door. "Good luck, Miss Brave or Crazy," she said.

Sparrow was in the taxi queue, and when Els pulled her luggage toward his van, he said, "At the port, they got steel pan music and everythin' to say goodbye."

"Take me to a place called Nisbet," she said. "I hear they have rooms available."

CHAPTER 13

While Tony drove the obstacle course to Jack's, Lauretta kneeled on the front seat facing backward, embracing the headrest. Els felt pressed against the back seat by the onslaught of her chatter. She'd grown up in a tiny East Texas town, learned she had a God-given talent for tennis, nearly bankrupted the family training with a famous pro, dropped out of college, married an assistant golf pro working at the same Houston country club, gotten divorced and answered an ad for a position at the Resort, even though she didn't know where in the wide world Nevis was, and had met Tony, and the rest was history. Did Els play tennis? Well, it was never too late to start, but teaching tennis was only a sideline now because she had started an interior decorating business, and if what Tony told her was true, Els's house really needed work.

Els sought Tony's eye in the rearview mirror.

"You'll be glad of a taskmaster if you want that place shaped up any time soon," he said.

"Always thinking, Tony," Els said.

Lauretta was a study in ginger—hair, eyes, freckles, lipstick, and nail polish, all were shades of tawny brown. "I've always wanted to see the inside of that house," she said, and, finally sitting down, adjusted the headband restraining her frizzy hair.

They drove through a scene made unfamiliar by the storm's rearrangement of just about everything. St. Thomas Church looked unscathed, but plastic grave flowers littered the knoll on which it sat. The swampy lagoon at Nelson Spring had inundated the road, and sand had washed across the low stretch near the riding stable. She made Tony drive to Oualie before doubling back to the house, and when she commented on the absence of boats, Tony said, "They're on the rocks, or in smithereens in St. Maarten's harbor."

Els shuddered that this might be *Iguana's* fate, again.

Barely five feet tall and balanced on the balls of her feet as if awaiting a serve, Lauretta stood in the graveled entry court at Jack's with a yellow pad under her bronzed and freckled arm. She was wearing a miniskirt, T-shirt, trainers, and tennis socks with white pom-poms at the heels. "Dear God in Heaven," she said. "Do we ever have our work cut out for us." She began making notes.

"It took two above-average hurricanes and one doozy to create this mess." Tony hefted aside a section of palm crown that was wedged between the Jeep and boat trailer. "Even you won't set it right in a day."

While Lauretta and Tony scrutinized the remains of the pergola, Els hung back, looking for signs of the monkeys and wondering how much of Lauretta's help she really wanted. "We'll never shift that pile," she said. "Tony, give me that tire iron." She climbed to the gallery and started to pry the plywood off the front door. A few minutes in, Tony grabbed the tool from her and finished the job. When they opened the door, light spilled into the lounge, making the room appear larger.

Lauretta examined the leather chair. "You'll be replacing this old thing."

"It stays," Els said. "We'll slipcover much of the rest."

Lauretta looked at her and made a note on the pad. The breeze from the open door sent the fire ashes swirling. "What the hell?" Lauretta said. "Was he fixin' to burn the place down?"

Els scooped the stack of photographs off the refectory table and tucked them into her tote.

"What stinks in here?" Lauretta said. "Promise me we won't discover a body."

"Maybe a dead primate or two," Els said. "No Jack, if that's what you're worried about." She headed up the stairs with Lauretta close behind.

She opened the study shutters and looked out at the sea. "Just exactly how do you propose to help?"

"I'm a wizard with lists," Lauretta said. "I get a real sense of accomplishment from checking things off." She pronounced it "accomplesh-mint."

Els leaned out the window. Hidden from view by the gallery roof, Tony grunted and cursed below.

"You're gonna need every trade to make this place fit to live in," Lauretta said. "Even if you was here all the time, you wouldn't want to go chasing them. Hell, I've dragged workmen out of bed or a bar, if that's the only way to make deadline."

"How do you charge?"

"By the hour," Lauretta said. She looked at Els. "Fifty bucks."

A piece of plywood sailed over the railing and crashed into the court.

"Of course, there's the customary markup on decorating services," Lauretta said. "Like if you was to have new curtains made or that window seat recovered. I got me the finest seamstress on the island."

For once, Els was disinclined to bargain, especially as she had no idea what going rates on Nevis might be. "I'll expect regular reports and receipts for everything," she said.

Lauretta smiled a pixie smile. "When we're all done, you'll put this place on the historical society house tour."

"Don't wager on that," Els said, recoiling at the thought of strangers ogling her home and commenting on her taste, Jack's taste. Already she felt protective of his possessions, wanted to understand their allure and purpose. She looked at the shelves stuffed with books and files. "And don't touch this room," she said. "I'll sort it when I can get back." She gathered up the papers on the floor, put them into the filing cabinet, and swept the items she'd removed during the hurricane back into the desk drawer.

Lauretta took in the bulletin board. "I hear he was quite the ladies' man." She walked into the bedroom and gestured toward the mattress and sheets. "Exhibit A. We might need to burn those."

"Just get me something I can sleep on without contracting a disease," Els said.

Lauretta opened the cupboard and ran her hand over the stack of dress shirts, yellowed on the folds. "I can give these to the church jumble sale," she said. "Long as I don't say whose they were."

"Leave them."

"What do you want with a dead man's clothes?"

"I can't explain," Els said. She wished she'd kept something of Mallo's, a favorite shirt that held his scent.

Lauretta nudged the basket chair. "My granny had one on her front porch." She picked up its stained seat cushion by the corner and dropped it onto the floor. The bottom of the chair was woven with a heart-shaped hole in the center.

"I doubt your granny's was a Japanese love basket," Els said. "Seems our Jack was a ladies' man, indeed."

Lauretta pulled off a faded gift tag that was tied to the edge of the hole with pink satin ribbon and read, "'Save this for me alone and let your imagination run. Love always, Amelia.' Granny'd be blushing to her roots." Lauretta snuggled into the chair and let it swing. "I gather you have experience with one of these."

Els imagined the pleasure Jack might have given his women and felt a bolt of desire for the first time since Mallo's death, as if the walls were exuding pheromones that she was no longer too numb to sense. She took Lauretta's hand and pulled her up. "You and Tony can experiment with that some other time," she said. "Here's the main job." She led Lauretta to the bathroom. "Hold your nose and be prepared to run," she said, and flung open the door.

"Sweet Baby Jesus," Lauretta whispered, and covered her nose and mouth.

Flies spiraled off the mounds of feces and rotting fruit. The stench made Els's eyes water. Rain had created a pool of dung slurry against the north wall and buckled the floor. The hole in the roof framed cloudless sky.

"I haven't seen anything this bad since goats broke into the Winchesters' villa over by Zetlands," Lauretta said. "One of them chewed the TV wire and electrocuted hisself." She fled, her trainers squeaking on the stairs.

On a shelf next to the lavatory mirror a queen conch shell bristled with toothbrushes beside several toppled medicine vials, each containing a few pills. Els didn't recognize the drugs. She dropped the vials into her tote. Shaving soap, like a farrier's paring from a horse's hoof, rattled in the bottom of a coffee mug. The brush was an antique Rooney with a bone handle, identical to one her father had used.

She poked at the mess in the tub enough to discover that the pages were handwritten letters. "Misguided S," one began; another, "Cursed S." The ink had run on some, and fire had consumed parts of others.

She tipped the mouse carcass into the tub and gathered up the readable pages. She closed the door securely behind her, went to the study, and put the mug and brush on the desk and the prescription vials in the top drawer. Inside was a sheet of letter paper dated September 21, 1998, with a one-line scrawl: *"I have subjected myself to the whip of my own remorse."*

Imagining the future treasure hunt the room promised, she put the letters in the filing cabinet, closed the windows, and pulled the door shut.

Els sat with Tony and Lauretta in the shade of the mango tree and ticked off the essential projects while Lauretta took notes in an oversized, round hand. Restore the current and phone service, hook up government water, repair the roof and water damage, install window and door screens, acquire a new mattress, clear away the fire pit, replace the fridge, rebuild the pergola, haul away the sodden contents of the chattel house and replace its roof, repair the cistern, clear the fallen palms and tidy the garden, get the Jeep running or find a decent used car.

She gave Lauretta the phone number to her London flat and said, "I'll call you with a fax number so you can send me that list. Remember, leave everything of Jack's precisely as it is."

"Locals won't go in there with Jack's belongings all around," Tony said.

"Then you'll find workers who aren't superstitious, won't you?" Els said. "How long and how much?"

Tony took the yellow pad and scanned the list. "You did your famous calculations," he said. "Double the cost and triple the time and you might be close. Lauretta will keep both in check if anyone can."

"When'll you be back?" Lauretta asked.

"I haven't planned that far ahead."

"You're some contradiction."

"How do you mean?"

"So definite about some things," Lauretta said, "and kinda drifty about others."

Els looked toward the sea. All her life she'd been obsessive, driven, competitive—anything but drifty—but now she felt unmoored, held fast only by Cairnoch and her father, and even he was slipping away into a mental fog different from her own but equally debilitating.

She stood up and paced the patch of bare earth under the mango tree. "I want real estimates," she said. "And a finished job as quickly as possible."

"Did you happen to notice the destruction from here to Charlestown?" Tony said. "Competent construction people will be in short supply."

"That's why I have you, isn't it?" Els said.

CHAPTER 14

It was Monday, but Els's trip to Nevis had erased her mental calendar, its relentless procession of meetings and deadlines. Hugging herself against London's pervasive November chill, she stepped into her flat, let furnished and offering the charm of a mid-range hotel suite. She would have felt disoriented without her yellow suede chair and her art. Her collection of splashy, challenging works—bought at auction on instinct and impulse—always welcomed her.

She skipped through phone messages from colleagues and the bank's human resources department. The last was from Ambrose Timmons, left that morning, requesting she ring back immediately and giving his home number. It was already half eleven. She flopped onto her bed and thought about phoning in the morning, but there was an unusual urgency in his tone.

"Where've you been?" he asked.

"Incommunicado in the Caribbean," she said. "Hurricane knocked out all the lines." She waited. Timmons always needed a moment to phrase precisely whatever he wanted to say.

"The housekeeper found Sir Harald dead on his study floor this morning," he said. "He might have been there all the weekend. His heart, presumably."

She swung her feet to the floor, her fingers locked around the receiver, and rocked on the edge of the bed. Her father's birthday letter, which had arrived just before she left for Nevis, was still on her bedside table, his writing gone a bit spidery, his affection camouflaged by details of the estate operations, the last roses.

"Miss Eleanor?" Timmons said. "My condolences. A lion of a man."

"That he . . . was," she said. Referring to her father in the past tense took concentration.

She went to her dresser and picked up a snapshot of Harald, taken at least ten years before. He was in the hills, leaning against the Rover and smiling into the evening sun of midsummer that burnished his auburn hair. She felt as if her bones were falling into the open spaces in her body—timbers in a collapsing mine—but in silence, except for the faint crackle on the line.

"I've taken care of the preliminaries," Timmons said. "The chairman and others await your decision on the service, as they all hope to attend."

"Tell them Saturday, midday, so they can make it a day trip," she heard herself say. "I'll go up first thing tomorrow and ring you from there."

When she dumped everything from her case onto the bed, the cheeriness of the bright summer frocks mocked her. An icy fury like that following Mallo's murder was pushing out any remaining Nevis glow of well-being. Her father had brought this upon himself. He'd been scheduled for quadruple bypass surgery, but after the cancer finally claimed Burtie the previous February, he'd canceled the operation and begun to decline in earnest. That raw sense of abandonment—first her mother's, then Mallo's and Burtie's, now her father's—gave way to rage crowding in. Harald had chosen to follow Burtie into oblivion instead of staying on earth, with her, and he'd made his decision months ago when Burtie was slipping away.

She'd been standing in her New York apartment kitchen dripping from her morning run when her father rang. "Doc's put her on the morphine," he said. "She was clear for a bit this morning and asked for you."

When she'd arrived at Cairnoch, Harald was nowhere to be found. Mary Partridge told her he spent much of his time lately driving the lands in the Rover.

She climbed onto the bed and rested her head on Burtie's once ample bosom, now shrunken and smelling of decay instead of violet water. Burtie's breathing was intermittent, and Els didn't immediately register the moment it stopped altogether. She covered Burtie's hand to hold onto her soul a moment longer.

They'd often been at loggerheads, two stubborn females, one trying to play a mother's role, the other resenting her for it. Burtie had grown bold in her criticism of Mum, and Els had angrily come to her defense, until they ceased speaking of her at all. It was only after Mallo's death that Els fully admitted the depth of affection she and Burtie shared.

On her bedside table, Burtie kept the triangle-folded Saltire that had draped Mallo's coffin and a photo of him at twenty-one, just out of university. Els took both.

When Harald bid her goodbye after Burtie's funeral, the last thing he said was, "It's time you got that posting to London."

Els swept her vacation clothing onto the floor, stuffed black cashmere and tweed into her case, and curled up on her bed. On her dresser was a miniature oil portrait of Mallo at about fourteen, her first clumsy attempt at a human face, which caught his lopsided smile and bright cheeks, and the cowlick that made his rusty hair poke out over his right ear, but not the intensity of his blue eyes. The whirling of her mind battling the exhaustion of her body, she stared at the painting and wished for the numbness she'd need to get through what was to come.

part four

CHAPTER 15

Scotland

November 22, 1999

From inside the revolving door at the Aberdeen airport, she could see Tommy McLaren already climbing out of the Rover and thought how he'd been drafted once again for a sensitive job. She dragged her bag outside.

"Welcome home, Miss Els," he said. "Ma and Pa and all the brothers send their condolences."

"Tommy," she said. "*Yir a sicht fir sair een.*"

"And ye, always," he said, and held the door for her, then stowed her case in the boot and climbed into the driver's seat.

"I'm surprised ye're not at school," she said.

"I'm only home the weekend. Got a major exam Tuesday, so I can't dally." He started the engine. "Pity Mr. Harald won't see me graduate, after all he did to encourage me studies. Of course, ye know he meant me to manage yer new livestock scheme."

It had been Els's idea to breed heritage pigs and to put Tommy in charge of the program. "We'll go right ahead with that," she said. "Chefs will pay a pretty penny for them."

He sat taller. When mist filmed the windscreen, he turned on the wipers. They drove through stands of Douglas fir and Scots pines that made the night all the darker. The mist turned to drizzle as they climbed.

"You're looking a mite fagged, if you don't mind me saying so," Tommy said.

"I am that," she said. Since the closing, she'd slept only a few hours in every twenty-four. A hare ran a zigzag course in front of the car before scrambling up the bank and into the heather. She closed her eyes and breathed in the smell of the Rover: faintly doggy, with an undertone of gun oil.

She snapped awake when they started into the bowl that sheltered Cairnoch House. Its tall windows were ablaze, but instead of the comfort of arriving home, she felt only dread as they crossed the stone bridge over the lake, passed the ruin of the original tower, and entered the empty car court. She took shelter under the portico while Tommy brought her luggage and opened the massive door.

The Great Hall was so silent she could hear the case clock ticking in the sitting room beyond. Neither Burtie nor Harald would have approved of leaving all the chandeliers lit. The suit of armor nicknamed Auld George was missing from the corner where it had stood for generations. The center table, which held a towering flower arrangement, had been pushed against the wall. The scent of lilies filled the room.

"Is anyone here?" she called.

Mary Partridge, who'd been helping out since Burtie became too weak to run the household and was now officially the housekeeper, hurried from the dining room, her clogs clacking on the stone floor. "*Fàilte,* Miss Eleanor," she said, and embraced Els, then stood away and clasped her roughened hands together. "Pity the night's so dreich. I'll warm up a bite for you."

"I'd love a bath first," Els said. "It must have given you a fright, Mary, finding him that way."

"And him cold as that fire dog, and as rigid too," Mary said. She stood with her arms crossed and her fists buried in the sleeves of her jumper.

"Ye've barely packed more 'n a hankie," Tommy said, lifting Els's bag onto his shoulder and taking the stairs two at a time.

"Naw but a wee black frock and city shoes," Els said.

"If only I'd insisted on staying through supper on Friday," Mary said. "Even if I couldn'a saved him, at least he wouldn'a been all alone." She drew a sharp breath and let it out. "*We'll no fin the brither o him in monie a lang day.*"

"Sure, and they broke the mold after him," Els said. She squeezed Mary's shoulders. Only about five years older than Els, Mary had been an extra in the kitchen, a spare girl at parties, for as long as Els could remember. Now, caved in by worry and loss, she looked old enough to be Els's mother.

The third step creaked, as it always had, and Els stopped on the landing to survey the Great Hall, the paneled walls lined with portraits of her forebears, laird after laird through two centuries. The only female subject among them was her grandmother, who'd commissioned her own portrait and posed resplendent in her tartan, an heirloom ring on her finger. Hanging next to "The Beatrice," as the family called the portrait, was a life-sized depiction of Harald with Ajax, his favorite Brittany spaniel, a wide black ribbon tied across the frame. The painter had captured perfectly Harald's chest-out, shoulders-back stance.

The black ribbon distracted her momentarily from noticing that the two most valuable portraits—those of her great and great-great grandfathers painted by Arthur Melville—were missing and the others had been rearranged, baring dark patches on the paneling. "Mary, what happened to the Melvilles?" she called.

"Mr. Harald sent them to London," Mary called back. "An exhibition, he said."

After the funeral mass in the family chapel, the line of people queuing to pay their respects snaked out the Great Hall door, and although the enormous fireplace was blazing, chilly eddies swirled around Els's feet. She felt she was growing heavier with each whispered condolence and sorrowful glance. Ambrose Timmons, minus the expected delegation of bank higher-ups, inched toward her, and when he took her hand he whispered, "We need to talk as soon as we can get a little privacy. You've read the news, I presume?"

"Not since Thursday," Els whispered back. "Nor even bothered with the telly."

"I'll explain later," Timmons said. "The chairman sent his condolences." He bowed and withdrew.

Els closed the door behind the last guests and went to the dining room, where Mary was clearing away the buffet. Candles guttered onto the damask banquet cloth. Mary put some sandwiches and a lemon tart on a plate and handed it to Els.

"Ye've eaten nu'in all day," she said. "Mr. Timmons is in the study."

When she closed the study door, Timmons rose from his chair by the fire. She set her plate on the desk and went to the trolley holding Harald's collection of single malt scotches.

"We've both earned a drink, Mr. Timmons." She poured Laphroaig into Edinburgh Crystal tumblers and handed him one.

She'd first tasted the peaty scotch in hunting camp when she was fifteen, after shooting the day's largest roebuck. Harald had passed around a flask, and Robbie, the gamekeeper, had handed it to her just like the rest of the men.

Timmons raised his glass and toasted Harald's life before reclaiming his seat.

Els retrieved her plate of food from the desk and settled into the other chair by the fire. Timmons gazed into his drink. "The bank has crashed."

She looked at him. "Standard Heb goes back almost to Stonehenge. I read a few days ago about some trading blip. Didn't sound too serious."

"Perhaps it wouldn't have been if the guy who started it all had fessed up," he said. "It's almost a rerun of Leeson's nightmare at Barings."

While she stared into the fire, the plate of sandwiches untouched in her lap, he explained that a rogue trader named Quartermain in the New York office had taken a disastrously losing position, then tried to hide it and work himself out. Everything had spiraled out of control. The bank didn't yet know the full extent of its losses.

A log shifted in the fire. She took a second's pleasure in having quit before her job imploded, but the victory was Pyrrhic. She was ruined, her investments obliterated. For years she'd been required to take a large portion of her earnings as deferred compensation in the form of Standard Heb stock, now worthless.

Timmons appeared to sense her absorption of this news. "It's even worse than that," he said. "Your father, against my recommendation, got into some schemes that weren't on—real estate in India and such. His judgment was faltering, as you know. Until he died, I had no idea what he'd done on the side. He used Cairnoch House as collateral for one particularly dodgy deal with a Russian energy baron named Smirnov or something, and that guy was in my office yesterday threatening to foreclose. He's salivating over the estate as a hunting lodge. It may have been his plan from the beginning to bilk your father out of it."

"How much did Father owe this Mr. Vodka?"

"Enough so that even if you sold it on the open market—money pits aren't exactly the rage these days—Cairnoch might fetch only enough to cover his debts with a hundred or so left for you. If we're lucky."

"I should have taken over everything sooner."

Timmons's little smile showed a career's worth of patience for the hindsight of his clients. "Sell what remains of the valuable items separately," he said. "And make your best deal with the Russian."

A new thought hit her. "Mum's as dependent on the income as I."

"She should be the last of your worries," Timmons said, and explained that Harald had long ago set up an adequate but not overly generous trust. "She's been living with a man for years," he said. "A retired doctor, Rinaldo Acquarone. They're quite comfortable."

"Do you have her address?"

"I'll send it, but I'm sure you'll find it here somewhere," Timmons said, and stood up. "I've left you some paperwork. Once I've cleared out my office tomorrow, I'm at your disposal."

"Ever loyal," she said. She felt a wash of sympathy for this careful, precise man who'd shepherded the family fortunes for decades.

He shrugged. "Maizie's been on me to retire. She's a saver, she is. We'll get by."

She saw his lie, and knew what a blow the loss of his lifelong employer was, not to mention the loss of her father, his friend and biggest client.

"I'll need your help, Mr. Timmons," she said.

"That's a comfort, actually," he said, and closed the door behind him.

CHAPTER 16

Els poured two more fingers of scotch and went to the partners' desk, the Laird's seat of power through the generations, where Timmons had left a stack of files. She dropped into the desk chair and stared at the pink ears and corkscrew horns of the kudu shot by her great-grandfather, contemplating the fact that her tenure as Laird would be the shortest ever.

The top file contained a sales slip from Christie's for £120,000 for the Melville portraits of her forebears. She'd always prized the one of her great-grandfather got up in "full Prince Charlie," with the tartan and heirloom *sporran* and *sgian dubh*. She discovered that one Maxwell Tierney had purchased Auld George for his private armory collection and had him shipped to Kansas City. On it went—pieces of silver she'd never seen, paintings she barely remembered by artists she recognized, carpets that might have been rolled in the attic for generations. Her father's attempts to stick his finger in the dike of debt. She wondered if he'd already liquidated the best of the best, leaving her so little of value that it would be more trouble to sell the rest than to let it go to the Russian.

The file marked Smirnikoff contained Mr. Vodka's offer on RussOil letterhead for Cairnoch House, furnished, in exchange for Harald's obligations. She imagined him, stout as a fireplug and a heavy smoker, sitting at this desk, and hated the idea of his loutish friends drinking here under the kudu's glassy gaze.

At the bottom of the pile was a yellowed file marked "G. Borelli." She opened it with trepidation as if her mother might waft out, genie style, from inside. Besides the details of the trust, there were letters from an Italian psychiatrist attesting to her mother's improved mental state and requesting that Eleanora be allowed to travel to Italy during her school holiday.

"Eleanora," Els said aloud, stringing out the syllables. She struggled for any recollection of her mother's saying her name and found none.

Eleanora was twelve now, the letters said, surely old enough to make the journey alone, and her mother pined to know her daughter before she was fully a woman. There was a carbon of a two-line letter from Timmons in reply stating that Harald denied the request. And later a letter from the same psychiatrist saying Harald's withholding of their child had caused his patient so serious a setback that she was once again in an institution. At the back of the file was a note in curlicue handwriting she imagined to be her mother's, pleading with Harald to assure their daughter of her constant affection and mentioning the enclosure of "this year's birthday painting."

In the thirty-one years since her mother's departure, Els had never received a single acknowledgment of her birthday, Christmas, or any achievement.

An unmarked key was taped to the inside of the file. Els tried it in every door, cupboard, and drawer in the study. Thinking the key must fit something private of Harald's, she went to his bedroom suite—a place she'd rarely visited, and never alone.

In his dressing room, she fingered the ranks of jackets, suits, and shirts. The drawers of his huge mahogany dresser weren't locked. She picked up his hairbrush, auburn and silver hairs trapped in its bristles, and the bay rum scent he wore hit her like a punch. She avoided her reflection in his full-length mirror. To its left, he'd hung a gilt-framed Constable depicting a bucolic scene with sheep, so evocative of the life at Cairnoch that she couldn't bear the idea that the Russian might get it. To its right was a keyhole in the paneling.

The key fit. Behind the panel was a shallow cupboard crammed with envelopes and packages in brown wrappings that smelled of dust and old paper with a hint of perfume. She pulled out a flat envelope addressed to her with an Ischia postmark. Inside was a page of colored pencil sketches of animals—rabbit, fox, squirrel, stag—with names printed in English and Italian. Where the signature would have been was a drawing of a gardenia, tiny as a shirt button, white with a red tear.

She spread the cupboard's contents onto Harald's bed. Flat as a letter or chunky as a book, all were unopened, addressed to her, and mailed from Ischia on 15 Ottobre, one for each year, designed to arrive in time for her 6 November birthday. The date stamps began in 1967 and ended in 1990, the year she left Scotland for Harvard Business School. She hugged herself and paced the room, atilt that a pillar of her life—the conviction that her mother wanted no contact with her—had crumbled into a lie.

As if celebrating each birthday for the first time, she opened the envelopes one by one. Inside those from the early years, she found cartoons and illustrations fit for a child; as the years progressed, the art gradually became darker and more sophisticated and abstract, shifting from pencil and watercolor to oil and acrylic. The works were dated on the back, but only the one from 1979 had a title, *Self-portrait*, and it was so powerful it felt almost violent. Each bore the weeping gardenia signature.

When she went to close the cupboard and take away the Constable, she found a creased black-and-white snapshot on the floor. Harald in a dark suit and her mother holding an infant, standing with a priest on the steps of the Cairnoch chapel. The infant, in a heavily embroidered gown, was wrapped in the clan tartan, which was secured by the family Luckenbooth brooch. Harald and the priest smiled at the camera. Her mother gazed into the middle distance, her expression blank. On the back in the same curlicue script was *4 December, 1966*. Els's christening.

She sifted through the contents of Harald's drawers. The fond memories summoned by his keepsakes, favorite ties, and medals couldn't compete with her churning well of sadness, her mourning of the father she thought she'd had as much as the one he was turning out to be.

She woke on Harald's bed, wrapped in his coverlet. The birthday gifts were stacked on the chair with the snapshot on top. Such had been her exhaustion that she had no recollection of placing them there, or of lying down or at what wee hour sleep might have claimed her.

Woozy and disoriented, she took the collection to her own room. When she splashed water onto her face, her red-rimmed eyes made her wonder if she'd wept in her sleep, though she'd been unable to weep while awake. She removed her funeral frock, pulled on jeans, a jumper, and her old hiking boots, and felt girded for the effort of that day, and those to come.

In the milky gray light of early morning, Mary Partridge was shoveling ashes from the Great Hall fireplace. The room smelled of fresh bacon and spent fire. "Had a good night, did ye?" she asked.

"Slept like a bairn," Els said.

"Ye must be starvin', barely touching a bite since I don't know when," Mary said.

The winter sun streamed through the conservatory's palm branches, casting their shadows onto the limestone floor. Els sat at the wrought iron breakfast table and gazed upward, stirred by a glimpse of blue sky between the fronds; it rekindled the memory she'd had in Nevis.

Mary wheeled in a trolley loaded with enough breakfast for six people—orange juice, melon, porridge, oat cakes, eggs, bacon, bangers, mushrooms, black pudding, toast, and marmalade. The smells of childhood Sunday mornings made Els tear up, and when she saw this, Mary stopped in the middle of pouring tea and made a sympathetic tsking sound.

"Join me," Els said.

Mary finished pouring and set down the pot, but didn't move.

"I can't bear to eat alone." Els had intended it as a statement, but it came out as a plea.

Mary sat stiffly and accepted a cup of tea but declined to eat. While they chatted about the village news, Els tried to make herself eat slowly, as she had in the Resort kitchen under Eulia's scrutiny, and managed to consume at least enough for two. As the sun climbed, the plants in the conservatory breathed out their fragrances and Els caught a whiff of the gardenia, now grown as tall as she in its enormous cachepot painted with koi. Legend was the plant had been a gift from Harald to her mother when she was born.

"Tell me about Mum," Els said.

"I heard she loved this room—spent a lot of time here, painting and just sitting. Reminded her of home."

It dawned on Els that her mother, though a banned subject of family conversation, had likely fanned gossip among the staff. She might have satisfied her curiosity had she only asked the right people.

"I was told she doted on that plant," Mary was saying, "but she could hardly take it along when she left, hurrying off as she did and the weather bitter at the time. Burtie'd have neglected the poor thing to death, but I loved its scent and I'd see to it whenever I was here."

"Why did she rush away?" Els asked.

Mary's gaze was still on the gardenia. "I'd only be repeating rumor," she said. "Me mum said we weren't ever to speak of it."

"Did Mum sing?"

"Once at that last Christmas. I was almost seven. I remember the lovely cakes. She had a pretty voice—deep-like and strong. Me mum said she was in her cups to sing that way, but I enjoyed it."

"Was she kind to you?"

"She yelled at everyone when she was in that mood, but never at Mum, nor me especially." Mary shifted on her chair and looked at Els. "We all think ye'll make a fine Laird."

Els rearranged the silverware on her plate. "I'm grateful for your confidence," she said, but as she contemplated the ancestral flatware and thought of the unavoidable sale of the estate, her face fell. Mary squeezed her hand, excused herself, and clacked away toward the kitchen.

Shredded from making hundreds of decisions every day, dealing with appraisers and auction houses, negotiating with Mr. Vodka's solicitor over the meaning of "furnished," bucking up the few staff who would remain, and bidding farewell with tears and stipends to those who would not, Els spent every evening in the study drinking scotch and staring into the fire. That afternoon, a month after Harald's death, she'd signed the sale documents for Cairnoch, and the finality of it clanged through her. In all her business deals, she'd given little consideration to the fate of the workers once the owners took their money and ran, just as she would do now. She felt the mourning numbness leaving her and sadness sneaking into its place, like blood returning to a tingling limb. Tears, long held in check, began to flow.

She'd propped her mother's self-portrait on the study mantel. Under its deranged eye, she pulled out Cairnoch stationery, thought better of that, and switched to a legal pad.

Dear Mum, she began, then sat for a half hour, at a loss for words, while she finished her scotch. She poured another, balled up the tear-splotched page, and started again:

> *After Father died, I found that he had hidden your birthday messages, drawings, and paintings from me. I always believed you'd never wanted to communicate with me. All*

my life I've felt rejected by you, and wondered what I did to drive you away.

Now that I realize you tried to be in touch with me all those years, I'm mourning not just the loss of Father but the connection you and I might have had that was denied both of us. I would have jumped to visit you during school holidays, and I even secretly learned some Italian in case the opportunity was ever presented.

Because nobody would speak to me about you, I know almost nothing. I hope we can meet, or at least correspond. I've had to sell Cairnoch and will be moving far away. I expect to be somewhat settled by Christmas. Please write to me c/o Mr. Timmons. He'll see that I get anything you send, and I promise to reply.

Your daughter,
Eleanora

She addressed the letter and left it on the entry hall table for Mary Partridge to post from the village. Though she imagined all sorts of replies, she braced herself for the possibility that there might be none at all.

Early on her last morning at Cairnoch, Els pulled on her hiking clothes and went to find Ajax. She found him lying on his tartan bed next to the AGA stove, looking despondent. At her approach, he heaved himself to his feet and leaned against her thigh, his stubby tail wagging.

"Can yi still make it up the Crag, boy?" she said. The dog barked and limped through the keeping room and out the scullery door, but he found his stride in the court and soon was leading her up the path through the heather and outcroppings.

Snow dusted the ground and the air was frigid, but she was determined to make this pilgrimage, and she needed Ajax's company as much as she'd needed Ariel's after Mallo died.

They stopped at the bothy, now looking well tended and recently used, and she took the tin cup she and Mallo had shared from the shelf. Standing in the open door, she watched her breath trail outwards—all the memories of that place escaping into the ether—then latched the door. She walked to the stream, dipped in the cup, and sipped, then held the rest for Ajax. When he was finished, she stuffed the cup into the pocket of her parka.

The sun broke through as they climbed the rise to the Crag with its view of the Munro. She sat on the ledge gazing over the countryside, as she and Mallo had done countless times, hoping for a glimpse of an eagle. Ajax stretched out and was soon asleep. A family of fallow deer browsed close by, and the buck raised his wide rack and sniffed in her direction. "Go on," she said, waving her arms, "or you'll end up on Mr. Vodka's wall." The buck wheeled and led his bounding entourage into the pines.

On the way back, she ushered Ajax into the family cemetery and they walked the lines of ancestors until they reached the new graves. Ajax lay down on the patch of earth in front of her father's just-erected stone. Harald Ian Gordon, April 5, 1940 – November 19, 1999. Next came Hannah Ailean Burton, September 22, 1945 – February 17, 1999. At rest between Mallo and Harald, her greatest loves.

In front of Burtie's stone, the new grass met the old in a neat rectangle. The wind moaned in the pines. Els pulled her hands into her parka cuffs and thought how hard Burtie had struggled to be the surrogate mother she didn't want.

As she had done just before leaving Cairnoch at the end of every visit since Mallo's funeral, she stood at the foot of his grave. Malcolm Connell Burton, May 26, 1965 – November 17, 1998. *He will raise you up on eagle's wings*. The flowers she'd moved to Mallo's grave after Harald's funeral had frozen. She tossed them over the fence and called, "Time to go, AJ." The dog let out a whining howl. She'd never imagined being barred from this place that was so alive with the spirits of her forebears, who nurtured her with their courage and ferocity. The last of the line, she would not be joining the others here. Who would she be now, separated from this soil, this rugged land? She gazed at the line of graves—her grandfather the Big Laird, grandmother Beatrice, Harald, Burtie, Mallo—and said a silent farewell.

A shipper's van sat under the portico, its doors agape, a stack of blankets at the ready. The agent and two burly men stood at the door with Mary, who looked disinclined to admit them. Els hurried up and led them into the Great Hall. It was full of everything she couldn't bear Mr. Vodka to touch.

Ajax hovered so annoyingly that Els took him to the kitchen. She stroked his ears, and he poked his cold nose against her neck. "Don't ye worry, AJ," she said. "Ye canna come wi' me, laddie. Ye'd never manage the trip and the quarantine. Robby McLaren will give ye a good home." She settled him into his bed and returned to the Great Hall.

After instructing the men to pack everything rowed up on the floor, she said, "Three more things: the case clock in the next room, my bed, and Grandmother's portrait over your head. Mary will get you a ladder."

"Surely ye'll be taking the one of Sir Harald too," Mary said.

Els looked at the portrait of her father, now devoid of the black ribbon. Since his funeral, she and Timmons had worked to exhaustion to settle the mess he'd left behind. He'd lost her home, and perhaps her mother. "Let the Russian have it," she said.

"Where are we sending all this, miss?" the agent asked.

"To a dot in the ocean."

part five

CHAPTER 17

Nevis, West Indies

December 23, 1999

As the Carib Breeze churned across The Narrows toward Nevis, Els stood alone on the open deck and clasped Liz's blue bead, now on an antique silver chain, hoping whatever powers it contained would bless her adventure. The wind smelled of salt and caramel, sweet and burnt. Except for the Resort's grounds, the shore before her was a nearly unbroken stretch of bush—wild, impenetrable—meeting the shallow beach.

In Charlestown harbor, the ferry passed astern of *Iguana,* locked up, Christmas wreaths in her rigging. The idea of her surviving the hurricane unscathed gave Els a jolt of relief tinged with something akin to hope.

Towers of shrink-wrapped cargo turned the damaged wharf into an obstacle course, and she was grateful for a porter's help in shifting her luggage to the Jeep, which was parked near the Ginnery as Lauretta had promised. The creased bonnet and round headlamps gave the car such a quizzical expression that Els decided not to repair the dents and that the vehicle begged for a name. Wilma.

Before entering the harbor road along the battered seawall, she stopped and watched *Iguana* tug at her mooring line. In her business travel, the reality of a place seldom penetrated her shield of meetings, hired cars, and posh hotels. The foreignness of this place was exciting, but her otherness and naïveté rang a warning bell. She knew by name only a handful of people who called Nevis home. She wondered if any of them, or anyone at all, would become her friend.

Jack's had a new rolling gate and cattle guard, and one of the drive's royal palms had sprouted opposite branches holding golf ball–sized fruits, red on one, green on the other, as if it had decked itself out to welcome her for Christmas. The fallen trees were gone, and the newly mown grass baking in the sun reminded her of haying season. With its polished windows reflecting the afternoon sun, the house appeared larger, more gracious. Lauretta had arranged outdoor furniture on the gallery. Nevis Pottery urns spilling pale blue flowers flanked the door.

A stroll through the rooms reassured her that their quirkiness remained intact, though they were tidy and bright with tropical fabrics now. She set about unpacking and arranging the few personal treasures she'd carried in her luggage. She placed her portrait of Mallo on the bedside table and the triangle-folded Saltire and bothy's tin cup on the study desk next to Jack's shaving mug and a piece of brain coral.

Crunching gravel and a slamming car door announced Lauretta's arrival in the court. At her call of, "Inside?" Els went to the gallery. She found Lauretta leaning against a gleaming white Lexus sedan.

"Where else would I be?" Els asked, suspecting her renovation had paid for the car.

"Hollerin' 'inside's' the Nevisian way of knocking," Lauretta said, "but from farther away, to respect people's privacy when they don't have normal doors." She hugged her yellow pad to her chest. "For only two weeks since you got title, are we making progress on this sow's ear, or what?" She looked particularly pixieish today, her ginger frizz held back in butterfly clips.

"Enough for me to stay here," Els said.

"Only if you plan to shower in the rain like a dumb chicken," Lauretta said. She climbed up the steps, and Els ushered her into the lounge. "The water permit got all twisted up—don't get me started—and there won't be any new hookups until after New Year's. The stonemason hasn't fixed the crack in the cistern yet. You're dry for at least two weeks. The new fridge won't arrive 'til then, either. If you hadn't rushed back, holiday coming and all, I'd have had time to get a lot more ready."

"I cleared out my London flat," Els said. "I needed a roof over my head."

Lauretta flipped the wall switch. The ceiling fan rotated. "You've got current and a working cooker. Only two of the big four necessities of civilization."

"Then I'm canceling the hotel," Els said.

Lauretta cocked an eyebrow.

"I made it through the hurricane wi' a lot less, didn't I? Look, I slept out on the moors all the time as a kid, sometimes in the snow." A memory stabbed her: warm dogs, shooting stars, falling asleep with Mallo to the voices of men telling tales. "The new mattress will be luxury enough."

"Top of the line," Lauretta said. "So you won't feel any peas." She walked to the window. "There's a flush privy and lavatory with its own cistern by that outbuilding that had its roof tore off. Stella insisted on scrubbing it, even though I told her you'd never use it. Don't even think about drinking that water unless you want bugs in your belly."

Els looked out at the shell of the chattel house she'd imagined as a painting studio and guest room once the roof was replaced. "Where can I get water?"

"Tourists buy bottled. People without their own cisterns like Jack's or government water use the public cisterns. There's one at the Westbury Road."

"Is it potable?"

"It's pure mountain rainwater, but you'd better boil it until your belly gets used to it."

"Then all I need are jugs."

Lauretta stared at her. "Jiminy. Well, Lady Eleanor, maybe neither of us is what people think." Amusement glinted in her pale brown eyes. "Welcome home." She dropped two envelopes on the refectory table. "Time you signed up properly with the postal service. And you'll want to paint your own name on Jack's mailbox."

Els stopped herself from commenting that Jack hadn't actually left yet and instead said, "What little mail I'll get can come 'Care of Jack' for now."

Lauretta gave a resigned shrug, her standard reply whenever Els mentioned Jack or his effects. "Tony sent some of your citizenship papers," she said. "And he said don't drive anymore until you get a local license."

"Surely my UK permit will do for a few days."

"Park in town somewhere and walk to the main police station as if you just arrived on the ferry," Lauretta said. "Don't let them see you drive up. One lady cop in the Newcastle station is strict enough to slap you with a summons. Go today or you might be grounded until after Boxing Day."

The concept that the island might shut down for days hadn't occurred to Els. "I'd no plans to go anywhere," she said, looking away. She'd no plans, period; the aimlessness that had felt so liberating now rang hollow.

Lauretta touched her arm. "I can't cook worth a damn, and

Tony loves a crowd on holidays," she said. "We go to Hermitage for their Christmas Eve pig roast and then into town to hang out with everyone and his brother. Come along."

"That's very kind of you," Els said.

"We've got a nice outdoor shower you can use any time," Lauretta said. She drew a crude map on her yellow pad with *X*'s marking the public cistern and her own house. "Good thing I left Jack's old beer cooler in the storeroom," she said. "Oualie sells ice." She ripped off the map and handed it to Els. "I thought we'd discuss some of the stuff on my list, but you look jet-lagged all to hell."

Before leaving, Lauretta slipped her an invoice. Els was glad to be alone when she opened it. Payment would wipe out most of her remaining savings, and the work was far from finished.

She parked Wilma near the port and wandered among vendors selling from tables in front of flooded-out shops. The wilting sun and the scents of barbecue, open drains, diesel, and roasted peanuts assaulted her. In the courthouse square a man played Christmas songs on a steel pan; his calypso "Frosty the Snowman" tormented her mind for the rest of the afternoon.

The only person in the police station, a young man in droop-ass shorts and a camo T-shirt who she hoped was an officer, said he couldn't help her about the license. "You needed to stop by this morning," he said. "Now you must wait until Tuesday. Where you staying?"

"I bought Jack Griggs's place."

He looked at her for longer than she wanted to be scrutinized by any policeman. "I trust we'll have no more trouble up there, then," he said.

In a sparsely stocked grocery, she selected a pricy bottle of cognac for Tony and Lauretta and examined with revulsion the freezer cases of cow heels, chicken claws, and boxed chicken parts that looked as if they'd been thawed and refrozen several times. She lugged back to

Wilma several jugs of water, bits and bobs of British and American packaged food, a child's watercolor set, and two sundresses from a tourist shop because she couldn't decide between them.

Fear of the constabulary was unknown to her, and she was relieved when she'd slid safely by the police station at Cotton Ground. Farther on, she spotted the public tap at Westbury, a concrete bunker covered with graffiti, only because a skinny boy was filling a bucket there. By the time she'd bought ice at Oualie and returned to the house, the papaya-colored sun was throwing palm shadows across the garden.

She settled into the study's creaky desk chair and opened the envelope from Timmons. Besides documents about the estate, it contained a letter with Italian stamps addressed in her mother's handwriting, dated ten days after Els had written from Cairnoch.

Mia cara Eleanora,

It is many years I do not expect to have your letter, but I am glad to receive it. I am in horror that your father kept you from me even more than I knew.

If you desire to visit Ischia, I will be happy to meet the woman you have become. It is not possible to make up for this time. We will be as strangers. Only our blood connects us. Even if we never meet, I wish to know about these silent years and to end them. If you are a mother yourself by now, perhaps you can understand my hunger for knowing.

I fear that you will be disappointed. I am sorry that I have not been the mother you want.

Con tanto affetto,

Instead of signing her name, her mother had drawn a tiny white gardenia with a red tear, just like the signatures on the birthday paintings.

Els read the letter over three times. Her elation at receiving it faded as she searched in the formal language for the loving mother she'd always imagined.

In Jack's desk she found a greeting card with a drawing of a palm tree on the front. She wrote *Dear Mum*, then stopped to stare out the window. A sadness—familiar, but more raw than before—washed through her at the thought of what her mother couldn't or wouldn't ever be. Unable to decide what to write, she pushed the note aside, folded her mother's letter into its envelope, and pinned it in the center of Jack's bulletin board.

After the sunset, the sky turned a yellow-washed gray that faded over the next hour. Els poured dark rum into a jam jar and sipped it as she ambled through the grounds in the bluing light. The garden cleanup had revealed the foundations of a stone outbuilding, its entry facing the sea. She stepped beneath its arch of magenta bougainvillea and into an intimate walled garden furnished with a metal café table and two chairs. Orchids, bromeliads, and ferns sprouted from crevices in the walls. A tangle of periwinkle, the source of Jack's spirit-banning nosegay, filled one corner. A passionflower vine twined among the bougainvillea, its flowers appearing to glow in the low light, marvelous in their complexity. She sat and savored her rum and listened to the sounds of evening swelling from the ghaut.

In the gloaming, she climbed the slope to the privy, pried open the door, and pulled the cord to light a bare bulb. There was a loud plop. A huge toad stared at her from the toilet bowl, its slitted amber eyes holding a malevolent gleam.

"Get out," she cried.

The toad curled its four-fingered front feet over the lip of the bowl.

She went looking for a stick, but when she returned the toad had disappeared. She hurried back to the kitchen, locked the door behind her, and put the privy pot back in the storeroom so she wouldn't encounter any creatures worse than mice during the night. She bolted down the rest of her rum.

She wrapped herself in her favorite shawl, a persimmon pashmina from Hong Kong, hoping to ward off the mosquitoes, and went to the gallery. Light from the lounge spilled down the steps and melted into the darkness in the court. She squared her shoulders, touched her bead necklace, and breathed in the perfumes of the place. She would be the proud protector of this ancient structure, these majestic trees. The weight of stewardship—a frisson of excitement mixed with apprehension—settled over her, but inside was again that glimmer of joy.

CHAPTER 18

Tony parked near the ruins of the Bath Hotel and the three of them strolled into Charlestown, where a boom box blared reggae from the courthouse steps and colored lights twinkled in the balcony railings. Nevisian families and tourists clogged all the side streets and squares.

The Hermitage pig had been succulent and Els had sampled every dish, including souse; only later had Lauretta told her with a smirk that it was stuffed pig's head. She'd also overdone it on the rum punch, and her stomach lurched at the aroma of grilling meat from a barbecue stand near the Chinese supermarket.

While a children's troupe clad in clown costumes stomped through dance steps that jingled the bells around their ankles, Els studied the faces of fellow bystanders.

Lauretta hung on Tony's arm, her eyes in dubious focus. "What are you looking for?" she asked. "You're craning around like a nervous hen."

"A sailor," Els said.

"How 'bout one of those?" Tony said. A knot of men chanted in German and held up Heineken bottles.

"Not just any sailor," Els said.

"Picky, picky," Lauretta said.

In the shadow of a balcony across the street, a black man stood a head taller than his companions. The holiday lights turned their shoulders orange, blue, and green.

"Be right back," Els said, and crossed the street. At her approach, one of the men shook the tall man's hand and wished him a prosperous New Year, then melted into the crowd with the others.

"The wooman who is all toughness, but fears the sea," Jason said. Though he spoke softly, his voice had a penetrating intensity. He was wearing the sunglasses and hair-stuffed hat she remembered from their sail. Against his ebony skin, his pale blue dress shirt glowed as if under black light.

"Merry Christmas to you too," she said. "Is Liz around?"

He looked at her long enough for her to wonder if he intended to answer. "Scarsdale," he said. "He father dyin' soon, mebbe dead already."

A memory of Harald at Christmas Eve Mass swam into her head. Not trusting her face, she watched a dog sniff at a pool of melting ice cream near her foot, lick it up, and slink away.

Jason looked over her shoulder. "We go collect him by English Harbour Sunday," he said. "Busy season. Long time before we see Nevis again."

"I saw that *Iguana* managed to outrun the hurricane."

"We was down by Aruba," he said. "Hide near Cumaná, Venezuela." A man stepped up, fist-bumped Jason and moved on. "How come you back so soon?' Jason asked. "You another one a' them tourists that just *falls in love* with Nevis?"

"I thought it a good place to welcome in the new century," she said. "Tell Liz I'm sorry about his father."

He nodded, a hint of a smile.

A choir on the courthouse steps burst into a gospel version of "Angels We Have Heard on High." Els threaded her way back to Lauretta and Tony.

"What were you doing, trying to score some dope?" Lauretta asked.

"He's a sailor, not a dealer."

"Ha," Lauretta said. "Just look at him."

Els remembered the roll of cash, the men who'd drifted toward Jason for whispered conversations at Sunshine's and again tonight. He could be shady, even on the wrong side of the law. "I've had enough of this crowd," she said. "I'll go lock myself in the car until you're ready to go."

"You can leave that New York London fraidy cat stuff behind," Lauretta said. "Come on, Tony, let's get the princess back to her tower."

CHAPTER 19

When a man called, "Inside?" from the court, Els carried her morning tea out to the patio, the flagstones dewy under her bare feet. It was the fisherman from the Resort beach.

"Mawnin," he said, and smiled broadly. "Sorry to intrude into you Boxing Day, Miss Els. It kinda urgent."

"My whole holiday could have used a little intrusion," she said. On Christmas, she'd taken her watercolors to Oualie, where families cavorted while she dabbed at a painting she'd later—after reducing the rum bottle by several inches—thrown into the bin.

"I help Jack build he boat," he said. "Me and Jack, we had a understanding. Anything happen to him, de boat is mine."

"It's a little late for a claim against Jack's estate. That boat and everything on this property were part of the sale."

"Jack do a lot by handshake."

"Handshake doesn't get you much in court."

"No fisherman getting mixed up with lawyer," he said. He sucked his teeth. "Enjoy you boat and all a' you property." He replaced his cap and turned away.

"Why don't we have a little tea?" she said.

He stopped, his back to her. "We doan need no tea to talk about that boat."

"You quit easily," she said.

He walked to where the boat trailer was backed against a new oleander hedge, a pale yellow cultivar specially ordered to complement the house trim. He untied the tarp and rolled it back. "Miss sell boat, de buyer need inspection."

She followed him, walking tender-footed across the gravel.

"Little *Maid* sit through three hurricanes," he said. "Maybe develop problems." He dangled a shriveled baby mouse by the tail and tossed it into the oleander. He held up a seat cushion to show where mice had chewed and tugged a length of gnawed line until it snapped.

"What makes you think I want to sell?" She lifted the varnished mahogany daggerboard. Painted across the stern was *Mermaid S*. "I might just take up sailing."

He removed the mast and sprit and made a business of inspecting the lines and wrapping them back around the spars and stowing it all again. Shaking his head, he ran his hand over a crack in the gunwale made by the fallen palm. "She take hard blow." He pulled off a splinter. "Smart miss doan try sailin' no leaky boat, or you goin' be makin' Jack's acquaintance. Where she sail?"

She led him to the storeroom and pointed to a folded canvas, woolly with dust and peppered with mouse droppings. He took the sail to the patio, flapped away the droppings, and spread it in the sun. Three ragged holes, a mildew stain along the foot. He rested his knuckles on his hips. "Miss, you not goin' far with this."

"Make me an offer," she said.

"Ah take she off you hands—holes, mice, and all—five hundred dollars."

"You must be joking."

"That US, not EC," he said.

"Two thousand," she said. "US."

He whistled. "Man gotta be crazy to pay that much for what already his," he said. He folded the sail and tried to hand it to her, but she averted her face and he set it on a metal garden chair.

"What will you use it for?" she asked.

"Tending pots," he said. "Most a' my livin' come from pot fish and lobster."

She paced a circle around the lumber stacked on the patio. "Fifteen hundred."

"Man like me cyan put his hands on that kind a' money, not legally," he said. "'Preciate you time." He walked toward the drive.

"I promised you tea," she called after him.

"This wasn't no social visit," he called back.

She strode into the restaurant at Oualie and rapped her knuckles on the bar. Barrett Cobb emerged from the kitchen, wiping his hands on a towel tucked into his jeans.

"Boxing Day special, Els," he said. "Conch salad."

"Someone named Finney fish out of here?" she asked. "He wants to buy Jack's boat."

"Why didn't I think of that?" Cobb said. "He designed the *Maid*, taught Jack how to build her. He's busting his behind over there right now repairing an old tub that got stove in so badly during Lenny the owner gave it to him." At the end of the beach, a shirtless black man leaned over a boat on sawhorses, planing. "He deserves a break."

As she approached, Finney was shaving a long curl off a new plank in the hull. "You're working hard on a holiday," she said.

He brushed the shavings onto the sand. "Gotta get some boat back in the water."

She slipped a curl onto her finger, a bulky ring. "What would you say to one thousand?"

He straightened. "Boat need repair," he said. "New sail cost plenty." He knocked a shaving from his plane. "Can't do more n' six hundred." His expression was a mixture of pride and need and he held her gaze.

"Okay," she said.

He set the plane down. "Ah doan have all that money in hand."

"What, you want installments now?"

"Hurricane bust up the whole fleet and most a' the pots. Ah got a stack a' new pots in me yard. Cobb goin' take anything me catch. Give you one hundred down."

She glanced toward the restaurant. Cobb was watching them from behind the bar. "Will he vouch for you?"

"I doing business with him steady," he said.

She drew circles in the sand with her toe. "Come at nine o'clock tomorrow morning."

"I goin' be punctual."

She marched back to the restaurant and asked Cobb for two bags of ice. When he put the ice into the Jeep, he said, "Deal?"

"He's giving me one hundred dollars down. I'm relying on your recommendation that he'll be good for the rest."

Cobb chuckled. "As soon as you leave, he'll be over here asking me for that hundred. Advance on the catch."

"Give it to him."

Finney surveyed the kitchen and said, "It almost like Jack still living here. If he was, he'd a' loan me the *Maid* long as I need her and we wouldn't be doin' business." He fanned five US twenties onto the table. "You want me sign a paper for the rest?"

"Might as well have a proper note," she said. She sat down at the table and flipped Lauretta's pad to a clean page. Finney leaned against the drainboard.

She asked for his full name and wrote on the pad in big letters, reading aloud as she went. "I, Finneaus Fleming, agree to purchase the sailboat *Mermaid S* from Eleanor Gordon for a total of six hundred US dollars, including an earnest money deposit of one hundred US dollars cash, paid 27 December, 1999, and the remainder of five hundred US dollars to be paid no later than . . . ." She looked up. "What should I put for the terms?"

He was staring at Jack's boomerang hanging above the window. "I doan promise outside my capability."

"Good principle," she said. "How's fifty dollars a month? Interest of, let's say, five percent."

He looked out the kitchen window at the mango tree. "No problem."

She handed him the note and he read it over aloud, took her pen, and signed where she had drawn a line. "One next thing, Miss Els," he said after she'd signed her name with a flourish. "I gotta borrow that Jeep to haul she down to Oualie."

"Let's go right now," she said. "See if she floats."

While Finney stood in the water directing her, she backed the trailer down the beach until the *Maid* floated free. He rigged the mast and sprit, raised the sail, and let it swing lazily. "T'anks for dat expert tow," he said. "I go to come back." He smiled. "Unless I end up at de bottom."

"For such a bargain," she said, "you could at least throw in a little ride."

He peered through a hole in the sail. "Better move that car. Tide comin' in."

She'd dressed for the sun—billowy white linen trousers, one of Jack's shirts, her floppy sun hat. After moving the car, she returned to the edge of the water and bent to roll the legs above her knees. Finney backed the *Maid's* stern to the sand and held out his hand. She grasped his broad palm and he helped her to the midship thwart, facing astern, and gave her the gnawed seat cushion.

He pushed off and settled onto the stern seat. When he slid the daggerboard home and trimmed the sheet, the boat heeled and leapt forward. Els clutched the thwart.

"Can you swim?" he asked.

She looked over the side at Oualie's white-sand bottom. "That depends."

"I hopin' you was goin' save me," he said, mischief in his smile, "if that time come."

The sun was hot on her shoulders. The little boat rocked and yawed, and when Finney changed tack she felt it hesitate and heel to the other side. He was at one with the boat, this burly man whose hand caressed the tiller. Older than she'd first thought: grizzle in the hair below his cap, yellow tint in the whites of his eyes.

"If you don't think she's seaworthy," she said, "don't go out over our heads."

They looked down at the bilge, which held a sheen of water, mostly spray.

"She good." He trimmed the sail and headed out of the harbor.

When the water turned from turquoise to dark green, Els's chest began to constrict and she gripped the thwart more tightly. "No junket to St. Kitts," she said.

"Just lookin' for a little real wind," he said. "See how she do."

Remembering Liz's tricks for easing queasiness and panic, she stared over Finney's shoulder at sturdy Wilma, which had shrunk to the size of a child's toy. She breathed in through her nose and out through her mouth. Her knuckles ached. "Who's the boat named for?"

"Mena know," Finney said. "Jack say something about mermaid in Greece what does wreck boats." He trimmed the sheet again, and the boat leapt forward and heeled more sharply. "He had something for the name Susie. Call every one a' his dawg Susie, gyull or bwoy."

The boat dipped and rolled with the growing swells, and the dark water was only inches below the rail.

"Keep talking," Els said.

"About what?" His frequent interjection of "anh?" gave his speech a staccato musicality, and his low register lent it a calming steadiness. His knees were pocked with white archipelagos of dried salt.

"Anything. Your family."

He told her his wife, Vivian, a former schoolteacher, had the "sugar," which had already claimed a foot and made her nearly blind. Their son was a lawyer in New York, and their daughter had worked at the Resort until it was destroyed. Vivian's father had been an influential, canny trader, and her older brother, Eugene, was part of the current government. "The higher he rise, the worse things get for Viv and me."

"Family in high places ought to benefit you."

"Not if you won't take from crooks and they despise you for it," he said.

A wave slammed the port bow, tossing cold pellets of spray, and she yelped and wiped her face with her sleeve.

"Miss not enjoying her ride," he said. He pushed the tiller and the little boat spun around. When she'd finished ducking under the sail, she was facing out to sea and he was squinting toward shore, avoiding her gaze.

While they zigzagged back to Oualie, she concentrated on a cruise ship steaming toward Basseterre, and he told her about diving for lobster and the beauty of the reef and all its creatures.

When the water turned turquoise again, she eased her grip and kneaded her aching hands. "You know the *Iguana* men?" she asked.

"I doing business with Jason long time," he said. "Like most a' we."

"What's his business?" she asked, hoping she hadn't written a loan to someone involved in drugs.

He shrugged. "Jason very discreet."

"Then tell me about Liz."

He signaled for her to duck and changed tack. "Jason bring him here, maybe ten year back," he said. "He have big trouble then."

"With the law?"

"If Jason know the circumstances, he doan speak about it." He eased the sail. "Liz a little like Jack," he said. "Make everybody laugh, but have a lotta sadness. Lotta anger." He squinted under the sail. "No ladies stay 'round him for long." He put the tiller over. "Keep you head low."

He raised the daggerboard and guided the *Maid* to a gentle crunch on the beach, stepped into the shallows, and steadied the sail.

"Lovely ride," Els said, accepting his help getting out. "I shan't be taking up sailing after all. See you in a month with that installment payment."

He grasped the painter and heaved the boat higher onto the sand. "You want some of it in lobsters?"

"Only if you cook them first."

"Ain't nothin' to cooking lobster. Viv show you in ten minutes."

"You said she couldn't see."

"She see with her mind and her ears."

"Tell her I look forward to that lesson, Finney," she said.

CHAPTER 20

Jack didn't have any flutes, so Els drank her first bottle of champagne from a jam jar and the second, since she wasn't sharing, straight from the bottle. In honor of what the Nevisians call "Old Year's Night," she'd put on a tangerine sundress and her great-grandmother's ruby matinee necklace. She'd splurged on a tin of caviar and was sitting at the top of the gallery steps spooning it messily onto crisps.

At midnight, car and boat horns blared and someone at Oualie sent up fireworks—a few sparkles and pops. Then it was dark again, and silent. Els began singing "Auld Lang Syne" in a faltering near whisper. After the first verse she swigged the champagne and said, "Here's to the new fucking millennium. Not exactly where I thought I'd be at Y.2.K."

She sang the second verse louder; the Scottish words on her tongue were a taste of home. "Ain't tha' fer true, me darlin' lad?" she said. "Many a weary, lonely foot have I wandered since I've seen yir fair face." Looking up at the stars, she began the third verse, but when she sang "But seas between us braid hae roar'd," she stopped and hugged her knees. "A great sea lies between us now, my love," she said. "And likely ever shall."

When she launched into the final verse, a man's voice chimed in—a baritone, tuneful and strong. He was standing in the shadows at the edge of the court with his hand extended to grasp hers, as the song lyrics said.

She squinted at him. "Is it you again?" she asked. "Stop skulking and come over where I can see you."

He stepped onto the gravel. He looked much as he had that night in her bedroom, but less tired, and naughtiness had replaced the pleading in his expression.

"Okay, Jack, so am I hallucinating again? I'm that pished."

He stepped closer. "You're so sad tonight, sweet. I thought I might cheer you up."

She held out her hand. "Shall we *take a right guid willy waught*, or did ye come to dance, perhaps? Been a while since I had a spin in a handsome man's arms." She stood up, lost her balance, grabbed the railing, and sat down hard. "Well, forget about cutting a bit a' rug." She looked at the midnight sky. "If you want to cheer me up, go off to heaven and bring back the two people I most want to see. If you can drag back only one, leave Father there and bring me Mallo. Father'd never answer all the questions I have for him, anyway."

"They'll have to find you on their own."

"Is there a time limit for yir wandering, a sell-by date, after which ye're just a stale spirit? Have I missed my window for seeing them again, and no goodbye for either?" She took another swig of champagne and set the bottle on the edge of the step. It tumbled down the flight, fizzing what remained onto the stones. "Bloody hell," she said. "Ach, just as well."

"Mark Twain is supposed to have said, 'Sometimes too much to drink is barely enough,'" he said. "My motto, but I hope you don't make it yours." He walked to the bottom of the steps. He seemed too substantial to be a hallucination, but her eyes were sliding in and out of focus. "So what did you think you'd be doing when the century turned?"

"My plan was to be the lady of the estate and my . . . my bonnie Mallo and I'd be managing it together, keeping it sound and strong. He'd be the darling of the devolution movement, and I'd be his secret weapon. Now it's all gone. Cairnoch. Him. No use crying in that beer."

"You like crying in your beer."

"And who cares if I do?"

"'First you take a drink, then the drink takes a drink, then the drink takes you,'" he said. "F. Scott Fitzgerald. And he should know."

"Is that what you do, wander in and drop er-u-dite quotes? Don't you have anything original to say? Look, Jumbiekins, if that's who you are, the last thing I need is someone visiting from the other side—and a poor example, at that—telling me how to live my life."

"It's seductive here," he said. "*Beguiling*. Easy to become a total slacker before you know it. Fall into the bottle every night and you could end up like so many expat prunes with their desperate, predatory eyes, pressing their butts against anything in pants." He stuffed his hands into his pockets. "Anyone might get a little tight contemplating the turn of the year, let alone a new century," he said, "but don't make a habit of it."

"I've got nothing to do, anyway, no reason to be all bushy-tailed of a morning, so who cares if I'm oot ma face night after bloody night?"

"You've got a life-and-death job to do."

"Oy, aye? And what might that be?"

"Forgive the past, embrace the future," he said. "Hard work, both. I failed the first and bungled the second, but there's still time for you." He looked at her a long time, as if trying to recall something. "'To forgive is to set a prisoner free and discover that the prisoner was you,'" he said. "A theologian named Smedes wrote that."

"I'd have guessed Hallmark."

"Hard to control how your work gets cutesied up after you're gone," he said. "We're all in prisons of our own making. I'll help you spring yourself if you'll return the favor."

"Just how do you propose we do that, Mr. Philosopher?"

"Make it our resolution: liberation in the new century."

One last firecracker shot up. She watched through the palms as its blue starburst disintegrated and rained down over the sea at Oualie.

"Happy New Year, sweet," he said, and when she looked back, the court was empty.

CHAPTER 21

It rained nearly every day in January, prolonged downpours that turned the garden into a mire. Whenever Els complained of construction delays, Rohan, head of the Guyanese crew, would say "It pissin' rain, lady, pissin' rain." The Christmas winds buffeted the house, rattled the palms, and made her fidgety.

While the workmen hammered overhead, she balanced on a ladder and stretched to roll paint onto the lounge's planked ceiling. The phone rang and she climbed down and threw back the corner of the drop cloth, dislodging the receiver, which clattered onto the table.

She answered, not bothering to hide her annoyance.

"Timmons here, returning your call," the voice said. "I've obviously interrupted something."

"Painting, and I don't mean on canvas," she said. "Trying to contain the ballooning cost of this bloody project." She rested her elbow on her grimy knee. "I need you to send more money," she said. "Fifty thousand—US—ought to do it."

A beat of silence.

"That will just about wipe out the balance of your trust," he said.

"I can't very well stop without proper plumbing," she said. "I'll still have a little savings."

Another beat of silence.

"I'll wire the money as usual. Look for it by week's end." He rang off.

She started a Dizzy Gillespie CD from Jack's collection and climbed back up the ladder. The music did nothing to improve her mood, and she wielded the roller with such force that she worked up a streaming sweat and was covered with celadon speckles by the time she'd finished the job.

She set the painting tools in the kitchen sink and turned the tap. Nothing. Again. Anger flaring, she crammed the water jugs Lauretta had advised her to save into Wilma's boot and drove dangerously fast to the Westbury public cistern.

Against one wall was a crudely rigged shower where an elderly black woman in a cotton shift was soaping her hair. The woman hummed as she rinsed, turned off the shower, and shook the water from her arms. She dried her face with a grayed pink towel and watched Els unload the plastic jugs.

"These bloody water stoppages," Els said. "A shower would be heaven right about now."

"This ain't my idea of heaven," the woman said. "But it better dan nothing." She slipped into her rubber sandals. "You almost as green as that Jolly Giant," she said. "Water alone never goin' get off that mess." She handed Els a sliver of soap. "Any left when you done, just leave it on that ledge." She flipped the towel onto her shoulder and walked up the hill, her dress clinging to her hips.

Els gasped when the cool water hit her skin. Being sparing of the soap, she lathered her hair and scrubbed the grime and paint off her arms and legs. She stretched the neck of her tank top and the waistband of her running shorts to let the water rinse the soap and sweat away.

When she reached to put the soap sliver on the ledge, a girl of about six was standing next to a puddle, staring. Her hair was divided into squares and pulled into knots held with pastel bow clips.

"Your braids and hair clips are pretty," Els said.

The girl ran toward the nearest house shouting, "Mammy, mammy, white lady using our shower."

A woman came to the door and looked at Els. "Get in here, gyull, you hear me?" she said, and pulled the child into the house. Els remembered Salustrio's taunt: *Just because they smile at you, don't get to thinking they* like *you.*

By the time she reached her gate, the rain was pelting again. A skinny black man was pulling weeds in the garden. She stopped Wilma and leaned out the window.

"What the hell do you think you're doing?"

He smiled and bent to his work.

The rain fell harder. She gunned Wilma up the hill and made a run for the kitchen door. On the step was a papaya and a calabash bowl holding several greenish-orange fruits with bumpy rinds. She carried them into the kitchen and mopped her face and hands with a tea towel. When she cut one of the fruits, loaded with seeds, it filled the kitchen with a scent somewhere between lime and orange. She squeezed a little juice into her mouth; her whole body seemed to pucker from its sourness. She took a fruit up to the study and riffled through Jack's books on tropical flora until she found the aptly named "bitter orange" and recognized the aftertaste of marmalade.

Still scattered on the desk were the calculations that had forced her to drain her trust. *When I'm flat broke*, she thought, *maybe I can go into the jam business, or live on mangoes and coconuts. Especially if that man, whoever he is, will deliver them.*

She went to the window and looked into the garden. The rain had slackened. The man had disappeared.

CHAPTER 22

Els paused from squashing and stacking the shipping cartons from her edgy artwork, so foreign to the customs inspector that Lauretta had successfully valued it at flea market prices, avoiding duty.

"These are worth more than the house," Els said.

"Everyone tries to cheat the system," Lauretta said, and flashed her pixie smile. She pulled a wad of price tags from her pocket and tossed them onto the refectory table.

"I can see why, if it's true that our taxes go straight to St. Kitts and we never see them again," Els said. "When did you remove all these?"

"While you were haggling over the furniture," Lauretta said. "You'd have paid sixty percent duty on all that fancy underwear if he'd seen it was right off the shelf. What does anyone need with matching bra and panties for every day of the year?"

Els shuffled the tags. In addition to US dollars, their denominations were in pounds sterling, French francs, yen, Hong Kong dollars, pesos, riyals. "Consolation shopping," she said. "I've always done it, but never so much as this past year."

"Consolation for what?"

Els fondled a bra, handmade of exquisite silk and lace. "A hole."

"What do you mean, 'a hole'?"

Els hung a Basquiat painting of a skeleton with a fish over the refectory table, crossed her arms, and stared at it. "A hole at the middle of everything," she said. The hole that had swallowed Mallo. The deeper hole that was her mother.

Lauretta settled the shade onto the celadon Chinese lamp from Cairnoch's sitting room and tightened its finial. "Throwing your money at this house won't fix that."

Els placed the lamp next to Jack's big chair. It looked perfect there, its bead fringe a jaunty counterpoint to the scuffed leather. "The first home that's all mine," she said, "is a gourmet meal after living on junk food."

"That sequined gown and the Dr. Zhivago coat aren't exactly Fritos."

"Should have donated all that to a London charity," Els said. "I've no closets for it. And a snowball's chance of wearing any of it here."

"You could add feathers to that underwear and parade through town during Culturama," Lauretta said, and returned to unpacking the lamps.

Els watched her buzz about the lounge, examining each item and placing it with conviction, though seldom to Els's taste. Finally, she said, "You just unpack the boxes. I'll figure out where to put everything."

"As you wish," Lauretta said. "As usual."

Els arranged her mother's twenty-three drawings and paintings in date order on the refectory table.

Lauretta examined the collection. "You'd never guess those were by the same person."

"In a way, perhaps they weren't," Els said. The emotional impact of the pieces varied—comforting, agitated, and furious—and their colors were alternately tranquil, festive, or gloomy. Her favorites were the earliest drawing of the animals, which made her feel as if her mother were reading her a bedtime story, and the self-portrait, which captured her own anger, all the more volcanic and disorienting since Mallo's death.

Lauretta ran her fingertip over the gardenia signature on a harbor scene with orange sails against a cobalt sea, but since Els had no answer to the unasked question, she said nothing. She put the animal drawing on her bedside table and hung the self-portrait in the study, where its unframed raw power felt right.

They worked all afternoon, and when they were finished, Els's belongings were melded with Jack's in a quirky mélange that made her smile.

The empty shipping container crowded the court, and, in the light of the full moon, its serial numbers and letters glowed against its rusty sides. Els sank into a chair and watched the clouds darken to smoke, imagining the container's travels. For the first time in at least five years, she hadn't been on a plane in over a month. A night heron squawked and lifted off, threading through the palms and over the ribbon of drive.

When her gaze returned to the container, Jack was leaning against it, his shirt silvery in the moonlight. She jumped up and grabbed the broom she'd been using to sweep the steps. As a weapon it was ludicrous, but she planted her feet and held the handle across her chest like a fighting stick.

"Good evening, sweet," he said. His voice was seductive. He walked soundlessly across the gravel to about ten feet from the bottom step.

She looked at her broom. Sparrow had warned her never to sweep at night.

"Did I . . . summon you?"

"Don't believe all that mumbo jumbo," he said. "It's hard work getting here. I waited until your gear arrived. You're less likely to flee now." He stuck his hands into his pockets. "We should try to get along, seeing as we have so much in common."

"I've nothing in common with a fancier of frisky young things, a drunken brawler."

"How about an unabashed romantic, inveterate questioner, recovering pugilist?" He took a step forward.

"That's close enough."

The breeze played with his shirttails. "This house," he said. "It called to you as strongly as it did me, once. We share more than you want to admit." He raised his hands in surrender, turned a full circle, and smiled rakishly. "You can put down your weapon."

She lowered the broom and hugged the handle to her chest. "I can't blame you on nightmares or booze this time."

He looked up at her. "Glad to see that getting some use."

She looked down. After her shower, she'd pulled on his pale blue linen shirt.

"I always loved the look of a woman in a man's shirt," he said. "Bare legs hinting at what might be just above the hem. This moonlight on your alabaster skin turns you positively celestial."

"Just how much of this alabaster skin have you seen?" she asked. The thought struck her that he might have been watching her naked in the rain during the hurricane, or on the shower platform—that he was always about, as if the wind had eyes.

"I don't spy," he said. "And I wouldn't join a lady in her bath unless invited. If you're so worried, put up a curtain."

"And spoil the view of the sea?"

"That's my girl," he said. "Joy over modesty all the way."

"I want my joy *and* my privacy," she said.

"And your *consolation*." His gaze was intimate, unnerving. "Now that you've patched up the roofs, how about fixing what's really broken?"

The moon's sparkling road over the sea merged with the bottom of the drive, tempting her to run away from his question and out onto the waves, straight to the ether, in pursuit of the spirits she preferred to his company.

"*Caelum non animum mutant qui trans mare currunt,*" he said. "'They change their sky, not their soul, who rush across the sea.' Horace."

"Fixing what's been broken most of my life isn't solely up to me," she said.

"Never is. Since I'm here, I might as well help you."

"What makes you think I want you around at all?"

"I couldn't be here if you weren't receptive," he said. "I can't visit just anyone, alas."

"I thought you spirits had the run of the place."

"Only in comic books," he said.

A bat made a loop over the steps, followed by another, and soon there were dozens of darting bodies, each on an acrobatic course, barely visible in the moonlight.

"I know they live under the roof because I hear them chittering to each other when they come home at dawn," she said. "But I never see them leave at dusk. They just appear. Like you."

"Some people are more afraid of bats than they are of spirits."

She swept a pebble off the step and sat down. "As children we were fascinated by bats," she said. "The barn and tower were full of them. Mallo made a collection of their skeletons, mounted against black velvet in a suit box. Tiny, intricate dinosaurs. Once we found a baby, no bigger than this." She touched her thumbnail to the first joint in her pinkie finger. "We made a bed with cotton wool in a kipper tin, hid it from Burtie, and nursed it with an eye dropper. Mallo planned to teach it to sleep in his cap during the day." She wrapped her fingers around the broom handle and rocked it. "When it disappeared, Burtie blamed the cat, but he could never have opened that cupboard." She smiled. "You have no idea who I'm talking about."

"I've got a hunch," he said. "Good first step, unearthing memories like that." Against the sky's pewter glow, the bat silhouettes careened between the dark trees, speeding, diving, pivoting. "Come down here." He extended his hand.

"I'll stay where I am."

"Admit it, you're curious."

She pointed the broom handle at him like a tommy gun, went slowly down, and stopped a few feet from him, the tip aimed at his chest. He was ashen, with dark circles under his eyes—or maybe it was just the moonlight. He cocked his head at the broom handle with its loop of string dangling from a hole in its tip. She jabbed it toward him. He stepped back and smiled.

"You appear to be different ages when you visit," she said.

"It was a big effort to show up the first time as that younger me," he said. "I'm too tired now to be so vain. You're probably stuck with this Jack. Or worse."

A bat flew so close that she felt a puff of air on her ear. The court was alive with hurtling shapes, sweeping through the space between her and Jack, or maybe even through Jack, but they were too fast for her to tell.

"Do you bring your own bats?" she asked.

"These come with the place," he said. "Without them to suck up all those mosquitoes, you could never sit on the gallery at sunset."

"I've never seen such a swarm," she said. Being immersed in a natural phenomenon so indifferent to her was oddly enchanting. It wasn't the first time she'd been arrested by the throbbing and largely invisible life all around her, but she hadn't felt that wonder since her rambles with Mallo through the magical kingdom of their childhood that was Cairnoch.

"It's a rare feeding frenzy. Full moon, perhaps?" His voice was intimate again, but no longer unnerving. He struck a St. Francis pose, inviting the bats to land on his hands. "I'm no scarier than they are, to the right person."

They stood barely the broom handle's length apart. "Could I sweep you away as easily as a cobweb?" She flipped the broom so that the tattered bristles nearly brushed his face.

"It's been years since a beautiful woman took after me with a broom," he said. "Go ahead. See what happens."

She looked at him and slowly lowered the makeshift weapon.

He smiled. "Another bunch of periwinkle might be a better deterrent."

"Sparrow told me to put rice in front of every door."

"Did he also tell you that jumbies like untying knots?" he said. "Hang a knotted rope by the door, and a jumbie'll get distracted and forget all about you."

"They say unfinished business keeps jumbies from their rest. What business has imprisoned you, Jack? I want to know what kind of *resolution* I might be getting into."

"Make you a deal. That's your forte, isn't it—deals?" he said. "I promise to wheedle you into recognizing—no, admitting—the obvious, and being brave enough to do what you need to do, if you promise to resolve what I was too cowardly to finish."

"I'm to be brave for both of us, is it?"

"Brave for real, not that pretend brave you're so good at," he said. "Or else neither of us will get out of prison."

"What if pretending to be brave is too hard a habit to break?"

"Start by agreeing to pay attention." He was staring over her shoulder at the upstairs windows.

She followed his gaze. His clues were in there somewhere. The moon bathed the facade in blue light.

"All right, Jack," she said. "I'll pay very, very careful attention."

He ambled down the drive and seemed to step right into the moon and disappear.

CHAPTER 23

The government water had been intermittent for a week, and when she had a strong flow for the first time in days, she hurried to try out the rebuilt platform shower. Her concept of luxury kept redefining itself and now included warm showers on demand and feeling truly clean. Her list of wonders was expanding too. When she rinsed, the low sun drew rainbows in the droplets bouncing off her shoulders.

A man called from the court, and she swore and retreated behind the shower's lattice screen. She climbed back through the window and kept an eye on the drive while she dressed, but there was no sign of his departure. When she went to the front door—barefoot, her linen shift clinging to her back—he was sitting on the gallery railing.

"Capital shower, isn't it," he said. His smile was mischievous. "Not to mention the view. No doubt you've noticed that it waters the ferns underneath."

"And just how would you know all that?" she asked, tugging at her dress.

He pulled off his cap. He was ash blond, bearded, gray-eyed, and weathered. Mid-fifties, she guessed. In the photo of Jack and the two other men holding the mahi-mahi, he was the one on the left with the boyish grin.

"Julian Crawford," he said. "Better known as Boney. I'm—was—a mate of Jack's. Enjoyed that shower many a time." He looked down, crumpled the crown of his cap, and shook it out again.

His words tumbled out in a rush. "I helped Jack board up the place. I've been on a boat out of St. Martin, and this is the first time I've been able to get to Nevis since he . . . ." He looked out to sea. "I just reconnected with the old Oualie gang, and none of us had a proper goodbye with old Jack, and we heard someone was fixing up the place, so I volunteered to scout it out."

She crossed her arms and waited. His smile was disarming.

"It'd mean a lot to us to come up for the sunset, like old times, if it's not too much of an imposition. They're down there waiting for my signal."

"Who's in the old gang?"

"The boys from *Iguana,*" he said. "Maybe you know her or them."

"They've been away since before New Year's."

"Came in this afternoon," he said. She wondered how she'd missed that huge sail.

A lorry accelerated around the curve, shifted gears, and roared toward Charlestown. Els stood up straighter. "Go tell them to come up," she said.

"I'll just fire off Bessie," he said. "The cannon that belongs on this pedestal. I'm relieved to see she's still here."

"You'll do nothing of the kind," she said. "I only kept that old thing for its decorative charm."

"Decorative," he said. "Sacrilege. Jack shot off the old girl whenever he was in an entertaining mood. We could hear her at Oualie and come up for a drink. Or several."

"Why couldn't he just use the telephone?"

"He never got ship-to-shore. Besides, it was the ritual of the thing." He smiled again, a pleading, little boy look. He glanced toward the sea where the sun was beginning its descent. "I could have her set up in a jiffy."

Except for Jack, her only visitors so far had been Finney, Tony, Lauretta, the workmen, and that mysterious black man who worked in the garden. While she explored the island methodically by day, she became reclusive at night, taking her first drink at sunset, picking at whatever food was about, and reading her way through Jack's papers and eclectic library. Time and again, she'd found herself ruminating about the exile she and Jack had chosen, both of them blustering through life, both nursing corrosive anger and guilt. The salve he found in the embrace of women. Her retreat into the embrace of memory. Even though she never passed the harbor at Oualie or Charlestown without looking for *Iguana,* she'd burrowed so far into herself that the prospect of company, Liz most of all, felt like an invasion. Her chest began to constrict, tiny stitches threatening to bind her as tight as a pearl on silk. She took a deep breath, forcing her ribs outward, giving her heart space.

"Okay," she said. "Only if you promise not to blow up the place."

"Hot damn," Boney said, and ran down to the court.

The struggle to remove the cannon from the alcove under the steps and reposition it on the pedestal left him red-faced. The sun appeared to gain speed in its dive toward the horizon. He hurried back to her. "Is the powder where Jack always kept it?"

"No clue," she said.

He went into the house; his flip-flops slapped on the kitchen steps. He returned breathless, holding yellowed newspaper and two Mason jars with rusted lids, one containing about two centimeters of black powder, the other kitchen matches.

He blew into the breach, poured in some powder, balled up a wad of newspaper, rammed it into the barrel, and stuck in a fuse. Waving her back, he arranged a small bundle of matches and, glancing at the sea, struck them, cupped the flame, and touched off the fuse. "Here you go, mates," he said. "Three, two, one." The cannon boomed, belched smoke, and recoiled almost off the pedestal.

Els cried out and fanned away the smoke.

Boney's eyes were full of merriment and anticipation. "Bet Jack left some Cavalier around. Let's crack it open while we wait for them," he said. "You live here long enough, you'll drink it like all the locals. A little ice and lime would be just the thing."

Rum would be just the thing to combat her rising jitters. She hurried upstairs and changed into a tank dress, slinkier than the linen shift but not too revealing, its dusky blue a good pairing with her eyes and the bead necklace, which she now wore most of the time. When she returned to the gallery, Boney had gathered glasses, rum, ice, and some of the limes she'd collected that morning and was sitting in one of two chairs he'd pulled close to the railing with his bare feet propped up on it.

"Make yourself right at home," she said, but her irony was lost on him.

He dropped two cubes into his glass, poured rum until they floated, then a little more, squeezed lime into it, and tossed the rind over the railing.

He raised his glass and waited while she splashed rum into hers. "To Jack," he said, "ecstasy in small things, and excess whenever possible." He sipped his drink. "This was his favorite part of the day," he said. "A big rum at sunset and a package of pork rinds was his idea of heaven."

She grimaced.

"Don't knock it," he said. "Those little morsels sustained Jack—many of us, actually—on more than one occasion. Got any around?"

"Nor much of anything else," she said. She sipped, the ice cold against her lip, the rum warm in her throat.

"If you wanted to eat well in this house, you brought the grub yourself," he said.

"Jack wasn't much of a host, then."

"None finer," he said. He poked his ice cubes and watched them bob. "Near the end, he drank his meals unless someone put decent food under his nose, and sometimes even then . . . ." He squinted at the sea, took a long swig of his rum, and wiped his mustache with the back of his hand.

Boney started to tell her the history of the house, but she put up a hand. "I've read all about that planter from the dry side, building this house for his mistress. Jack wrote pages about fiery Sophia, the lover of sunsets."

"He had a serious crush on her," Boney said. "That she died a hundred fifty years before he was born didn't faze him one bit."

He told her Jack had been as kookily inventive as he was handy, cobbling together the original shower platform and figuring out how to divert some of the torrents in the ghaut to a cistern under the chattel house and run piping from there around the garden. "How the hell else could he have so many friggin' plants?" he said.

"I'm on the government water now," she said.

Boney gaped at her. "And be at the mercy of the powers that be, or wannabe? Jack had reasons beyond pure cussedness to be keen on self-sufficiency."

When the gate rattled, Boney jumped up and waved his arms, and a pickup truck with a sun-seared paint job rolled up the hill. He vaulted the gallery railing—right into the newly planted birds of paradise below. "Who put these fucking things here?" he asked.

"A very expensive landscaper." Els scowled down at the smashed plants.

"Just think of it as pruning." Boney thrashed through the bed toward the truck, scattering leaves onto the court as he went.

Liz climbed out of the passenger seat, looked up at Els, and gave her a surprised grin, his eyes the color of the sea.

Jason uncoiled himself from behind the wheel. "When we hear that cannon," he said, "we want to believe old times have come back again." His laugh flowed through his sinewy body. He was wearing his sunglasses and crocheted hat.

"Sadly, no," Boney said. "Step up, lads, and meet our hostess. She says her name is Els, whatever kind of name *that* is."

Liz twisted the broken stems off the birds of paradise and carried the flowers up the steps. "I heard a crazy Brit bought the house, even camped out here during Lenny," he said. "Jason said he saw you at Christmas, but I never put it together."

She went to the top of the steps; he remained standing on the one below. "Your father?"

"Died Christmas Eve," Liz said. "Had a stroke a week before and never spoke again."

She touched his arm. "It's hard."

"He was hard," he said. "Mister Big Shot CEO."

She removed her hand.

"I see introductions are superfluous," Boney said.

Jason leaned against the truck, watching them.

Liz handed her the flowers and reached up to touch the blue bead. "It worked," he said.

She caught his salty, soapy smell. "What did?"

Boney climbed up behind Liz, squinted at the bead, and pulled his beard. "That can't be the same one," he said. "I thought you'd never part with it." He looked searchingly at Els.

"What worked?" Els said, cradling the bouquet. The spiky flowers scratched her bare arm.

"Quit the palaver, or the sun will go to bed without us." Boney stepped around them and hurried to the cannon.

"I suppose you need Bessie to tuck the sun in too," Els said.

"Part of the ritual," he called over his shoulder.

While Liz and Boney prepared the cannon, Jason stood in the court looking toward St. Kitts. Els retreated to the doorway. Boney went through his countdown, and the cannon boomed just after the sun winked green on the rim of the world. In silence, they all watched the sunken sun's rays gild the wisps of cloud.

Jack stepped to the railing, smiled at the sunset, and nodded at Els. The men gave no sign of seeing him, but Els cried out in surprise, and when Liz looked at her, Jack bowed and disappeared behind the hibiscus. She avoided Liz's gaze, pretending to be entranced by the sunset.

"Got dinner plans?" he asked.

"A doggie bag from Unella's."

"Barrett Cobb let us raid his provisions," he said. "We were heading to Jason's house, assuming the new owner here would kick our asses out after five minutes."

"A fair assumption," she said.

"Let us make you dinner," he said. "As a welcome. And in honor of our friendship with Jack."

The rum had nudged her from apprehensive toward what-the-hell, but she wondered if being receptive to Jack also meant uncorking a stream of his erstwhile pals. She opened the door and gestured the men inside.

Jason, his expression still unreadable, lifted a cooler out of the truck, stacked two six-packs of Red Stripe on top, and strode toward the kitchen door.

"I take it you know where everything is too," she said.

He kept walking toward the patio. She stepped into the lounge and let the screen slam.

Anger pricked her—a flash of distant lightning—and she wondered why Jason, with whom she'd exchanged only a few words, should exude such annoying disapproval when Liz, to whom she'd been bitchy and ungrateful, should take her in his amused stride.

Liz took in the lounge and its celadon ceiling. "Unusual color."

"The inside of limpet shells," she said.

He examined her mother's harbor scene near the door and the Basquiat over the refectory table. "The whole place is part Jack, part revelation."

"Am I to take that as a compliment, Captain?"

"If you'll accept one."

Boney stepped over to the wall that hid the staircase and examined the six black-and-white blowups in museum frames she'd hung on it. "What are these weird pho-tos?"

"Nudes," she said. "I found the negatives upstairs."

"I'd have guessed sand dunes in the desert," he said. "You can't hardly tell they're of a lady, much less the sweetest part of one." He traced a line. "That's an elbow all right, and there's a boobie."

"No drooling, Bones," Liz said, elbowing him as he started down the kitchen steps. He stopped to inspect The Beatrice. "A relative?"

"And a role model," Els said.

"I wouldn't want to tangle with her."

"People say that about me too."

"They're right."

The aroma of frying onions and potatoes welcomed them to the kitchen, where Jason, wearing a faded orange New York Mets tank top, was chunking tomatoes and tossing them into a bowl.

"A chef too," she said.

"Unless you plan to eat only junk, you learn to cook," Jason said.

"What makes you think I eat junk?"

"Nothin' here but junk."

"So you've rummaged in the cupboards."

"At least you got salt," he said.

Liz shot Jason a glance and dumped red snappers from the cooler into the sink. Oversized black eyes stared.

"She doesn't seem crazy to me," Boney said.

Jason waved the tip of his knife toward Els. "She mad but she no crazy," he said. "Ambition bury her passion." He pronounced it "ahm-bee-shun" and "pah-shun." He cubed slices of baguette and scattered the pieces over the tomatoes.

"That's one hell of a pronouncement," Els said. "Based on a few hours of eavesdropping on your precious sailboat." She stuck the flowers into a vase and plunked it on the table.

Liz picked up the knife Jason had been using and glanced from Jason to Els.

"You forgetting our evening at Sunshine's," Jason said. He sprinkled salt and pepper onto the salad and flipped the bowl with a practiced hand.

"Where you were *conspicuously* silent," she said. "Is that your game, Jason? Hiding behind those sunglasses and passing judgment on everyone you meet?"

"Something Jason say hit a nerve," he said. He tore basil leaves into the bowl, releasing their peppery anise fragrance. "Angry? Ambitious? Repressed? All a' dem?" He scooped the tomato cores into his hand and tossed them out the door.

"Why don't you just settle for 'bitch,' like your partner?" Els snapped.

Liz looked down.

"If the shoe fit," Jason said.

"Mates, mates," Boney said. "We're celebrating here." He handed rums around.

Liz raised his glass. "To unburied passion." He swallowed half his rum, put the glass on the drainboard, and began cleaning the fish, using the back of the knife as a scaler. When he was finished, iridescent scales clogged the drain.

Els took her drink out to the patio, where she sat in the shadows and watched the men through the window. The aroma of the onions and potatoes and the men's easy camaraderie tripped her hunger, as much for a shared meal as the food.

The house filled with music—Latin, insinuating, sexy, nothing she recognized. Liz sashayed onto the patio with a platter piled with fish and his rum.

"Are you the self-appointed DJ?" she asked.

"Bachata," he said. "Got it in La Romana." He put the platter on the table. Holding an imaginary partner, he mimed a hip grind. "Great dance music." He picked through the pile of construction scraps and built a fire in one end of the long grill. While he tended it, he swayed to the beat and sang phrases in Spanish.

"When Jack was alive, did you guys just take over the place at will?"

"He had an open door, loved company at any hour."

"Well, that's over," she said.

The music shifted to slow and sinuous, with a weeping trumpet over the steady beat. Liz spread the fire and arranged the fish. Embers flared when the drippings hit them. Inside, Boney's voice rose and fell, punctuated occasionally by a rumbling comment from Jason. Insect ticking and chirping filled the night. Els had finished her rum. Everything was pulsing.

"Tell me about this bead," she said, running it back and forth on its chain.

"Statia is what we call Sint Eustatius, which is over there near Saba on the other side of St. Kitts."

"I know where Statia is. Jack left books on every subject."

"So did you also read that Statia was once an important Dutch trading port?" He reached for his glass and brushed her arm when he set it back down. "The blue beads were used to buy slaves." He slid a spatula under the fish and flipped it. Boney was laughing and shouting Jack's name. Liz chuckled. "There'll be no stopping him now." He poked the fish and licked his finger. "The beads were also used to pay free slaves for their labor. A free man could buy his wife out of slavery if he saved up enough beads to go around her waist."

She gathered her dress to her waist. "A lot of beads," she said, "even for a slender wife."

He flicked his eyes over her. "And a lot of labor for each bead. After emancipation, the slaves threw the beads into the sea. They're as rare as doubloons now, but sometimes show up after storms. I found that one about twelve years ago when I was diving with . . . a friend." He gestured for her to hold the platter. She picked it up, and after he lifted the fish onto it, he squeezed lime over them and tossed the rinds into the garden. "The legend goes that if you find a blue bead of Statia, you will return."

"And if you're given one?"

"It got you back here."

"Lifted me out of slavery."

"Last I checked," he said, "slaves didn't get big salaries."

"Bondage nonetheless."

"Of whose making?"

Boney had moved the flowers and put candles in the center of the table. Everyone took their places, Els and Boney facing Jason and Liz. Jason removed his sunglasses, put his huge pink palms together, and bowed over his plate so quickly that it took Els a second to realize he was saying a private grace. His eyes were as black as his skin.

"Don't you ever take off that hat?" she asked as Jason served himself some fish.

"You really don't want him to unleash that Medusa hair, Fair Lady," Boney said.

They'd finished the Cavalier and the remains of a bottle of Mount Gay. Liz passed around beers, and they bent to their meals.

In the silence after the bachata CD ended, Boney raised his bottle. "I never thought I'd be sitting here like this again."

"To you, Jack," Els said, "wherever you are."

"He is all around you, if you believe it to be so," Jason said. He replaced his sunglasses.

She wondered if he was also receptive, or just superstitious. "Do you guys think he committed suicide and his jumbie can't find rest?"

"Goddamn local voodoo," Boney said. "Last thing he said to me when we finished boarding up this place was, 'Catch you later.'"

The wind had come up; the candle flames leaned and guttered.

"What could be accidental about standing on a seawall when the waves are twenty feet high?" Els said. "If you ask me, he certainly was self-destructive."

"You got evidence for *dat* judgment?" Jason lowered his sunglasses and looked at her, his eyes hard.

"Don't tell me I don't know a thing or two about Jack," she said. "Sometimes I feel as if I've moved into his life as well as his house."

"You tired a' you own life," Jason said, "so you tink you can just appropriate his, like buyin' a new dress?" He stabbed and ate a chunk of tomato.

"I think I've made this house a marriage," she said. "An overlay of my life and belongings onto his."

"Jack doan marry nobody," Jason said. "'Specially no jus' come woo-mon tink she can be some jumbie tourist."

"You cheeky bastard," she said.

Liz, his eyes gone a shade darker, looked at Jason.

"Jack belong to he friends and to Nevis," Jason said. "He ain't you property to spread you fantasy on."

"You clowns are the ones living a fantasy if you think you can waltz in and take over the place in Jack's name. It's my house now."

Jason stood up and dumped his plate into the sink. He strode to the door and let it slam behind him. Liz followed him. The truck engine started. They were arguing; Els went to the patio to hear them better. Liz's back was to her but Jason saw her, leaned out the driver's window, and said, "You wrong, mon. Fust bump she hit, she runnin' back over there, full a' stories. She want she adventure at all a' we expense. Fuck dat." He gunned the engine.

"Wait!" Boney raced out of the kitchen. Jason braked at the gate.

"Sorry to eat and run, Fair Lady," Boney said. "Gotta catch a ride to town." He clapped Liz on the shoulder and ran down the drive. As soon as he climbed into the cab, the truck lurched through the gate and rumbled away toward Charlestown.

Els walked up behind Liz. "Don't bring Jason back here again," she said. "I don't choose to be baited by some ignorant local."

"Wrong on two counts, neither ignorant nor local." He was still looking at the gate. The truck's dust settled. "Jason saved my life. He's a fiercely loyal friend." He looked at her. "Are you saying I can come back without him?"

"Jury's out on you," she said.

"Will helping clean up improve my odds?"

"Not helping would banish ye forever."

Liz put on James Taylor's *Mud Slide Slim* and sang snatches of the songs as he moved about the kitchen with the familiarity and confidence he'd shown on *Iguana*. Els was tipsy enough to drop and shatter a glass; at that, he told her to sit down and let him take care of things.

"Our dinners here, back in the day, always ended with a round of darts," he said.

"No way," she said. "It's half one."

"A last bit of old ritual." He shoved open the storeroom door, releasing the smell of damp earth. "Lot of stuff in here."

"My childhood," she said. "Best kept behind closed doors."

He shifted some boxes, pulled a dartboard off the wall, and carried it outside. A bright light came on, and Els stepped out into the glare of a floodlight she'd never noticed before. Shining from the mango tree, it illuminated the kitchen's end wall and the dartboard, which now hung from a hook driven into the mortar.

Liz took his position on the grass at the edge of the patio. He twirled a dart between his thumb and index finger and set his bare toe at the edge of the flagstones, the dart poised at his ear. He threw straight and hard, three darts in quick succession popping into the cork.

"Ton 80," he said. "Perfect score."

"Don't expect me to kiss you," she said.

"You have to lose first." He sauntered up, extracted the darts, and dropped them into her hand.

"I'm a total novice."

"Captain Liz can fix that," he said. He took two of the darts. "Step up to that line. No, not over it."

She adjusted so her toe was planted where the spongy grass met the stone, held the dart close to her ear as Liz had done, and leaned forward.

"Leaning ruins your throw," he said. He stepped behind her, circled her waist with his left arm, and pulled her against his chest. She wobbled and his arm tightened and she leaned against him, feeling his warmth on her bare shoulders. He ran his hand down her right thigh and pressed her leg against his so that she stood with one foot slightly behind the other. His mouth was next to her ear. He curled his fingers around her right hand, leveled the dart, and pulled her hand gently back and forth. "You want to throw straight, not up," he whispered. He wrapped his right arm over his left, crossing her stomach. She threw the dart. It clicked against the wall to the right of the board and landed on the patio.

"Captain Liz is naw the teacher he claims to be," she said.

"You just need another lesson or two," Liz said. He released her and she stepped away. The breeze made her miss the warmth of him immediately.

"Another time," she said.

He looked at her for longer than she found comfortable before dropping the darts into her hand. "Another time," he said, and walked down the drive. A snippet of song she couldn't identify drifted up to her when he closed the gate and turned toward Oualie.

CHAPTER 24

When Finney called from the gate, she was weeding a bed of plants in arresting colors: dried blood, bilious green, acid yellow. She fanned her face with her floppy hat while he labored up the hill.

"Jack call that his spooky border," Finney said. "All dem weird plants want the sunniest place." He set down his bucket. "You gon' get heatstroke, working so hard this time a' day."

"I can't bear idleness," she said. She put the hat on, folding the brim back so it didn't hide her face. "Only a month ago, Lauretta had this place shipshape. Now just look at these weeds."

He pulled a roll of bills from his pocket. "Boat payment day."

"You'll want a receipt," she said.

"What for? I got a calendar and I know how to subtract."

"A business arrangement based on trust," she said. "How refreshing." She looked from the half-weeded bed to the sun that grew higher and hotter by the minute. "My head's going to pop if I don't take a break." She peeled off her gloves and tossed them into the wheelbarrow. "Hang on while I splash water on my face, and I'll give you a lift home on my way to town."

She sped toward Charlestown, the wind whipping her hair. "A skinny man's been hanging around, Finney," she said. "I saw him once filling a gourd bowl at the cistern. A few days ago I found him pulling weeds in the rain and yelled at him, but he ignored me."

Finney chuckled. "Pinky reach back."

"Pinky?" she said. "He's black as coal."

"Pinky doan speak since he born," he said. "But he hear fine. He live in de bush, never go to school, but he bright. He and Jack assemble all a' his pipes and machines, and he help Jack and me build the *Maid*. He and Jack bin pretty close. When Jack disappear, Pinky go back in de bush."

"He gives me the creeps." After dark, she imagined all manner of eyes, human and animal, watching from the bush.

"He won't do you nothing. He observe what you need and he do it."

"He left fruit by the door. I've discovered bitter orange juice is delicious in rum."

"Pinky trying to tell you not to fraid him. You give him a bit a' food, he become very useful to you. Pull all a' you weeds. Prevent you drop dead in that sun."

"Even if he's not dangerous, he's loony enough to weed in the pouring rain."

"He know 'bout plants," Finney said. "You wish to eradicate a plant, you doan try when it holding fast in the soil. It leave roots behind, grow back tomorrow. When it rainin' and those roots busy drinkin', you surprise that plant and pull out the whole thing, and it can't come back."

She wondered how one might distract grief enough to yank it out whole.

"For a fisherman, you know a lot about the psyche of plants," she said.

"Got to grow if you want to eat," he said. "When I ain't fishin,' I in my provision ground. Vivian love my tomatoes."

They'd reached the cistern at the Westbury Road. "Put me out here," he said.

"Nonsense," she said, and turned into the road. She waved to the pigtailed girl from the shower incident who was sitting on the steps of her house. The girl stared, then waved with enthusiasm when she saw Finney.

"It just past Josie's Snackette," he said. "The light blue with the new patch a' roof."

She pulled over at the gate and pushed her sunglasses into her hair. The dwelling looked as if a wooden chattel house had sprouted a larger concrete box. Where a flamboyant tree cast a patch of shade onto the dirt yard, a woman wearing a cantaloupe-colored dress sat in a wheelchair. *The real Nevis, you gotta find on you own*, Sparrow had said.

"My Beauty, we got company," Finney called. Els followed him through the gate.

The woman looked in their direction. "You're early, Husband." Her right leg was propped on an overturned bucket, a bandage covering the stump, and her hands were busy crocheting an afghan square in primary blue and red.

"Miss Els give me a drop." He leaned in to kiss the woman; their kiss was a beat longer than perfunctory, reverent. "She wish to say hello."

The woman sat straighter and smoothed her hair toward the bun at her nape. "What a lovely surprise."

"I don't want to intrude," Els said. The woman beckoned.

Els approached and took her offered hand—soft, its grip an invitation to intimacy, the first human touch Els had felt in months that carried affection.

"I've been wanting to meet you, Mrs. Fleming," she said. "Finney's that proud of your cooking."

"Vivian," the woman said. Her smile teased out the wrinkles around her eyes, making her look both older and younger at the same time. She had an elegance, prominent cheekbones and almond eyes dusky with cataracts. “Child,” she called toward the house, “bring that baby out here and say hello to our visitor.” A copy of *Pride and Prejudice*, a long seedpod as a bookmark, sat on a plastic chair near her elbow.

A young woman appeared in the doorway, a drowsy child on her hip. Els had to look twice to recognize Eulia, who was wearing an African print dress in the colors of a cowrie shell that set off the figure her Resort uniform had masked.

She crossed the yard and stood behind Vivian’s wheelchair. “So, that jumbie ain’t scared you off yet.”

“What kind of hello is that?” Vivian said.

“When that storm finally done, I dyin’ to see my baby,” Eulia said, “but de boss make me cook she something to eat first ’cause she been hidin’ out in Jack’s house all that time.”

The child pointed his finger and let out a stream of babble. Shame pricked Els. A new mother, trapped serving over-entitled Resort guests while her infant was wanting her at home.

Els tried an appeasing smile. “And what’s your name, wee one?” She touched the baby’s hand, and he grasped her finger.

“We call him Peanut,” Eulia said. “He seven months, just about.”

The baby’s hair resembled brass springs. He peered into Els’s face with a world-weary look, as if an old man lived behind his eyes, which were camouflage green with brown flecks.

Finney moved the book to the ground and gestured for Els to take the chair. He lowered himself onto the bucket and rested Vivian’s stump across his knees. They all barely fit in the patch of shade and were sitting close enough for Els to catch Vivian’s scent, a mixture of talcum and something herbal.

When Vivian asked Eulia to bring tea, Els said, “I wouldn’t put you to that trouble.”

Eulia didn’t move. “Maybe she doan drink bush tea.”

“Viv ain’t had company in a while,” Finney said.

"I mean . . . I'd be honored," Els said.

Peanut on her hip, Eulia carried Finney's fish bucket into the house. The door hung open crookedly. The new metal on the roof caught the sun, shining like a scrap of foil. A row of nearly ripe tomatoes lined the sill of a screenless window.

"Eulia could probably use a hand." Els stood up. "One of the few things my grandmother taught me was how to serve tea." But the image that evoked—silver service, cubed sugar with tongs—felt excruciatingly wrong. She went into the house.

Eulia was in the kitchen, which occupied the entire wooden section of the structure. A pot sat on a lit burner of the old cooker. There was a small fridge with an extension cord running out the window and a handmade table and shelves. Outside the window, a platform held a washing pan and bucket and beyond it a privy and the vegetable garden. In the block section of the house, a bed, dresser, and straight chair, all painted the pumpkin orange common on local fishing boats, stood against whitewashed walls. The bed's coverlet was appliquéd with a tropical forest scene worthy of Rousseau. Even from the doorway Els could tell the handwork was exquisite. White lace curtains framed all the windows. The sparseness struck her, as if the family's scant possessions were displayed in a gallery.

"Someone's quite the seamstress," she said.

"Mamma sew everything—clothes, uniforms, curtains," Eulia said. One-handed, she arranged mismatched mugs on a tray. "'Til she run over her finger with that machine 'cause she can't see good enough. She doan like to talk about that."

"I didn't mean to pry," Els said. "I came to help."

"Then take him," Eulia said.

Peanut averted his face and Els stepped back. "I'm hopeless with bairns."

"You okay with pouring, then?" Eulia pointed at the pan on the stove, which contained a pinkish honey-colored liquid. She gave Peanut a rag to suck.

Els poured the brew, releasing a vegetal, minty aroma, and put down the pot.

Peanut flapped the rag. Els stroked his soft hair, and he jerked away. "Your father must be handsome," she said, "and very proud of you." Peanut looked solemnly at her.

"He daddy doan know he exist," Eulia said. "This baby is all mine."

"What, some swine left you pregnant?"

Eulia turned off the burner. "Happen every day a' the week," she said. "Even in merry old England."

Imagining the father as some Resort guest, Els wondered if the union—and issue—had been desired or not. Eulia nuzzled Peanut, picked up the tray, and walked outside, Els following behind.

With a practiced transfer, Eulia handed Peanut to Vivian. He patted her face until she gently removed his hand. Els returned to her chair. There was a glimmer of mischief in Eulia's eyes when she extended the tray ceremoniously toward Els and said, "Hope this tea up to you standards."

Els chose a mug and cradled it with both hands while Eulia offered the tray to Finney, who wrapped Vivian's hand around a mug and took one for himself.

"Welcome to our home," Vivian said.

"I love its simplicity," Els said. "Nothing superfluous."

Finney's smile was wry. "We leave superfluous behind long ago."

Els colored, fearing that instead of complimenting, she'd dropped another clanger, and anything further she might say would only make it worse.

Vivian moved her mug out of Peanut's reach. "Nothing in there to trip over," she said. "Or run into."

With Eulia watching, Els raised her mug, hesitated.

"Might taste a little unaccustomed," Finney said, "but probably work some benefit on you." He sipped. "What this one good for, gyull?"

"Fancy company," Eulia said. She put the tray on the ground, took Peanut, and sat down with him in her lap. "Mamma's herb doctor friend Miranda mixed different tea bush and hibiscus, what give it that pretty color. She say doan drink it too hot." She took the remaining mug. "Go on," she said to Els. "It ain't poison."

Els took a sip. The brew tasted swampy and floral and made her throat tingle.

"You've probably made big changes at Jack's," Vivian said.

"Repairs, a little paint, a few of my own things here and there."

"And his books?" Vivian asked.

"I'm reading my way through them."

"Was a time Jack share those books with Viv," Finney said. "They talk and talk about history and literature."

Els had imagined schoolteacher Vivian as upstanding, even priggish, and the notion that she and Jack had shared an intellectual friendship increased the intrigue about both of them. "So that was before your . . . foot." Vivian's forehead creased, and Els sensed another gaffe. "You must come and borrow anything you please," she said.

Vivian flashed an eager smile at Eulia. "We just hit the jackpot." She chuckled at the pun. "Eulia and Finney have already read me everything we have, more than once. There are few books to be had here besides the occasional Mills & Boon from the church jumble sales."

Els cringed that Vivian might look down on the romance novels she found so comforting, but this gracious former teacher didn't seem the type to discourage reading in any form. "What about the steps?" she asked.

"If Finney takes my one arm and Eulia the other, I think I could run right up to reach that treasure." Vivian's glance at Eulia had a pleading quality.

Peanut squirmed out of Eulia's lap and crawled under Els's chair. Eulia watched him, her lips compressed. "Let she help Daddy haul you up," she said. "Doan need me."

"You must come see what I've done to the place," Els said. "Let's go right now." She looked at Eulia. "Would you help me move things about to make room in the boot for the wheelchair?"

A car roared past, throbbing music trailing it like a tail. Eulia glanced at Vivian, then clasped Peanut to her chest and stood up in one motion, a spring uncoiling, and handed the baby to Finney.

When she and Els reached the Jeep, she touched Els's elbow. "He visit like they say?"

Els stowed a water jug and beach towel and squinted at a hen and three chicks that stopped pecking near the roadside to scatter, amid peeping and beating wings, for no apparent reason. "Why would he?" she asked.

Eulia looked toward the sea. "If is something he want, Jack never leave 'til he get it."

"Any idea what that might be?"

"Guess you gotta ask that jumbie."

While Els carried the fidgeting Peanut, Eulia struggled to push the chair across the court, its wheels digging deep grooves in the gravel.

"Help me up, Husband." Vivian grasped the chair arms.

"You just hang on," Finney said. "We gon' roll you right up." He backed the chair to the stairs, and he and Eulia pushed and hauled Vivian up. By the time they reached the gallery, sweat beaded his face.

Els swept open the door and Eulia maneuvered the chair over the sill. "Tell me what you see, Child," Vivian said.

"Same leather chair, table, books everywhere," Eulia said. "New cushions and pretty things all around. A clock over there, taller than me with sun and moon faces on it and gold hands, new strange pictures, and a paintin' of an old lady in a big gold frame hangin' by the stair. She looks vex."

"Child!" Vivian said.

"My paternal grandmother," Els said. "A warrior's heart trapped in a woman's body." She handed Peanut to Vivian, popped open the secret door, and said, "Tour of the upstairs, anyone?"

"I goin' keep Viv company," Finney said. "You go 'long, gyull." He put his hand on Vivian's shoulder and she leaned her cheek against his forearm, making Els long for such tiny caresses.

"None a' we got any business up there," Eulia said, eyeing the nudes.

"Go on, Child," Vivian said. "I want to hear everything you see."

Eulia trailed Els up the stairs, past the study door and into the bedroom. Staring at the carved mahogany bed frame hung with voile curtains, she said, "You got youself a house inside a house."

"That bed had tapestries woven with all the wild animals and flowers on the moors," Els said. "As a child, I'd close them to shut out the world."

"You gon' need more dan curtains, if you wan be safe from that jumbie," Eulia said. The cupboard door was ajar, admitting a view of Jack's shirts. She stepped closer. "You just invitin' trouble keepin' he things."

"I like their man smell."

Eulia plucked at a sleeve, yellowed on the crease, and sniffed. "Get youself a live man for that." She poked her toe at a pair of shoes stretched on Brooks Brothers shoe trees and green with mold. "He doan never put he feet inside, but he polish them every week." She hugged her elbows. "These things pullin' him," she said. "You toss them out, maybe he leave you 'lone."

"Never said he was bothering me."

Eulia closed the cupboard and secured the latch.

In the bathroom, Eulia leaned out the new casement window that served as a door to the rebuilt shower platform, ran her hand along the rim of the tub, and fingered a monogrammed hand towel. "House doan look like a man place now."

"I'd call it a draw," Els said.

On the way back, Eulia stopped at the study door. "Jack doan like nobody in there," she said. "He doan even let me dust."

Els stepped inside, but Eulia leaned against the doorframe, her big eyes darting around the room. "He leave more than I thought," she said. "The day before August Monday, he drink 'til he vex. Make a big fire in the court and burn up papers and pictures." A faraway expression tinged with sadness came over her face. "He destroy lot a things."

"I heard he could be a bit, well, crazy. Violent, even, especially when drunk."

"He say nasty lies, burst bad words," Eulia said. She dropped her eyes. "He say he can't bear to look at me no more." The case clock rattled into action. Eulia started. Three bongs rang through the house.

"How long did you *do* for Jack?" Els asked.

"'Bout eighteen months." Eulia walked to the desk and peered at the postcards and photographs tacked above it. She pulled off a snapshot of a Japanese woman on the Resort wharf, a blazing sunset behind her.

"That bonfire night was the last time you saw him?"

Eulia tossed the photo onto the desk. "No reason to come back."

When fat raindrops began to splatter on the gallery and the lounge slipped into gray, Els lit all the lamps and served her guests iced tea and fingers of banana bread. She tried to answer Vivian's questions about her former job, struggling to put the financial jargon into lay terms.

"Jason know all about fi-nance," Eulia said.

"*Iguana's* Jason?" Els said. "What could that smartass know about investment banking?"

"He loan Daddy money for his motor," Eulia said.

Vivian looked at Finney, who was glaring at Eulia. "Did he now?" she said.

"Miss, you make this nice cake?" Finney said.

"Jamaican bakery," Els said. "I'm clueless in the kitchen."

Eulia's lip twitched and she looked down at Peanut, asleep in her lap. Els mentally ticked through the skills that gave women status here, all of which she lacked: mothering, cooking, housekeeping, tending to neighbors, teaching. She was no good at praying, either.

After the rain, the garden steamed in the sun, releasing its fragrances. Els placed a sack of books into Vivian's lap. Vivian clasped it and smiled. "Husband," she said, "see if you can get me back down without shaking the teeth out of my head."

Eulia put Peanut in the Jeep and went back to brace the front of the chair while Finney eased Vivian down. Finney's flip-flop slid on the wet step and he sat down hard; the wheelchair lurched, the handle twisting out of his grip. The chair tipped and Vivian let out a cry. Eulia tried to steady the chair, but the weight was too much and it fell over, pinning her leg and spilling Vivian into the plantings below.

Els yanked the chair off Eulia. It bumped down the steps and crashed into Wilma's fender. Peanut started to wail. Els hurried to Vivian, who lay facedown in the muddy flower bed next to the new clump of heliconia. One of its lobster claw flowers dangled on a shredded stalk above her head. Vivian mumbled and pushed herself up a few inches, moaned, and sank back.

"Finney, call the ambulance," Els said. "Eulia, bring a blanket." She felt for Vivian's pulse, which was steady but weak. Vivian's right arm was caught beneath her. Els didn't dare move her. "Can you talk, Vivian? Where does it hurt?"

"Hurts . . . to . . . breathe," Vivian said, her eyes pinched shut.

Finney hobbled down the steps and knelt next to Vivian. "They comin'," he said. Eulia slid a pillow under Vivian's cheek and spread the blanket over her. Finney took Vivian's hand. "My Beauty," he whispered. "I just a weak old fool."

Vivian opened her eyes. "Husband," she said. "Don't take blame for the rain."

Eulia, her shin bleeding, sat on the bottom step rocking Peanut, who refused to be consoled. Finney squeezed Vivian's hand and stroked her cheek. Els paced the court, unable to comfort herself.

When the ambulance finally swung into the drive, Els was amazed at how small it was, how spare of flashing lights.

The attendants examined Vivian with tender respect, and she yelped when they gently rolled her over. Finney watched their every move.

"Miss Els, meet Hamilton and Marcus," Vivian said in a hoarse whisper. "Students of mine at one time. Boys, I hate to be such a trouble."

"That what you get for tryin' out for the Olympic wheelchair slalom, Miss Viv," Hamilton said.

Vivian laughed, then moaned. "I was so happy, I thought I could fly," she whispered.

The attendants loaded Vivian's stretcher into the ambulance and Finncy climbed in with her. He promised a full report before they shut the doors and sped off.

After the siren faded, Els darted a glance at Eulia. "This is all my stupid, bloody fault."

"This is Jack's fault," Eulia said.

"How the hell d'ya figure that?" Els said. "Tempting her with Jack's library was my idea."

"We all just dancin' 'round to his music," Eulia said. "He must want something real bad, he got to knock Mamma down to get it."

CHAPTER 25

Late the next afternoon, Finney appeared in the court with his fish bucket.

"Come cool off in here and tell me everything," Els called to him from the kitchen.

He stepped inside and wiped his brow. "Viv crack two ribs and break her wrist," he said. "Doc say rest got to heal her now. He suggest she go mend by her muddah, who got a big house in Gingerland, but Viv say she won't never go there."

"They fell out?"

"Nod to each other at church." He dropped into the chair she offered. "Sometimes not even that. All 'cause a' me."

"Tea or beer?"

"Tea's fine."

"No drinking before sundown?"

"No drinkin'," he said. "Cyan be dull-witted if Viv need something."

She poured a glass for each of them and pushed the sugar bowl toward him. He dumped a heaping spoonful of the local brown sugar into his glass, where it formed a sludge at the bottom, and stirred until he seemed embarrassed by the clinking and took a sip.

"Doan keep sugar at home," he said. "Not fair to tempt Viv."

"You've given up a lot for her," she said, and felt a twinge of longing for a love powerful enough to cause willing sacrifice.

"Viv been suffering on account a' my romance impulse ever since we meet," he said.

Els pulled a packet of Peek Freans biscuits from a tin, shook them onto a plate, and settled into her chair. "Tell me," she said. "I could use a tale of impulsive romance."

He took a jam tot. He told her he'd met Vivian on Anguilla, where he grew up fishing and building and racing boats and where she'd gotten a teaching job in The Valley after university. "Her girlfriends bring her to the Easter Monday races. She look like a tigress dressed up as a schoolmarm. I sweet her up a little and make her promise to come to a bashment after the races if we win," he said. "We take second, but she go with me, anyway. Next thing you know, she pregnant with our son Tibby and we get married. Her mudda hate me the minute she rasp her eyes over me, and everything I do since only make it worse. I too black, too ignorant, too poor, too radical."

"Politically?"

"Dyed into the bone secessionist," he said, and took another biscuit. He explained that Britain had once lumped Anguilla into a territory with St. Kitts and Nevis, where St. Kitts made the rules and got most of the goods and kept Anguilla in such poverty that it still lacked paved roads in the 1960s. His father and uncle joined the revolution for Anguilla's independence, and his father was jailed after a skirmish on St. Kitts. "When we finally prevail," he said, "Anguilla Separation Day, 1980, was a big celebration day fuh my whole family. But by then, Viv and me already here, 'cause her father got the sugar, too, and ain't doin' so good, and she want to come home. Since then, I barely see Anguilla or any a' my family."

"You're an exile too," she said.

"You put Viv in this hand and Anguilla and all a' dem in this hand," he said, holding his palms like scales. "Not a contest." He stirred his tea. "But now seems to me Nevis under Sinkits thumb as bad as Anguilla ever was."

"A rabble-rouser," she said. *Like Mallo*, she thought. *Like I would have become*. "You should stand for office, fight for change."

"Was a time I enjoy stirring it up," he said. "Back then, our house always full a' my compatriots, drinking beer late into the night, plotting our campaigns, eating Vivian's goat water and coconut cake. I back a guy who beat out Viv's brother Eugene." He took another jam biscuit. "That guy winnin' 'gainst Eugene mean we mostly cut off from Viv's people. Customers mysteriously start going away from me. I lose my boat buildin' business. After that, I step away from politics 'cause we got babies to feed. Anyway, Anguillian fisherman like me what leave school by twelve cyan achieve no position of authority here."

"From what I read in the papers, you've got more sense than anyone now in office."

"Papers only good for wrappin' fish," he said. "Gorment and opposition each got they own, nothing objective."

It was true that each publication was so partisan Els often wondered where the truth hung between them. As she studied Finney's proud profile, she thought of the children she and Mallo might have had, despite her terror of motherhood. A bunch of red-haired hooligans. But Mallo would never have traded his political dreams for Scotland for the comfort or safety of his family, and she would have plunged into the fray, drawn as much by the force of his passion as her own.

"Viv put up with what we got, but she deserve more'n that damn shack we rent from her skinny-ass cousin," Finney said. "Doc doan like her livin' with water from a hose, doin' her business in a bucket." He flashed a smile and spun his spoon. "I got a plan," he said. "With that boat, I coverin' all a' my financial obligations, some weeks even a bit over." He watched the bananaquits darting from the mango tree to the plate of sugar on the patio table. "I got my eye on a house in Newcastle. Shaded gallery, real plumbing, pretty vine growing up."

She thought of her introduction to the airport four months before and Sparrow's excited expectations for the new field. "Newcastle's nothing but a construction zone," she said. "With all that dust, every blade of grass is as gray as cement."

"Up Shaw's Road they's only a bit a' dust and you got a nice view a' the sea." He reached toward the biscuits, reconsidered, and sipped his tea instead. "New airport's just another gorment stupidness. Cyan make the airlines send planes just 'cause we got a place they can land. That Eugene claim he can buy his shiny new car because his earth shiftin' business been good. He neglect to mention he negotiate the contracts for the airport and the new road, and it's dat keep his machines goin' solid for two years."

She put the rest of the biscuits back into the packet and handed it to Finney. "Wrap your catch in that government rag over there," she said. "We'll get Eulia and go cheer Vivian up. But first, I want to show you something."

At the restored chattel house, she joked about the carved wooden toad she'd placed in the privy and the hand-painted sign reading "Toad Hall" she'd hung over the cottage door. She showed off the new outdoor shower and deck connecting it all, and when she ushered Finney into the cottage and propped open the shutters, the golden light hit the easel and made her unfinished sunset painting glow.

"You got a fine paintin' place," he said.

"The studio's finer than the painter." She removed the canvas and leaned it against the wall. "What if you and Vivian stayed here, just until she recuperates?"

Finney took in the whitewashed walls, Jack's brass bed strewn with bright pillows, the lemon suede chair from her London flat, jars bristling with paint brushes, paintings and sketches of flowers, leaves, shells, and monkeys. "These pretty," he said. He put the sunset canvas back on the easel. "Thanks all the same."

"I could move all this to the study in five minutes."

"We doing okay."

"If it's a battle of pride we're in," she said, "I warn ye, I come well armed."

Vivian shared a ward with a very pregnant teen and a crone who was curled up facing the wall. Her casted arm, resting across her stomach, rose and fell with her shallow breathing. Her hair made a salt-and-pepper halo on the pillow. At Finney's "Hello, My Beauty," she looked toward the door and greeted his false heartiness with a wan smile.

"Back so soon?" She tilted her chin to accept his kiss.

"Els had to see for herself you ain't dead," he said.

"Help me up a bit," she said.

Finney eased her forward while Eulia wedged pillows behind her. Vivian settled back with a wince. She looked shrunken, her face the color of putty.

"I leave Peanut by the snackette with Josie," Eulia said. "She say to tell you howdy and mus' get well soon."

Els leaned in to kiss Vivian's cheek. "I feel dreadful about all this," she said.

"The world has guilt enough," Vivian said.

Eulia smoothed her mother's hair. "Let me do this up for you."

"Leave it," Finney said. "She wear it that way when we first meet. Make her look twenty-two all over again."

"Foolishness," Vivian said. "Never mind. I'm past caring if my hair's not combed."

"You not sounding like yourself, My Beauty," he said.

"I'll be myself again when I get out of here."

A doctor entered the ward, said something that made the pregnant girl laugh, and came to Vivian's bedside. After checking her pulse and listening to her lungs, he looped his stethoscope around his neck. "I was worried all this might trigger that infection again. I've given her an antibiotic as a precaution." He extended his hand to Els. "Andre Lytton," he said. "Vivian tells me you've rescued Jack's. I called him friend long before he became my patient." He slipped his glasses into his shirt pocket. "Finney, either help me convince Viv to go to Tavie's for a few weeks or get her to accept that I have to keep her here."

Vivian squeezed her eyes shut. "Home," she whispered.

"Daddy and me can care for she just fine," Eulia said.

Lytton looked at her. His smile was tired. Eulia looked away.

Els touched the doctor's elbow. "May I have a word?"

The corridor smelled of bleach and curry. "I blame myself for Vivian's injury," Els said. "I'd be honored if she recuperated in my cottage as long as necessary. We can even roll the wheelchair right into the shower."

"It's a war of attrition, fighting diabetes in someone as indomitable as Viv," Lytton said. "She fights to bounce back, but each bounce is lower than the last. You might be committing to shelter her for far longer than you think."

Els looked out the windows to a chain-link fence entwined in coralita vine. "I stand advised, Doctor."

The only home touches Finney and Vivian brought to Toad Hall were the appliquéd coverlet and a blue glass vase Vivian filled with the zinnias Finney grew for her in his provision ground. Seeing this, Els painted splashy flower images and hung them on the walls.

Over the weeks, while everyone made efforts to respect each other's privacy, Els's eagerness to break her isolation with whatever companionship her guests could provide only grew. As her solitary routine included swimming vigorous cross-harbor laps at Oualie every morning, never venturing beyond the turquoise shallows, she took to walking there with Finney when he left to fish. One Sunday they bundled Vivian into Wilma and made the trip to Oualie, where Finney and Barrett Cobb carried her, wearing a shift dress, shower cap, and plastic sack taped over her stump, into the water for her first leisure swim in years. The freedom of her buoyancy made her weep.

Eulia, delighted to have the Westbury house to herself and Peanut for the first time, came daily to Jack's to care for her mother, see to the house, and cook for them all. Els happily paid her a salary and provided everyone's groceries. At least once a week she took Vivian along to the farmers' market, where the vendors crowded around the Jeep to tout their wares, calling Vivian "Miss Fleming" or "Teacher Vivian," and Els "darlin'." At the house, she lingered in the kitchen while Vivian and Eulia cooked and laughed, Eulia fusing her mother's specialties with Resort dishes and herbs from Miranda into a culinary language all her own. The chatty lunches they all shared became the high point of Els's day and erased her wraith look.

When Vivian asked for rides to church, Els found herself tugged into the community, and though she considered Reverend Stillman's sermons overwrought, she enjoyed her weekly glimpses into the island's social currents and politics. Vivian's company bestowed a certain standing on Els, as if the parishioners didn't find it necessary to hold back in her presence, and she treasured the fragments she could understand of "dem say"—local gossip. But she found no comfort in Vivian's God.

She made a mission of restoring some of the life Vivian's near blindness had stolen from her. Serving as her chauffeur and going along to doctor's appointments, sewing circle, and ladies' meetings gave Els purpose and nascent feelings of belonging.

In the privacy of the Jeep, the women tiptoed into more intimate topics. Vivian confessed her fears of the dangers Finney faced daily at sea, her frustration at being unable to supplement his earnings, and her sadness at Jack's despair and Eulia's bitterness. Delicately, she drew Els out about Mallo, as well as her confused emotions about her father and what might have been had she known about her mother's paintings.

One day, as they were driving through Gingerland, Els said, "I wrote my mother after Father died. She replied that she was sorry she couldn't be the mother I wanted. It's made me wonder what a mother is supposed to be." She didn't admit that she studied Vivian and Eulia, trying to understand how a mother and daughter might bond, hold each other separate, or compete with one another.

Vivian pointed out a house, the highest and most elaborate on the hill, with ranks of concrete balusters painted two shades of salmon. "There was government reparation for families who owned homes in Newcastle that were demolished for the new airport. Finney and I got nothing because we were only renting, but my mother put all of her reparation and most of her savings into building that ostentatious thing so she can look down on everyone." She looked away, toward the sweep of grassland and the sea beyond. "Some rifts don't heal."

They rode in silence almost to Coconut Walk.

"Beware of romanticizing maternal love," Vivian finally said. "It's not always guaranteed, and it's often complicated. Mamma expected me to marry smart. Continue the family's upward trend toward prosperity and light skin. She never forgave me for falling in love with a fisherman, not to mention one as dark as Finney. From Anguilla, in the wrong party, and a secessionist to boot. Eulia's shame, as Mamma sees our Peanut, is purely my fault." She laughed her girlish laugh. "My sins are legion and I repent none of them."

"At least you know what sins she might hold against you."

Vivian touched Els's arm. "Write again," she said. "Give her a way to imagine you now, your home and life here. Help her think of you as any mother would want—safe and happy."

"Safe, perhaps." Els stopped to allow three cows trailing their lead ropes to file across the road.

"Happiness and sorrow are jealous siblings, always vying for attention," Vivian said. "We need to be on the lookout for happiness, though. Sorrow can find us on its own."

A pair of cattle egrets crossed after the cows with their beaky struts. One flew up, landed on a cow's haunch, and pecked.

"The world is full of relationships we might not predict, just like those cows and egrets. Finney calls them 'gawlins,'" Vivian said. "You just don't know who'll want to peck the bugs you can't reach off your hide until they step up and volunteer."

CHAPTER 26

Els returned from grocery shopping one mid-March afternoon to find Jason's truck in the court, Vivian crocheting and Finney playing dominoes with Liz and Boney on the shaded patio.

Liz jumped up and strutted toward her. "Dinner's on me," he said. "I bought enough of Finney's lobsters for all of us."

Els shook her head. "I don't see you for two months, and suddenly you commandeer my dinner plans?"

"It's high time I gave you that lesson in cooking them," Vivian said.

"Fair Lady," Boney said. "Knowing your dislike of surprise visitors, we decided you needed an improvement over Ol' Bessie." He stood up and hurried toward the north end of the house.

"What, a starter's pistol?"

"No noise this time," Liz said, already pulling her after Boney. Whenever he took her hand, her life shifted.

He stood behind her and put his palms over her eyes, his calluses against her cheekbones. She smelled something like oil, metal.

"Ta-da!" He removed his hands.

Boney was standing under the shower platform, grinning. A metal flagpole lashed to the shower railing poked high above the roof. He hurried to where they stood and held out a flag folded into a tight triangle.

"Cor," she said, and took a step back. A dove pursued another across the court. The gliricidia tree, still naked of foliage, was raining its pink blossoms onto the grass.

Liz steadied her against his chest. "Something the matter?"

The sight of the flag sent her back to Cairnoch's graveyard and Jerry Grimes presenting the folded Saltire to Burtie while Els stared into the rectangular hole next to Mallo's coffin.

"Think of flying it as an engraved invitation," Boney was saying. When she made no move to take the bundle, he flapped open a handmade rendition of the Nevis flag. On the green triangle was an appliquéd image of Jack smoking a cigar, his face encircled by a horseshoe; on the red triangle, an image of crossed darts.

"I especially like the little skulls and crossbones we put on all the stars," Boney said.

"We copied the face from a photo I found on *Iguana*," Liz said.

The handwork was worthy of Vivian in her prime; Els wondered if she'd had any role in this.

"When you want company, you just hoist 'er up there," Boney said. "You can see 'er from the dock at Oualie. We checked. I'll rig you up a spotlight so you can send a signal after dark. Come on, I'll show you how she works." Boney slung the flag over his shoulder and sprinted up the steps and through the front door, Liz close behind.

By the time Els reached the bathroom, they were both on the shower platform. She'd stopped in the door of each room on the way there, looking at what they must have seen on their trips through her private space: a black negligee tossed on the bedroom chair, her unmade bed with the lacy pillows askew, a flowered bra and matching panties hanging on a towel rack, a streak of makeup in the sink, a box of tampons on the bathroom chair.

She stepped over the muddy footprints crisscrossing the floor and climbed out the window onto the shower platform. The flagpole looked salvaged, a little bashed up, maybe tossed about by Hurricane Lenny, but had a new cleat, pulleys, and rope. Yellow nylon cord, the ends wrapped and tied off, secured it in the corner of the railing. The flag hung limp from the halyard. Her bathing suit, left to dry on the railing, was in the ferns below.

Boney held out the halyard. "Here, give 'er a yank."

"I know how to hoist a fucking flag, assuming I'd ever want to," she said. "What gave you guys the idea you could barge in and rig up anything you want?"

"I thought you'd be tickled," Boney said.

"Get off of here, both of you, and out of my bathroom."

Boney looked at Liz. "What did we do?"

"Out."

Boney slid through the window and stood with his cap in his hands. "It's just the sort of thing Jack would have loved. I'm surprised he didn't think of it himself."

"He had that bloody cannon," she said.

"Do you want us to take it down?" he asked.

"I said *get out*."

Boney flipped on his cap and hurried down the hall. He looked back once before clumping down the stairs.

Liz's eyes had darkened to Prussian blue. "We won't disturb your privacy again," he said. He climbed over the railing and shimmied down the support, strode to where Boney was standing in the drive, and whacked him on the shoulder. They exchanged words Els couldn't hear and then got into Jason's truck, and Liz slammed the door and drove out of the court with a spray of gravel.

She sagged into a seat at the domino table opposite Finney and put her hands on the tiles, seeking steadiness in their antiquity. They were real ivory—Finney said they'd belonged to Jack's grandfather—and were as yellowed and shot with brown as old teeth, the pips stained with India ink, a tiny brass stud in the center. Their clack was richer, deeper, than the plastic bones available now, as if they held the stories of every sweaty hand that had cradled them, and all the banter and foolishness of generations of men bragging about boats and fish and revolution and women and more women.

Finney squeezed a double six in his palm. "Wha'appen?"

"Those presumptuous fucking guys," she said. She stood up and began circling the table and Vivian's wheelchair, hugging her arms tightly to keep herself from flying apart.

"Such language," Vivian said. She extended her arm to stopped Els's pacing.

"Best not to let Liz get vex," Finney said. "He doan recover quickly."

"Go after him," Vivian said. "Once he cools down, he'll want to apologize, but he'll need some encouragement."

"Tell him we need help eatin' all a' them lobsters," Finney said.

Iguana, riding on her distant mooring, looked deserted. Els spread the flag on the dock, lay down on it, propped her chin on her arms, and stared at a school of fish swirling between the pilings. Calm flowed through her, as it often had at the Crag when she'd run there as a child to recoup after a tantrum.

An osprey raked up a fish and flew to the masthead of a sloop to rip at it. *These are the eagles of this land*, she thought, *and beware the little creatures below*—but she could not bring herself to feel sorry for the fish, as she often had for the hare.

She felt footsteps on the dock and turned to see Liz and Boney approaching. Boney elbowed Liz, said something, and doubled back toward the bar. She stood up and draped the flag over her arm. Liz leaned against a nearby piling.

"What is he, chicken to face me?" she asked.

"Cut him a little slack," he said. "He was just hoping there could be fun and carousing again."

"Where does he get off thinking I want Jack's friends making free with my home? Why do you hang out with him and Jason if you have to apologize for them all the time?"

"They can do their own apologizing."

"I'll wager neither of them feels a pinprick of contrition," she said. "What about you?"

He looked across the harbor. "We should have asked first. Boney would take the rap, but I wanted you to have that flag at least as much as he did."

"What makes you think I'll ever use it?"

"Jack's place needs people. Maybe sometime you will too."

Over their heads, two least terns screeched, one carrying a fish, the other harrying. As was often the case after one of her rages, Els felt disoriented, unsure where to place blame, as if everyone involved had held a match and it was unclear whose had set off the conflagration.

She draped the flag over her arm. "You guys really know how to trip my switch."

"Not pretty," he said. "But I'm no stranger to anger."

"People have warned me about that."

He looked at her. "So neither of us is exactly a picnic."

Standing like a pole, she held the flag by two corners and let the breeze belly it. "You could redeem yourselves a little by helping us eat the lobsters."

His eyes remained a cloudy blue. "Least we can do."

CHAPTER 27

Wearing one of Jack's shirts, caught by only two buttons, Els lit the candles on the refectory table and sheltered them with hurricane globes. Liz, Finney, and Boney had cajoled her into joining their after-dinner dominoes, a competitive game with much slapping of tiles. The contest between Els and Liz had edged toward playful by the end, but his leave-taking had still been wary.

She restarted the Bob Marley CD Liz had played during the domino game and danced around the shadowy lounge, singing along about getting together and feeling all right. When Marley launched into "Don't Rock My Boat," she went to the gallery, where the frogs were chirping a counterpoint to the reggae beat. Candle glow spilled through the front door and a fingernail moon hung in the western sky, its horns pointing away from the satellite that always appeared first and blazed brightest, a man-made star that never budged or wavered.

"So which is it, sweet?" Jack asked from among the heliconia below the gallery. "Get together and feel something, or leave your little boat unrocked?" He stepped onto the court.

She went to the railing. "Mother of God."

He was naked, the dark hair on his torso descending like a braid to his crotch, which was lost in shadow. He held a pirate stance, fists on his hips. "You can't have it both ways," he said. "Dive in and get wet." He swiveled his hips. "Or float around above it all, missing the fun." He looked about her age—fit, tanned, bearded, and ponytailed.

"I refuse to have a conversation with you in that condition."

"You'll talk with a jumbie, but not a naked jumbie?" he said. "Don't go all prissy on me." He walked into the garden, his buttocks a pale stripe between his bronzed back and legs, and disappeared among the sago palms. After some thrashing and cursing, he reappeared holding the pleated leaf of a blue latania palm, big enough to cover him from chest to knees. "I hope my fig leaf satisfies you, Miss Priss. No—I hope my leaf does the trick, and I wish my fig could satisfy you." He clapped his hand over his mouth. "I guess I shouldn't say 'trick,' either."

"What's this, Adam in the Garden?"

He held out his hand. "Come be my Eve."

"You're not my type."

"And what type would be?" he said. "I thought you *liked* 'em dead."

Far away, a dog barked.

"How dare you," she said.

He began to pace, his gait a little wobbly. "We dead guys have a lot going for us," he said. "Frozen in our prime, all our manly splendor intact." He looked down, held the leaf away from his body, then swept it back into place. "A lot of women—I mean, really a *lot* of women—came flocking to get a taste of this manly splendor. But not you. Oh no, you're immune from mine or any man's charms, because you're married to a memory, a figment."

"Fuck you, Jack."

"My fondest wish," he said. "Or it would have been if you'd chanced along sooner." He looked up at Orion's Belt. "I wish, I wish, I wish I were your figment, even if I could never be your fig man." He stood with his back to her, admiring the stars.

"You're drunk."

"At this age, I nearly always was," he said. "Amazing what a body can endure. In my thirties I still thought I was invulnerable." He turned and dropped the leaf and held out his arms. "Look at me."

The soft light touched the planes of his chest, his narrow hips, taut muscles. Leonardo's Vitruvian Man. With a huge erection.

She looked away. His magnificence was that of a long-ago Jack; the effort he must have expended to reach that state was touching but mystifying. He resembled her memory of Mallo only in stature, but even that similarity plucked a long untouched chord that sent deep vibrations through her, their tremors a threat to the brickwork that walled in her grief.

"What, does this embarrass you?" he said. "Offend you?"

"I don't like this you."

"You can't choose," he said. "Although I grant, some of me is more likable than the rest."

"So now I get to see your scary side."

"What's so scary about a man aching with desire? A man who would love nothing more than to find your very core and caress it until you come moaning and blinking back into this world?" He swatted at a passing bat. "Ah, the places I could have taken you. Lucky you, there's still time. But you won't dare go there again, assuming lover boy even got you there in the first place."

"It's none of your bloody business what ecstasy I did or didn't reach," she said. "What makes you think that hard-on of yours is such a prize?"

He thrust his hips forward. "Some women would be impressed, honored, by this."

"As you claim hundreds were."

"Goddamn right, you prissy, icy bitch."

"*Icy*," she said. "You slobbering exhibitionist. All talk, no action."

"My *action* was legendary!"

"Have you got a point?"

He looked down his torso. "Less and less." He picked up the palm leaf and studied it, running his fingers over its folds, then swirled it like a fan dancer before settling it over his crotch. "Obviously my exhibit is a distraction from my message."

"Out with it."

He stood at the foot of the steps, swaying slightly, and looked up at her. "You're no more here than I am. Dead before your time."

"You're jealous."

"You got that right, Ice Queen," he said. "I'm seething with envy that someone left such a mark on your heart. But that's not my point."

"Get to it."

"Too late to resurrect me, but maybe this man can bring you back from the dead if you give him a chance."

"What man?"

"You know damn well who I mean."

"If I want a matchmaker, I'll let you know."

"You're quite the pair, now that I think about it," he said. "He's as guilty as you of obsessing on the dead, and as unwilling to make the move."

"If you know so much, who's his obsession?"

"He never told me," he said. "Even in his cups, and believe me, he was there as often as I for a time." He walked to the edge of the garden and stepped in, tossing the leaf over his shoulder. It flopped onto the court, a crinkled, dark shield against the pale stones.

CHAPTER 28

From the study window, she watched Liz swing one tanned leg out of Jason's truck, examine his reflection in the wing mirror, and rake back his hair. He climbed out, eased the door shut, and straightened his shirt. It was the cornflower-blue linen he'd worn that night at Sunshine's, which turned his eyes the same color.

When he looked up at the house, she ducked behind the curtain. The sun was just striking the court. He leaned against the truck and closed his eyes, and she wondered how it would be to watch him sleep.

He opened his eyes. "Inside?"

She dropped her paintbrush into a jar of thinner. "I thought you might have sailed already," she called back.

"In an hour." He grinned and peeled himself away from the truck. "Request permission to come aboard."

"Granted, Captain."

He took the steps two at a time. She wiped her hands on a rag and started to remove the shirt of Jack's she'd appropriated for a smock. He burst through the study door, pinned her arms to her side with an embrace, spun her around, and set her down, still holding her elbows.

She caught her breath, felt the warmth of his hands on her arms.

"I hope I'm the first to wish you a Happy St. Patrick's Day." He kissed her quickly on the cheek and stepped back.

"Aye, laddie, but ye've got yir Celts confused," she said.

He looked slowly around the study, examined her oil painting on the easel—a still life of a cut papaya, its seeds glistening fish eggs against the peachy flesh—and the watercolors of flowers she'd propped against the wall. "That passion flower is really good," he said. "And the hibiscus."

"My first daubings since high school," she said. "It's forcing me to really see again, not go about in oblivion." She hung Jack's shirt on the easel. "Vivian encouraged me. She and Eulia are writing a cookbook of her recipes, and she asked me to illustrate it."

He considered her mother's self-portrait without comment. While she leaned against the wall, he walked around the room, picking up paintings and sketches. She watched him flip through her watercolor pad full of scenes of Oualie. The room was too small for the two of them.

"Do you ever paint people?" he asked.

"Most of them don't sit still long enough."

"Paint from memory," he said. "Or imagination." He took her notebook and looked a long time at her pencil sketches of Jack. "Well, obviously you know what I mean. This one here got him perfectly."

"Those are just doodles," she said. "Private doodles."

He turned the pages slowly.

"Stop," she said. "That's as bad as reading someone's diary without invitation." She grasped the corner of the pad, then let go and crossed her arms. He reached a page with a series of sketches of his own face. He held her gaze and handed her the notebook. She turned away and tossed it onto the daybed.

"I brought you a present," he said. He took her hand firmly. His boyish excitement ignited her curiosity, and she let him lead her down both flights of stairs. On the way, she looked at how his tanned hand—which gave no sign of letting go—encircled her pale one, and remembered when he had helped her aboard *Iguana*. But that had been all business, and this was not.

"The last time you dragged me anywhere, we fought over that damn flag," she said.

"Sometimes the only way to get you anywhere is to drag you," he said. He opened the truck's passenger door. In a carton on the seat was a tiny puppy. He cuddled it against his chest. It nibbled his thumb. "If you're going to live here, you need a dog."

"You think I need protection."

"I think you need to rescue this adorable, abandoned creature."

He handed her the puppy, and she wondered if this was his idea of an apology. She gathered the ball of fur into her arms, felt the puppy's warmth, its fragility, the tiny ribs beneath its loose skin, its racing heart. While she stroked its head, it licked her hands.

"What makes you think I even like dogs?"

"The way you were with Trixie," he said. "If I guessed wrong again . . ." He reached for the puppy, but Els held on tighter.

The dog was honey colored, with a white chest blaze and paws. Above its blue-gray eyes, lighter patches formed blond eyebrows. Holding it under its front legs, she let the body dangle. A female.

"Susie," she said, and rubbed noses.

"You'd continue Jack's naming tradition."

"Why not?" She carried the puppy into the kitchen.

Liz followed with the carton and unpacked a heating pad, baby bottle, and liter Coke bottle of milky liquid with a recipe for puppy formula and feeding instructions taped to it.

"Jason's known as a softie for abandoned pups," he said. Susie squirmed and yipped. "Someone left a litter in a box on the dock at Oualie, all of them badly dehydrated. He couldn't save the others." He reached over and tickled the puppy's chin. "She'll probably need nursing for at least another two weeks."

"You've presumed a lot about my own soft spots, much less any maternal instinct." Els poured a little of the formula into the baby bottle and put a bowl of water into the microwave to warm. "But as it happens, we raised hunting dogs at home. There was often a whelping box next to the Aga. When we lost one of Father's prize bitches in labor, a . . . boy who lived with us and I raised the pups with droppers. Six of them." She put the bottle into the warm water.

"I imagined you growing up with lots of boys," he said. "To get so tough."

"There was a gang around the estate. I hardly knew any girls until I was sent away to school. And most of them were mean. I was a country hick to them. They aped my accent mercilessly until I gave one of them a bloody nose." Because of them, she'd learned to temper her brogue, become a speech chameleon as a shield against otherness, but since reuniting with Mallo, she'd embraced her accent as a badge of honor.

"I'll remember to steer clear of your left hook," he said.

She tested the formula's temperature on her wrist. Cradling Susie in her palm, belly down, she offered the nipple and the puppy took it eagerly. She kissed the puppy's downy head and breathed in her milky smell.

"They can abandon us, but they'll never keep us down, right, girl?" she said.

"The princess was abandoned in her castle?"

"No fairy tale," she said. "My mother left when I was nearly as helpless as this little thing. I wasn't allowed to know why." When the puppy released the nipple, Els gently burped her.

"Come sailing when I get back," Liz said.

"And leave my new dependent?"

The puppy peed all over her arms, and she laughed and set the ball of fur into the box. While she was washing, she heard the screen door close and turned with a dishtowel in her hands to see Liz climbing into the truck. "You guessed right," she called. "She's a brilliant gift."

"We don't allow pets on *Iguana*," he called back, "but we'd make an exception for Susie."

Els kept Susie with her constantly under the guise of building trust and speeding house training, but she found herself talking to the dog more than seemed sane. It hit her that she'd allowed her work, travel, and living in flats to deprive her for decades of canine companionship—the affection that had helped her weather childhood and adolescence, and the loss of Mallo.

One morning in late March, she dumped her paintbrush into her turpentine and looked around for Susie, who was nowhere in the study. Calling, she searched the bedroom, lounge, and kitchen before she heard a yip and a growl from the patio. Pinky was standing still, holding out his hands for the puppy to sniff. Susie approached him cautiously; after he caressed her ears, she let him pick her up. When she licked his chin, he broke into a broad smile and laughed, a mere rush of air.

From February onward, the calabash bowl had reappeared several times a week with fruit or vegetables, once a jar of honey, once a few eggs. She'd returned it each time with sugar, cornmeal, coffee, biscuits. She would occasionally spot Pinky working in the garden, or washing himself at the hose tap at dawn.

Today, there was a papaya on the patio table. Els opened the door. "Pinky, Finney says you can hear me."

He put Susie down and stepped back. Susie jumped at his shins, barking her playful bark. He was very dark, weathered, his hair matted, his eyes wary, his smile tentative.

"Do you want work?" Els asked.

He gave a quick nod.

"Can you see to the garden, weeding, mowing?"

He nodded again.

"Would you want to be paid in wages or food?"

He touched the tips of his fingers to his lips. He handed her the papaya.

She held the door wider, and he stepped shyly into the kitchen. She opened the fridge and asked, "What di yae like?"

He pointed to the beer and Vivian's mango cheesecake. Els filled a carry sack with those choices, plus packets and cans, and handed it to him. "Come every day at lunchtime. I'll ask Eulia to provide a meal for you."

He smiled, thumped his chest, and made a low whistle, like someone blowing into a bottle.

"I'll pay you fairly besides," she said.

Carrying Susie, Els followed him outside and watched him stroll to the back fence and step through a makeshift gate into the bush. "Well, Suze," she said, "the place comes with jumbie, jumbie pals, and now a mute gardener, all with their own agendas."

CHAPTER 29

Though it was officially spring, the days marched on with little variation beyond an almost imperceptibly later sunset. Els countered the loneliness that crept in with the dark by sipping rum and reading, making a game of choosing a book at random from the shelves. But tonight she was fidgety, and when she searched for the comforting cadences of the King James Bible, she found it stashed among the novels, a surprising departure from Jack's meticulous shelving system. Its pages had been glued together and their centers cut out to form a well that contained a packet of letters.

She took the Bible to the chair, untied the jute twine, and examined the envelopes. Ten, all addressed to Jack Griggs, Nevis, West Indies. The cavity also held a man's gold signet ring, its bloodstone carved with the entwined initials *JGS*.

She poured more rum and settled into the big chair with Susie in her lap. She sorted the letters into date order and opened the earliest one, written in a round hand on lined pages torn from a notebook:

February 3, 1978
My Dearest Disappeared Jack,

85 days and not a word from you!

I miss you so much—not just the sex, which was beyond groovy—but just, well, YOU. I'll keep this short 'cause I don't even know if you'll get it—they do have mail down there, don't they? I finally broke down and called your mother—told her I was married to one of your college buddies and was putting together a surprise 30th birthday party for him and needed your address—and she said she'd gotten a postcard from Nevis. I had to use a magnifying glass to even locate it in the atlas. She's as snooty as you always said and it sounds like she doesn't give a hoot where you are, but I do—so please, please write me back right away. Send it to Becky Wickage's address below. Daddy will make confetti of anything from you if he gets hold of it first.

I can't bear that we've been cast apart by these cruel forces. I wish I could have stood up for you—for US—and fuck Daddy and old Traftie. Can you ever, ever forgive me?

I'm lying on my bed all naked right now. Imagine me wrapped in your musty old fur rug under the stars in our favorite spot, on a cold night like tonight, with my nipples standing at attention, waiting only for you.

All my love, forever,
Susie

There was a heart over the "i."

The next letter had a border of pink flowers:

May 18, 1978
My Beautiful Pirate,

All I did today is cry. I'm 18 now—legal—and you're not here to celebrate with me. Or fuck with me. Or take me away with you. Where the hell are you, Jack? You could at least let me know if you are OK and if I'm even sending this to the right little speck of an island.

You always said I had a good imagination, and I'm fantasizing like crazy these days to keep from going nuts—I've decided that you turned pirate and are off plundering ships and taking their wenches hostage. I wish I was one of those wenches. Please take me hostage. You can even beat me—I deserve it. Even so, I don't think I deserved to be left behind with these bastards and fools. Daddy is watching my every move and makes me be home by 9:00. I'm sure he's tapping my phone.

They gave me a car for my birthday, with a big bow on it just like in the commercials—can you BELIEVE it's a Dodge Intrepid? Daddy said it won awards for safety, as if I care. I just couldn't think of a thing to say —it's so totally old lady—at least it's red. The seats fold down and someone even as tall as you could lie in the back. It would make our little "meetings" way more comfortable than your Ghia. I drove it out to your favorite place on the golf course and crawled in the back and looked out the back window at the moon and talked to you and made myself come. I do that a lot now—no way am I going to let any of those pimply Weston Hall guys get what you once had all to yourself—and I have to do SOMETHING or I'll go insane.

I'm totally depressed. I've been stealing Mom's pills—I have a good stash now. I've also been stealing

Daddy's cash—I've got a good stash of that too. Just tell me where you are and I'll get the next plane, or boat, or canoe, or whatever they have down there. If I am stuck here much longer, I'll take those pills and whatever happens will be ALL YOUR FAULT. Or maybe I'll drive that red car right off the Currier Street Bridge. Think of me at the bottom of the river. Ophelia.

Your ever-loving Susie.

At the bottom of the page she'd drawn an upside-down car with heart-shaped bubbles rising along the right margin.

The next letter was written with purple Biro on notepaper with a university crest:

September 12, 1978
Dear Sexy Professor,

Hello from the halls of higher learning. I'm officially orientated now. OU is so big I feel like I could just disappear, or maybe start over and make less of a mess of everything. I thought it would be a good idea to room with Ginny Feldberg—you remember her, the one with the frizzy hair—but some days I think she's Daddy's spy.

Since you left me in nowhereland, I was hoping to meet some real men here, but the upperclassmen are nothing but boy-men in varsity sweaters with little dicks and big egos. They hang around our dorm checking out the freshman crop. Droolers. I'm going for a sorority, if only to get away from GF.

Here's my address for now. Please, please write. No Daddy to monitor my mail now—unless GF is doing it for him ☺. Just tell me you got this and that you're OK. If you still love me, tell me that too. I will love you always, always, always.

Forever your sprite,
Susie

Enclosed was a heart-shaped slip of paper with a dorm address at Ohio University.

November 10, 1978
My beloved partner in crime,

Well, it's the anniversary of the worst day in my life. I'll never forget that meeting in Traftie's office—Daddy's face so red I thought he might have the big one right there and I'd have his death to be guilty about on top of everything else. I kept willing you, begging you to look at me—I thought it would make me strong if I could just look into your eyes—but you were looking everywhere but at me. I've thought a million times what my life might have been if that snot Margie Thompson hadn't squealed. Just like her to blame it on her Christian morals, but I know it was because she had her own crush on you—can you imagine, that flat-chested, pear-shaped little mouse? I hate her for what she did to us and I told her so, at graduation, in front of her smarmy parents. She called me a slut.

Enough of old times. I'm a Chi-O now (see new address). I love living in the house and couldn't wait to get away from GF. Please, please write.

On the envelope flap was Susan Grant, Chi Omega, and an address on College Street in Athens, Ohio.

May 26, 1979
Dear Man of My Dreams,

I had a dream about you last night. More than a dream—a visitation. We were in the school darkroom and you had those nude photos hung up all over the place. Me, me, me, from every conceivable angle. You made me look so pretty, so ripe. You pulled beauty out of me into the lens, and I felt you were reaching into me and finding something that I didn't even know was there. Do you remember the incredible sex we had in that red light—you hoisting me up onto the table and me holding onto a pipe above our heads and making it go on forever? I came in my sleep and woke up missing you SO much. I thought maybe you were trying to communicate with me.

I had this guy in the bed—a gorgeous but totally unimaginative basketball center who's been chasing me, and I finally said what the hell. I was so hot from the dream I had to shake him awake and do it, slowly, on top the way you like it, and he said I was the best fuck he'd ever had—I guess I have you to thank for that ☺. I wish it would make you jealous that I'm squandering all your lessons on these college clods, but you always said you wouldn't waste your time being jealous, or on people who are.

I'm spending the summer in Cincinnati with my sorority sister Nancy Whitman—what a relief not to be home for two months with THEM. If you decide to break your silence between now and August 20th, I'll be at the address below, and after that back at Chi-O.

I cut off all my locks—no more Lady Godiva with tresses covering my breasts—and I'm not answering to Susie any more.

Write to me, PLEASE.
Susan

The next—dated June 2, 1982—announced that she had graduated, was taking a parent-funded trip to Europe, and would return to a job as a copy editor in an advertising firm, courtesy of a connection of her father's. She continued to beg for some word from Jack, at least confirmation that he still lived, but the tone was more distant.

She wrote on formal personal stationery with the script monogram *SGT* on December 1, 1983, that she was engaged to Charles Whitman, the cousin of her sorority sister, and that her parents were over the moon about throwing a huge wedding at the club on the following June 25th.

> *I almost refused to have it there because of all the memories of us out on that golf course under the stars at all times of year, but I couldn't exactly tell Daddy why I wasn't thrilled about the location when Mother had her heart set on that little gazebo with the pink roses. It's time I accepted that you are dead to me, by your choice, but if I am wrong about that, this is your last chance! Just kidding . . . well, not really.*

She signed it "*Fondly always, S.*"

The letter had a P.S.: "*I REALLY need the ring back. Daddy's totally fixated on it now that I'm getting married and (he expects) will produce a male heir—no, I'm not pregnant—yet ☺. I told him I just knew it would turn up when I cleaned out this apartment to move into the grown-up house Chip is buying for us.*" She'd enclosed an engagement photo clipped from the *Cleveland Plain Dealer* of a young woman, more saucy than beautiful, with blond hair and pale eyes, wearing a chaste drape and pearls.

Els returned the letters to their hiding place, closed the Bible's scratched cover, and felt its weight on her knees. She gazed at the nudes on the wall—so sensuous, so full of the photographer's yearning. He had sought to hold Susie's soul in his lens, to capture the ideal of woman shimmering in his mind's eye.

In the study, she aimed the desk lamp at the wall above the daybed—Boney said Jack dubbed it his Pariah Wall—where he'd hung framed rejections for literary submissions. When first setting the study to rights, she'd puzzled over a document typed on browning bond with an embossed school seal and placed high above the others. She stood on the mattress and lifted it down.

November 15, 1977

Mr. E. Jackson Griggs
Simpson 304
Carrolton Academy
410 Highland Hills Road
Cleveland Heights, Ohio

Dear Jack:

Per the binding ruling of the Faculty Grievance Committee, I write to confirm that your appeal is denied and your employment at the Academy is terminated.

I take this step with great personal sadness, as I shall miss you as a colleague in the Department and the students will miss one of their favorite teachers.

Given the circumstances of your removal, the Chairman of the English Department, Head of the Upper School, and I prefer not to be listed as references for any future employment. However, if there is other assistance I can provide, in friendship, please feel free to call upon me.

Yours sincerely,
Trafton S. Williams
Headmaster

The signature read "Traft." Over one corner, Jack had scrawled *The Traft Shaft* in ink that had faded to gray.

She rehung the letter and glanced at the other documents. "Poor bugger," she said, and climbed down and switched off the light.

When the puppy stood up on Els's lap, bared her teeth, and started to growl, Els was surprised to hear so threatening a sound coming from so small a creature. She peered into the blackness that had swallowed everything beyond the court, but could see nothing.

Jack stepped from between the sago palms. Susie's growl deepened. He was wearing the familiar white shirt and frayed shorts, but he'd aged again. She'd floated a gardenia in a snifter on the table; its scent was so aggressive, she wondered if it had summoned him.

"I owe you an apology, sweet," he said.

Susie sniffed and fell silent but kept staring at him, her hackles bristling.

"Narcissistic nutter."

"I thought my appearance last time was pretty slick, if I do say so," he said. "But my, well, manifestation of sincerest admiration was never meant to offend you." He broke off a stalk of lily of the Nile from the copper in the center of the court and set it on the bottom step. "None of us are at our best when drunk."

"What di yae want, Jack?"

He looked at Susie. "Isn't it nice having a warm body next to you in bed? They say jumbies can take the form of animals. I could circumvent my off-limits promise by inhabiting that adorable creature. Make myself at home at your very breast."

"She prefers her box."

"I suppose Miss Discipline would never encourage the nasty habit of sleeping on the furniture."

"She's already better at understanding boundaries than you." The puppy gazed up at her with rapt attention. "Why did you name all your dogs Susie?"

"Easy to remember."

"An excuse to say her name, perhaps?" she said. "You went to a lot of trouble to hide those letters. Why desecrate a Bible?"

He straightened and gathered himself together. Bats, invisible against the dark sky, zoomed in front of his white-clad shape, which appeared to be a bit out of focus, lacking sharp edges between it and the night. "My father went Pentecostal a few years before I left the States. Righteous hypocrite, ruined the Bible for me forever."

"She's the one in your photographs who's half kitten."

"Half vixen, half harlot, all lost," he said.

"Those images I enlarged are worshipful."

"Her essence reduced to an abstraction, one exquisite curve standing for the whole," he said. "My best work, never exhibited before now. I swore under oath I'd already destroyed every negative. A condition of my freedom. Such as it was."

"Was she the love o' your life?"

He paced the court, his hands deep in the pockets of his shorts. "Love, obsession, what you will. She was so supple, so yielding, so eager. The sex was addicting, all the more delicious for being forbidden. But then, I think you know all about that." He looked out to sea, where the moon cast a band of silver sparkles. When he turned back, he wore an expression of sadness and defeat. "They trumped it up as rape. She went along with them, her father and their fancy lawyer and that milquetoast of a headmaster." He looked up at the bedroom window. "I'd *never* do *anything* with a woman that she didn't welcome."

"She wiz a child."

"I'd lay bets you were rolling in the hay with some red-haired swain at that same age."

She looked away. "Only fantasizing about it."

Susie wriggled and whined. When Els set her down, she started sniffing in circles, so Els carried her down to the grass near the patio. The puppy squatted, then, with a sideways look at Jack, scampered back to Els, who praised her and carried her to the bottom of the steps.

Jack was only a few feet away. He looked exhausted, ravaged.

"Taking advantage of one's student is not on at any age," she said.

"She asked me for a passport photo. Daddy was taking the family skiing in the Alps. She showed up with those spectacular boobs stuffed into a fluffy sweater. Then she began stalking me on campus. Sat in the front row of class with her skirt up to here and no panties on. Came to my office on the slimmest of pretexts and stood so close I could smell her shampoo. Apples. She always smelled of apples."

"And poor Adam couldn't resist Eve in an angora sweater." *It's always beauty's fault*, she thought.

"It was torture to resist as long as I did." He stared up at the sky. "I should have burned all her letters unopened."

She sat on the bottom step with Susie in her lap. "Was that the whole lot?"

He began to pace again, slow, wobbly circles. "She wrote every few days, then every week or so for at least a year. Chatter, chatter, chatter. Every detail of her family drama, her pimply boyfriends, like I was her fucking diary. She slacked off eventually. I kept the ones with new addresses."

"But left her begging for any sort of reply."

"I wrote plenty of them," he said. "When the mood struck me, I'd tie one on and let 'er rip. Christ, I filled pages with excoriating prose, caustic enough to take the paint off that Jeep. Trotted out a whole dictionary of five-dollar words like 'vapidity.'" His smile was devilish. "You saw that stuff in the bathtub."

"The ravings of a complete nutter," she said. "What little I could make out of it."

"So you see why I never sent them," he said. "In the cold, semi-sober light of dawn, I didn't think she was worth the trouble. I only read hers to see if our li-ai-son had had any lasting effect. With me, she glimpsed life's stunning possibilities, but she tossed it all away. Slid into the unexamined torpor typical of her ilk. Daddy's little angel, Chip's little wifey. No reply from me, nasty or not, would have halted her descent once she decided to lie about me."

"That ring implies you made promises."

"I gave her my great-aunt's ruby. Worth almost nothing, apart from sentiment. We had a mock wedding on the golf course at midnight. She wore a white gown from the secondhand shop." He chuckled mirthlessly. "The campus cops probably could have seen it a mile away in that harvest moon, but it turned out one of the girls was up in a tree watching us, that night and others. Our *wedding* was the beginning of the end. But that's true for most couples—end of the romantic illusions, start of festering resentments."

"Mr. Romantic reveals his cynical soul," Els said.

He was looking at the bed of birds of paradise. "She put her hair up in this fancy twist and pinned fake gardenias in it." His smile was ironic, sad. "She'd worn a gardenia wrist corsage to her junior prom. I was a chaperone. She ditched her date long enough to pull me into the field hockey coach's office. We did it on a pile of pinnies on the floor. She gripped my head when she came. That flower was right next to my ear. She wasn't a virgin, if you were wondering." He looked up toward the lounge windows. "That ring you found was her great-great-grandfather's—supposed to go to the oldest boy, but she had no brother. She believed it had powers. She gave it to me to spite her father. I was one big rebellion against Daddy, until she realized what it could cost her."

"One seldom anticipates the cost of rebellion," Els said. A dog barked far away. Susie's ears pricked. In all her wailing and gnashing about why Mallo had been torn from her, she'd barely considered that his loss might be the price of rebelling against Harald. Nor would she have chosen differently had she known then of her father's deceit and cruelty.

"I should never have taken that ring," Jack was saying, "or polluted this place with its evil karma. It's the cause of a lot of bad stuff."

"You cannae blame that lump of stone for any of your ill fortune," she said. A bat flew so close to her arm she could feel the air it stirred. "And you cannae be expecting me to track down this Mrs. Charles Whitman and return the steamy evidence."

"Burn the letters for all I care," he said. "The ring is bad juju."

"Why don't you just fly up to Cleveland and shove it through her mail slot?"

"I'd never make it. Probably drop it in the ocean, and that's as bad as taking it to my goddamn grave." He looked at the sea for a long time. "Look, just give it to Teal, the solicitor."

She shooed Susie off her lap and stood up. One bat flew between her and Jack, then another. *Highly personal items the heir would like returned.* She looked at him. "You're not saying you left her this house after all these years."

"I assumed Gravy told you her name and you'd pieced it together with that razor sharp brain of yours."

"He hid every detail of *the heir*," she said. "Except that she was no relation of yours, making me wonder which of your many women she might have been."

"She wasn't first, best, or last," he said. "Just consequential."

"So the fortune I paid for this house went to that wee bitch?"

"Some of it. A moment ago you were calling her a child."

"If she was acting like a woman, I can call her a bitch," she said. "But bitchy, sexy, needy, none of it gives any man license to swing his dick around."

"You can't beat me up about what I did any more than I've already beaten myself up. Just get rid of that damn thing."

"Is it what's holding you here?"

"And make sure Teal gets proof of delivery," he said, and dematerialized.

She picked up Susie and rocked her, wondering if all love was doomed from the start and the lovers too besotted to notice the warnings.

She dropped the ring on Teal's desk. "I believe this is what your heir hoped I'd find."

Teal picked it up and examined the engraving. "Just so. She also mentioned some letters."

"You said at closing you didn't have a list."

He responded with a tight smile. Through the open windows, the sea wind carried harbor smells of fuel and seaweed, along with curry and fry smoke from the roti trucks serving up lunch beside the destroyed seawall.

"Jack burned many letters," she said. "Nothing left but charred fragments." She pulled from her tote a package wrapped in her hand-painted paper. "Put this in along with the ring," she said. "I'm sure she'll find the subject of interest. Kindly send me confirmation that your package has been received. I'll be relieved to be shut of this burdensome obligation."

She stood up, and before Teal could rise from his chair she was out the door and gulping sea air.

Darkness had fallen an hour ago, but she hadn't moved from the big chair. Barking furiously, Susie leapt off her stomach and knocked Els's near-empty rum glass to the floor.

Els sat up and turned on the Chinese lamp. She grabbed the bandana that served as Susie's collar, pulled the puppy against her knees, and shouted, "Enough," and Susie subsided into yelps, then growls, then tense silence. There was no sound but the faint hum of the fridge, the palm fronds rattling, and the faraway barking of dogs.

Els felt alone, not just in the house but in the world. She gathered Susie into her arms, a talisman against whatever or whomever might be skulking about in the dark outside.

Jack stepped forward, gradually taking form in the lamplight. "I still can't get the hang of being a good guest."

"Thank God it's only you," she said.

"That feels like a promotion. How quickly the terrifying becomes the merely annoying." He was fit and spry, in his thirties again. He stopped to admire the photo of Susie-as-sand-dune—her ribs, the intimation of arch to her back, a suggestion of passion. "This one's my favorite," he said.

"Now that I've done your dirty work," she said, "does yir karma feel any better?"

"'Like a kite cut from the string, lightly the soul of my youth has taken flight,'" he said. "Japanese poet, name of Takuboku. They named a comet or something after him. What are you going to do with the letters?"

"What would you suggest? Publish them?"

He looked at her, a flash of malice in his eyes, then turned pensive again. "Best to pretend they didn't survive."

"Precisely." She shot him a conspiratorial smile. "I never said *whose* letters you torched in the tub."

"If you'd returned them, she'd know you read them. Only a saint could resist that."

"No halo here," she said. "I sent her a little gift through Teal. Three-by-fives of those nudes."

He laughed, Pirate Jack for a second. "That's my girl." He looked at her a long time, smiling, then said, "See ya," and floated down the kitchen steps.

"Is that it?" she called. "Are we all done? Are ye gone?"

She hadn't contemplated the consequences of complying with his request. At the idea that he might have left so abruptly and for good, she felt anew the prick of abandonment. Though she knew it was pointless, she checked the kitchen and went out to the empty court. A pearly-eyed thrasher sang from the mango tree, two notes up, two notes down, another two notes down.

CHAPTER 30

On the first of May, Lauretta stopped in to bring her previous month's invoice. She refused a beer and stood in the kitchen with her arms crossed, twitching with nervous energy.

Els dropped the invoice on the table. "I'll give you part of it now and the rest as soon as I can."

"How long does that mean?"

"I'm talking to some bankers."

"Those workmen are really bugging me."

"Give me a week."

"Like I have a choice," Lauretta said, and went outside. The screen door slammed behind her. Els didn't move until she heard the Lexus rumble over the cattle guard at the road.

The bank manager stood behind his desk and gestured toward a chair. "I regret your wait, Ms. Gordon." The office smelled of curry.

She sat and crossed her legs. The skirt of her navy Armani suit was too short for this meeting. She uncrossed her legs and pressed her knees together. "I appreciate your giving me this time, Mr. Leonard," she said. "I hope you've had a moment to review my CV."

His desktop was empty, save for her letter and CV, a partially consumed bottle of Fanta orange soda, and a few crumbs. He sat down and picked up the papers.

"Royal Bank of Scotland. Sanders & Sons. Standard Heb," he read with a slight twitch of his mouth on the last. Her family bank, now the butt of jokes. He was wearing a boldly flowered tie and a short-sleeved shirt. On the wall behind him, crayon drawings in plastic frames hung askew beside posters trumpeting a better life through loans.

"Help me to understand how experience in mergers and acquisitions would benefit NevisOne." He brushed the crumbs to the edge of the desk, used her CV as a dust collector, and shook them into his bin.

She'd saved this bank for last, and the meeting was clearly heading toward perfunctory rejection, as had all her other interviews. "NevisOne leads the local banks in corporate lending," she said. "You've spearheaded turning our island into an international investment haven. As investment in Nevis grows, so will your capacity to lend to local businesses."

"We will continue to support Al's Auto Shoppe and Muriel's Snackery," he said. "But when international investors want to reinvigorate one of our sugar hotels, do you suppose they come to us? The last such group took its business straight to Argeron Capital."

"I've done deals with Argeron, and most of their ilk," she said. "I have connections in New York, London, and elsewhere." His bland expression did not change. "I could be of value in marketing and customer service. Help you attract that offshore money. I speak their language."

He folded his long brown fingers over her CV and regarded her. "We all speak English here, Ms. Gordon."

"I meant . . . money talk."

"NevisOne is dedicated to creating opportunity for our local people," he said. "We have our full staff complement at present.

Perhaps you should inquire at ECCB or Bank of Nevis, or the international and regional banks—Nova Scotia, RBTT, First Caribbean."

She unclasped her hands and fanned her fingers across her lap. "They've been encouraging. But the best fit is here, because you've got the jump on attracting a global customer base. My own money is with you, in case that matters."

"We appreciate your custom, Ms. Gordon." He glanced back at the CV. "Banks serving more of an American clientele—in Puerto Rico or Barbados, because of the embassy—or those in the more developed islands, Trinidad perhaps, might welcome a background such as yours." He held out her papers.

"That would be some commute," she said. She stood up, took the CV, and dropped it into his bin. She thanked him for his time, squared her shoulders, and walked past the winding queue of customers staring blankly at the CNN monitor. *If you hired me,* she thought, *the first thing I'd do is put on more tellers at lunch hour.*

When the humid blast of the early May afternoon hit her, she could barely draw a breath. She walked to Wilma—parked near the slave market square—tossed her ridiculous designer jacket on the front passenger seat, and sat behind the wheel, listening to the seemingly unemployed young men flirt with the passing girls.

Knowing *Iguana* had returned that afternoon, she raised the flag just before sunset and sat on the gallery, pretending to read. The knife of rejection cut deep into old territory, and her tumbler of rum had done nothing to quell her rising sense of panic.

Against a flaming sky, Jason's truck chugged up the hill. When it rolled to a stop, Liz hopped out and snapped to attention at the bottom of the steps. "You rang?"

She tossed her book onto the other chair. "It was a bad idea," she said. "I'm shitty company tonight. Go on back to yir floating palace."

He took the steps several at a time and pulled her to her feet. "Captain Liz has a cure for the blues. First I'm going to make you a drink"—he glanced at her glass—"well, maybe a refresher. Then you're going to tell me all about it while we rustle up something to eat."

"You know I'm not even competent in the kitchen," she said.

"Just do what I tell you for a change and we'll manage."

Lubricated by her second stiff rum, she'd confessed to being flat broke and terrified. "It's not too late for me to get back in," she said. "Somewhere."

"And give up all this?" he said.

"I can no longer afford *all this*."

"Look," he said. "Everyone here lives by their wits and their luck. You've got plenty of the first and you have to make your own luck, like the rest of us."

"I'm at my wits' end and I'm shit out o' luck," she said. Her vegetable chopping had become vengeful.

Liz took the chef's knife from her and gave her the job of whisking the eggs. He finished mincing onions, tomatoes, and herbs from Finney's garden, and when they hit the hot olive oil, they filled the kitchen with an aroma that made Els feel cosseted, and hungry.

When he saw her clumsy whisking, which produced only globs of egg white wobbling like jellyfish in a lemony sea, Liz took the bowl from her and whisked energetically, then poured the mixture over the vegetables. A few minutes later, he was dishing out an inviting scramble.

She took a bite, sucked air to cool it, and nodded her approval. "I mean, a type-A workaholic like me can handle only so much paradise." She ticked off her accomplishments with her fingers: "I've hiked Nevis Peak, tramped up to Montravers, visited Philippa's grave, poked about the Hamilton and Nelson museums, put in a massive number of plants, adopted a local mutt, painted every shell, flower, and fruit on the island. What else is there for an unemployed person to do here?"

"Become a drunk."

"Working on that," she said, and sloshed a bit more rum into her glass. "Tony had the cheek to tell me a few days ago that he has a buyer for the house, as long as I swear I've never seen the jumbie."

He looked up, the fork halfway to his mouth. "You've put it on the market?"

"It was just Tony fishing for a deal. Maybe he thought my plan was always to flip it for a profit and run back to the UK."

"Jason thinks the same thing. I told him you were putting down roots."

"Jason can go fuck himself. This is my home now." She ate another bite of eggs. "Ye're not bad in the kitchen fir a water rat."

"The way to a man's heart is through his ego."

"Lauretta has been all over me to let her turn the house into a special events place," she said. "*Venue,* she calls it. Weddings and such. Thinks she and I can make a business of it."

"There you go," he said. "Daddy walks his princess down the steps to get hitched in the court. Wedding photos with a perfect sunset as backdrop."

"I hate the idea."

"You could charge a big price for letting people in for a few hours."

"As usual, ye're awfully free with someone else's privacy."

He sat back in his chair. "I'm just saying you should deploy your assets. You've taken one fantastic house and made it even better. And the garden, the way you sort of paint with plants and how the sun shines through them."

She looked at him. "Thank you for noticing."

"It's my job to notice, remember?" He finished his beer. "Look, if you have something like this house or *Iguana,* that's one of a kind, people will pay up for it, and talk about it for the rest of their lives.

You can be choosy, exclusive. Get into the right circles, and word of mouth takes care of your advertising."

"So now ye're a marketing whiz."

"Jason and I run a good business, and yes, I'm the marketing whiz and he's the money man, and I bet his investment record could give yours a run any day."

"Kick her when she's down, why don't ye?"

"Who had all her eggs in the same basket?" he said. He got himself another beer. When he sat back down, she thought he might reach for her hand, but he only leaned forward on his elbows.

"Do I detect Mr. Marketing Whiz cooking up a package deal—storybook wedding at the Jumbie House and romantic honeymoon aboard a 'piece o' history'?" she asked.

"Hadn't thought of it, but it's not a bad idea. One plus one equals four, isn't that investment banker math?" He did take her hand now, and sought her eyes. "Just do it one time, make a few bucks, and see where it goes."

"You wernie listening," she said, pulling away. "I really, really hate the idea."

CHAPTER 31

To top off the barbecue celebrating Peanut's first birthday in mid-May, the men proposed a game of horseshoes on Jack's pitch between the house and Toad Hall, which Liz and Boney had persuaded Els to allow them to restore. Vivian sat under the mango tree, smiling at the men's rivalry.

While she helped Eulia wash up, Els stole glances through the kitchen screen at Liz—clowning, making a graceful toss, and helping Peanut lift a shoe and heave it a few inches. Boney and Finney cheered and Pinky whistled. Els went to the door and joined in the applause, but hers was for Liz's gentleness and patience with the child. Jason, who'd kept his distance from Els and said little except in dialect to Finney or Eulia, was raking the pitch while Pinky collected the shoes.

Els handed Eulia a small package. "This was mine." Eulia unwrapped the gift and smoothed the paper as if she meant to frame it. Inside the box was a silver baby spoon with "E" engraved on the looped handle.

Eulia lifted it out and slipped her thumb through the loop. "Well, ah guess you born with a silver spoon in you mouth," she said, "but I never exspeck one to touch Peanut lips. This too valuable to use."

"It's been chewed, banged, and thrown to a fare-thee-well," Els said. She gave Eulia a second package, which she unwrapped as carefully as the first. It contained a miniature silver picture frame, engraved with "EJG" and holding a photo of a curly-headed white child looking saucily into the camera. Eulia ran her thumb along the edge of the frame.

"I found it in a cigar box in the study," Els said.

"What this got to do with Peanut?"

"It's Jack at about the age Peanut is now."

"Anybody know Jack know this is him." Eulia held the frame out to Els.

"It's rightfully Peanut's," Els said. "His likeness to Jack at that age is unmistakable." A horseshoe clanged against a stake. "I did the math." She looked at Eulia, who dropped her eyes to the picture. "What's your baby's real name, anyway?"

The women gazed out the door at Peanut, who tottered up to Liz, dragging a shoe. Liz lifted the boy to his hip, took the shoe, and lofted it, and it clanked and thumped. Peanut shrieked and the men hollered and clapped.

"He named for his daddy and us," Eulia said. "Elliott Jackson Fleming."

"Did Jack die without knowing you were pregnant?"

"Last I saw him, I didn't know myself," Eulia said. "I doan tell nobody but Doctor Lytton and Mamma and Daddy. Daddy was so vex, mostly at Jack. Mamma, she just sad. All dat time, I let them believe I was just doing for Jack, never talk 'bout the res'. Things turn 'round once Peanut come." She looked at the photo. "Arright, I goin' save this for when Peanut start asking about he daddy." She smiled ruefully. "Jack look cute when he was small."

"Maybe Peanut got the better part of his nature," Els said.

"Jumbie been sweetin' you up," Eulia said.

Still watching Liz play with Peanut, Els said, "He visits now and again. I'm what he calls 'receptive.'"

Eulia glanced around the kitchen as if Jack might pop out from behind the stove. "Receptive mean you could see jumbie?"

"He must believe you aren't, or I'm sure he'd visit you as well."

"I doan want see he at all," Eulia said. "That finish long ago."

Having invited themselves over on the pretext of helping Pinky repair Jack's waterworks before leaving to sail the Mediterranean for the summer, Liz and Boney raised beers to celebrate the restored flow of water throughout the garden. While the women sat in the mango shade, they challenged Finney to a domino game that became more boastful than usual.

The shadows of the palm trees stretched across the court, everything washed in caramel light. Boney came out of the kitchen with another round of beers, sashaying to the beat of Martha and the Vandellas's "Dancing in the Street" pumping from the lounge. He stopped to straighten the dartboard, which was still hanging on the stone wall near the kitchen door, and stood there a minute, pulling on his beard.

"Hot damn," he said. "I've got the answer to your dye-lemma, Fair Lady." He set the beers down ceremoniously. "Just start charging for these here drinks."

"I may be broke, but I can still stand you to a few beers," Els said.

"Resurrect old Jack's bashments," Boney said. "Offer some tasty grub, good drink, friendly competition, and com-ra-de-ree, all at a fair price. They'd come running."

Liz lowered his beer slowly. He was shirtless, a turquoise bandanna around his head. "Bones is onto something," he said. "Look, Els, you can make money off the house without losing all your privacy. Put a few tables out here, crank up the grill, maybe make a bar up there in the big room, but keep the top floor off-limits. Let Eulia do her kitchen magic."

Eulia looked up from the book she was reading to Vivian.

"Domino nights again," Finney said.

"All the old games," Boney said, his eyes shining. "Dart tournaments. Crab races in the ring."

"What ring?" Els said.

Boney walked to the circle of bleached conch shells about ten feet in diameter where the soil had been tamped so hard that only a few tufts of grass had broken the surface. He yanked out the grass, stamped down the divots, and struck a *ta-da* pose.

"I've been trying to get Pinky to dig that up so I can plant something there," Els called. "But he pretends not ti understand, and one day I caught him sweeping it."

Pinky laughed his puff of air and whistled.

"Dig it up?" Boney called back. "Sacrilege. I'm not the only one to lose a month's wages over those godforsaken crustaceans on this very spot." He crouched and straightened one of the conch shells, patted the tamped earth, and walked back to the patio. "We raced on Sundays. Best fun of the week," he said. "But the dominoes and darts would keep 'em coming night after night."

"Night after night?" Els said. "The prospect of the occasional wedding was odious enough."

"It'll take a lot of beers to equal one fancy wedding," Liz said. "But you get a great pub going, and the weddings could be optional, a little boost to the bottom line."

"Pub is it, now?" Els put a hand on her hip. "Do yi think me a bar wench?"

"You just run the business end. Eulia can manage the rest with her hands tied."

"Need all a' my hands and a big cooler besides," Eulia said. "And a new stove." She was staring toward the kitchen, her eyes narrowed, a calculating little smile on her lips.

Els looked around at their expectant faces. "You want a sizeable investment in equipment? Darts and horseshoes flying, crabs threatening people's toes, wagering? I suppose you want me to shoot off that cannon at sunset, put a sign at the road, and call it 'Horseshoe Jack's.'"

Boney looked at her, a slow grin crinkling his eyes. "Purely inspired, Fair Lady."

The entrance to Lover's Beach was a washed-out track through the undergrowth. Els maneuvered Wilma through mud wallows, past a termite mound nearly as tall as the car, and under the canopy of poisonous manchineel trees to a spot large enough to park a few cars. Carrying Susie in her pack, which she wore like a baby sling, she walked the path through the sea grapes onto the night-chilled sand.

Lilies erupted in white starbursts from crevices in the lava ridge behind her, and the empty beach stretched east toward the airport. The rising sun touched the reef, turning its curling surf gold. She marched along the sharply sloped sand, forcing herself forward. The coral sand on the west end sucked her feet in to the calf, but as she neared the airport, the sand turned hard and black, glistening like obsidian where the wash slid over it and barely accepting her footprints.

She retraced her steps and paused to watch a great blue heron fish in the lagoon behind the dunes. Back at the entrance, she let Susie sniff among the nests of seaweed above the wrack line while she dunked in the shallows, turned milky with stirred sand. She sat on a rock watching the ghost crabs tending their holes until her clothing was dry and her skin was prickling with crusted salt. She'd turned her options over and over, and there was no way out but to take the least unappealing of them.

"Come on, Suze," she called. "Time ti get to work."

While Els charged around the property, spilling out plans and ideas, Lauretta followed her, taking notes on her yellow pad. By the time they finally reached the kitchen, she'd filled several pages.

"See if you can round up at least thirty wooden chairs, doesnae matter if they match," Els said. "And get Fred up here so he can build us some tables."

"This is going to be a mishmash," Lauretta said.

"We'll paint everything in a mix o' tropical colors," Els said. "It'll be charming, romantic." She handed Lauretta a beer and poured herself a rum, and they went to the gallery and flopped into chairs. The May humidity encased them like a second skin.

"Let's review who's got what," Els said. She held her sweating glass to her cheek. "I'll get Fred to build a bar in the lounge. You and Eulia will scout out the kitchen and service equipment. I bet the Resort has cast-offs we could get for a song. You'll get the licenses and insurance rolling, but I'll go meet all the bureaucrats. If they're going to run my life, I want to look them in the eye." She rattled her ice cubes. "I'll paint the furniture, a sign for the gate, and a big portrait of Jack for above the bar."

"What about the food?" Lauretta said.

"Eulia's been recipe testing like mad. Come for lunch sometime and join the jury."

"We'll never get this joint open in three months."

"We'll start small in late August, maybe dinners a few nights a week, and build to a fuller schedule when the season opens."

"It's dead empty here then," Lauretta said. "You got some magic plan for getting customers into those romantic, mismatched chairs during hurricane season, with the Resort still closed?"

Els swigged her rum. "Counting on your genius to create the buzz," she said. "We've got to build a base of locals. Have promotions for the taxi drivers, concierges. Advertise. What else can you do to launch a business?"

"Pray," Lauretta said. She sipped her beer. "This is going to be one long, hot summer."

part six

CHAPTER 32

Nevis, West Indies

September 2000

In Horseshoe Jack's first weeks, business was spotty and plagued by power outages, an island-wide shortage of bottled gas, and a tropical storm billed as minor that dumped rain for two days. Els struggled to become a gracious hostess and competent bartender, and once she'd mastered classic cocktails using Jack's tattered *Old Mr. Boston* as a guide, she branched out into signature drinks for the pub, including Jack's Rum Wallop, her riff on Sunshine's lethal Killer Bee. Her role as bar wench took so much concentration that she swore off drinking whenever patrons were on the property.

Eulia hired her cousin Genevra and a friend named Luleesha as her kitchen and wait staff. Together they pushed the makeshift kitchen to produce inventive dishes that pleased the locals without intimidating the visitors. Lauretta's PR campaign succeeded in getting one dessert, an improbably light cornmeal and pumpkin concoction served on a sculpted banana leaf, featured in a glossy tourist magazine. Eulia had dubbed it "honkie conkie" but instructed her girls never to call it that in front of a guest, and they all hooted with laughter. Els didn't get the joke.

One morning Pinky appeared with a lumpy sack of charcoal he'd smoldered in a pit on the mountain and, after a negotiation with Eulia, was installed as the grill master.

"He cookin' over charcoal and wood his whole life," Eulia said.

"We cannae have the guests see him looking like that," Els said.

"Buy him some shorts," Eulia said. "I gon' cut he hair. We give him one a' them pub T-shirts you gettin' made up, who gon' know he live in a shack in de bush?"

Thereafter, Pinky also took over firing off Bessie at sunset, and Els flew Jack's flag whenever the pub was open, floodlighting it after dark to be sure it was visible from Oualie.

Vivian's church friends started dropping in for lunch or tea. Finney asked permission to return the domino table to its former place of honor under the mango tree. Soon, a group of older men began playing there, joking it up and nursing their beers. Expats dribbled in to try this new addition to their short list of dining options, but none had yet returned. Though Lauretta kept insisting traffic would pick up, Els became obsessed with the daily cash flow, which was alarmingly in the red.

Early in one lunch shift, when the domino players were chatting up the kitchen girls and laying out the bones, Finney finished cleaning snapper for dinner, stepped out onto the patio, surveyed the lunch crowd, and said, "Trouble, Els."

Els delivered her tray of drinks and followed his gaze.

"Them guys at the orange table," he said. "The big one wid the stylish shirt and mouth like a fish is Viv's older brother Eugene. The one with all them freckles, that her younger brother Clarence."

"Introduce me," Els said.

Despite her effusive welcome, neither man rose or shook hands. Eugene slid his sunglasses down his nose and looked her over. Clarence nodded and grinned, rather idiotically, she thought. When she offered them drinks on the house as members of Finney's family, Eugene smiled, an important man smile.

"Hear you two real cozy," Eugene said. "Finney, you got a nice little house, nice boat, catch all pre-sold. Looks like you got yourself a benefacture."

"Or maybe a little luck flowing my way for a change."

"You want to keep it flowing," Eugene said. "You know what I'm sayin'?" He jutted his chin toward the domino men. "Dem say you got meetings here most every day."

"They're just playing dominoes," Els said. "And bragging about the fast women and cars of their youth."

"What you think, fool?" Finney said. "Those old guys is hatching a plot to toss out you party?"

Eugene shrugged. "Anything can happen over dominoes."

Els glanced around the unusually busy restaurant, anxious to attend to other guests.

"You here to ask after Viv, or maybe you on official gorment business?" Finney said.

"How she doin?" Clarence said.

"She sleepin' now. Got all the comforts." Finney tipped his head toward Toad Hall.

Eugene shrugged again. Clarence continued to smile.

"Try de soup," Finney said, stepping away. "Eulia make it from Viv's recipe."

"Tell Viv to talk some sense into you," Eugene called.

"She give up on that long ago," Finney called back.

"S'long, Bobo," Eugene called, and he and Clarence laughed.

Els followed Finney to the court, stopped him, and searched his face.

"'Bobo Johnny' what Nevis people call Anguillans they wish to insult," Finney said. "It mean we backward, gullible. Eugene been tryin' to get me vex wid dat since we first meet. One time I rough him up about it, but Viv make me promise no more fighting."

When Eugene and Clarence had finished their meal and started down the drive without comment or farewell, Genevra called from the patio. "Els, water quit again."

"Pretend you upset long as Eugene watching," Finney whispered to Els. "I go switch over to the cistern. Doan let on we got a backup."

"What are you implying?" Els said.

"Lotta reasons water might stop flowin'," Finney said. "None a' them the water's idea."

At half three, when the last table had asked for their check and the domino men had left for their siestas, Els found Finney sitting in the shade behind Toad Hall mending a cast net.

"Are the domino players putting my business in danger?" she asked.

"Mr. Big just paranoid," Finney said.

"Enough to engineer a water stoppage?"

"Could be coincidence," Finney said. "You want me tell them doan come no more?"

The domino men were fun to have around, and on Friday nights when the old league turned out and they set up extra tables, they drew a crowd. Els didn't want to lose those liquor sales.

"Just tell them no politics," she said.

"Politics in everything," Finney said. "What bank you use, where you buy you groceries." He tightened a knot and cut the thread. "I tell them no loose talk. None a' we want anyting do you."

CHAPTER 33

As Lauretta had promised, the jewelry shop in San Juan was full of glittering cruise passenger bait. A smartly dressed Mr. Hidalgo ushered Els to a conference room, and while he inspected each of her items, she caught herself tapping her nails—manicured for the first time in months—and knotted her hands in her lap.

"The diamonds are excellent quality," he said, and arranged the pieces on his velvet board—two pairs of earrings, a three-stone pendant, and a tennis bracelet, all consolation gifts to herself. She'd kept only the stud earrings she was wearing. "The necklace and ring . . ." He gave a shrug of regret. "I could be interested in those only for the stones."

She poked at her great-grandmother's matinee necklace, a lattice of rubies and diamonds she'd worn exactly once: on New Year's Eve to welcome in the new century, alone but for Jack's appearance. She picked up the ring. "My grandmother wore this every day." A family heirloom of generations, the ring was a cabochon star sapphire surrounded by diamonds. The portraitist of The Beatrice had perfectly rendered its glint.

"A treasure to you," he said. "But I cannot foresee a customer for it."

Thinking of Beatrice's feistiness, she sat taller and slipped the ring onto her finger. "Give me your best price for the rest."

The airport restaurant's glacially slow service left her staring through its windows into a corridor full of tourists, departing ones bronzed and pink, arriving ones pale. A very tall, very black man walked by with two pink men dressed like American bankers on casual Friday. He wore a form-fitting blue dress shirt and pressed slacks and carried an alligator briefcase. What arrested her were his hair twists, which were caught in a thick ponytail that fell halfway down his back.

Jason. Barely recognizable without the crocheted muffin hat and sunglasses.

Unable to get the waiter's attention, she chugged the rest of her wine, stuck some cash under the salt shaker, and hurried out. The men were clustered near an exit door, laughing and clapping each other's shoulders as they parted. Jason's back was to her. "Thanks for making time, guys," he said. "Enjoy the golf and give my regards to Hank." His Jamaican accent and patois had disappeared; he sounded like an educated northeasterner.

She followed him to the Nevis departure gate, where he leaned against a pillar and opened a prospectus.

"I thought *Iguana* was still plying the Mediterranean," she said. When he looked up, there was a flicker in his black eyes. "Is Liz back too?"

"He in St. Maarten," he said. "You enjoyin' a little taste a' the States after all deez months in paradise?"

"Merchandising Jack's gift shop," she said. "I've just spent a bloody fortune on logo T-shirts." She looked him over. "Did you take lessons from the Italians on how to clean up your act? And from those Americans about how to speak like a Yank?"

He studied her, perhaps debating his reply, stuck the prospectus under his arm, and grabbed his briefcase. "Let's sit over there," he said, no trace of the Jamaican accent.

She chose a seat. When he sat, he left an empty seat between them and put his briefcase on it.

"Who the hell are you, anyway?" she said.

He looked across the terminal. "Liz and I argued about you this summer. He's wanted you to know about our business for some time."

She thought of all those shadowy men, the roll of cash, the whispered conversations. Here it was, the truth she'd been denying, that would dash all her fantasies.

"Ever since you called him a rental captain, it's been bugging him that you think we're just employees of some fat cat." He looked at her. "We own *Iguana*."

"He could have told me that himself."

"I didn't trust you enough," he said. "But he does, in spite of anything I say. And he doesn't trust easily." He shifted in his chair. "He doesn't need some spoiled rich girl leading him on and running home when things get tough."

"Nevis *is* home."

"You don't know the first thing about what you're getting into. The undercurrents, the politics. You better watch who you associate with."

"Including you?" she asked. "Including Liz? Who appointed you his keeper?"

"He's easily hurt."

"And I'm in no hurry to let myself get fucked over by some sailor who's never around."

He looked at her, challenge in his black eyes. "Then you and I both hope your little business adventure succeeds. Give you your own life. On land."

"I have every intention of achieving that," she said. She pulled on her shawl against the aggressive air-conditioning. "Why does he trust *you*?" she said. "A guy with a fake patois who pretends to be from Jamaica?"

"Jamaica, Queens," he said. "But my mother grew up in the hills above Montego Bay. We spoke creole, *patois*, as you call it, at home."

"A chameleon," she said. The charge could as easily be leveled at her, sliding as she did from brogue to Brit to American inflection, depending on the circumstance.

"Change your accent," he said, "you're still black. But sometimes I prefer to appear more black than others."

She glanced at the prospectus he'd tossed on top of his briefcase. "Those gringos give you a little bedtime reading?" She watched him weigh his answer.

"They're fund managers from Boston, here on a boondoggle. I flew home early to meet with them." He turned to look at her, held her gaze. "I manage money for private clients."

He was wearing Italian loafers, no socks. She'd never seen him in anything but flip-flops.

"I discounted it as pure boast when Liz called you a financial whiz," she said. "I'm not alone in assuming you deal drugs."

"Ah, assumptions," he said. "I deal only money. And use some of the proceeds for micro-lending."

"A loan shark."

There was that flicker in his eyes again. "You also assume usury," he said. "My rates are a few basis points over prime. My clients are people like Finney. The working poor. Fifty bucks here, a couple of hundred there. The banks won't give them the time of day."

She rearranged her shawl. "If you're any good at investing, why put up with the likes of Salustrio and your other charter clients?"

"*Iguana* and my investment business are mutually beneficial," he said. "But she's a separate division that Liz runs. He isn't happy long anywhere but at sea."

At the pre-boarding announcement for their flight, he dumped the prospectus into his briefcase and she feared he'd clam up.

"So Liz taught you to sail," she said.

"When I decided it was time to leave New York," he said, "I wanted to explore my Caribbean roots, and sailing was a way to know the whole region. I couldn't tie a single knot, but I signed on with any boat that would hire me, worked my way up. Who'd think a big black guy could be invisible, but for most of the charter clients, I could have been part of the mast. They discussed their business openly."

"Eavesdropping for investment tips."

"Not my fault if the Man assumes I'm too ignorant to understand what he's saying. I learned how those guys thought, where the value was, the risk. I studied hard, got strategic, made smart buys."

Els straightened and leaned away. "Mother of God."

"What?"

"You've involved Liz in insider trading."

Jason looked at her. "The only time I got even close to that—the *only* time—was when we had a bunch of British M&A guys aboard, totally shit-faced and arguing *indiscreetly* about a possible merger involving a company already in my portfolio. I did my homework and decided it warranted a bigger investment, merger or not. That deal cratered, but eventually another company bought them. Big payday. Liz and I bought *Iguana* with the proceeds." He chuckled. "She was a wreck then. We practically stole her. Finney and Jack helped us restore her."

"Does Liz have a double life too?"

"People believe what they want."

"But you actually mislead people."

"I never said one untruth to you."

"You've barely said anything to me."

"Smart mon know silence doan betray him," he said, waggling his head, then dropped the accent. "Silence leaves room for the imagination. You're like all the other visitors. You make up our stories for us based on your own fantasies. If you know the truth about us, we aren't so picturesque."

She pulled her shawl tighter. "What's your deal with Liz?"

"He and I own *Iguana* 30/70."

"He's a minority captain, then."

"But the better sailor. Besides, he's lousy at taking orders. We share all the decisions. I take care of his money."

"Of which he has a lot, I'm sure, no small thanks to you."

"Would I violate client confidentiality with such an indiscretion?"

"Would it violate your *ethics* to tell me how you two came to be partners?"

"You'll have to get that story from Liz," he said, sliding on his sunglasses. Her face was reflected unflatteringly, all nose, in their lenses.

"Hiding behind those sunglasses may be the most irritating thing you do," she said.

"Being irritating is something we have in common. That and knowing how to make money work." He handed her a business card: *Iguana Nevis Holdings, LLC*, with addresses in Charlestown and San Juan.

The agent announced their flight. Jason motioned her ahead and took his time joining the queue. The last passenger to board the shuttle, he hung on a strap near the door and was already halfway to the plane when she stepped out of the bus. He was bent over the prospectus when she passed by in the aisle.

On the flight home, she replayed their past exchanges and couldn't catch Jason in a lie. She mulled over those men in the shadows, customers of a sort she'd never imagined. Staring out at the clouds, she thought about Liz, the rental captain and self-proclaimed water rat who had seemed so rootless—homeless save for his berth on *Iguana*, which she'd assumed was a condition of his job but now realized was his choice. Exiled from his country and family, leading a life afloat and alone, a man with roiling anger and an obsession with the dead. None of that squared with the boyish man, the bearer of impulsive gifts.

When Nevis appeared in a break between the clouds, she gazed down at its white-laced reefs and the mountain's rumpled green folds and felt as excited as she had when flying home to New York and catching sight of the skyscrapers of Manhattan with their grids of light against the night sky.

CHAPTER 34

Els was sitting in the leather chair, a yellow pad on her knee and a calculator and dinner plate on the chair's wide arm, humming along with Billie Holiday's "God Bless the Child." The aroma of garlic and fish from her half-eaten dinner lured Susie; without looking up from her lists and calculations, Els shooed the puppy away each time she nosed the plate.

"Glad you're no longer subsisting on Cheez Ums, sweet."

Els jumped. The plate slid to the floor. Susie dove for the fish bones and Els grabbed her collar. "Could you figure out a way to announce yourself that doesn't startle the shit out o' me?" she asked, leaning down to pick the bones off the carpet.

"Leave some old chains by the door and I'll drag them in, or maybe ring a bell, like Marley," he said. He was standing in the dim light near the refectory table. His hair was on end, his beard unkempt.

"I thought you'd disappeared forever," she said.

"Or maybe you wished it."

"Not without a proper goodbye."

"Nobody else got one." He stepped closer to the light. His eyes were bloodshot, darkly circled. "Most expats go away in the heat of summer, why not me?"

"There have been days this bloody summer when I might have fled back to London just to get a proper bath, if I'd had the money."

"Maybe now you appreciate my waterworks, all the Aladdin lamps," he said. "You have to be prepared here to bounce back a century without notice. Good move, though, resurrecting the water system and buying that generator."

"A costly necessity. We can't close every time the current clicks off."

He gazed at the refectory-table-turned-souvenir-shop: T-shirts with the pub's logo, a version of his likeness on the flag with the cigar and horseshoe. His nude photos and Els's flower paintings made into notes and postcards. Vivian and Eulia's cookbook. He walked to the bar and gazed at his portrait, a swashbuckling counterpoint to The Beatrice. "Your preoccupations have changed."

"The pub is more than a preoccupation." She stroked Susie's ears. "You're jealous."

"Jealousy," he said. "The only vice that gives no pleasure. I swore off it long ago." He picked up a postcard with an image of the flag and the legend *I got walloped at Jack's.* "You've filled my—our—house with boozy life again, gotten my best work out there. My little measure of immortality. How could I be jealous of that?"

She stared at him, sipped her drink. He looked less substantial than in earlier visits, his shirt a misty blur. "Have you been spying on my customers?"

"Who could resist?" he said. "All these people drawn to the legend of Horseshoe Jack? Whispering to each other about illicit sex, political overthrow?"

"Sex I'll grant you, but overthrow's a bit dramatic."

"You watch out for those domino guys or your fine establishment might suddenly start having trouble with the powers that be."

"They're just playing and watching the girls."

"Don't bet on it. Power is money here, and don't you forget it. You flirt with the opposition and see what happens."

"I'm not flirting with anything. I'm just trying to run a business."

"My point precisely," he said. "You're not just a white private citizen anymore. Pay attention that you don't get on the wrong side of power."

"Why shouldn't they push for Nevis independence?" she asked. "I don't see that we get much out of being yoked to St. Kitts."

"You need to stay the hell out of all that."

"Did ye come back just to warn me where not to stick my nose?"

"Partly." He gazed at the carpet. "It was two years today that I died."

September 21: the autumn equinox and the day Hurricane Georges slammed into Nevis in 1998.

"Damn, I should have observed the anniversary," she said. "A special night at the pub, drinks half-price at sunset in celebration of a life recklessly lived."

"There's always next year," he said. "Stoke the legend. Should be good for business."

She looked up at him but couldn't catch his eye. "Jack, how insensitive of me." She stood up and Susie huddled against her shins. "I never knew the exact date." She picked up her drink, decided a toast was inappropriate, and crossed her arms. "It's only just occurred to me that there's no marker for you."

He shrugged. "Even if you plant us, we dead don't hang around some graveyard address you can visit."

In the family plot at Cairnoch, she'd sought her beloved spirits in the keening wind, piney scent, stones ancient and new, and had always drawn strength from their presence. She thought to argue with Jack, but he was sliding in and out of focus, and she knew it couldn't be the fault of her few sips of rum. She swirled her slivers of ice, trying to pin down what made him so ephemeral.

"Your death," she said. "What was it like?"

"Falling," he said. "No, being pulled head over heels, arms

wheeling, down the drain. I was standing there on the wall, daring the storm and thinking about jumping, and then a gust of wind hit me from behind, and my feet went out from under me and the wave grabbed me and I thought, *Oh shit, I'm going to be ground to a pulp on those rocks.* Vain to the last gasp, I imagined what a disgusting corpse I'd make. Luckily, the sea decided to keep me." He looked at the slowly turning ceiling fan. "I always wondered where the fish went in a big storm. I called out for them and they were all around me, squirming like salmon against the current, bumping me with their bellies, slapping me with their tails. An enormous grouper sped by in the murk, looking surprised, and said, 'Mon, this is far out,' and then my clothes dragged me down and the water was the color of slate and there was froth everywhere. When I stopped trying to swim it got easier, and I just rolled and rolled and rolled."

A cock crowed in the distance and another challenged it.

"And that was it," she whispered.

"The end of Jack as we knew him."

The case clock scrabbled into action, and they looked away from each other until it finished its nine bongs.

"I have dreams where the water is dark and all I can see is faint gray light way far above me," she said. "My arms are pinned, my clothing is pulling me down. I wake up in a panting sweat. Do you think I'm imagining my death?"

"How would I know?" he said. "I certainly never imagined mine. I imagined a funeral, witnessed Tom Sawyer style, where I could hear all the sweet and sappy things people would say about me and see all the weeping women try to throw themselves into the grave. But the moment of death, no." He stepped closer, haggard in the lamplight. "Whatever you imagine won't be what happens anyway."

"Were you planning suicide?"

"Who isn't?" he said. "We all have to go sometime. Better at fifty and in reasonable shape than drooling and peeing in your pants. You wouldn't be nearly so receptive if I appeared with a walker."

"What's changed to make you so fragile tonight?" she asked.

"That has more to do with you than with me, sweet. I was bound to lose my charm sooner or later. Story of my life with women." He backed into the shadows near the kitchen stairs.

Susie took a step after him and let out three tentative barks. Els reached for her collar and when she looked up, Jack had disappeared.

CHAPTER 35

Els and Eulia huddled at the domino table, Els scribbling columns of figures and drawing arrows and boxes to answer Eulia's questions. The air seemed to be stockpiling moisture in preparation for hurling another September storm their way. Genevra was in the kitchen with the radio turned low, but now and again preaching or a hymn drifted to their ears.

Finney lumbered across the court carrying his bucket. "Boat payment due yesterday," he said. "Wha'appen nobody here?"

"Eulia and I decided we can only serve three nights a week," Els said. "At least until the Resort reopens."

"That new road mess gotta be keeping people away too," Finney said. "You wanna get here from Oualie today you gotta walk."

The road project's path of destruction inched daily closer to Jack's, shaving front lawns to leave houses almost teetering at the curb, removing hairpin curves at the ghauts, and creating straightaways that would invite even worse speeding. Protective of what had so charmed her about Nevis, Els was ambivalent about the government's "improvements."

"Maybe I'll sue the government for business disruption," she said, thinking of how the construction must be enriching Eugene and what pleasure he might take in sending a layer of dust over everything at the pub.

Finney pulled US bills from his shorts pocket and flattened them on the table. "Double installment. Now the *Maid* really mine."

Els weighted the bills with her glass. The hundred dollars was significant money to Finney, but a drop in the sea of her debt. "When we first inked this little business relationship, I thought I'd see you only when the payments were due. Now you're practically family."

"Zat true?" Finney said, and though he smiled, Jason's taunt returned to her. She had to admit that her need to snuggle into the Flemings' lives vastly exceeded their need for her shelter and patronage. Now that Vivian had regained so much of her strength, Els wondered when Finney's independence or Vivian's pride would send them back to the Westbury house.

She poured Finney a glass of the iced tea mixed with bitter orange juice that the pub would feature as long as the crop held.

"Good lobster catch today," he said. "I sell it all to Cobb, thinkin' you not here." He sat down and took a gulp of the tea. "You can call him. Jason limin' down there, he can bring some up."

"Is Liz back too?"

He nodded. "Jason say Liz comin' up for dinner tonight, bringin' the Jammer crew."

In the four months since she'd seen him, she'd tried to put Liz out of her mind, but there had been many days when she'd gazed out to sea imagining *Iguana's* huge sail heading for Oualie. The prospect of seeing him raised her jitters a notch.

"I'll surely need those lobsters, then," she said. "We have a big family party from Golden Rock. It's so bugger-all hard to plan, but maybe that's to be expected until a place catches on. Or doesn't."

"We goin' do fine once we get that new cooler," Eulia said. "She teaching me the business, Daddy. Today we studyin' financial planning. It gon' take a lotta cookin' to pay for all the stuff we got to buy. Even that old walk-in we can get from the Resort. They askin' three thousand for it. US."

"Better snatch it," Finney said. "You get a new one, gorment grab most a' that in duty before you get it down the wharf."

"Jack's got a cash flow problem," Eulia said, rolling out the words like a schoolgirl testing new vocabulary. "I just tellin' her she gotta axe Jason."

"Miss not like ar we," Finney said. "She can go to the bank."

Maybe not, Els thought. "Eulia claims he's an understanding lender," she said.

"Understandin' got nothin' to do with it," Finney said. "He got to know you honest, one. Then you mus' convince him you got a sure plan for de money." He drank the rest of his tea. "From time to time a lotta us cyan make it widout him. If he agree to help you, that make you local, fuh sure."

Half an hour later, Jason pulled into the court, lifted Finney's cooler from his truck bed, and said, "Lobsta fuh you tourists." He carried the cooler into the kitchen and emerged with a beer, strolled to their table, and sat down.

"Is okay I take this, payment fuh the delivery?" he said.

"Fair enough," Els said.

"You welcome." He took a long pull on the beer.

"Els need axe you for a loan," Eulia said.

"I need nothing of the kind." Els gathered the pages.

Eulia jabbed a finger at the yellow pad. "You gon' listen to your new *minority partner*?"

Jason's eyebrow lifted over his sunglasses.

"I offered her a profit-sharing scheme to keep her from jumping ship back to the Resort," Els said. Eulia shot Jason a look full of pride and mischief. Els refilled her glass even though the caffeine and sugar were already making her buzzy.

"You choose a perfect partner," Jason said.

"If you doan tell he about the stuff we need, I do it myself," Eulia said. "I ain't cooking my tits off for nothin'."

"We'll manage," Els said.

"We flat-ass broke," Eulia said. "Worse." She dropped to a whisper. "We ain't got enough to pay the girls beyond Saturday, and I ain't layin' off my own cousin."

Els slowly handed her calculations to Jason. "It took everything I had left to get us this far," she said. "If we don't get proper refrigeration and replace that relic of a cooker, Eulia can't feed a full house. We should add a pavilion in the garden for extra tables and build a guest loo so Finney and Vivian can have their privacy back. I've done cost and revenue projections by activity—pub, gift shop, even weddings."

Jason studied the pages while she finished her second glass of tea and poured a third.

"Forget it," she said. "Give those back."

"What the rest a' you financial picture?" he asked.

"I said, give them back. I want nothing from you."

"Then I got me a fool for a partner," Eulia said. "Unless you thinking somebody gon' give you big money for Missus Beatrice, them Haring squiggles, or the other weird pictures up there."

Bananaquits ganged on the plate of brown sugar on the patio tipped their heads to shovel up grains. Something spooked them and they burst away.

"When the renovations soaked up just about all I had left," Els said, "I borrowed against the house to outfit the pub. I'd never had a penny of debt before."

"All bankers should try the borrower's side," he said. "See how it feel."

She tried to gauge his irony, but he was stone-faced. "I can't make the payments right now, much less invest in the business. I risk losing my home."

"How much you need?"

"One thirty-five," she said. "US."

Eulia looked at her. "You ain't borrowing all that against *our* restaurant?"

"Welcome to the concept of leverage," Els said. "It's what makes the world spin."

"I go tink about it," Jason said.

"Who said I want your help?" Els said.

Jason finished his beer. "I give you a answer tomorrow."

Eulia followed him to the truck. They stood in animated but hushed discussion for a few minutes. When he drove away, she returned with compressed lips and spoke little for the rest of the day.

Els was working the bar, her head pounding, while Genevra and Luleesha waited tables and Pinky manned the grill. When Liz appeared with the windjammer crew, she'd been too busy to do more than show them to a table. The sound system pumped a mix of Jack's jazz favorites, leavened with reggae, the Beatles, and R&B, but tonight she longed for a little Debussy or Vivaldi.

"Yer table will be ready in a jiff," she said to a waiting group's white-haired paterfamilias, pouring on the brogue that always eased a crisis. On the patio, Liz and the crew had finished their meal and were on their third round of beers. She beckoned Liz to the court.

He walked over to her, the torches bathing his face in amber light.

"A round on the house if you'll finish yer drinking in the lounge," she said. "I'm desperate for that table."

"Deal," he said. "You look a little fried. Let me take over the bar for a while."

"That's beyond the call," she said, wondering what Jason had told him and if the two of them might feel entitled to horn in if they decided to invest.

He smiled his gee-whiz smile. Maybe Jason hadn't or wouldn't even consult him and her assumptions were working overtime again.

"If I swallow some aspirin and lie down for ten minutes," she said, "I can manage the rest of the night."

"Take as long as you need," he said. "I'm a rattling fool with a cocktail shaker."

"Call me if anyone wants their check," she said.

She never let a guest see her open the secret door; she waited until Mr. Whitehair and family were in the court before slipping upstairs.

Her waking was a kind of swimming into consciousness. When she opened her eyes, Liz was standing beside the bed. He wore an expression she'd never seen before, tender. Light from the torches danced on the gauze curtains. A Keith Jarrett arpeggio wafted from the lounge.

"I called and knocked, but you were out cold," he said. "Several parties are ready to leave. I can handle the checks."

She hadn't intended to sleep; her head felt stuffed with cotton. The headache had faded to a thickness behind her eyes. She rolled onto one elbow. "I'm fine."

He held out his hand and she took it, and he drew her up. He turned her around and massaged her shoulders, his work-roughened fingers kneading the knots in her neck, making them yield. She melted against his hands and caught his familiar scent. "Is massage another service you provide your guests, Captain?" she whispered.

"On very, very rare occasions," he whispered back. His fingers circled her neck and touched the blue bead hanging from its silver chain just below the hollow of her throat. "This becomes you," he said. "Makes your eyes more blue than stormy." He massaged her scalp, drawing the pain out through the top of her head.

"Burtie, my nanny-mother, called my eruptions 'fireworks,'" she said. She relaxed against his chest, and he crossed his arms over her waist. "I've been working very hard on being less volcanic." She leaned her head against his collarbone.

"I'm trying to tread very carefully in your space," he said.

Laughter burst from the gallery. The frog chorus sang from the ghaut.

He inhaled. "That fragrance. It's not tropical. Why can't I place it?"

"Roses," she said.

"Who'd think a guy from up north could ever forget that?" he said. "But it's all new, anyway, on you."

"Els?" Genevra called from the gallery. "People need pay dey bills."

"Right there," she called back, and moved to step out of Liz's embrace. He ran his hands up her arms, squeezed her shoulders, and let her go.

"Don't come down with me," she said.

"Why?"

"Gossip."

He grinned and sang the chorus of "Let's Give 'Em Something to Talk About." When she frowned, he said, "I'll go out the shower window."

He sat on the bed while she checked her makeup in the bathroom. When she passed the bedroom door, the light from the torches illuminated the tips of his unruly hair, but his expression was lost in shadow.

She walked over and kissed his forehead. "See you at the bar."

She loved sitting on the patio in the early morning, the light diffuse and gentle with the sun still behind the peak and the sea calm. She cursed out loud when the gate rattled. Jason had parked his truck outside and was walking up the drive.

She squared her shoulders and stood, determined not to appear as needy as she felt. "Aren't you the early bird."

"I'm busy later."

"And your answer is?"

He gestured to the chairs behind her. "Can we sit down?"

She nodded. "Tea or coffee?"

"No time for that." He settled into a patio chair and removed his sunglasses. "I'll do the deal."

She looked toward the sea. A tiny sail—surely Finney in the *Maid*—was already far beyond the protection of Oualie. "I detect a 'but' in your tone."

"There are conditions."

"I'd be a fool not to expect that."

He teased a hatpin with a lion's head from the ribbing of his hat and reinserted it. "I want a piece of the action."

A lamb or kid bleated; she sat up straight, fearing one might have gotten into the garden, but caught sight of it scampering down the road.

"I need a loan, not a partner," she said.

"We'll all be better off if we treat this as an investment."

She stood up and paced. "Next thing I know, you'll be telling me how to run things."

"I already have several businesses to run."

"Does Liz know about this?"

"It's not his capital," he said. "But I'll tell him if you accept the deal."

She hugged herself and looked out to sea, wondering how or if Liz figured into his thinking. "Why are you doing this?"

"It's convenient for one of my investors to stash some money," he said. "If there's a tax loss for a year or two, that would be welcome."

She bristled at the implication that Jack's would be in the red that long. "Would it have anything to do with making sure I don't hightail it back to the UK?"

A hint of a smile. "Nevis needs this kind of business."

"Give me a minute," she said.

She walked through the garden and citrus grove to the back fence, the highest point on the property, and looked down at her home—the sturdy house, the gardenias gleaming in the sun, Toad Hall, the cascade of bougainvillea at the secret garden, the lilies of the Nile bursting from the copper, the wide swath of sea and St. Kitts. She threw a rotting lime as hard as she could into the bush and heard it strike leaves and thud to the ground. Then she gathered the ripe limes and returned to the patio, where she set the yellow-green fruits on the table. Jason had helped himself to a glass of water. She felt a wash of anger and wondered just how proprietary he might become.

"I'll cut you into the business but not the real estate," she said.

A little smile. "I expected you to say that." He picked up two of the limes and rolled them in his huge hand. "The business isn't worth much by itself. Yet." He spilled the limes onto the table, caught them before they rolled off, and lined the harvest up in a row. He sat back and looked at his handiwork. "Can't separate Jack's from Jack's."

She turned her back and watched the mountain doves chase each other around the court while she took deep breaths and tried to quell her mental noise. "I guess I have a new partner, then," she said.

"An excellent one," he said.

She bit back a remark about his arrogance.

He stood up and extended his hand. His long fingers closed around hers more gently than she expected. When he released her, she leaned against a pergola support, suddenly woozy. While he spoke of having his Puerto Rico staff draft up the agreement, she stared into the garden, puzzling at her simultaneous rush of relief, hope, and apprehension. Her home and livelihood were secure for now, but with what future strings or entanglements, she could not guess.

"We'll keep it as simple as possible," he said, and left her. She watched him go through the gate and drive away, then gathered up the limes and carried them into the kitchen.

CHAPTER 36

The bonfire shot sparks into the night sky, and its glow turned the beachfront palms into shaggy silhouettes. Liz parked Wilma behind the cooking shed, came around to the passenger side, and opened Els's door. He took her hand and led her toward the blaze, where dancers kicked and shimmied in the sand.

She hadn't visited Sunshine's in months, and the bar, rebuilt more sturdily since Lenny leveled it, had already taken on the quirky ambiance of its predecessor.

"Bee?" Liz asked. She nodded and he plunged into the scrum at the bar, high-fiving and shaking hands as he went.

When he'd invited her to dinner on his last night in port before charters would keep him away most of the time until Christmas, she'd debated what to wear and settled on her batik sundress and the blue bead. She sat on the end of a picnic table bench and stared at the flames, enjoying the fire's warmth when the sea breeze ruffled her hair.

Liz returned with their drinks, sat on the opposite bench, and looked into the fire. After several minutes he rapped his beer bottle on the table and said, "Let's dance."

When they joined the dancers near the fire, the sand was warm on the surface, cool underneath. Elvis was rocking and twanging about his burning love. Liz pulled her into his embrace and ignored the beat. Resting her chin on his shoulder, her lips close to his ear, she inhaled and then let her breath out in a sigh that caused him to draw her even closer.

"You know I ran into Jason in San Juan," she said, trying for a casual tone.

"He told me about the loan, too, but it's none of my business."

"He's raised as many questions as he's answered."

He spun her under his arm and back into his embrace so her back was to him. "I guess it's my turn, then." He spun her out again and gathered her chest to chest. "What do you want to know?"

She pulled away enough to look into his eyes. "He refused to tell me how you and he met, became partners. How you came to be here."

The song ended, but he continued to hold her and sway gently in place. "Let's go for a walk," he said.

Hand in hand, they walked to Charlestown and back, and he told her he'd been a huge disappointment to his corporate executive father because he dreamed of being a rock musician and a sailor. He'd messed about in boats from the age of seven, anything to be on the water and away from his suffocating mother. A summer crewing job on a superyacht led to a winter berth in St. Thomas. He'd dropped out of Wesleyan in the middle of his junior year and sailed the Caribbean ever since.

"I never saw my mother again," he said. "She died about fifteen years ago. I thought I'd try to reconcile with Dad this past Christmas, while there was still time, but he lay there with tubes coming out of him and got all red in the face and said he no longer considered me family."

They were nearing the bonfire, its shrunken remains glowing. The bar was still crowded, and the aroma of grilled chicken and fish hung on the breeze. The music was Motown. He led her to the trunk of a fallen palm where they could sit facing the water. The firelight burnished the right side of his face.

"How is following the call of the sea a disownable offense?" she asked.

A dinghy crossed the moon's path and its wake set the masthead lights bobbing against the black sky. "I chose an unacceptable woman," he said. "He accused me of wanting to pollute the family bloodlines."

"That sounds like something out of another century."

"He was an unapologetic bigot," he said. He sifted a handful of sand through his fingers. "Okay, here goes," he said. "Dora was part Arawak, part Venezuelan, part Portuguese, raised in Miami. She was a tiny thing, barely five feet. But fiery, a bundle of enthusiasms. As far as my father was concerned, she was a nigger, and when he called her that, we stopped speaking."

He picked up a stick and began drawing in the sand between his feet—a child's rendering of a sailboat. "Dora and I sold everything we owned to buy a small sloop named *Feather.* The plan was to sail her to Venezuela and get married in Dora's grandfather's village. She was pregnant, barely showing."

The story came out haltingly. When they were just north of the Los Roques archipelago heading for Bonaire, they were overtaken by pirates in a speedboat who'd mistaken *Feather* for a boat carrying drugs. The pirates spoke little English and Dora knew some Spanish. Holding Liz and Dora at gunpoint, they ransacked the cabin, and when they didn't find any drugs, the leader grabbed Dora and ripped open her shirt. Liz knocked him down. The other two pirates grabbed Liz, and one of them hit him with the butt of his rifle.

"When I came to, I was sitting on top of the cabin," Liz said. "My torso was bound to the mast with duct tape. They'd taped my wrists and mouth, and I could taste blood and my right eye was swollen shut."

He propped his forehead on the back of his hand for a few seconds, then gave his shoulders a little shake and began speaking again in a softer voice.

He described how the pirate leader instructed the others to hold Dora and began to unzip his jeans. She clawed at her captors, screaming in a mixture of English and Spanish, and when the leader stepped closer, she kicked him hard in the genitals and he doubled over. When he recovered, he grabbed a gun and shot her twice in the abdomen. She crumpled onto the deck. Liz yelled against the tape. The pirate smiled, flicked open a switchblade, and cut a zigzag on Liz's calf that healed into that lightning bolt scar. Laughing, the pirates got back in their boat and set *Feather* adrift.

"Dora couldn't move to cut me loose," Liz said. "We stared at each other until her eyes closed. It took her hours to bleed out."

The music shifted to Etta James belting out "Tell Mama," and he cocked his head to listen. He'd drawn a stick figure next to the mast on the sailboat. He erased the drawing with his foot. "If I hadn't been such a goddamned hothead and gone for the guy, maybe . . . ."

He looked out at the boats long enough that Els thought he might end the story there. Etta switched to a yearning ballad backed by dissonant horns. He tapped a few bars on his knee.

"Jason was delivering a boat to Aruba and came upon us," he said. "I don't know how long we'd been drifting."

He said that the rest of Jason's crew regarded *Feather* as a cursed death ship and wanted nothing to do with her, but when Jason came aboard and saw Liz was alive, he sent the other boat on its way and sailed *Feather* after them. He took gentle care of Liz and cleaned up the boat. He washed Dora's body and, praying over her the whole time, wrapped her in a sheet and put her in a sail bag. Liz wanted to slip the bag over the side, but Jason persuaded him that dealing squarely with the police in Aruba was the best course.

Liz was so weak he could barely trim a sheet on the run to Aruba. Once there, Jason dealt with the authorities, arranged for the sale of *Feather*, which Liz never wanted to see again, and got them berths on a crew delivering a ketch to St. Kitts. From there he took Liz home to Nevis. Along the way, they scattered Dora's ashes at sea.

A car revved its way out of the sand behind them. Liz stood up. "I need a beer."

Els pulled her knees under her skirt, gathered her shawl around her shoulders, and watched wisps of cloud scud across the moon's face.

Liz returned with his beer already half-consumed and handed her a Killer Bee. He sat closer this time, his thigh touching her elbow. He screwed his beer into the sand between his feet. "You really want to hear this?" he asked.

"Everything."

"Jason saved my life, and I don't just mean on the boat," he said. "For over a year I was drunk most of the time, got into a lot of fights. Jack and I became good buddies, but I was never a match for him in the drinking and brawling department. I crashed at his place a lot. We were both just rotting with anger."

He told her Jason repeatedly got him out of jail, got him sober, but sooner or later he'd end up on another tear. One night Jack decided they should break the Killer Bee consumption record. After the eighth, Sunshine said the rest were on the house and a crowd gathered. Jack made it to fourteen, two over the previous record, still spouting poetry, but Liz only learned that afterwards, having passed out at nine. He woke up on a picnic table the next morning. Jack was under the bar, naked, a dog licking his balls.

"I decided I'd better shape up or I'd succeed in killing myself," he said. "Which I guess is what I'd been trying to do. Jason was buying his first boat, a sweet cat. He let me earn my way into the business. We did day sails, sunset cruises. He wanted me to do the talking, said I had all the charm."

"He said he lets you pretend to be the boss."

"He and I are real clear on what's what." He took a swig of his beer. "He gave me good work at sea, which is the only place I belong.

It helped me pull myself together." He looked into her eyes. "Only the three of us know what I've just told you. Many of his debtors know how kind he is. People think what they want about him. Most of them are wrong." He looked out at the boats. "I never picked another fight or drank like that again."

"Or loved," she said.

A motor yacht with underwater lights that made it seem to float in a private emerald pool slipped its anchor and headed for St. Kitts, twinkling like a small liner.

"Or loved." He set his beer on the sand again and cradled it with his feet. He showed his teeth. "I could have gotten this fixed," he said, running his finger over the broken front tooth that gave his grin a cartoonish air. "I barely notice the eyebrow scar anymore, but then I'm not a guy who looks in the mirror much. But the tooth, I feel that all the time."

There were whoops from the bar and chants of, "Six, six, six." Liz smiled. "Some fool trying to break Jack's record. Nobody's come close." He took her hand. "I promised you lobster."

At a table made from a weathered wire spool, they sat close together facing the water. He freed her lobster from the shell, cut up the tail, and fed her the first bite with his fingers. As they ate, he coaxed out her stories: Cairnoch, Harald, Burtie, her childhood with Mallo, school, work, the chain of impulsive decisions that resulted in her self-imposed exile to Nevis and Jack's. He looked at the boats as she talked, as if studying her face would be an invasion. The bar crowd was thinning, and the Killer Bee record challenger was cheek down on a table.

"You keep touching on this Mallo guy, then changing the subject," he said.

The near-full moon, low in the western sky, was tangled among the boats, speared by the tallest mast. She felt equally impaled, as if her heart had been lanced. Whenever she mentioned Mallo's name the fury flared, and she had to tamp it back down or be unable to speak. She pulled her shawl tighter. He moved closer and put his arm around her, and she nestled into his shoulder.

"As a wee laddie, all he ever wanted was to be a soldier," she said. "Serve his Queen, return to the estate, and raise children and dogs. But at university he fell in with the separatists and became passionate about Scotland's independence."

Her hand went to her face. He entwined his fingers in hers and drew her closer. His collarbone against her ear, she counted his heartbeats.

She told him how Harald had expelled Mallo, and about their unexpected reunion nearly two years ago. "That childhood friendship boiled over into this other thing," she said. "This force. We were foolish enough to think we could keep it secret. When we hatched plans to elope, I thought Father might banish me, too, but Mallo so believed in his political future, was so sure his—our—side would eventually prevail. He was confident we could mend anything."

She looked out at the boats. Liz ran his thumb over her palm. When she was able to speak again, she told him about Mallo's death.

"At least he lived to see the act pass," she said.

Someone poured water on the remains of the fire. There was a sharp hiss. A plume of smoke rose up and covered the stars, and she watched until they twinkled through it and the sky was clear again. The breeze brought the smell of wet ashes.

"Senseless violence robbed us both," she said.

Liz tightened his arm around her and touched her chin. She settled her head against his shoulder again.

"I packed away all my feelings and dove into work," she said. "The Yanks assumed I was a workaholic with no love life, making it possible never to speak of him. To think, I traded a year I could have been married to him on the chance of a bloody promotion."

She described Burtie's death, her transfer to London, Harald's mental decline and death, and their financial ruin.

"I thought I could keep it all in, but in the months before I first came here, I began leaking emotion like a cracked bowl. I believed paralyzing grief was best shared only with a dog."

"Beats drowning it in booze," he said.

"Maybe you were smarter, going on a rampage and getting it out of your system."

"Some things neither of us will ever get out of our systems."

A couple wandered up from the beach and stood looking into the bar, then moved on.

"Jason sometimes has to remind me how hard I fought to survive on *Feather*," Liz said. "He says I have to 'embrace da choice a' life, mon.' When I slip, he's tolerant of my moods and black spells."

"I've never seen a black spell."

"Yes, you have," he said. "I get really quiet, go away. Around you, they're short."

She squeezed his hand, which was still wrapped around hers.

"Maybe you keep me from going all the way to the bottom," he said. "If I do, I can be there a long time."

"Liz," someone called from the bar, "cash up?"

He glanced at his watch. "Right there, Junior," he called. He helped Els stand up, and she leaned into him on the way to the bar.

She thought he might try to sweep her up and carry her across the court, but he folded her arm under his and guided her to the steps. Light from the kitchen window cast a golden grid onto the gravel. Her whole body was humming.

He pulled her into his arms, lifted her chin, and looked at her searchingly. He kissed her cheek so softly she barely felt it, despite yearning for it, and then he kissed her a little lower and again on the corner of her mouth. Whole minutes seemed to pass between kisses. When finally he kissed her full on the lips, she rose on her tiptoes to put her hands in his hair and held him there and returned the kiss again and again, deeper and deeper. His arms went around her back and she clung to him, her tiptoes barely touching the ground.

He loosened his grip, and she felt for her footing and laid her cheek against his chest. He kissed her hair. "I've felt protective of you from the minute I hauled you out of the water," he said. "A scared little kid trying so hard to be tough." His hand drifted to her neck, his fingers tracing the silver chain, the blue bead. "Even when you really piss me off, which is often enough, I can't forget that terrified, brave little girl for long."

The idea that he'd seen the very thing she'd struggled to conceal all her life, and that it was what bound him to her despite her moods, left her too unmasked, too confused, to form a reply.

He kissed her again, this time tenderly, lingeringly, as if her lips and mouth were a new country he wanted to explore and remember forever, then looked into her eyes. "Thanks for tonight."

He put his arm around her shoulders and walked her up to the lounge. He switched on the Chinese lamp, and in its gentle light his eyes were the color of blueberries. She sought the refectory table for balance, wondering what would, should, come next, but her head was a pudding of revelations and emotions that needed sorting. She wanted him both to leave her alone and never to leave her.

When he turned to go, she reached for his arm, and he stopped and looked at her for a long beat.

"My fantasy goes like this," he said. "We spend some unhurried time together on *Iguana*. Put that stateroom to proper use."

The fantasy was so similar to her own she almost laughed. Finally, she found her voice. "Would that be a dare, Captain?"

He grinned. "If that's what it takes." He leaned in and kissed her left eyelid. "I'll make you coffee and fresh grapefruit juice in the morning." He kissed her right eyelid. At the door he paused. "I've been thinking about that for a long time." He stepped out and closed the screen gently behind him. The frogs chanted in the still night.

CHAPTER 37

From their table in Golden Rock's garden, Els and Lauretta looked through the hedge-high poinsettias at the hazy profiles of Montserrat and Redonda.

Lauretta agitated her lemonade with her straw. "*Condé Nast Traveler* is running a piece on the Resort reopening and wants to include us in their Nevis 'must visit' list. *With* a photo. Just so you know, I've turned down two wedding requests. And I've been busting my butt to mend fences after you were so rude to that historical society woman."

"She had the cheek to pull weeds on her way up the drive," Els said. "Then she went nattering on about an encounter with Jack years ago. Said he was drunk at ten in the morning and wearing only a shirt." She sipped her iced tea. "She seemed to believe it was his civic duty to open the garden for their fund-raiser."

Lauretta twirled a curl around her index finger. "You aren't Jack. Why turn down high tea among the flowers for a bunch of ladies we'd love to have as regulars?"

When their food arrived, Els made slow business of unrolling her silverware, spreading her napkin, and tasting her snapper. Lauretta plopped ketchup onto her plate and dipped a French fry.

"Book it soon, then, before the season really kicks in," Els said.

"What's the matter with you?" Lauretta said. "You're barely listening to me."

Els stared out at Redonda and chewed a slice of cucumber. "I've invited my mother to visit."

Two weeks before her thirty-fourth birthday, she'd spent a boozy, blue evening mulling over all that had happened since she turned thirty-two, her last birthday with Mallo in the world. Though she'd found purpose again, and glimmers of a sense of belonging, she knew that immersing herself in the pub was barely keeping at bay her loneliness, and doing nothing for her blooming obsession with her mother. Before she could second-guess herself, she'd fired off a letter that said, in part, "*I can't have a life unless I understand what's happened to me, to you. I must see you and try to know you, if you'll let me. Please Mum, for this birthday, make your gift a visit.*"

Jack had appeared as she was signing the letter, read it over her shoulder, and said, "Atta girl, sweet." He'd smiled his pirate smile. "Grab life by the throat and give it a good shake." He'd looked so self-satisfied, she'd wondered if he imagined the letter his own idea. The next morning she'd gone to the Nevis philatelic bureau, selected its most beautiful tropical stamps, and posted the letter before she could chicken out.

Lauretta looked at her over her flying fish sandwich. "I thought she wouldn't budge off that *Eye-talian* island of hers."

"I begged her to come while she still can."

"She sick?"

"Fine, for all I know, but Father didn't make sixty." She pushed the snapper around her plate. "I've got questions only she can answer, I can't risk her going senile, and I want her on my turf."

"When's she coming? We'll have a party."

"In about a fortnight," Els said. "She might make the party or ruin it altogether."

With her brief acceptance letter, her mother had enclosed a color photo of herself in a flowered bathing suit that accentuated her voluptuousness. She was talking to the camera operator, a hint of flirtation in her eyes. She seemed vibrant, animated. Els pulled the christening photo out of the study desk and compared her mother's vacant expression with this flirty one, hoping the mother who visited would be the Ischia version.

Susie threw her front paws into Els's lap, and Els stroked her ears. "Dum-da-dum-dum," she sang. "Moment of truth, girl. If we're lucky."

Her mother had proposed to arrive just before Liz's next time in port, and Els was apprehensive about how this collision of her unexplained past and barely coalescing present would work out. She reached for a piece of stationery and Harald's fountain pen and wrote her reply slowly, reading over each sentence before starting the next.

When she finished, satisfied she'd cloaked her anxiety in cheery enthusiasm, she was unsure how to sign off. Her mother had closed with "*baci—G.*" Els wondered if she wanted to be addressed by her given name now, as if they were peers. She spoke it aloud, Giulietta, and tried to imagine saying it to her mother's face. Finally she scribbled, "*I can't wait. Ciao, Eleanora.*"

By midafternoon the mango shade extended to the deck of Toad Hall, where Vivian sat in her wheelchair crocheting an aqua baby blanket for the church jumble sale. Els passed around sweet iced tea and a plate of biscuits.

"Doc Lytton would scold me," Vivian said. "Find me a lemon crème, Husband."

"What we celebratin'?" Finney popped a jam tot into his mouth.

Eulia walked up the hill from the house, Peanut in tow. She carried herself in a square-shouldered, fluid way now, and the cropped hair from her Resort days had given way to a crown of braids.

Peanut threw himself at Els, and she kissed his forehead and offered him the biscuits. He took one in each hand, looked up at Eulia, and put one back.

"My mum is arriving Monday week," Els said. "I need all of you to help me get through her visit."

"She some kind of dragon lady?" Eulia asked.

"It's one of the possibilities."

"How long she stayin'?" Finney asked.

"No clue," Els said. "I've booked her a week at Oualie." She swirled her tea. "She's Italian, so I hope she's into food. Vivian and Eulia, maybe you can show her some of your specialties. Finney, would you take her snorkeling?"

"You sure she up to that?"

"She's only fifty-four. I believe she swims."

Vivian drew herself straighter. "Husband, it's time we gave Els back her cottage."

"Nonsense," Els said. "I might want to keep a little distance between Mum and me." A kestrel swooped down over the court and rose with a gecko in its talons. "She's been mentally unbalanced in the past. I've no idea what to expect."

"Nevis can have a calming power over people," Vivian said. "You know that yourself, Els."

"I need more than calm," Els said. "I need answers."

The sight of Jack leaning against the kitchen sink made her drop the container of ice cream. Susie flattened her ears and skirted where he stood, but darted over to investigate the windfall. Els shooed her away and put the container on the table.

"I can't wait to meet that mother of yours," he said.

"You stay away from her," she said. "She might be *receptive* too. The idea of the two of you conspiring is beyond unnerving."

"Then I can't wait to see *you* meet that mother of yours."

"I'm having dreams—nightmares—about it," she said, watching a moth circle the candle. "The last one wasn't even the scariest, but it was the most vivid and coherent."

She recounted being in *Iguana*'s cockpit with Liz and her mother, a Sophia Loren look-alike with big sunglasses and an ample bosom filling out her string bikini. The sea was angry, the wind blustery. Something popped and the sails began to flap. Liz shinnied up the mast and fixed whatever had broken, and when he swung back down, Giulietta gave him a sexy kiss and called him her hero and he was smiling. Giulietta put her hand on Liz's naked chest and said, "*Bellissimo.*" She grabbed Els's hair, dragged her to the rail, threw her overboard, and yelled, "You don't deserve him." The wind filled the sails and *Iguana* sped away, leaving her alone in the heaving sea.

"She may be a piece of work," Jack said, "but I doubt she's traveling halfway around the world to drown you."

"She could turn Liz against me," she said. "Or bring out my inner bitch so that I drive him off myself."

"When are you going to give Liz any credit? That boy's one determined SOB when he sets his heart on something." He stepped toward the door and started to vaporize.

"Don't leave yet," she said. "I need to talk to you about Liz."

"You need to talk to Liz about Liz."

The candle flame flattened when a gust of wind knocked it sideways, but no breeze stirred the mango leaves outside the door. She thought she saw a shape moving in the garden. When she looked out, all was still and empty.

"I would," she called, "if he would ever stay home for more than a heartbeat." She opened the near-empty carton of ice cream, ate a runny spoonful, and set the rest down for Susie.

CHAPTER 38

On the day Giulietta was to arrive, Els returned from grocery shopping in Charlestown to find her mother asleep in Jack's big chair, her bare feet on the ottoman and a half-finished glass of white wine at her elbow. Els studied her: hair a shade redder than russet, tawny skin that, in repose, was nearly without wrinkle, toe- and fingernails lacquered a deep rose. In her turmeric-colored linen dress and a Hermès scarf printed with seashells, she was elegant, alluring.

Giulietta opened her eyes and smiled. Els felt trapped by her gaze, caught in a trespass. Swinging her feet off the ottoman, her mother opened her arms and said, "El-e-a-nor-a."

Susie waggled up to her, and Giulietta cupped her muzzle and kissed it. Els felt a stab of alarm that her mother might steal the dog's affections.

When Els leaned in and pecked her mother's cheek, Giulietta grasped her face in both hands and looked it over, committing every lash and freckle to memory, before kissing her firmly on both cheeks. She gave off that exotic scent—flowers, a hint of nutmeg—that had permeated the cupboard where the paintings were hidden.

Els sat on the corner of the ottoman. "Why didn't yi call from St. Kitts so I could meet your plane?"

"I am not bothering with local coins," Giulietta said. "You didn't say your airport is so *primitivo,* but Mr. Sparrow is there. Polite fellow. He tells me all about this house, how he is the first to show it to you. He says this Jack man is a jumpy ghost. He says your restaurant is *un grande successo.* He says a sailor might be your *amore,* but you are not letting him."

"You already know more about me than I do about you," Els said.

"You want to be private," Giulietta said, "don't live on an island."

Els imagined traveling to Ischia incognito and researching her mother and wondered if her life there was an open book, if she was a local celebrity.

Giulietta pushed herself out of the chair and stepped into her wedge sandals. "You painted these, yes?" She straightened Els's watercolor of one of Pinky's offerings, the calabash bowl full of skinnips, which was propped in the bookcase. "You understand color," she said. "The sunsets and the portrait of that man—he is Jack, yes? Those are full of emotion. They pull you in. Most of the others are safe. Pretty, but safe."

"They happen to be very popular," Els said. She'd thought painting might create common ground but now saw it could be a source of competition, one her mother would always win.

"You need to paint from here," Giulietta said, placing her hand over her heart. "Not from here." She tapped her temple. Els thought of the self-portrait, which she'd imagined springing from a tortured mind, but maybe a tortured heart too. Her mother walked over to her own harborscape hanging next to the door and touched the gardenia signature. "*Cara,*" she said, "this home you have made is *bellissima.*"

Els glanced at the wine glass. "You've obviously given yourself the tour."

"The kitchen is pleasant," Giulietta said. "Cool. But the light up here is better." She stared at The Beatrice hanging over the stairs, her lips tight.

"Where's your luggage?"

"In frog house," Giulietta said. "When we arrive, your friends Finney and Vivian are leaving to go back to house with daughter and *bambino,* and they tell Mr. Sparrow to put it there."

Els stopped caressing Susie's ears; the dog pressed her hand, wanting more.

"Vivian says she makes this plan herself."

"They were adamant you should stay here instead of Oualie. We compromised. I've moved to the study, and you're to have my bedroom."

"You would want me gone in three days, like fish," Giulietta said. "Your bed upstairs, too much reminder of that house, even though you make it very tropical now." What might have been a shudder passed through her, and then she was bright again. "Put your things back in the bedroom. I am already unpacked."

Toad Hall was spotless; Finney, Vivian, and Eulia must have been plotting their move ever since she'd announced her mother's visit. She felt both abandoned and a little panicked to be without their company and buffering. Giulietta's case was small, enough for only a short visit, and Els began to fret that she might run off, leaving her questions unanswered.

Giulietta settled into the lemon suede chair and looked around the walls at Els's canvasses. "This is *perfetto,* this frog house," she said. "I wash off the jet lag in that shower *simpatico* outside, then we make dinner, *va bene*?"

"We're closed tonight. I thought we'd go out."

"*Assurdo*!" Giulietta said. "Your kitchen is full of food. We make a little pasta, have a little wine. Talk."

"Talk," Els said. "My fondest wish." But she sensed a wariness in her mother that matched her own.

Wearing a red linen shift, with one of Eulia's chef's aprons tied under her breasts, Giulietta moved instinctively around the unfamiliar kitchen, finding any implement she needed, making the restaurant stove her own. She gave Els jobs to do—chop the garlic, test the pasta. When they sat down to eat, Els felt pride in helping to create the meal, that she deserved to share it, that it was already shared.

Giulietta recounted her trip and, with much laughter, caught Els up on their family in Italy, cousins her own age she'd never met. When Els tried to talk about Harald or Burtie, her mother cut her off, and when she teared up in describing Mallo's death, Giulietta stared into her wine and said, "So much sadness for you, *cara*, all together." When Giulietta dismissed the bank failure and the struggle to create and manage the pub with a wave of her hand, it dawned on Els that her mother was both engaging and self-absorbed—as gifted a storyteller as she was a spotlight hog—and not nearly as empathetic as the fantasy Mum she'd carried in her heart all these years. When Els described finding Giulietta's birthday paintings, her mother looked away toward the screen door, where insects had clustered.

By the time Giulietta poured the last of the red wine into her glass, Els had nearly finished a bottle of white and the candles had puddled wax onto the table. Els grasped the blue bead and ran it along its chain, and the talisman combined with the wine made her bold enough to ask, "Mum, why would Father have kept your gifts from me?"

Giulietta looked at her. "I cannot go into all that."

"You came halfway around the world to see me, for Christ's sake."

"*Cara*," Giulietta said. "We both drink a lot of *vino*. My head is tired from all the planes."

"Mum," Els said, "I'm desperate to know why you abandoned me . . . us."

"Is that what they tell you, those Cairnoch people, Grandmother Beatrice? Your father, Mr. Big Laird?"

"Nobody would speak to me about it. I worked it out that it was your idea."

"*Bastardo*," Giulietta said.

Els reached for her mother's hand. "Promise me you won't leave until you give me some answers."

Giulietta gave Els a wan smile and squeezed her hand. Els squeezed back. The walk-in's compressor clicked on and the lights dimmed. Insects ticked against the window.

Still holding Els's fingers, Giulietta sipped her wine. The candlelight softened her face, shaving away some of the twenty-one years that separated them and making her hazel eyes look almost green. "Who is this sailor?" she asked.

"Just a friend," Els said, removing her hand. "American."

"When do I meet him?"

"He's mostly away on charters." She ran her index finger and thumb up and down the stem of her wine glass. "How long are you staying?"

"We go *giorno per giorno*," Giulietta said. She swept bread crumbs onto her plate. "Tell *tuo amore* I want to visit his big boat." Resting her chin in her hands, she closed her eyes. "It is four in the morning in Napoli," she said. "I sleep only two winks on the plane from Milano to JFK."

Els stood up. "I'll wash up."

Giulietta rose with a little wobble, and Els took her arm.

"I am not so old, yet," Giulietta said. She slipped her arm free and walked ahead of Els up the path lit with fairy lights. At Toad Hall, she leaned against the door and Els reached to turn the handle.

Giulietta held Els's face and kissed her again on both cheeks. "I never want to see you in New York or London," she said. "There, I fear you are too much your father's daughter." She touched Els's chin with her fingertips. "Here, you are mine." She stepped into Toad Hall and closed the door.

CHAPTER 39

Els kept a watchful eye on the gate the day Liz was due back. She was stunned when the Jeep raced up the drive with Liz at the wheel and Giulietta in the passenger seat, her hands and hair flying, both of them laughing. Els set down Rum Wallops for the sunset drinkers on the gallery and hurried to the court.

Liz jumped out, grinning, but a question hung in his eyes. The blue of them reminded her of mountain harebells, as it had that first moment on *Iguana*.

"I don't see you for a month," Els said, "and my mother finds you before I do?"

"I am at Oualie," Giulietta said. "This huge boat sails in, and Mr. Barrett tells me it belongs to your sailor. I swim there to meet him."

"Jason and I were setting things to rights on *Iguana* when Mama G here climbed up the ladder and invited herself aboard," Liz said. "You should try it sometime."

"And trigger another panic attack?" Els said. "He saved my life, Mum. I may be a regular fish in a pool, but I've always been terrified of dark water, and I got tossed into the sea the day we met. I might have drowned if he hadn't pulled me out."

That fleeting shudder passed through Giulietta again as she looked from Els to Liz. She climbed out of the Jeep and kissed Liz on both cheeks. "*Ciao, Capitano. Grazie mille.* I make you special pasta when you come back." She walked across the court, her hips swaying with what Els thought was a slight exaggeration. The back of her red linen dress bore a wet mark in the shape of a bikini bottom.

"That was the longest month on record," Els said. She stepped into Liz's embrace and nestled her cheek against his chest. He kissed her hair and took a breath. As he let it out, he pulled her closer with a fierceness that surprised her. "Anything wrong?" she asked, leaning back to look into his eyes.

"I had plenty of time to worry that your feelings might have changed."

"What, a stubborn Scot like me?"

"Stubborn as her father, and sexier than her mother," he whispered.

Giulietta was on the gallery chatting up the guests. Els was sure she was watching them behind her sunglasses. Surprising herself, she kissed Liz with abandon, a real movie kiss. When she let him go, he faked a swoon and grinned. She led him to the palm shade near the drive, in clear view of the gallery but out of hearing range.

"You didn't tell me your mother was coming," he said.

"I invited her after you left. I've been a mild wreck ever since."

"Why? She's charming."

"To you."

She turned her back to the gallery and put her arm around Liz, pulled his hip against hers, and slid her fingers into the back pocket of his shorts. The low sun was a golden ball caught in clouds that would soon drape the sky with flaming gauze. Pinky stood at the ready to shoot off the cannon.

"It's hard enough meeting my mother for the first time when we both have so much history," she said. "But she's elusive about hers, at least as it regards me. If I ask her an important question, she blanks me or changes the subject."

"She complained you were elusive about me."

"What was there to say? This intriguing man and I spent an evening pouring our souls out to one another and I haven't heard from him since, except for a few radio messages via Barrett Cobb?"

"I've never been any good on the phone," he said. "But we had some beautiful days, and I wished you were there."

"Is that how I'm going to see more of you, become a deckhand? Your drinks waitress, perhaps?"

"If I get you onto *Iguana*," he said, "there won't be any guests around."

"What's this Mama G business?"

"She went into perturbed Italian when I called her Mrs. Gordon," Liz said. "Jason gave her the nickname."

"What did she worm out of you?"

"Besides my marital status, financial prospects, and zodiac sign? Not much." He tightened his grip on her shoulder. "She asked me if we're lovers. I told her that was none of her business, which I'm sure she took as a yes."

Els found her present display of possessiveness perplexing, unsure if it was aimed mostly at Giulietta or Liz, and recoiled at the idea of how "dem say" would feed on it.

"I'd love to join the two of you tonight," he said. "But a Swedish family arrives in less than an hour and wants dinner aboard. We're back in a week. First time in years we aren't booked for Thanksgiving weekend." He kissed her shoulder. "I'll have four whole days to make it up to you."

She bumped his hip. "I'll be counting the ways."

The sun oozed into the sea. Pinky fired the cannon.

Els sat on her heels, her bare knees deep in the red soil of the newly turned herb bed Giulietta had pronounced a necessity for any restaurant. Giulietta, her hair bound in one of Jack's bandanas, wiped her brow with the back of her wrist, leaving a streak of mud. They were both perspiring freely, though the sun was barely peeking over the mountain.

"How soon can we eat it?" Els asked.

"When they are about this high, you pinch the tops to make them grow full, and we eat the tops. Maybe you order mozzarella from Puerto Rico and we make *caprese* salad for Christmas with Finney's tomatoes."

"You plan to stay five more weeks, then?"

Giulietta shrugged. "Rinaldo visits his daughter and grandchildren in Amalfi for Christmas."

"Tell me about him," Els said, keeping her eyes on her mother's hands, which were placing the basil seeds at precise intervals along the row.

"He is four years younger than me. His wife dies of cancer six years ago. He was my *psichiatra*. He falls heads over heel in love with me, so he sends me to a colleague."

"Some other doctor wrote about permission to visit you when I was twelve," Els said. "Had I known, I'd have badgered Father until he let me come."

Giulietta stopped seeding and looked at Els. "After that, I am hopeless for a time. I visit this shrink and that one. *Stregoni.* They try every medication in the sink. I become too bright, too black, too blah. Rinaldo finds the right combination. No up and down now."

"You seem constantly up to me."

"You prefer I am in a pit of blackness, hiding in your frog house?" Giulietta said. "Even Rinaldo cannot love me like that."

Els kneaded the dirt. The confirmation that her mother was bipolar answered some questions, but raised the specter that her own moodiness came from the same cause. She didn't think of herself as either manic or depressive, just explosive, and even that was abating since she'd moved to Nevis. She tickled dirt over the row of seeds and firmed it gently, the way Harald had taught her to do. "Am I to have a stepfather?"

"*Forse si, forse no,*" Giulietta said. "Rinaldo proposes every year on my birthday. He asks me to allow a divorce."

"Why did you hold out all these years?"

"I do not give Big Laird his freedom, his happiness." Giulietta tamped down the soil Els had already firmed.

Els stood up and slapped the soil off her knees. "What did Father do to deserve such spite?"

"He thinks he is God in that house, makes rules for everybody." Giulietta heaved herself to her feet. Her smile was cold. "Only one real God." She looked heavenward. "I tell Big Laird I cannot break His rules."

"Since when are you devout?" Els said. "Don't pretend you aren't living in sin with Rinaldo."

"That is not your business."

"I won't speculate on your sex life if you don't speculate on mine. When did Father ask for freedom to remarry?"

"First time when you are about five, then three more times," Giulietta said. "I tell him his *puttana* becomes honest woman only when I am dead." She yanked off her bandana, shook out her hair, and strode to Toad Hall.

The next night, when the guests and staff had departed and Giulietta had gone to bed, Els took a glass of wine to the secret garden. Even though it was now outfitted as a dining space for private parties, it was still her favorite spot for late-evening or early-morning solitude and appreciation of the forest and ocean sounds and smells. With the moon overhead, the white Phalaenopsis orchids she'd nestled into the foundation crevices hung like moths among the ferns.

"May I join you?" Jack stood under the bougainvillea arch, smiling his most ingratiating smile.

"What, you finally figured out a civilized way to arrive?"

"Is it hunky-dory with Mummy, or is the four-day fish turning smelly?"

"She's clearly staying beyond a week," she said. "And since she's been tight-lipped about anything I want to know, I'm prepared to wait her out. That fish can stink all it wants as long as I get my answers." She looked up at the traces of clouds. "As a guest, she's both easier and harder than I expected. As a mother, too, actually."

"What did you think, that she'd fall on your neck, prostrate herself to make it all up to you?"

"That she'd be more curious about me. More sympathetic."

"You've got me for sympathy," he said.

"You're as sympathetic as a drill sergeant."

"I know what anniversary this is." His voice was gentle.

The palm shadows along the drive melded and parted in the breeze. "Kind of you to take note," she said. "It's so isolating, grieving alone. The world is supremely uninterested. Nature shrugs." She sipped her wine. "Well, I got through the day. What a difference a year makes. New home, new business, partially reclaimed Mum." She bent and yanked out a shoot of coralita vine. "So, both of us have passed the two-year mark—your death, Mallo's. I hear that's the big healing point. Aren't we now supposed to just *move on*?"

"I will if you will," he said.

"I already have," she said, struck by the truth of it, the sea change in her only clear in retrospect.

"Then try working on what's holding me."

"Jealous of my progress?"

"Running out of time."

She scrutinized him. He was even less substantial than the last time, as worn through as old cloth. "If I can't manage your release in time, are you doomed to stick around forever? My own private jumbie?"

"I'm not a pet."

"Pets are supposed to give us unconditional love," she said. "All I get from you is unspecified wheedling. Come on, Jack, stop being so cryptic and just tell me what will release you."

"Admitting the truth," he said. He thinned, became lacy, and then there was only the bougainvillea.

Giulietta injected activity and laughter into the daily life at the pub. She often bested the men at dominoes and was the most boisterous player, encouraging the female customers to join in and cheering on the old men. Els watched the guests respond to her and tried to adopt a more welcoming demeanor.

Every day, Els brought Eulia, Peanut, and Vivian to spend the morning in the kitchen with Giulietta, who babbled in a combination of English and Italian while she taught Eulia to make pasta, gnocchi, and ricotta. Els mused that she might have learned to cook and be hospitable had her mother stayed at home.

On a Tuesday when the pub was closed, Giulietta announced she would make dinner for Els's "new family." Els wondered if she thought Vivian had accepted or even usurped her motherly role, and whether Giulietta might be affronted or relieved to be shut of it. Giulietta was a bit standoffish around the Flemings, except for Eulia, with whom she was more affectionate than with Els.

"It's true, they're more than friends," Els said. "You'll leave me again, and they'll be here."

With Els guiding her around the stocking clerks at Best Buy, Giulietta made up her menu, scowled over the produce, and held her nose dramatically at the odor of dried salt fish that permeated the back of the store. There was the usual chaos at checkout, little sense of a queue in the cramped space around the registers. When a young man in a Miami Heat tank top began flirting with one of the cashiers, Giulietta sent a burst of Italian his way, telling him to do his courting in the street.

He squinted at her. "You interferin' with me?"

"Mum, let's not have a scene," Els said.

Giulietta stepped toward the man. "Who else but you make pretty girl forget her business, make customers queue all the way back to that stinky fish? Burning balls don't make you hot stuff." A few customers chuckled; others stared at the floor.

The young man patted the flaming basketball logo on his chest, turned to the cashier, and said, "Hear that, baby? Plenty hot stuff, all for you."

"Big hot nothing," Giulietta said.

"Woman, keep outta dis." Mr. Heat turned to the other customers. "All a' you my witness. She start this." He backed away and slouched out the door, throwing an incomprehensible comment over his shoulder.

Giulietta followed him, berating him in Italian. Els left their basket and hurried after them. When she got outside, her mother and Mr. Heat were shouting at each other in the gravel car park. Els grabbed at Giulietta's arm, but her mother swatted her away.

The altercation soon attracted an audience. Schoolgirls giggled into their hands. Young men clapped and hooted.

When a policeman pushed his way through the bystanders, Mr. Heat said to him, "De woman mek big ruckus when ah wasn't even talkin' to she."

Giulietta said something in Italian Els couldn't catch.

Els gave her a warning look. "Mum, I'll take care of this."

"She with you?" The policeman looked at Els. "Ah, yes, Jack's," he said with a little smile. "We heard you had a foreign visitor up there."

"Wired in to immigration, are you?" Els said.

The officer's smile tightened.

"Bad business you let a bum like him insult the *turisti*," Giulietta said.

"I just sweeting up Tishiana in there, and she starts comin' with her fatness into my affairs," Mr. Heat said.

"Throw him in jail," Giulietta said.

"Mum, wait in the car," Els said.

Clasping his hands behind his back, the officer said to Giulietta, "We apologize, madame, for any unpleasantness. But I suggest you refrain from starting arguments with our citizens." He waved away Mr. Heat, who hesitated before thumping the logo on his shirt, grinning at the crowd, and hurrying off. Giulietta sauntered to the Jeep.

"The Cotton Ground station has received complaints," the officer said, turning back to Els.

"About Mum?"

"About disturbances at your establishment."

Probably fewer than when Jack was alive, she thought. "I specifically have permission to fire Bessie—the cannon—at sunset," she said. "Otherwise, we're positively sedate."

He looked at her. "It is unwise to contribute to disruption," he said, and walked toward the police station.

By the time Els returned to the Jeep with their groceries, Giulietta had refreshed her lipstick and was filing a fingernail.

Els slammed the shift into reverse. "If you're going to get me and my business in trouble, Mum, I'll leave you home from now on."

"You brag to be so tough in your bank," Giulietta said. "What makes you shrinking flower all of a sudden?"

"The government could close me down in a heartbeat."

"Because I refuse insults from *un nero*?"

"It's their island, Mum."

CHAPTER 40

Jack's had been busy all of Thanksgiving weekend. On Saturday night, Els was frantically doling out drink orders when she spotted Paul Salustrio and a familiar-looking man coming up the drive.

She intercepted them in the court. Salustrio, cigar in hand, flicked his eyes over her.

"You've changed," he said. "Or is that stiff little investment banker still under there somewhere?"

She was wearing a strapless batik sundress and the blue bead necklace.

"I believe you know each other," Salustrio said, pushing his companion forward.

Franklin Burgess. She'd failed to recognize him because a sunburn had replaced his normal pallor except for patches around his eyes. A raccoon in negative.

"I snagged him right after the Standard Heb debacle," Salustrio said.

"What do you think, boss," Burgess said, "can Lady Eleanor, the legendary Fire and Ice Queen, have mellowed a bit?" He stuck out his hand.

She crossed her arms. "Did that deal you stole from me nail your promotion, Foghorn?" she said.

"It would have," Burgess said. "But Paul hired me away—as a *managing director*—the minute the shit hit the fan."

"Are you here because Goldman's throwing some group grope over at the Resort?" she asked.

"A private cruise," Burgess said.

"Not on *Iguana*."

"Wouldn't charter anything else," Salustrio said.

Glass shattered on the patio. Genevra bent over the dropped tray. Pinky bolted from the kitchen, dustpan in hand.

"Without your families at Thanksgiving?" Els asked.

"They're resting up tonight," Burgess said. "It's a hell of a trip to your little paradise here."

"Keeps out *some* of the riffraff," she said.

"I wondered where you'd disappeared to," Salustrio said, "until I saw that *Condé Nast Traveler* bit." He tapped cigar ash onto the gravel.

"We can't seat you until at least nine o'clock."

"How continental," Salustrio said. "We'll wait in the bar." He scanned the restaurant. "Who's the voluptuous vision?"

"My mother."

Giulietta, in a flowered silk dress with ruffles at its deep V-neck, a glass of red wine in hand, was visiting each table, laughing and speaking her English-Italian mix and telling people what to eat. Salustrio watched Giulietta cock her hip and flirt with a patron.

"So I was right about the red-hot mama," he said. "I can't wait to hear her take on Sir Harald, rest his dour soul. Sorry for your loss, by the way."

"Talk to her about Father at your peril," she said.

"A little protective of family secrets?" Salustrio said.

"She parts with them harder than I do with my virtue."

Salustrio's Diet Coke was watery and Burgess was on his third scotch and they'd consumed a platter of coconut shrimp and two orders of bruschetta. The lounge stank of cigar, Salustrio having challenged the men to sample Els's supply of top-of-the-line Cubans and Dominicans. Cigar sales alone would make it a decent night.

She finally got the bankers seated, and when she'd reeled off the remaining menu choices, Burgess said, "Some career shift you made, Gordon." In the year since she'd seen him, he'd put on a stone and switched to contact lenses. The contacts had turned his stare glassy, but the real change was in his air of entitlement, the way he lifted his chin and looked down his nose.

"That strapless number would knock 'em dead back home," he said.

"It's a relief not to have to dress for success," she said.

"And those nifty cashmere sweaters were, no doubt, a large part of your success." He exchanged a look with Salustrio. "Tell me, is waiting tables an improvement over M&A?" With his voice at its customary blare, he broadcast this question all over the restaurant, causing other patrons to stare.

A burst of laughter rose from the table at the back of the garden. Els imagined they were laughing at her, but it was Giulietta charming them, leaning in to flirt with the host, her bosom brushing his shoulder.

"It beats having my chain jerked night and day," she said.

"I bet the pay's fabulous too," Burgess said. He was sporting a Patek Philippe watch that might have set him back the pub's annual gross. "Paul's given me free rein to build my own London team. I could use someone like you. If you haven't lost your deal edge, that is." He produced his card with a practiced flourish. "No hissy fits, though, eh, Paul?"

She put the card on her tray. At one time she'd have jumped at a chance to work at Goldman—even under Burgess, even under Salustrio. "My life is here now," she said.

"Finding yourself any local action?" Salustrio said.

"None of your fucking business."

"Bet she's got her pick of refugees from civilization," Burgess said. He smiled at Salustrio. "The Ice Queen might have to lower her standards. I'll have the lobster."

Salustrio ordered spaghetti puttanesca, emphasizing each syllable as he stared at her breasts.

When Giulietta floated down the kitchen stairs, replenished wine glass in hand, Els said, "Mum, stay away from those two guys in the garden pavilion."

"What is harm?"

"Either of them will turn any morsel of information to his own advantage somehow."

"I can handle them."

"Don't bet on it."

Giulietta swanned out the door, and Els imagined her making a beeline for Salustrio and Burgess, even agreeing to go sailing with them on *Iguana*. Salustrio wouldn't be above making a pass, and she wondered what her mother's response might be. She threw her tray into the sink, shattering a plate and sending Burgess's card into a pan of suds.

"That make two plates and six glasses we down tonight," Eulia said.

"Fuck the dishes. Fuck them all." Els sat on the steps and rested her forehead on her knees. "I've got a restaurant full of assholes."

Eulia pulled Els into the storeroom and closed the door. "If you can't handle assholes, we ain't goin' have no restaurant," she said. She'd been more assertive lately, but the vehemence of this statement took Els aback. Eulia pointed her finger at Els's chest. "Who you tink dat money Jason *invested* in us come from?"

"Somebody besides Liz."

"Jack leave me half a' this house," Eulia said. "It more money than I would see in two lifetimes. He make Jason exactor to watch over my inheritance. Peanut can go to college—Harvard, even. I axe Jason to buy me into our business. He declare the risk okay."

The condenser clicked on, making the room hum.

Els stared, agape. Her own inheritance coming full circle. "You could have told me."

"Jason say mus' be confidential." Eulia's eyes narrowed. "You gotta understan' you ain't the only one gotta lot at stake. I ain't takin' orders from no Resort boss again." She opened the door. "But we still got to take shit from them Resort guests. Think whatever you want, as long as you paste on that smile." She returned to the kitchen.

Els backed against the chilly walk-in door and stared at the bare bulb over her head. Though she was irked at Jason's secrecy, the flood of relief that his mysterious co-investor had real skin in the game, was a partner in every sense, made her break into an astonished grin, which she wore back into the kitchen and out into the thronged restaurant.

Els hadn't yet tamed the new espresso machine, and on her first attempt, it spewed coffee slurry all over the bar. She bit back her curses and made a joke with the patrons in the lounge. On her second attempt, she managed to make four decent cups. When she delivered the coffee to patrons in the garden, Giulietta was standing at Salustrio and Burgess's table, laughing, and all three of them were watching Els. At the same time, she saw Liz jogging up the drive.

She reached the court too late to head him off into the privacy of the sago palms. He kissed her quickly, his two-day-old stubble prickling her lip, but she felt many eyes on them and avoided his embrace. He smelled rank and his T-shirt was streaked with grease. "I expected you by Wednesday night," she said. "We even made a Yank Thanksgiving dinner."

"Radar problems," he said. "I thought I could get the parts in St. Maarten and fly right over, even beat them home, but everything got screwed up by the holiday, and I had to wait for a shipment and take whatever flights I could get as far as St. Kitts. I came straight here from the ferry."

"And three of your four days home are gone," she said. "Do I need to give you lessons in how to use the telephone?"

"My making-it-up-to-you list just gets longer and longer."

"Go get a beer. And something to eat, if there's anything left."

"You look done in," he said.

"Mum had this grand idea of doing an Italian Night," she said. "It's been mad here since six o'clock."

"Mama G seems to be holding up."

"Belle of the ball." She tipped her head toward Salustrio's table. "You might have warned me that he was back, and with that toady Burgess to boot."

"I just found out myself," he said. "We had a cancellation and Mr. S jumped on it. Some kind of bonding trip with a new star on his team."

"They deserve each other."

"I'd better say hello." He walked over to their table. When next she looked, he was pulling up a chair.

She climbed up to the lounge with a tray of checks and credit cards, her sandal straps digging at every step. Giulietta was chatting with a couple nursing cognacs, and when she whispered something, the man rocked back in his chair, pointed his cigar at her, and guffawed.

Smoke burned Els's eyes. Someone, probably Liz, had changed the music to a frantic calypso, and the steel pan music pinged in her throbbing head.

Liz was busy behind the bar, boogying as he poured. He'd showered and was wearing one of Jack's shirts.

"What do you think you're doing?" Els said.

"Making *sambuca con la mosca*," he said.

"How dare you help yourself to Jack's shirt?"

"I couldn't lend a hand wearing something I'd worn 24/7 for two days."

"Nobody asked you to lend a hand."

The couple stared.

Liz frowned. "You wear his shirts all the time."

"He left them to me."

"He left them, period," he said. "Okay, so I invaded your privacy again. Didn't know your goddamn *space* included Jack's effects." He unbuttoned the shirt, tossed it into the big chair, and walked out, letting the screen slam behind him.

She sank onto the ottoman and pulled the shirt onto her lap. The couple looked at one another, finished their cognac, and slipped out the door.

Giulietta rested her hand on Els's shoulder. "*Cara,*" she said. "Go catch your sailor."

Els looked down at her tray.

"Girls can finish this." Giulietta pulled away the tray and held out her hand for the shirt. "Go, *cara*. Bad business, sleeping on top of fight."

Salustrio and Burgess were climbing into a taxi van at the gate. "Hop in," Salustrio said. "We can all go in hot pursuit."

"You can go fuck yourselves," she said, and headed down the hill toward Oualie, the lights of the van casting her shadow far ahead on the empty road.

The harbor was calm, the ensigns hanging limp. She tossed her sandals onto the *Maid* and cooled her sore feet in the water while she scanned the beach and dock for Liz.

He was sitting at the bar, slouched over his beer. Barrett Cobb said something and Liz shook his head, grabbed the beer, and headed for the dock. She expected him to jump into *Iguana*'s zodiac, but he walked to the end of the planks and stood there facing the sea.

The running lights mounted on the last pilings glinted off his bare shoulders.

The wharf planks were rough under her feet. When she was about ten feet from Liz, she hesitated. He chugged the rest of his beer and turned.

"That wasn't about the shirt," she said.

"You think I don't know that?" He tossed the bottle into the dinghy, where it clanked against the gas tank. "It's real easy to love a ghost."

"Well, you'd know all about that, wouldn't you?" she said.

"Make that two ghosts."

She'd long realized that her feelings for Jack were a kind of love. Denying it now seemed cowardly, but necessary. "I love one memory," she said.

While she dreamed of him, Mallo had never appeared to her, taken on form, or made demands like Jack. She wondered how it would be if he did, if she could switch him for Jack, perhaps become a batty old maid, living alone in exile, visited by the specter of her first and truest love.

Liz cupped his hands and shouted toward the moon, "This woman loves the ghost of a guy she's never even met."

She imagined the sound waves gliding among the boats and wondered if all men were out to embarrass her publicly this night.

He buried his fists in the pockets of his shorts. "You've made Jack more of a legend than he was in real life. Don't you think you've done enough for his immortality?"

"Fuck you."

"Now you're talking." He crossed his arms. There was just enough light for her to see his chipped smile. "Unless you've been prowling Sunshine's, you've had quite a dry spell. Or maybe old Jack can service you from the great beyond."

"He said he'd be game," she said.

"He *said*? What are you doing, communing with the spirits of the dead? Never worked for me." He stepped into the zodiac and kicked the beer bottle into the bow. "Go ahead then, get yourself a little action from the self-proclaimed Lover King of the Caribbean. In case you haven't heard, he was a little prone to exaggeration." He started the engine and cast off.

"I'll let yi know how it goes," she yelled.

"You think I care?" he yelled back, revving the engine, and skimmed over the sea toward *Iguana*.

She scrubbed the night's frustrations away in a long shower and tied a pareo above her breasts. Although it was nearly half midnight, she poured a generous rum and sipped it, staring at her portrait of Jack.

"'Make use of time, let not advantage slip,'" he said.

She jumped and knocked a vase of agapanthus flowers, but caught it before it toppled off the bar. He was lounging in the big chair, dreamily watching the ceiling fan twirl. Susie glanced in his direction, sniffed, and rolled onto her side.

"'Beauty within itself should not be wasted: / Fair flowers that are not gather'd in their prime / Rot and consume themselves in little time.' Shakespeare," he said. "'Venus and Adonis.' You should take her example."

"Pursue an unwilling man?" She crossed her arms to hold the pareo closed. "Why court humiliation when it seeks me out?"

"I bet he's more willing than you think."

"He's unwilling enough, and I can't manage to avoid being a complete bitch." She looked at him. "It's all your fault, Jack." She sipped the rum, the ice cubes resting against her lip. "I should banish you. Become as unreceptive as Eulia."

He sat up straight. "Eulia has good reason."

"And I don't?"

"Only if you decide it's him or me," he said.

They looked at each other. The ice in her drink shifted.

"You're the one who demanded I choose life over ghosts," she said.

"You know perfectly well I meant your childhood chum, never *moi.*"

"Our relationship is getting in the way."

"And what exactly is our relationship?" he said.

"I've allowed my house—"

"*Our* house."

"*My* house to be haunted," she said. "I've allowed you into my head."

"Your heart."

She swirled her drink. "My heart."

"And what damage have I done to this house, head, heart of yours?"

"I'm thinking about prevention," she said.

"Oh, Christ, I'm finally getting you to stop obsessing on the past, only to have you start fearing the future."

She retied the pareo knot. "Okay, Jack, you've done me no serious harm. Yet."

He stood up and walked over to the bookcase. "I wish that were true of Eulia."

She sipped her rum. The frogs chanted from the ghaut.

"I researched those medications you left around," she said. "It was AIDS, Jack, wasn't it?" His back to her, he caressed the ebony carving of an African woman's head. "Tell me you didn't drive Eulia away to prevent further sex."

"A wise man knows his own weakness."

"Even if celibacy was your penance, was that terrifying enough to kill yourself?"

"The storm killed me," he said. "I owed her a future—especially now, with the boy." He faced her and spread his arms to embrace the lounge. "My olive branch to her, however bountiful, came too late."

His eyes were full of pleading. "Get me a few words with her." He walked to the door and turned. "Then, if you're bent on my exorcism to clear the way for your captain, go get help from Miranda."

"The herbalist who treats Vivian?"

"She's got powers you wouldn't believe," he said, and drifted through the screen.

CHAPTER 41

The mountain road led through a village of dilapidated wooden houses, kept standing by bright paint and corrugated iron patches. Els gave two elderly women using black umbrellas as parasols a wide berth, then eased Wilma around a deep pothole.

"Sheep can drown in there," Finney said. "Gorment spend all the road-fixin' money in they own neighborhoods."

The houses thinned, the bush began.

"That old witch doctor live up ahead with the trees and the monkeys," Finney said.

"Miranda's no witch doctor to Vivian."

"She come by every now and again with some kinda bush to drink or use for pain. It does give Viv some comfort." He looked out the window. "Some believe she a obeah woman. Els, what kinda trouble you wanna get de rid of?"

"Just checking out my options."

They followed a switchback deep into a ghaut and continued through a neighborhood with security cameras and million-dollar views of St. Kitts. The way turned to gravel and entered lush forest—coconut palms with an understory of banana and heliconia—where the air was markedly cooler. When the road became little more than a track with volcanic stones pressed into the mud, branches smacked the windscreen.

"This one of the oldest bits a' road on the island," Finney said. "Built by slaves. Plantation owners lived up high to enjoy the breezes. Some ruins over there behind that baobab tree, all cobed up. Rich folks in those villas we just passed doing the same thing. Paradise Gardens." He sucked his teeth. "Fuh dem, mebbe."

Miranda's house was barely visible behind the flaming hues of a croton hedge. "Wait here," Finney said. He hopped out of the Jeep and let himself through the gate with a hand-painted sign that read, "Don't leave in sheep or goat or donkey or cow." The tiny wooden house was double-peaked and on blocks, its shingles weathered, its trim the bright red-orange of flamboyant tree flowers.

Finney's shout of "Inside?" brought Miranda to the porch. She wore an African print turban and caftan, dangling earrings, and silver bangles on both wrists. After she and Finney had an exchange full of her chuckles and his "anhs," she stepped inside and returned with a Ting and handed it over the railing. Finney beckoned to Els and went to sit on a wicker settee in the shade of a mango tree.

"Go ahead, Finney, drop asleep if need be," Miranda called. "We goin' be a while." As Els climbed out of the Jeep, Miranda moved deliberately, almost regally, down the porch steps and out to the gate. "Miss Els, I expectin' you for some time," she said. "Come in, darlin'. You doan need to 'fraid me."

Els latched the gate and extended her hand. Instead of shaking it, Miranda grasped her fingers, peered into her palm, and read her pulse.

"I'm not here ti have my fortune told," Els said, tugging her hand, but Miranda held it fast.

She studied Els's face. "Some people buy Jack house, show up here de nex' day, lookin' to toss him out." She gave Els's fingers a little squeeze and let go. As she walked toward the house, her rhinestone mules slapped the pink undersides of her heels.

Els followed along a path of crushed volcanic stone that snaked through a landscape of plants in Nevis Pottery pots and car tires.

"This my pharmacy," Miranda said.

The house smelled of thyme, vanilla, and jasmine. On the shelves were jars of dried leaves, bark, shriveled berries, bones. Miranda shooed a tiger cat off a recliner and ushered it out the door with her foot before facing Els, her knuckles on her hip. "What you need from Miranda?"

"Are you really an exorcist?" Els asked.

"Could be," Miranda said. "Exorcism forever, though. No going back."

"Death wasn't permanent enough."

Miranda invited her to sit at a Formica table under an open window. "You as jumpy as a tree frog. You needs a dose a' special bush tea." She dropped a pinch from three different jars into a small pot, poured in water from a pitcher, and set the pot to boil. She hummed as steam began to rise and fill the room with a vegetal scent. She took down a cup and saucer—pink flowered with gold at the rim—and poured the tea, then drizzled in local honey.

"Let that cool a minute," she said, and set the cup in front of Els.

Els contemplated the twigs and leaves floating in olive-green liquid. "What will it do to me?"

"We goin' see," Miranda said. "Everybody react different." She lowered herself into the chair opposite Els. "This knee carry me fuh seventy-one years, and it like it doan wan' carry me seventy-one more."

"I'd taken you for much younger than that."

Miranda smiled. She was missing a molar on one side, and another flashed gold. "Drink that now."

Els lifted the cup and sniffed.

"Go on. It just settle you nerves, help you story roll on out."

Els sipped. The tea had a raw floral sweetness from the honey and a woodsy, bitter undertone.

"Too many spirits in you head," Miranda said. "You loving all jumbled. You prefer a straight way." She waved her arm, jingling the bracelets. "But love go its own way."

"Some of my spirits are becoming obstacles."

Miranda looked out at the garden. "You studyin' too much 'bout Jack." Yard fowl cackled from a pen near the fence. "Some tink Jack use woman, but dey could use him too. Twis' him and knot him right up. He need dem like he need oxygen." She tapped her maroon fingernails on the windowsill. A gecko poking its head over the edge looked at her, tasted the air, and scampered into the mandevilla vine. "That Jack, he pull 'ooman like magnet pull iron. And he know what make dem happy." The soft light in Miranda's amber eyes made her look under fifty and exotically beautiful; perhaps she and Jack had found each other irresistible at one time.

"I take it he was a good lover," Els said.

Miranda laughed, a throaty chuckle. "Spile a woman for the rest a' men."

Yearning for Mallo surged through Els. She blinked and managed not to drop her gaze. "Jack's never touched me."

"He can't do that, darlin', but he can touch your mind all the same."

"Can he be all in my mind?" Els said. "Some kind of hallucination?" She stared into her cup, seeking whatever answer might be lurking in the tangle of leaves at the bottom. "Am I crazy?"

"There's all kind a' madness."

"He appears when I'm wide awake, but never in full daylight. I dream about him. Well, not exactly *about* him, but his visits can provoke these dreams. Some leave me weeping for a loss I can't name." Els swirled her cup and watched the leaves rearrange themselves. "We made this bargain. He's certainly keeping his side. Always pushing me to chase what I most fear."

Miranda took the cup, reheated the tea, and poured Els a refill. "Tell Miranda about that fear."

"You experience deep love with this Mallo man," Miranda said.

Peering into the dregs of her third cup of tea, Els felt as if she'd had a glass of wine: loosened but not yet wobbly, and far more candid even than when drunk. "More than that," she said. "I believed only he, who knew me so well and for so long, could ever love the difficult person I've always been."

"But you angry at him too."

"I'm furious at him for dying. For leaving me." Els hid her eyes in the heels of her hands to squeeze in the tears. "Since he died, I've no place for all that love to go."

Miranda clasped Els's forearms, her touch encouraging, knowing. "You got to forgive him that he can't be here no more to soak up all that love." She pried away one of Els's hands and looked at her. "Darlin', you must be just drownin' in love pushin' to flow out."

"I'm trapped in ice."

"Ice doan last long in a place like this," Miranda said. She heaved herself out of her chair and put Els's cup on the counter. "Liz not an easy man. Fighting inside, even though he stop boxing down everybody. He got his own load a' sadness. Maybe you help it, maybe nobody can."

"Am I a fool?"

"Love make all a' we a bit foolish."

"I'm terrified."

"Of Liz?"

"Of no Liz." The words were iridescent soap bubbles, too delicate to touch lest they dissolve. A pair of hummingbirds flitting around the porch sent their thrumming through the open window. Els felt tears welling, blinked them back. "Liz is absurdly jealous of Jack. It's unfair to have to choose between them. But even if I wanted him gone, Jack won't leave until Eulia lets him in, and she's too bitter."

Miranda shook some of the herbs she'd used to make Els's tea into a small jar and handed it to her. "You brew this like I show you. Drink it down before you go sleep."

"Will it send him away?"

"No, darlin'. You drink it for clar-i-ty in you own spirit. We got work to do before you done with Jack. Come." She went out to the porch. "Finney," she called. "Miss Els goin' now." Finney emerged from the shade and returned to the Jeep.

"If I decide Jack must go," Els said, "can you make Eulia receptive to him?"

"Only she can do that," Miranda said. "I go tink on it."

She led Els to the gate, brushing her hand along the croton hedge as they passed. "This plant got a strong heart," she said. "You make a row all one color, it throw out a stem like this one or that one, spile your design." She broke off a shoot—burgundy leaves with red spots—from a plant that was otherwise acid green with yellow veining, and handed it to Els. "You heart takin' you its own way."

Els stepped through the gate. Miranda fastened it behind her and said, "I mus' consult my wisdom."

Twirling the croton leaves, Els watched Miranda return to her house, her mules slapping.

CHAPTER 42

When Els explained Miranda's plan to Pinky, he'd nodded his quick nod, thumped his fist against his chest, and whistled. Ten days later, he'd summoned Els to the patio and presented the mahogany coffin he'd made of wood from the mountain, hand planed and sanded until its surface was as smooth as baby skin. His eyes had been moist when she embraced and thanked him.

The next morning, as she dumped all of Jack's clothing onto the patio table, it sighed out his scent and a hint of cigar. Though the sun had just crested the peak and was beginning to illuminate the mountain's western folds, she could already tell it would be a stifling day.

In the volcanic dust from neighboring Montserrat that had settled on the lid during the night she wrote with her finger, "RIP Jack," then wiped it away with a kitchen towel. She stared into the box and listened to the cooing of the doves, a rooster far away, his call echoed by another even farther.

She scattered the photos of women from Jack's bulletin board over the bottom and laid his moth-eaten tennis sweater on top of them. After layering in everything else, the coffin was as full as a well-packed suitcase. The aroma of new wood might soon overcome the traces of Jack, just as the aromas of Nevis had erased her memory of Mallo's scent.

She arranged Jack's dark trousers and tucked a yellowed dress shirt inside his only jacket, a tuxedo. After struggling with the fish-print bow tie and only succeeding when she filled the shirt neck with boxer shorts, she fastened the skull and crossbones earring into the top buttonhole like a formal stud. She stuffed the trouser legs with Jack's partially burned letters to Susie and the charred photos of her and the other women. Taking a last look at the shapely legs and feet she now knew to be Eulia's, she nestled the fragment inside the shirt where the heart would be.

She picked up Jack's shoes. "Can't imagine you wearing these," she said, "much as you prized them." She propped them against the inside of the coffin foot and tucked in the trouser cuffs. Last, she arranged his faded Foxy's baseball cap where the head would have been. The effect was of a deflated body, the cap over its face, as if Jack had wafted out of the clothing as easily as he drifted through the screen door.

She sat on the gallery with Liz and Jason and stared at the sea through the midafternoon heat shimmers, fanning herself with a paperback book of Dylan Thomas poems. She'd chosen her black cocktail dress and diamond ear studs; Liz's eyes, made all the bluer by his cornflower shirt, had widened when he saw her. Boney, sporting a fresh haircut, was weeding and stamping down the dirt in the crab ring. Miranda, Finney, and Vivian waited on the patio, drinking lemonade. Giulietta, wanting nothing to do with the scheme, had claimed a headache and was holed up in Toad Hall.

"What if she doesn't show?" Liz asked.

"Miranda and I have no Plan B," Els said.

"We could start without her."

"I told you how this has to go."

"I'm getting a beer. Jason, want one?" He started to rise.

"Don't ye think that would be disrespectful?" Els said.

"We're talking Jack, here," Liz said, but he settled deeper in his chair. "What's with the poetry?"

"Dylan Thomas was a favorite of Jack's," she said. After packing the coffin, she'd found the dog-eared book on the seat of the leather chair, a brass candlestick weighting it open. "I came across some lines this morning that will be just the ticket for today."

Eulia's newly acquired car rattled over the cattle guard and into the court. She sat for a minute before sliding out. She was wearing a white dress and her church hat, a swoop of persimmon straw and tulle that shaded her face.

"Thought you'd chickened out," Els said.

"Mamma made me promise to come," Eulia said. Hugging her elbows, she leaned against the car, and Els feared she might get back in and drive away.

"Come on, child," Vivian called. "This home-going ceremony's already long overdue."

Eulia lifted Peanut from the car, went to the patio, and said something to Vivian, who reached up and took her hand. Carrying Jack's Bible and the poems, Els led them all to the top of the garden, where Liz and Boney had set the coffin on some cinder blocks next to a long, narrow hole, the dirt piled behind it. At the coffin's foot, Els had placed an arrangement of the garden's wildest assortment of croton boughs. Pinky emerged from the bush and came through the back gate to join them.

The family of monkeys Els had dubbed "the bathroom gang" and tried to keep out of the restaurant were gathered on the back fence, a mute choir. Miranda, wearing a white caftan and turban, her nails painted bright red to match her lipstick, took her place at the foot of the coffin with her back to the sea. When she brought her palms together and nodded, Boney stepped forward and opened the lid.

Everyone gathered closer.

"Well, hello, Old Jack," Boney said. "Looking nattier than the last time I saw you, or maybe ever."

"She got all a' his things in there," Finney told Vivian. "I see a corner of that Anguilla T-shirt I brought him, what left of it after he wore it clean through. She got him laid out like a undertaker would do."

"Liz, I want you to know *all* his shirts are in there," Els said.

He stared toward the sea. "Seems a good time to part with them."

Eulia stepped closer and looked in. "I told you to get rid of all a' that. I thought you'd a' burned it by now."

"I wasn't ready," Els said. She placed the Bible in the coffin and arranged the empty sleeves over it.

"You want ol' Jack to rest easy, you might not want to put that in there," Boney said.

"Trust me, he'll rest easier if this particular Bible is underground." She looked around the group. "Anything else you want to send along with him?"

Boney tucked a dart into the jacket pocket, its flights a jaunty boutonniere. Jason unrolled a tattered burgee and placed it across the chest like a sash of honor.

"His drinkin' flag," he said.

Liz propped a Bob Marley CD next to the cap where the ear would be. "Dance the night away, mon," he said.

"Doan never forget how I taught you to shape them boards," Finney said, and placed a small block plane next to the jacket's elbow.

"Eulia?" Miranda said.

"He got everything from me he gon' get," she said.

The monkeys began squabbling, and one jumped into a tree and screeched at the others. When the commotion subsided, everyone shuffled and looked at the ground.

"Read your piece, darlin'," Miranda said.

Els stepped to the head of the coffin. It was a still, oppressive afternoon with enough of Montserrat's ash in the air that the sun hung like an orange halfway down the sky. "As Jack wasn't a religious man," she said, "I thought I'd read a few lines of poetry that he might well have chosen for today."

She began:

"And death shall have no dominion.
Dead men naked they shall be one
With the man in the wind and the west moon;"

She caught a movement in the periphery. Jack appeared behind Eulia, his beard clipped, his hair shining; he, too, had cleaned up for the occasion. He'd never appeared in full daylight before. He stood with his hands clasped low, merriment at the corners of this mouth. Miranda glanced at Els and nodded. Peanut squirmed in Vivian's lap and pointed at Jack, his expression crinkling toward a wail, but Jack raised a finger to his lips and Peanut looked at his mother and back at Jack and only stared. A quick scan of all the faces told Els that nobody else could see Jack, though Eulia hugged herself as if she was chilled.

Liz touched Els's elbow. "You okay?"

"Brilliant," she said, and continued reading:

"When their bones are picked clean and the clean bones gone,
They shall have stars at elbow and foot;
Though they go mad they shall be sane,
Though they sink through the sea they shall rise again;"

Jack looked into the coffin and smiled. He stepped in front of Eulia and turned to face her, but she stared through him at the coffin, her mouth in a tight line, her nails digging into her upper arms. Jack reached toward her face, then lowered his arm. His shoulders drooped.

Eulia looked at Els. "That all?"
Els resumed reading.

"Though lovers be lost love shall not;
And death shall have no dominion."

When she closed the book, Jack was gone. Peanut gasped and blinked.

Watching Eulia, Miranda spread her arms. "All a' we here to help our friend Jack find peace. His spirit been very troubled, since long before that wave carry him into the next land. He need our assistance. He need our forgiveness for all he done on this earth." The corner of Eulia's mouth twitched. "Each and every one a' we need to reach deep in our hearts and find that forgiveness and welcome him, yes, welcome him back from that spirit land where he been trapped." When she raised her arms higher, her bracelets slid to her elbows. "Reach into your hearts. Reach."

Miranda began whispering, and soon the whispering turned into a sort of hum, and then a chant in a language Els didn't understand. Miranda closed her eyes and swayed side to side. Eulia looked at the coffin as if she expected the scarecrow to sit up. Els worried she might bolt.

Miranda lowered her arms and seemed to reinhabit her body. "Now, I want all a' you to think about something Jack loved and some way you loved him." Her head was bowed, but Els saw her sneak a glance at Eulia, who was looking at the sea, tears caught in her long lashes. "We gon' gather Jack back to us with love so he can leave us with love."

A breeze rattled the palm fronds. A cattle egret landed on the crab ring and regarded them with its yellow eye, strutted a few steps, and lifted off again, tucking its feet. It winged over their heads and up the mountain.

After a nod from Miranda, Boney closed the coffin. Miranda placed both hands on its lid and began whispering again. Finally, she straightened and said, “Gentlemen, set him down.”

Using the lengths of nylon rope Boney had run under the box, the men eased the coffin into the hole. Pinky approached the dirt pile, loaded the shovel, and tossed earth onto the coffin. Pebbles rattled on its top. He handed the shovel to Liz, who followed suit and handed it to Jason, and it made the rounds of the men twice before Eulia, eyeing the grave, stepped forward.

She grasped the shovel handle, sank the blade into the earth, and stamped the shoulder deeper. Straining, she lifted the blade and dumped the dirt into the hole, then reloaded the shovel and tossed again. She wiped her brow with the back of her wrist and stamped the shovel down again. Her church pump slipped off the side and she lost her balance momentarily, but she went back at it, panting, for two more loads.

Everyone stood back, Els watching the coffin disappear, the rest watching Eulia.

“Let us finish this, Eulia,” Liz said.

She glared at him and dug up another load. “This ain’t gon’ finish nothin’.” She threw more dirt into the hole.

Pinky touched Eulia’s arm. She pushed the shovel handle toward him. Her face was running with sweat and maybe tears. Her church hat was still in place; dirt marked the hem of her skirt and was caked onto her shoes. She brushed off her hands, took Peanut from Vivian, strode to her car, and drove away.

The men regrouped around the grave and Liz tried to take the shovel, but Pinky tightened his grip and lifted his chin in a gesture of dismissal. Blinking back tears, he set to his task. Only Miranda was smiling, her hand on Vivian’s shoulder, her eyes on the sea.

“That’s not what I call receptive,” Els said.

“Heart got to shift in its own time,” Miranda said. “We open it a crack.”

"What the devil are you talking about?" Boney asked.

"Jack's last wishes," Els said. She started walking toward the house. "Come along. It's time to get out of this sun, and Liz has needed a beer for hours."

CHAPTER 43

She flapped the Dylan Thomas book at the moths that gathered to her torchlight beam and shifted on the stack of cinder blocks next to the closed grave. In a whisper, she resumed reading "Fern Hill," over and over, until tears splashed the page, as if the last iceberg of her anger had thawed and was rushing to escape. Susie lay in the soft earth at her feet, gazing up with her concerned expression.

"That would have been my other choice," Jack said.

Els aimed the torch toward the lime trees.

"But I knew it would break you up to read it in front of everyone." He shielded his eyes.

She pointed the beam at the book. "This might have been written for Mallo." She read:

> *"And as I was green and carefree, famous among the barns*
> *About the happy yard and singing as the farm was home,"*

Jack recited the rest of the poem, walking a slow circle around the grave, his hands clasped behind his back. He finished:

> *"Nothing I cared, in the lamb white days, that time would take me*
> *Up to the swallow thronged loft by the shadow of my hand.*

In the moon that is always rising,
Nor that riding to sleep
I should hear him fly with the high fields
And wake to the farm forever fled from the childless land.
Oh as I was young and easy in the mercy of his means,
Time held me green and dying
Though I sang in my chains like the sea."

"Time holds us all green and dying," he said. "Only the lucky among us sing in our chains."

"Sing he did," she said. "He was fairly bursting with life and determination."

"I've been hard on you about him," he said. "Everyone needs their own time, I guess, and it's never over, is it? The mourning, I mean. Maybe the anger too."

"Maybe Miranda is right. Only love can force either out."

"Or forgiveness." He sat on the other stack of concrete blocks and looked at the sea. "Nice try today."

"Miranda thinks this grave might give Eulia a place to seek you out, if she wants to," she said. "I'll add a bench and a proper stone, maybe plant croton in honor of indomitable hearts."

"*Cara,*" Giulietta called from Toad Hall. "Who's there?"

Susie sat up and pricked her ears. Giulietta was in her nightgown; the moonlight touching her bare shoulders cast a blue shadow onto the deck.

Els glanced at the emptiness where Jack had just sat. "I wiz just reading aloud," she called.

Giulietta crossed the grass barefoot, with enough of a wobble that Els wondered if she'd been tippling in Toad Hall. "I heard a man's voice," she said.

Els was relieved she'd skipped the funeral. "See for yourself how alone I am." Els flicked the torchlight around the grave and into the citrus grove.

Giulietta peered into the darkness, then sat on the stack of blocks Jack had vacated. "Your tears, *cara*, can't be for this man you never knew."

"This burial reminded me I can't visit everyone left behind at Cairnoch."

Giulietta's shoulders moved the way Els had seen before, somewhere between a shrug and a shiver. "Nobody there I would visit, even if that Russian serves us cakes and vodka."

Els studied Giulietta's silhouette against the glow from Toad Hall. "You never loved Father."

Giulietta swatted a mosquito. "Not in your romantic way," she said.

Els removed her shawl and draped it over her mother's shoulders. "Did he ever love you?"

"Maybe. For a while." Giulietta gazed toward the lights on St. Kitts.

"Tell me the story, Mum."

Giulietta stared out to sea long enough for Els to worry she might not answer, then she smoothed her hair and sat up straighter. "I am barely twenty," she said. "My father drives a truck delivering vegetables. When he drinks, he beats my mother, sometimes all of us. My two older sisters are married and complaining always about money, and I do not want the life any of them have. I work at any job I can find to pay for school, but it is nothing like your fancy university. Mostly a place for young people to become angry. In the mid-sixties, there is great poverty, protesting. Terror in the streets. Student strikes and riots."

"Were you passionate about politics?" Els asked, wondering if she'd inherited her rebellious streak.

"Politics matters to my friends, my lovers," Giulietta said. "All I care about is art and staying alive." She shifted on the blocks. "Your father is working in Naples—some assignment with the bank. His colleague rents a house on Ischia and they come many weekends and they like to drink at a place where I am tending bar. He thinks I'm exotic, talented. It excites him to be, how you say, 'slumming' with me. He is handsome in that pink English way. He has the confidence of a rich man, and he is the only person I meet who is *ottimista* in the middle of so much *agitazione*."

"He wooed you with promises of a posh life," Els said.

"Nobody is wooing anybody. I am throwing everything I have at him and he is falling for it. He is my way out."

"Were you always so cynical?"

"*Disperata*," Giulietta said. "What is there for me but a life of poverty, painting in obscurity, marrying some fool who goes to fat in a few years and smashes my face for fun?" Susie poked her nose into Giulietta's lap, and Giulietta fondled her ears. "I tell your father I am carrying his child. Soon enough, it is not a lie. The local priest marries us. I am wearing a lace tablecloth for my veil." She kept staring at the necklaces of light on St. Kitts. "It is good, living in Naples with money. When your father's work there ends, we go to Scotland and I see the trap I have made for myself. He travels to Edinburgh, to London. By then we speak very little. He leaves me in that freezing house under the evil eye of Beatrice."

"So you ran away," Els said.

Giulietta looked at Els and then to Toad Hall, as if she was gathering strength either to tell Els why she left or to run for the safety of the cottage. She stood up so abruptly that Susie jumped back; then she tossed the shawl into Els's lap and hurried to Toad Hall. When her mother looked back before shutting the door, Els wasn't sure if she was weeping or if it was simply a trick of the moonlight.

CHAPTER 44

Els looked around the Christmas Eve dinner table at her mother, the Flemings, Tony and Lauretta, and the Oualie gang: Liz, Jason, and Boney. She'd found her tribe. To humor Giulietta's insistence on making a traditional Feast of the Seven Fishes, she'd closed the pub for the day and set up the secret garden for eleven, using Cairnoch's formal linens and silver. When they all toasted the cook, Giulietta preened. Els could have sworn she was flirting even more than usual with Liz, too, but she didn't want to call her on it and disrupt the holiday merriment.

At half ten, after the guests departed with overstuffed bellies and armfuls of gifts, Giulietta retired to Toad Hall to ready herself for Midnight Mass.

Announcing he'd help wash up, Liz drew Els to the gallery, where he and Jason had rigged a Christmas tree in Jack's tradition: a dried century plant stalk in a bucket of sand, its skeletal branches twined with fairy lights and hung with empty beer bottles on ribbons. The breeze tinkled the bottles.

"I failed Gift Wrap 101," Liz said, and pulled a package from behind the bucket. It was swaddled in newsprint and tied with yellow nylon rope.

"I hardly deserve a gift."

"The giver gets to judge worthiness," he said.

Jack would have had some pithy quote to that effect, but when she looked into Liz's eyes—deep blue, expectant—she bit back that observation and tore off the paper. Inside was his cornflower-blue linen shirt, the one he'd worn on the first night at Sunshine's, the day he'd given her Susie, the afternoon of Jack's funeral.

"I thought your wardrobe might be a little thin," he said.

She shook out the shirt, freshly laundered but unironed, pulled it over her sundress, and hugged it to her. Liz leaned in and kissed her lightly, and she put her arms around his neck and kissed him back. "I have something for you too," she whispered.

She led him to the lounge, where she'd stashed a flat package behind the bar. He weighed it in his hands before gently removing the wrapping.

She'd cribbed *Iguana*'s lines from the photo in Liz's brochure to paint a watercolor of the boat in full sail against a muted sunset. She hoped the painting would touch him as much as the shirt touched her. That it might demonstrate that her envy of his love for the yacht and the sea had softened into a kind of acceptance.

"I'll give it a place of honor," he said. "In the saloon. No, in my cabin." He tucked the painting under his arm. "Got a day group tomorrow. My guess is that they'll want to end up at Sunshine's. Meet us there if you like." He kissed her, and again, and then walked down the hill. At the gate, he looked back at her for a long beat, waved the painting, and turned toward Oualie.

Christmas was two hours old, but Els was still pacing the gallery, trying to sort out her mother's shift in mood toward agitation and wariness since Mass. She wished she'd never committed to open for brunch later that morning, even though reservations were strong, so she could hang out at Oualie with Giulietta. She feared that any day now her mother would announce her departure, or simply disappear, leaving her with so few of the answers she craved.

Jack bubbled out of one of the beer bottle ornaments, a crimson hibiscus behind his ear. He stepped back and admired the tree. "How did the sinners enjoy Mass?" he asked.

"Mum got all chummy with the priest afterwards, gushing over his sermon about God's infinite love and forgiveness, blah, blah, blah. I thought she was aiming it at me."

"We could all do with a little forgiveness." He was standing so close she could have smelled him, but the only scent she detected was melting candle wax and salt air. "That grave isn't working," he said. "Eulia's been there at least five times since you planted that damn box. Sneaks up after work and sits for a few minutes on the bench you put there. Cries, even. She was there tonight."

"And you didn't appear to her?"

"You think I didn't try? Whenever I get close, I'm in a tornado, whipped this way and that." He looked toward the grave. "I hoped Christmas might soften her up. People get sappy at the holidays."

"You think?" she said. "Mum was teary when she went off to bed, and I'm positively inside out." She gathered her shawl tighter. "I dreamt of Mallo last night. You were in the dream, too, Jack, both of you standing at the foot of my bed, and when I reached for him, you pulled him out the window."

"Don't blame me if your heart is cracking open and letting him escape," he said. "Ever consider he was pulling *me* out that window? All of us need a little help letting go."

"What'll it take to make you let go?" she said.

"I can see you're done with me."

"You're in the way."

His eyes narrowed. "You're in your own way. Admit what you feel. For that matter, damn it, *feel* what you feel. If you want *me* to be done with *you*, try that." He stepped toward the tree. "And then, Miss Ice, if you can accomplish that, just get me a few minutes with Eulia and we'll be square."

He condensed, became one of the fairy lights on the tree, then flared and winked out.

CHAPTER 45

She'd never worked so hard on Christmas in her life. Between delivering drinks and helping to wait tables because she'd given Genevra the day off, Els kept glancing at Toad Hall, but by half two Giulietta still hadn't appeared.

When her mother finally ambled into the kitchen wearing her red linen shift and turban with a beach towel slung over her shoulder, Els said, "I thought you might be hiding."

Wariness swept over Giulietta's face, then she shrugged. "Seven fishes is big effort. Maybe swim wakes me up." She grabbed the remains of some eggs Benedict off a guest's plate before Els could sweep it into Susie's bowl and walked out the door. As Els watched her cross the court, a wave of disappointment and fear coursed through her.

Once the last brunch guest finally departed at four o'clock, Els gave in to the heat, peeled off her sundress, and stretched out on her bed. When she woke, it was already dark. The peculiar stillness that was common on Nevis holiday evenings was broken only by the surf and the faraway barking of dogs. She went to the lounge and noticed when she poured a glass of wine that Giulietta had left a used one on the bar. A faint light burned in Toad Hall. Her mother was a puzzle, at times so animated and seized by her schemes and at others nearly a recluse who ate and drank at odd times and discouraged conversation. Whenever Giulietta became distant, Els feared she might be slipping into depression.

Els carried her wine upstairs and out onto the shower platform. It was the dark of the moon; even the stars were muted. She took a long shower, and as she was shutting off the taps, she thought she heard the gate rattle as if someone had closed it carefully. A sedan drove away toward town. It was nondescript, like all the other used cars shipped by a dealer in Florida to rust out their remaining years on Nevis. "Drink someplace else, boys," she muttered. Despite a sign clearly noting the pub's opening hours, people persisted in testing the gate and sometimes even walked up just to be sure.

She toweled off, pulled on running shorts and a T-shirt, and went to the lounge, planning to rummage in the kitchen for a snack of leftovers.

She smelled smoke, different from grill smoke, and stepped out onto the gallery to sniff. Susie was sprawled on her side on the court and didn't move when called. Els hurried to her and lifted her head. She was breathing, but shallowly. Els tried to rouse the puppy, who looked at her in an unfocused way and flopped back down.

A flicker caught her eye. Flames under the pergola, licking the legs of the domino table. She ran for the kitchen bucket. No water at the tap. By then, flames were devouring the table and starting to scale the pergola. Black smoke rose, thick and noxious. She sprinted to the tool shed, grabbed a shovel, and raced back to the patio, where she beat at the flames and tried to scatter the fire. Fighting choking smoke, she dragged the dining furniture to the safety of the gravel court. Flames leapt from the pergola toward the shutters and the house's wooden story above.

Giulietta screamed for Els from the deck of Toad Hall.

"Stay where you are," Els screamed back.

"Get out, *cara*! Fire will fall on you."

"Go upstairs and call the fire brigade." She broke off in a fit of coughing. Giulietta hurried across the court.

Pinky appeared as if he'd taken form from the smoke and disappeared as quickly, and Els wasn't sure she'd seen him at all. Moments later he reappeared with the hose from the cistern. In her panic, she'd forgotten all about it. He sprayed the base of the fire until it stopped rekindling, then doused the side of the house and the flaming pergola. He shoved Els so hard that she hit the stone wall, scraping her elbow, just before a section of pergola fell in a shower of sparks where she'd been standing. Giulietta, now on the gallery, began screaming again.

After wetting the grass all around, Pinky handed the hose to Els, took the shovel, and beat at the remaining flames. He scooped up something and tossed it into the court. Susie rallied at this, walked unsteadily farther away, and collapsed again.

Els plied the hose until a puddle of water and floating char formed at the edge of the court. Pinky made a cutting gesture at his throat and disappeared. The water dribbled to a stop. The substance in the court continued to smolder. Everything smelled of wet ash and burnt rubber. Above the charred remains of the pergola, stars winked in the inky sky.

When Pinky touched her elbow, Els jumped. She hugged him. "Thank God for you, Pinky. And thank you, Jack, for your wacky waterworks."

Pinky exhaled in a puff and stepped away when Giulietta arrived at the edge of the court. "Stay out there, Mum," Els said, and surveyed the jumble of timbers—reminiscent of the pick-up sticks after the hurricane, but far more sinister. She took stock of her own condition: soot everywhere, a small burn on her left foot, a gash on her right ankle where she'd hit it with the shovel. Though she'd fought the fire in flip-flops, her feet were mostly unharmed. She stepped over a beam onto the court. Giulietta flew at her and embraced her so hard she thought her bones might crack. She clung to her mother, gasping in that spicy scent. Pinky smiled and disappeared into the night.

Giulietta released Els but continued to grasp her shoulders and search her face, her eyes glistening. "My only baby," she said.

"I'm fine, Mum," Els said. "Really."

Still clutching Els's shoulders, now as if for balance, Giulietta looked down at their feet.

"Susie," Els said, and eased herself away. The puppy was still lying on the court but was no longer flat on her side. Els felt her warm nose and carried her to the kitchen. In the light she examined every inch of the pup; except for her bleary eyes, nothing seemed amiss. Els encouraged her to drink a little water and settled her into her bed.

The siren's distant warble cut through the still night. Els lit the floodlights on Jack's flag, walked to the gate, and waited, breathing consciously to balance the adrenaline still surging through her. When the fire truck arrived, she shielded her eyes against its blinking lights and said to the man at the wheel, "All under control."

"Let us make sure," he said.

She rolled open the gate and followed the gleaming truck into the court. The three men roamed their torches over the fire scene and surrounding area.

"You put this out by youself?" the lead man asked.

"I had some help."

The fireman glanced at Giulietta, who was sitting on the steps in her nightgown, pristine compared to Els, and more agitated. "One of my employees," Els said. "He . . . lives nearby. He's gone home now. He thought to hook up the cistern. Fine time for the government water to cut out."

She told them how the fire appeared to have started near the domino table, now a charred fragment, and how fast it had built.

The headman eyed the grill. "Any kind a' accident can happen if you don't exercise care with an open fire, 'specially by a wooden structure."

"We're extremely careful," she said. The grill was upright and closed. She opened it. The unspent charcoal and ashes had been removed.

Speaking quietly among themselves, the men picked around the fire scene. When they started toward the truck, one of them kicked the chunk Pinky had heaved onto the court and called the others over to look. The headman dispatched one of his underlings to the gate.

"That thing wouldn't quit smoldering," Els said.

"Bit a' tire," the headman said.

The colleague returned from the gate and whispered something to the boss.

"Government water fine," the boss said. "The valve turn off."

She stared at them. A scrap of combustible rubber, placed among some of Pinky's charcoal and sticks and palm fronds from the compost pile. The water turned off. No accident.

The truck radio squawked. One of the men said something into it, but all she could catch was, "Domestic fire. Damage limited."

The headman took the shovel, dug a hole in the mud at the edge of the court, and buried the scrap. "Leave that 'til after the holiday," he said. "Make sure it out good, then bring it in for evidence."

"What do yi expect to find, fingerprints?" she asked.

"I tell the inspectors," he said. "They going stop by soon, get the details."

"What, a car that could be anybody's at the gate, a fragment of tire that could have come from anyone's yard? What possible motive could anyone have?"

He shrugged. "Come by the station for you report. You gon' need it for you insurance."

She looked at the mess, mentally calculating the cost of cleaning up and rebuilding the pergola. The house had survived with only a little blistered paint. It could be weeks before repairs were done, but she couldn't afford to close the pub at peak season for even a few days.

She closed the gate after the fire truck drove away and looked up the hill. From that angle, the house looked normal, perfect, and she mentally caressed each beloved detail. She climbed the driveway and found her mother still sitting on the steps in a daze. Els left her to sort herself and went to check on Susie, who lifted her head and slapped her tail once. Els gathered the floppy creature into her arms. "I know you would have barked to warn us if they hadn't done this to you, sweet thing," she said. "We're lucky it was only drugs instead of poison."

The screen door to the lounge slammed. "*Cara*, where are you?" There was an edge of panic in her mother's voice. Els put Susie back in her bed and hurried up the steps. When she reached the lounge, Giulietta sprang forward and embraced her again.

"Mum," Els said. "Nothing's harmed that can't be fixed."

Giulietta sank onto the ottoman, her eyes crazed. "You were surrounded by flames, like the fire would turn you to ashes. I cannot lose you again."

"Nor I you."

"I come here with big curiosity, to see who you are. You want answers, but I don't plan to speak of it, ever. Yet I am thinking and thinking about how dark water terrifies you. You say in your letter that you don't have a life unless . . . ." She clasped her upper arms. "Unless I tell you. I want my daughter back, but I am so afraid I will lose my daughter again."

Els sought Giulietta's eyes, but her glance was flitting around the room; her agitation was so infectious that Els's heart began to race again. Susie padded up from the kitchen and rested her chin on Giulietta's thigh.

Els went to the bar and turned on the tap, which gushed air, then water. *The valve turn off.* She suppressed a shiver, took a glass of water to her mother, and sat in the big chair so that their knees nearly touched.

Giulietta stared into the water as if direction might be found there. Afraid to say anything that might derail her mother's urgency, Els waited. If it took a near disaster to shake loose the answers she so craved, all the damage would be worth it.

"Okay," Giulietta said. "Okay." She fixed her eyes on her cobalt and orange painting of the ships. "We are in battle, you and me," she said, "from when you are a tiny fish in my belly. You fight me in the womb; you are already fierce the second you are born. You steal all my strength. You are greedy at my breast, but you refuse to be cuddled."

Els balled her hands in her T-shirt. *Prickly from the start. Unlovable.*

"The only thing I do that pleases your father is to produce you. He adores you, and when he is home, he puts you in a dog bed in the Rover and drives you all over the hills. I wish to show you off in the little dresses I order from London, but I am not invited by the neighbor ladies. They talk only of horses and dogs and are competitive about their flowers. In the shooting season the Big Laird invites many bankers, and Cook makes huge, terrible food, and the men are laughing late into the night. Grayness is filling me up. I begin to drink in bed. Soon I am not leaving the bed."

"Was there nothing about Cairnoch that you enjoyed?" Els asked, hoping she'd brought at least a little joy into her mother's life.

"The only place in that house I am content is the glass room. I fill it with ferns, orchids, palm trees."

"You sang to me there."

Giulietta's frown softened. "You stay with me sometimes when I paint. You fuss a lot, get on my nerves. Singing is a way to make you quiet. When you reach two, *cara*, you are as terrible as they say. Such a temper."

Els ached to stand up and pace, but she pressed her knees together and ran the blue bead back and forth on its chain.

"About that time I fall into real blackness," Giulietta said. "I believe you are a little demon, sent to prove I fail as a mother. The village doctor says I have *depressione* after birth—a little late, maybe, but all the same."

"Surely you got more qualified help than Doc Gowan," Els said.

"The only mental places then are like prisons," Giulietta said. "Anyway, nobody admits to a problem, as long as I hide myself. Oh yes, I yell at the servants sometimes, but I keep away from the village, and nobody visits but the hunters."

Els thought how Cairnoch in winter—the isolation, ancient stone, low gray skies, and muted colors she loved—must have compounded her mother's misery.

Giulietta sipped her water. "Beatrice believes fresh air cures everything. That December we barely see the sun, but every day I am pushing you up and down the hills until I am exhausted. You behave a little better in the pram. We watch for animals, and I tell you their names in English and Italian. *Scoiattolo, coniglio.*"

"*Volpe, cervo,*" Els said. "I love that first drawing."

"One day I choose my favorite little coat, and you are fighting the sleeves, the pram, everything. You scream the whole way that you want to walk." Giulietta raked back her hair, twisted it, and let it go. The telling etched the lines more deeply into her cheeks. She looked at Els. "Once I say the rest, there is no going back."

"Already there is no going back," Els said.

Giulietta went to the bar and poured a glass of wine, took a gulp, and returned to her seat. She took Els's hand and looked at their intertwined fingers.

"At the bridge," she said, "you always want to see the ducks. I hold you on the *parapetto* and you are calling 'duck, duck, duck.' My head is aching. I cannot make you shut up. The wind is so cold. I try to lift you. You twist and scream until your face becomes purple. All I want is for the noise to stop." Giulietta looked toward the door and took her hand away. "I let go, *cara,*" she whispered. "I make a little push. You splash into that gray water. The ducks make big noise. Your pink hat floats under the bridge."

In Els's recurring dreams, cold drove her breath away. Wan light glittered at a surface she couldn't reach. Her arms and legs were bound too tightly to move. The terror of those dreams bloomed now in her chest and her lungs refused to take in air. Desperate to avoid another panic attack, she recalled Liz's soothing voice as she breathed raggedly in and out on a count of ten.

Giulietta grabbed both of Els's hands. "*Cara*, this is as bad for you to hear as for me to say. I fear this moment for years."

Els managed a deeper breath. "That fear I have of dark water. It actually helps to know why."

Giulietta held on tight until Els's breathing calmed.

"And then you fished me out, right?" she asked.

Giulietta released her grip and looked away. "I start walking back to the house," she said. "I reach the front door. Then I become afraid. I am yelling to everyone for help. Clyde, the ape who works in the garden, has already pulled you out. He hears the ducks and comes running."

Els stood up, went to the bar, and splashed water on her face then dabbed her eyes, turning a bar napkin gray with soot. Her mother's story felt both raw and rehearsed. Had she confessed it to one psychiatrist or another, one priest or another, until the truth of it became distilled or wrung out in the retelling? Susie padded over and leaned against her shins.

Giulietta cradled her wine glass and stared into its ruby depths. "I tell everyone you run away from me and fall in the lake and I cannot swim," she said. "There is big commotion in the house. Cook makes a warm bath and turns you from blue back to pink. Clyde is big hero. He gives me a look that says he saves me as much as you. But then the servants begin to whisper to Beatrice. She whispers to your father, and they decide I am a no-good mother and I must return to Italy. If I will go to doctors they choose, they will send money. I cannot see my child unless the doctors approve. They make me sign papers. I leave the next morning."

Harald had been so forceful, so practical. By reputation, steely in business. With Els, he'd been strict, hard to impress, and often distant, but never unkind. Perhaps he had been as vindictive as Mallo often claimed.

"I accept to be banished because I am convinced an evil woman lives inside me and I cannot control what she will do," Giulietta said. "I renounce my child."

Susie scratched at the door, and Els let her out and leaned against the doorframe. "But you sent the birthday paintings."

"When I hear nothing back, I decide maybe your father and grandmother teach you to hate me. Maybe even tell you what I did."

"You persisted."

"After a while, it becomes as much to poke at Mr. Big Laird," she said. "Remind him he shares the blame that his daughter has no mother."

The case clock scrabbled and bonged ten times.

"I've always known your leaving was somehow my fault," Els said.

Giulietta finally looked at her. "The path of blame begins long before you are born. I work hard all these years with those doctors to step off it." She finished her wine. "That is why I write you I am not the mama you want." Her smile was rueful. "When you invite me, I fear you imagine we have big tears and all is forgiven. The real world is not like that."

"I believe the real world piles more shit on you than you could ever imagine, and turns its back and lets you deal with it alone," Els said.

"*Cara*, your path has always been up to you." Giulietta stood up and carried her glass to the bar. She touched Els's arm. "I do wish for some forgiveness, though, like in your books."

Els looked at her mother and covered her face with her hands. "Not just now, Mum."

"*Finché siamo vivi,*" Giulietta said, "*tutto è possibile.*" She went out to the gallery, letting in Susie, who threw herself against Els's legs.

Els carried the puppy to the leather chair and curled up with her, wetting her fur with tears.

CHAPTER 46

She showered and pulled on the long sundress she'd tossed onto her bed hours before and her lavender cashmere cardi. In the lounge, she looked around at her treasures and Jack's, then turned off all the lights and threw herself into the big chair. Her hair still smelled faintly of smoke. To the ceiling fan's tick, visions and admonitions looped in her head. *Unlovable, bitch, ice queen, where there's life there's hope, admit what you feel, icy water, duck bellies, paddling black feet, unlovable, rotting weeds, my fault, his fault, her fault, unlovable, feel what you feel, hope, your path, your path, your path.*

The case clock announced midnight. As Boxing Day began, all was silent but for the frogs and the distant roosters, whose waves of screaming sounded like the tortures of the damned. She went to the kitchen and set the kettle to boil, but killed the flame before the water was tepid.

Your path, your path, your path.

Closing Susie inside, she stepped onto the patio and breathed in the scents of the tropical night—ylang-ylang, damp earth, gardenia—mixed with damp ashes. She navigated the charred debris and headed down the drive. Her shadow, thrown by the flagpole floodlights, was that of a giantess.

In Oualie's harbor, mast lights cast broken streaks over the water's ragged surface. She'd thought to borrow a dinghy, planning to row as she'd no idea how to use an outboard motor. No dinghies were tethered to the pilings. From the end of the dock she could see one illuminated porthole on *Iguana*. The few other boats were dark. She cupped her hands and shouted for Liz, but the breeze scattered her voice over the waves.

Iguana was anchored in deep water, almost beyond the harbor's shelter. She gauged the distance—fifty pool laps, maybe. A tough workout, but doable. She sat on the planks and swirled her feet in the water, boiling the phosphorescence, and imagined creatures rising to gulp in the shimmering plankton.

She stood up and tied her cardi to the railing. Eyes on the porthole beacon, she grasped the blue bead, ran at the end of the planks, and launched herself over the water. Her skirt bellied as her feet knifed through the chilly darkness and quickly touched sand. She sprang off the bottom and burst into the air, gasping and sobbing. The dress twined around her legs. Panic tightened her chest and she fought to breathe.

She was surrounded by blackness, deep and impenetrable, full of creatures with scales and teeth, tentacles, lidless eyes. She stroked to the ladder and held on, shaking. When she'd caught her breath, she stripped off her dress, stuffed the skirt into the smocked bodice, and looped the straps over her shoulders, a light backpack. She took a few strokes, naked but for her panties. A wave splashed her face and she swallowed water and began to cough.

She floated on her back, searched out Orion's Belt and the North Star, and willed her breathing to settle. Rigging clanged. The surf raked the shore. She rolled over, fixed on *Iguana*'s porthole, and began to breaststroke toward it. A mat of floating seaweed enveloped her, and she recoiled from its slippery fingers but pushed through it.

Buffeted by waves, she struggled to find a rhythm. In a pool she'd be watching the tiles slide easily by, but here she could think only of what lurked beneath her, how distant the bottom. She imagined Jack's bones among the rocks, shreds of his linen shirt waving, hollow eyes beseeching. *Feel what you feel.* As she passed the last boat before the long haul to *Iguana,* a gust sent the hull seaward, and the mooring line snapped out of the water and rasped against her foot. She cried out, took a wave in the face, and kicked frantically away.

She forced herself to rest and float again, her milky skin the only marker of where black sky met black sea. A wave knocked her, and when she righted herself, the dress was flowing behind her like a cape. *Dump it*, she told herself, but instead she struggled to stuff it back inside itself and pressed on, her arms and legs burning. She'd miscalculated the distance; she'd come only halfway, and the rest was open water.

She pressed on, more and more slowly. About two hundred feet from *Iguana*, the dress came loose again. She balled it under one arm and side-stroked the rest of the way.

The yacht's looming hull dwarfed her. There was no ladder.

More spent than she had ever felt in her life, she pounded the hull with her fist, a hollow thud, barely louder than the slap of the waves. When she heard movement inside, she called for Liz.

A torch beam searched the water, found and blinded her.

"Jesus," Liz said. The ladder came over the side, there was a splash and a ball of phosphorescence, and he surfaced next to her. He held her fast and stroked to the ladder, untangled her from the dress, and lifted her foot onto the lowest rung. "Hang on," he said, and climbed onto the ladder behind her. His arm around her waist, he rested her against his thighs and eased her up one rung at a time. When she tried to stand on the deck, her knees gave out. She crawled to the cockpit and collapsed on a banquette.

He tucked a towel close around her. He was wearing shorts. The warmth of his naked chest against her back on the ladder came back to her now. She watched him wring out her dress and drape it on a lifeline.

"I had some silly notion I could put that back on before I got here," she said.

"A blue bead and a pair of panties are more than enough for me," he said. "Let's get you a hot shower."

He helped her climb down to the saloon, led her to the stateroom, and switched on a lamp. In the full-length mirror on the head door she caught her skim-milk skin, bluish lips, red-rimmed eyes.

He wrapped his arms around her from behind and smiled over her shoulder at their reflection. He teased a piece of seaweed out of her curls. "A fetching mermaid visitor is unusual, especially at this hour," he said. "Even more so if she smells like a campfire."

"That's a story for later," she said, and pressed her back against him. "You've saved me twice now."

"The first time you were panicked. This time maybe just stupid. What if I hadn't been aboard?"

"Didn't consider that," she said.

A wave slapped the stern, slid under the hull, lifted the bow, and moved on toward shore. In the safety of the cabin and his arms, she tried to allow herself just to feel, but her mind continued to lash her with irony and regret. She'd swum competitively to conquer her fear of the water. She'd elbowed her way through a career to impress Harald, only to lose Mallo, to whom her success was a given. Becoming prickly to everyone had just proved she was as unlovable as she'd always believed. She'd imagined that solving the mystery of Giulietta's departure would produce a loving mother. How foolish not to see that any relationship would require effort on both their parts.

She turned in Liz's embrace and pulled him close enough to eliminate any space for doubt or recrimination. "My whole life has been one huge compensation," she said into his shoulder.

He kissed her hair. "And risking death to swim here is compensation for what?"

Her mother's confession filled her head; she pushed it away.

"Nothing," she said. "Everything. An admission." She kissed him, concentrating on his lips, nothing but that, and he sighed into her embrace. "Show me your lair," she said.

A tiny smile crinkled his eyes, which were the blue of morning wood smoke, questioning.

He led her through the "Crew Only" door to a tidy cabin on the port side. Cast by the bedside lamp, his shadow ran up the wall and onto the coffered ceiling. She glanced quickly about, taking in lockers with brass fittings, a bunk with drawers underneath and a batik spread. Sailing books, *Treasure Island*, poems of Pablo Neruda. A framed snapshot, faded to amber, of a deeply tanned woman squinting into the lens, wind in her black hair. Her painting of *Iguana* propped on the shelf.

She closed one of the porthole curtains.

"Nobody can see us," he said.

"I'm closing out the darkness," she said. She looked at the feeble streetlamp at Oualie and up the hillside to the pinpoint of light that marked Jack's flag. The eastern sky was graying just enough to reveal the outline of Nevis Peak. She slid the other curtain shut.

His kiss this time was hungry, and she returned it with a fervor that surprised her. She dropped her towel and met him, as if she'd shed all reticence in the sea. He stripped off his wet shorts, scooped her up, and set her on the bunk, then stretched out facing her. She gazed down their lengths, his skin walnut against her ivory, and snuggled closer, seeking his heat.

He touched the blue bead, which had slid against her collarbone. "When I gave you this, I wasn't sure if I'd see it again."

"Did ye put a love spell on it?"

"If it brought you back, that's magic enough." His fingers traced the hollow of her throat, the curve of her breast. He looked into her eyes. "Anything you like is okay with me."

"Trust your imagination," she said.

As a lover, Liz was a combination of fun-loving and careful, teasing her through the awkwardness of finding their fit and rhythm, making her laugh, moving her with hands as confident as they were tender. "It's like *Iguana*," he said. "You have to feel the wind lifting her and let her go with it."

When she came, the tension wires of longing, grief, and anger binding her snapped, and in her release, she began to sob. He pulled her against him and let her cry until she finally stilled, overcome by a deeper exhaustion than she had ever experienced. Her mother's revelations had hollowed her out and the sea had rushed in, rinsed every cell in her body, and poured its salt out through her eyes.

Liz got up and tucked the spread around her. "I always make one last safety check before I turn in," he whispered.

"Good principle," she said.

She was asleep before he returned.

As rosy light rimmed the curtains, Els rolled onto one elbow and watched Liz sleep. She kissed him awake and they made love again, taking their time, learning.

Afterward, she rested her sticky leg on his thigh. "Challenge you to a skinny dip."

She rolled off the bunk and opened the curtains. The sun was still hiding behind the mountain, giving it a golden rim, and the sea was glassy. She let him chase her to the cockpit. Her dress hung limp from the mizzen in the still morning. Standing on the stern deck, she hesitated at the sight of the purple-mauve water. Liz came up behind her and held her shoulders, but she flashed a brave smile and executed a perfect dive. She sliced through darkening purple, righted herself, pawed toward the surface, and broke into the air.

Her breathing labored, she tread water and gasped out, "You coming or what, Captain?"

While he watched her with an expression of wonder, she stretched out on the surface and let the water spread her hair into a russet mane. He dove, his splash washing over her, and she inhaled some water, began to cough, and lost her float. He rested one hand under the small of her back, steadied her at the surface, and kissed her nipple. The clouds over the mountain turned from pink to white, and she closed her eyes and felt the first rays warm her lids.

Back on the boat, they wrapped themselves in *Iguana*'s terry robes and Liz made coffee and hummed as he squeezed local grapefruit. The spicy citrus scent filled the saloon, and the juice he handed her was thick with pulp and sweeter than anything she'd imagined such speckled and dented fruit could produce. Mallo had given her sweet orange juice, but since life had ripped away sweetness and replaced it with bittersweetness, she'd come to crave the taste of the limes, bitter oranges, and grapefruits that were the bounty of this land.

They foraged in the galley and took bread, cheese, and mango to the cockpit. Though her immersions in salt water had washed away the taint of smoke, they'd turned her cuts and scrapes lurid against her pale skin.

He ran his finger over them. "What dragon were you slaying last night?"

While she nibbled a slice of mango, she considered her reply. Too many dragons to choose from, and she wanted none of them crowding into the cockpit. The idea of arson and its implications made her shudder. Whatever the cause of the fire, she was in deeper than she'd thought. Liz caught her change in mood, moved closer, and took her hand. "We had a minor fire last night," she said. "Some embers from the grill."

He looked at her in alarm.

"Pinky took care of it. Just an expensive nuisance."

"And that propelled you to beard me in my den in the wee hours?"

"It shook Mum into telling me what I've been dying to know," she said. "It turns out near drownings have rerouted my life more than once." She squeezed his hand. "But I can't talk about all that until I've sorted it a bit."

"Remember, I don't ask unless I really want to know."

"And so you shall." She squinted up at her dress. "Would you haul that down, Captain?"

"I'd like to keep it," he said. "My version of your flag."

"If I walk home in this robe," she said, "tongues will wag."

He lowered the dress, slipped off her robe, and looked at her before easing the dress over her head and smoothing the smocking across her breasts. He pulled her close. "Will you give it back to me when I get home next week?" He kissed her earlobe. "And the girl in it?"

"With a bow?"

"Only if it's easy to untie." He licked the salt crystals off her shoulder and kissed her again.

She tasted the salt on his tongue and nipped it playfully. "And you so proficient in knots," she said. "I really must get back. Mum will be worrying."

"I think she'll applaud," he said.

And so will Jack, she thought.

He handed her into the dinghy and ran it back to the wharf. Barrett Cobb glanced up from sweeping out the restaurant and gave them a thumbs-up. News of their tryst would be all over the island within hours.

Liz sprang onto the wharf, helped her up, and gathered her into his arms. "I'd much rather spend New Year's with you."

"We rental captains and bar wenches don't get holidays off," she said, and melted into a last kiss, the most tender so far.

As she watched him zip through the harbor, the breeze carried to her a few notes of whatever song he was singing.

Els found Finney down the beach, working on the *Maid*.

"Is boat fixing your holiday ritual?" she asked. "Last Boxing Day I found you right here doing the same thing."

"Same spot, better thing," he said, and poked his screwdriver into the sand. "Fortune turn her smile on both a' we since then."

"I hope she's not just playing with either of us," she said. The glow of Liz's kiss was wearing off, and she felt an icy shard of dread that he might leave her or be snatched away, that the pub might go under, that she would cease to belong here.

Finney looked at her searchingly. She told him about the fire, the scrap of tire.

"Luckily, I'd put the dominoes away," she said, "but Jack's special table is a goner. I was terrified I might lose everything."

His eyes narrowed. "Is my fault. They sendin' a message."

"If that was a message, I want to think it just got out of hand. Surely they didn't aim to burn down my house or harm Mum or me."

He gazed at the sea. "I goin' tell de fellas not to come no more."

She watched Liz coiling a line on *Iguana*'s foredeck. "They're all part of the pub now." She didn't want to think of afternoons without Manny, Trigger, Stormy, Spink, and the others who came by on tournament nights. "Political partisanship cost me the love of my life. When I moved here, I'd lost everything I cared about. Now that I have plenty to care about, I'm not caving to some bully."

"Cyan let they presence encourage vandalism," Finney said. "Or worse."

"If I'm to belong here, I have to belong to all of it, otherwise I *will* be just a tourist living in my own fantasy. I have so much to learn." She imagined herself sucked into the criminal and legal systems. "Self-determination is in my bones, Finney. We Scots can be damned fierce about our homes and lands." She wriggled her toes to sink her ankles deeper into the sand. "Crazy acts can be blamed on politics, but they're the acts of crazy people." She put her hand on his shoulder. "Ye can tell the domino men they're welcome any time."

CHAPTER 47

All the way up the hill from Oualie, Els anticipated sharing with her mother the news of her triumphal swim with all its implications. Giulietta's small case was on the gallery. Els ran up to the lounge to find her finishing an espresso. In her turmeric-colored linen shift and Hermès scarf, Giulietta looked much as she had the day she'd arrived, except for her deeper tan and a cowrie shell necklace. Despite the rigors of the previous night, she looked rested, younger, as if her confession had erased years.

"You were planning to run off with no goodbye," Els said.

"Rinaldo calls to say he misses me," Giulietta said. "Mr. Sparrow comes soon to take me to the plane."

Els clenched at how narrowly she'd missed returning to an empty house, maybe not even a note. "I want to drive you, Mum," she said. She carried the case down and tossed it into the boot. Giulietta stopped on the gallery, took a few deep breaths while she eyed the destruction of the pergola, kissed Susie's muzzle, and swanned down to the Jeep.

Els left a note with a tip on the gate for Sparrow. When they passed Oualie, she looked between the casuarina trees for a glimpse of *Iguana*. "Mum, I swam to Liz last night."

Giulietta peered over her sunglasses and touched Els's arm. "Tell Captain *Amore* to be careful of you."

"Careful as in watch *out* for me, or watch *over* me?"

Giulietta considered this while they crested the rise at Hurricane Hill and dropped into the straightaway along Lover's Beach.

"Both," she said.

At the airport counter, Els glanced at her mother's ticket and saw that she'd always planned to leave December 26th.

The passengers milled while the agent weighed each person and piece of luggage. When Giulietta stepped onto the scale, she pronounced it a liar and everyone laughed. She embraced Els—too fleetingly, enveloping her in that spicy floral scent—and stepped out onto the tarmac. Els tried to follow, but the agent directed her back to the car park. She gripped the chain-link fence separating her from the field.

Giulietta walked over and covered Els's fingers with her own. "Only *bambini* are free of sorrows and regrets, *cara*." She looked over Els's shoulder at the mountain. "Rinaldo puts up with enough spite. I will let him marry me." She smiled. "I send you invitation. Bring Captain *Amore*."

"Lady," the agent called. "De plane gon' fly away widout you."

Giulietta's eyes were moist. "You make new chance here, *cara*. Don't waste it." She squeezed Els's fingers and walked toward the plane.

"*Ciao*, Mum," Els called after her.

Giulietta blew a kiss. She said something to the attendant that made him laugh and pretended to need his help to climb into the plane.

The house was unbearably empty, a hollowness Susie tried to fill by getting underfoot. In Toad Hall, where her scent lingered, Giulietta had propped a drawing in the buttery suede chair: a colored pencil sketch of Els, her copper curls a squiggly mane, her eyes more blue than gray. She was wearing the blue bead and persimmon shawl, and, though she wasn't smiling, her eyes held a spark of joy. Across the bottom Giulietta had written "*figlia*" and "daughter." The tiny gardenia drawn in the corner had no tear.

CHAPTER 48

During Friday's hectic dinner service, so many customers inquired after Giulietta that Els worried the appeal of Horseshoe Jack's might be dangerously diminished by her absence. When the guests were finally gone, she spotted Eulia at Jack's grave and climbed up to find her sitting with Peanut asleep in her lap, her tear-slicked face gleaming in the moonlight.

"Jack must love the view from here," Els said.

Eulia moved over to make room for her. "You pick a good writing."

The new grave marker read:

Horseshoe Jack
July 30, 1949 – September 21, 1998
How strange this fear of death is!
We are never frightened at a sunset.
—George MacDonald

"It's from an author he loved," Els said. "Me as well. I hope it's not bad juju that I pointed his feet west, but he'd take a sunset over a sunrise any day."

Susie lolled on the bare earth. A fog-like wisp wreathed the stone and assumed greater density until Jack took shape. He smiled at Els. "Well done, sweet. On all counts."

Eulia gasped and pulled Peanut closer. "Move from me, Jumbie."

"I've waited only for this, my love," he whispered. His white linen shirt was diaphanous in the moonlight. His hair was tidy, his eyes pleading.

"Oh Lord, oh Lord, I too frighten," Eulia said, and pulled Peanut so tightly against her that he squirmed and muttered.

Els started to stand up, but Eulia clamped onto her wrist and forced her back onto the bench. "You seein' this too? We both crazy?" She sheltered Peanut's face.

"I treated you savagely," Jack said. He stepped closer. When Eulia put up her hand, he stepped back again. "I did it to protect you."

"From you cussin' me? All you had to do for that was stop gettin' drunk."

"Tell her, sweet," he said.

Susie stood up and nudged her nose under Els's elbow. Els stroked her ears, silenced by the fear that she might squander Jack's chance. His eyes were pleading. Finally, Els looked at Eulia. "Jack lied to you. He learned he had AIDS and was terrified you'd get it, so he pretended not to love you."

Els thought of Eulia in the study that first visit, the sadness and bitterness in the girl's face. Jack leaned against the headstone, gazing at Eulia and Peanut.

"He decided it was best to . . . end it, end himself, rather than put you in further danger."

Eulia touched her forehead to Peanut's. "They can test everyone now," she said. "I didn't catch it."

The frogs' urgent cries filled the air.

"Safe sex means he gotta throw heself into the sea?" Eulia said. "Make my baby grow up never knowin' he daddy?" She looked at Jack. "You the biggest fool I ever know."

"Guilty," Jack said. He held her gaze. "But I never stopped loving you."

"Lovin' my baby is the only way I can still love you," Eulia said.

Water from the afternoon's downpour gurgled in the ghaut, carrying some of the mountain into the sea.

Peanut opened his eyes and Eulia tried to turn his face away, but he wriggled free, stared at Jack, and said, "Ma?"

Jack smiled at him. "He's got my eyes."

"Let's hope he got my brain," Eulia said. She sat Peanut up. "That man just visiting, baby. He doan live here no more."

Jack reached out as if to caress his son's brassy curls, smiled ruefully, faded, and was gone. Peanut blinked and pointed to where Jack had stood. "Ma?"

Susie barked once.

Eulia looked around. "He come and go just like that, poof?"

"When he damn pleases," Els said.

"He comin' back?"

Els pulled Susie close, looked out to where a lemon slice moon cast a glittering path over the sea, and said, "I think we're done."

On the kitchen table, under a bottle of olive oil, was a note scrawled on a bar napkin: *Where are you? Guests cut charter short to spend New Year's Eve at Sunshine's. Come sailing—no guests for four days. Champagne aboard. Bring Susie and bathing suit.* He'd scratched out the bathing suit. *I'll show you where the blue bead came from. ~Liz.* The *Z* was extended, spiked, and curled into a lizard's tail.

She went up to the bar and splashed a little rum into a glass, toasted Jack's jaunty portrait, and stepped onto the gallery. A perfect gardenia sat on the railing. She closed her eyes and breathed in the scents of this land—the sea, the gardenia, the damp earth in its endless cycle of fertility, something always blooming, something always dying. The night air pressed on her as if crowded with spirits, Jack's and all the others she'd loved and lost. She picked up the gardenia. In the moonlight, its petals gleamed like silver.

ACKNOWLEDGMENTS

It's impossible to thank by name all the people who have encouraged and helped me during the prolonged birth of this novel, but a few deserve special mention. My agent, April Eberhardt, whose enthusiasm for my work and whose energy propelled me through dark days and twisting paths and eventually into the arms of my publisher, She Writes Press. The SWP team of Brooke Warner, Lauren Wise, Krissa Lagos, and Barrett Briske. My Vassar writing teacher, the late Bill Gifford, whose sly smile offered the first encouragement. My Vineyard teacher and editor John Hough, Jr., who decades later helped me claim my voice and hone my craft. My editor, Rebecca Faith Heyman, who showed me how to reshape the narrative and gave me the title. My Italian translator, Lori Hetherington, and my Scottish and Nevisian sensitivity readers, Ruth T. Pollock and Isabel Byron, respectively, who together brought realism and sparkle to my characters, dialects, and settings. My readers Arlan Wise, Jimmy Rubens, the late Karen Harris, Jennifer Tseng, Carol Newman Cronin, Larry Hepler, and the many members of John Hough's Indian Hill Writer's Workshop, who gave me the huge gift of their honesty. My tough-love critique partners Sue Hruby and Elle Lash, both gifted writers and acute listeners, who helped me kill darlings and mourn their loss. My talented neighbor

Laurie Miller, for decades of friendship, cups of tea, and the beautiful map of Nevis that graces the front of the book. The welcoming and generous people of Nevis, led by Kay and Henry Loomis, whose Seahorse Cottage has been our Nevis home and whose garden inspired Jack's, and Louis de Geofroy and Karen Overtoom, whose home in Cades Bay was our introduction to the island in 1996. Our Anguilla hosts Roy and Mandy Bossons, Claire and Patrick Lynch, and the whole Roy's crew, whose hospitality sustained me during annual retreats for writing and editing. Patricia MacDonald Bourgeau, who lead the way for decades. And never last nor least, Larry Hepler, who couldn't avoid a front row seat for the creation of *The Moon Always Rising* and who rarely complained about foregone holidays and beach afternoons, distracted conversations, late dinners, and occasional temper flares and anxiety binges. A story he told me in 1996 inspired Finney's character. It all unspooled from there.

Please write a review

Thank you for reading my novel. I hope you enjoyed it, but whatever your reaction was, please consider contributing an honest review on Amazon and Goodreads. A book finds its true audience when one person recommends it to another, and other readers rely on all of us to help them find their next great read. Please pay it forward for their sake. With ideas and entertainment bombarding us now in a dizzying array of forms, I believe we must all work together to spread the joy of having one's imagination captivated by words on a page.

ABOUT THE AUTHOR

Alice Early's career spans academia, international executive recruiting, commercial real estate, career transition coaching, and always writing. All her life, people have entrusted their stories to her to shape and share. Her studies in creative writing and counseling and her decades of work easing clients' career and life transitions have all contributed to her writer's ability to see and listen, and to touch others. *The Moon Always Rising* is her first novel. Alice and her partner have visited Nevis annually since 1996 and otherwise share a hand-built life on Martha's Vineyard in view of the sea.

Alice is available to meet with your book group, virtually or in person. For book group and readers' guide information, please visit www.aliceearly.com.

SELECTED TITLES FROM SHE WRITES PRESS

She Writes Press is an independent publishing company founded to serve women writers everywhere. Visit us at www.shewritespress.com.

A Drop In The Ocean: A Novel by Jenni Ogden. $16.95, 978-1-63152-026-6. When middle-aged Anna Fergusson's research lab is abruptly closed, she flees Boston to an island on Australia's Great Barrier Reef—where, amongst the seabirds, nesting turtles, and eccentric islanders, she finds a family and learns some bittersweet lessons about love.

Play for Me by Céline Keating. $16.95, 978-1-63152-972-6. Middle-aged Lily impulsively joins a touring folk-rock band, leaving her job and marriage behind in an attempt to find a second chance at life, passion, and art.

Size Matters by Cathryn Novak. $16.95, 978-1-63152-103-4. If you take one very large, reclusive, and eccentric man who lives to eat, add one young woman fresh out of culinary school who lives to cook, and then stir in a love of musical comedy and fresh-brewed exotic tea, with just a hint of magic, will the result be a soufflé—or a charred, inedible mess?

A Cup of Redemption by Carole Bumpus. $16.95, 978-1-938314-90-2. Three women, each with their own secrets and shames, seek to make peace with their pasts and carve out new identities for themselves.

Anchor Out by Barbara Sapienza. $16.95, 978-1631521652. Quirky Frances Pia was a feminist Catholic nun, artist, and beloved sister and mother until she fell from grace—but now, done nursing her aching mood swings offshore in a thirty-foot sailboat, she is ready to paint her way toward forgiveness.

Magic Flute by Patricia Minger. $16.95, 978-1-63152-093-8. When a car accident puts an end to ambitious flutist Liz Morgan's dreams, she returns to her childhood hometown in Wales in an effort to reinvent her path.